PENGUIN CLASSICS

VICTORIAN VERSE

George MacBeth was born in Scotland in 1932 and was educated at New College, Oxford. He joined the BBC in 1955 and was until 1976 a producer of radio talks and documentaries. He has published fifteen books of poems, among them *Poems from Oby* and *The Long Darkness*. His nine novels include *Anna's Book*, *The Rectory Mice* and *The Lion of Pescara*, and he has edited six anthologies of verse including *Poetry for Today*, and, with Martin Booth, *The Book of Cats*.

Victorian Verse

A CRITICAL ANTHOLOGY
INTRODUCED AND EDITED BY
George MacBeth

PENGUIN BOOKS

Penguin Books Ltd, 27 Wrights Lane, London w8 5TZ (Publishing and Editorial)
and Harmondsworth, Middlesex, England (Distribution and Warehouse)
Viking Penguin Inc., 40 West 23rd Street, New York, New York 10010, USA
Penguin Books Australia Ltd, Ringwood, Victoria, Australia
Penguin Books Canada Ltd, 2801 John Street, Markham, Ontario, Canada L3R 1B4
Penguin Books (NZ) Ltd, 182–190 Wairau Road, Auckland 10, New Zealand

First published as *The Penguin Book of Victorian Verse* 1969
Reprinted 1975, 1982
Reprinted in Penguin Classics as *Victorian Verse* 1986
Reprinted 1987 (twice)

Copyright © George MacBeth, 1969
All rights reserved

Made and printed in Great Britain by
Hazell Watson & Viney Limited,
Member of the BPCC Group,
Aylesbury, Bucks
Set in Monotype Imprint

This book is
dedicated to the memory of
ALFRED MILES
1848–1929
editor of *The Poets and the Poetry
of the Nineteenth Century*

Contents

CONTENTS

CONTENTS

9

CONTENTS

CONTENTS

CONTENTS

CONTENTS

Acknowledgements

FOR permission to publish poems in this anthology acknowledgement is made to the following:

For Austin Dobson, poems from *The Complete Poetical Works of Austin Dobson*, Oxford University Press; for Lord Alfred Douglas, 'Rejected', Martin Secker & Warburg Ltd; for John Gray, 'Les Demoiselles de Sauve', The Prior Provincial of the Dominican Order; for Thomas Hardy, for poems from *The Collected Poems of Thomas Hardy*, by permission of The Trustees of the Hardy Estate, The Macmillan Company of Canada Ltd, Macmillan & Co. Ltd, and The Macmillan Company of New York, copyright 1925 by The Macmillan Company; for Alfred Edward Housman, for poems from *The Collected Poems of A. E. Housman*, The Society of Authors as the literary representative of the Estate of the late A. E. Housman and Messrs Jonathan Cape Ltd, copyright 1922 by Holt Rinehart and Winston, Inc., copyright 1936, 1950 Barclays Bank Ltd, copyright © 1964 by Robert E. Symons. Reprinted by permission of Holt, Rinehart and Winston Inc.; for Rudyard Kipling, poems from *Rudyard Kipling's Verse: Definitive Edition*, reprinted by permission of Mrs George Bambridge, Methuen & Co. Ltd, The Macmillan Company of Canada Ltd and Doubleday & Company Inc.; for Alice Meynell, five poems, Alice Meynell's literary executors; for Sir Henry Newbolt, poems from *Poems New and Old*, Mr Newbolt; for Agnes Mary F. Robinson, for a poem from *Collected Poems*, Ernest Benn Ltd; for Arthur Symons, for poems from *The Poems of Arthur Symons Vol. I* and *The Poems of Arthur Symons Vol. II*, William Heinemann Ltd and Dodd, Mead & Company, Inc., and for 'Scènes de la Vie de Bohème – I. Episode of a Night in May', Martin Secker & Warburg Ltd; for William Butler Yeats, for poems from *Collected Poems of W. B. Yeats*, Mr M. B. Yeats, Macmillan & Co. Ltd, and The Macmillan

Company, New York, copyright 1906 The Macmillan Company, renewed 1934 by William Butler Yeats.

Although the selection of poems, and the opinions expressed in the Introduction and notes, are my own, I am indebted to a number of friends, anthologists and critics who in print or by word of mouth drew my attention to poems I would otherwise have missed. These include Ian Fletcher, who first interested me in nineteenth-century poetry; Sir Ifor Evans, John Heath-Stubbs and Jeremy Warburg; John Betjeman, John Bielby-Wright, William Empson, Geoffrey Grigson, John Hayward and Peter Porter. I am also indebted to past editors and anthologists of Victorian poets from Q to Auden. My largest debt, however, is acknowledged in the dedication of this book.

Introduction

THIS anthology faces a difficult task. Victorian poetry has for a long time been the subject of neglect, misunderstanding and abuse. The Victorian Age has been frequently revalued – very notably in a giant series of fifty broadcasts in the Third Programme in 1949 – but the emerging image has always been one of a society very different from our own. At the moment this society seems most readily available as a source of décor and jokes. Television serials are able to combine an appeal to admiration for the visual elegance of the Victorian period with an appeal to amusement (admittedly often sympathetic) at its language and attitudes. Victorian literature, in fact, has not yet begun to enjoy the appreciative revival already being accorded to Victorian painting and design. One reason for this is the widespread view that Victorian literature – particularly poetry – often provides an extremely ineffective, hypocritical and incomplete picture of its age.

For example, despite its attractive freedom from major foreign wars, the Victorian Age seems to many modern observers to be sullied by a whole range of social inequalities and cruelties going hand in hand with a purposeful public neglect of them. Why didn't the poets of the day (one might argue) do more about these evils? Why did they withdraw so frequently into history and fiction? The reasons are complex. One thing, however, is immediately clear. If an explanation of their behaviour is to be found, it will first entail some examination of our own assumption that a poet's duty – though not a painter's – is to provide an imitation of, rather than a substitute for, the life of his time. Moreover, there is often confusion about the facts of the case. For the middle classes – who produced almost all the Victorian poets – society seemed a well-ordered and well-run affair. The conditions in the schools and factories of the day were often no better known at first hand to the middle-class writer than the war in Vietnam or the state of apartheid in South Africa is to his modern critic. At the same time, he certainly had some general idea of what went on, and often preferred to forget about it. There were strong social – as well as moral and religious – pressures to do so. Neither the widespread practice of prostitution in London, nor the oppression of junior clerks in offices, was felt to be a safe subject for extended public ventilation. It was increasingly felt to be incumbent on a man of eminence – and poets *were* men of eminence in the Victorian period – to present an optimistic and public-spirited view of his age, at least when speaking *in propria persona*. This inevitably led to a special sort of balancing-act, a studied compromise between apparent forthrightness and underlying hypocrisy. The Victorians believed that they had to turn a blind eye to certain abuses if they were to preserve the stability of society. They also believed that an open denial of these abuses would be unacceptable. The only solution was to pretend.

As far as society was concerned, this encouraged atrocious and lasting inequities. As far as poetry was concerned, there were both good and bad consequences. The good consequence was the rise and immense development of purely imaginative writing, a literature springing from, and dependent upon, a willingness to invent situations which were not real or true. The bad consequence was a widespread superficial smugness, a preaching tone almost always brought on by a writer feeling that he had to be optimistic when he knew there was little cause for it. At its worst, this comes out in the immensely popular series of 'Proverbial Philosophy' brought out from 1837 onwards by Martin Farquhar Tupper. Although technically original, and intermittently accomplished in phrasing and imagery, these poems are marred by a drearily conservative moral tone. They always say exactly what the reader wants them to say. This vice recurs in the work of far better writers – very notably Tennyson and Arnold – and it was particularly apparent at the turn of the century in the sort of anthology which aimed to present Great Thoughts. Poems of this kind inevitably tended to be reasonably short and hence well suited for extraction and presentation in anthology form. Even that most careful anthologist Alfred Miles felt it necessary to devote no less than two volumes out of his twelve to the sacred, religious and ethical verse of the period.

It isn't altogether surprising that even a fairly perceptive foreign critic in the early twentieth century should have identified the mass of Victorian poetry with a pompous, shallow and fundamentally dishonest kind of moral exhortation. Certainly, this seems to have been the view of T. S. Eliot, to whom the current critical misfortunes of Victorian poetry can largely be traced back. This isn't entirely Eliot's fault. Like Freud, he had a specialized problem in hand, and it was the side-effects of his pronouncements that led to misunderstanding. It was never Eliot's intention to attack the Victorians head on. Indeed, again like Freud, he presented his doctrine in the tone of voice, and with the high seriousness, of the Victorians themselves. The macabre spectacle presents itself of a stern father accidentally eaten alive by the last of his children. Of course, Freud's theories went far further than Eliot's, penetrating, as they did, not only into psychology, politics and anthropology but eventually into the intimate behaviour of almost everyone now alive. Eliot's revolution was only of the mind, and the literary one at that. Nevertheless it *was* a revolution, and its effects in its own sphere were Ptolemaic: it put the clock back to 1640. English literature emerged as a remote golden age clouded by centuries of dissociation. Poems re-grouped themselves like iron filings round the magnetic personality of John Donne. Long-admired minor figures such as King and Carew began to swell (though no one actually *said* so) into the status of near major poets. The desired quality was no longer the sanity and poise looked for by Dr Johnson, nor the criticism of life expected by Matthew Arnold, but the intellect at the tips of the senses. Not unnaturally, the early seventeenth century began to glow with a special radiance.

The brilliance and lasting interest of Eliot's analysis are, of course, undeniable. For 250 years the importance of metaphysical poetry had been neglected, and its widespread reading and praise by the Victorians – and later the Georgians – only emphasized their inability to see its real merits. From Palgrave's *Golden Treasury* onwards the record is one of distortion. Herrick, for example, is given a consistently false prominence because of his sweetness and clarity. Ironically enough, precisely the same fortune has attended a number of minor Victorian poets as a consequence of misapplying the theories of Eliot, as I shall show in a moment. To be fair to Eliot, his own practice in dealing with major figures like Swinburne and Kipling is reasonably just: his admiration for why they work as well as they do is allowed to come through. Nevertheless, he was historically and temperamentally very ill-placed to sort out the minor Victorian trees from the wood. Apart from anything else, he was led into his revival of metaphysical standards partly as a practising poet reacting against the dilute (as he believed) sub-Victorian gentility of poets like Brooke and Bottomley. Actually, he went too far in condemning this, even by his own standards. Abercrombie, for example, was our best writer of dramatic blank verse since Beddoes, and his work lends itself well to analysis by the techniques Eliot applied to Ford. Nevertheless, a distaste for a culture tottering from the verge of Tupper to the brink of Drinkwater is historically explicable.

After all, the Victorians were not the Georgians, and their poetic achievement was hugely richer. As I suggested earlier, its central excellence lay in the development of narrative fiction, a replacement of the Romantic concern for subjective emotion with a quite new concern for imaginary situations. It was this which Eliot's own preoccupations blinded him to. Perhaps the extent of his neglect can be indicated by suggesting that Tennyson – whom he treats chiefly as the author of *In Memoriam* – is the most consistently successful writer of symbolist narrative in the nineteenth century, and tends to be at his weakest when directly aiming to reveal his own feelings: that Browning – whom he scarcely treats at all – is perhaps the most effective creator of character in English, after Dickens and Shakespeare: that Arnold – whom he treats as a critic – is the author of the only two poems apart from *Beowulf* and *Paradise Lost* which have an obvious claim to be classed as English epics: and that Evans, Lee-Hamilton, Brown, Dobson, Meredith, Morris and Newbolt – most of whom he never mentions – are the richest cluster of minor verse fiction-writers our country can show at any one time. All these poets – without exception – were for many years sunk into the slough of abysmal neglect.

The one Victorian poet who survived, and was – and rightly – admired, was Hopkins. The reason is the obvious one that – apart from anthology appearances – his work had never been published until 1918. Its arrival on the scene at the very moment when Eliot was recommending the metaphysical virtues of ambiguity and concision allowed a superficially attractive re-ordering of the Victorian scene with him at its centre. Unfortunately, though Hopkins seemed well suited to play the role of the Victorian Donne, it was not so easy to find candidates for the other roles in the metaphysical pantheon. It took many years for the two alternative possibilities to be fully worked out. The first began to appear in 1950 in books like Geoffrey Grigson's anthology *The Victorians* and John Heath-Stubbs's critical study *The Darkling Plain*. The Heath-Stubbs book – together with the ingenious anthology he edited with David Wright, *The Forsaken Garden* – provides an excellent example. It enshrines – with much skill and sound argument – what might be called the retrospective fallacy. This consists in accounting for the inadequacy of Victorian poetry by explaining it as a falling away from the high

standards of what preceded it. *The Darkling Plain* is sub-
titled 'a study of the later fortunes of Romanticism in
English poetry', and its conclusion is that no poetry which
fails to satisfy both the intellect and the senses – as much
Victorian poetry does – can ever last. In the poetry of the
great Romantics we obtain this necessary synthesis, but in
the Victorian period, with the exception of Hopkins, and
his ally Patmore, it must usually be sought for in vain.
Certain minor figures like Hawker and Doughty emerge
from the murk but, on the whole, the central figures of the
tradition – Tennyson and Browning, in particular – must
be regretfully abandoned.

The second way of looking at the period emerges in the
work of slightly later critics such as Frank Kermode and
Ian Fletcher, who have concentrated on the 1890s. They
present a case of what might be called the prospective
fallacy. This consists in beginning with the merits of the
great twentieth-century figures and tracing back the seeds
of their achievement to its primitive origins in the last
Victorians. The latter part of the nineteenth century is
presented as a process of gradual acceleration towards the
modern movement, with Symons and Gray appearing as
forerunners of Eliot, and Yeats emerging as the appro-
priately Donne-like major poet round whom the whole
analysis can be grouped. Superficially, this view has more
plausibility, since there is little doubt that Yeats is a
genuinely key figure, and one of a peculiarly hybrid nature,
with one foot in the nineteenth century and one in the
twentieth. Unfortunately, the only poet who shares this
fate is the very minor figure John Gray, whom the prospec-
tive fallacy extensively over-values. Of course, purely
nineteenth-century poets like Symons and Stevenson do run
counter to the tone of the Victorian period by being at their
best with autobiographical material, but their achievement
is not on a scale to provide an adequate buttressing of the
theory against the counter-example of Kipling, a poet of
the 1890s who is squarely in the fictive tradition of Browning

and Barnes. Moreover, very little is done by the prospective analysis with any writer active before about 1870, and the solution for Tennyson and Browning becomes one of relative neglect. Obviously enough, no theory which avoids or shrinks Tennyson and Browning is going to make sense of the Victorian Age, any more than one which avoids or shrinks Milton and Dryden is going to make sense of the late seventeenth century. The reason why neither the retrospective nor the prospective analysts have noticed this is not so much their indebtedness to Eliot's conclusions – which in the case of the seventeenth century they sometimes condemn – as their (often unacknowledged) indebtedness to the tools with which he reached them. Most of these tools were forged in the battle for the metaphysicals, but the passage of time has extracted them from context and enshrined them in – or rather *as* – the common critical arsenal, with their predecessors relegated to the basement. Unfortunately, neither detailed textual analysis, nor a correspondence theory of value seeking to match effects with states of mind, nor a moral revulsion from the hortatory and the sentimental, will get the critic very far with Kipling, Sebastian Evans or later Tennyson.

To take an example. It seems to me that the greatest of Victorian poems is *The Idylls of The King*, a work to which the most accomplished verse technician of his age devoted fifteen years of his life. The Victorians themselves were divided about this poem, and it was sometimes heavily criticized. Modern opponents have argued against it largely on grounds which are irrelevant. These grounds have included flaccid looseness of rhythm, thin diction, artificiality of characters and situations, and an absence of Miltonic narrative structure. As observations, these grounds are accurate, but as value-judgements they are not. To take the points in reverse order, the poem's construction is based on techniques of cutting which anticipate the cinema; its diction depends on a stripping away of non-relevant adjectives and characters in the interests of classical allegory, and the rhythm arises from Tennyson's attempt to create the illusion of a dream-world by a musical smoothness of metre, as Dali in our own time attempts in his paintings to create the illusion of a dream-world by a glossy clarity of outline. This last point is a crucial one. Tennyson is a vital link between Surrealism and the Pre-Raphaelites, and his concept of the idyll – the basic structural unit of his serial-poem – is more that of a psychological icon than a genre painting. To understand *The Idylls of The King* one must distinguish between the symbolic narrative of Burne-Jones and the realistic narrative of Frith. In Tennyson every picture tells a story, but not every picture tells a story in the way Milton – or even Queen Victoria – would have understood.

The Victorian age is the great age of fiction in English poetry. In the course of it, the ways in which narrative could be used for poetic purposes were developed and exploited more widely and ingeniously than ever before or since. The joint architects of this development were Tennyson and Browning. As an innovator, Browning's role is the more significant of the two. Whether or not Browning and Tennyson invented the dramatic monologue independently, the publication precedence goes to Browning with the anonymous appearance of *Porphyria's Lover* in the *Monthly Repository* in 1836. The seeds of this incredible poem were already scattered in the work of Hood (*The Last Man*), Shelley (*The Cloud*), Praed (*A Letter*) and Moore (*The Fudge Family in Paris*), to take only four examples. It took the genius of Browning, however, to grasp its full potential for development, and it took even Browning six years to publish a collection of poems exhibiting it. If we compare the 1842 volumes of Tennyson and Browning, there are at least nine monologues of Browning's (including *My Last Duchess*, and *Soliloquy of the Spanish Cloister*) compared with Tennyson's two (*Ulysses* and *St Simeon Stylites*). With the possible exception of *Locksley Hall*, the remainder of Tennyson's monologues in this and his earlier volumes – including *Sir Galahad* and *St Agnes* – are essentially lyrical and narrative poems in the first person, rather than dramatic monologues proper. They do not involve opinions distinctly other than the author's own. Nevertheless, the independent role of Tennyson in developing this kind of poem has never had its full due, and should be stressed.

At first sight, it may be puzzling to see just why the Victorians found the dramatic monologue so invaluable. The reason, however, is not far to seek. Put bluntly, the dramatic monologue was a way of lying while seeming to tell the truth. It enabled the Victorian poet to indulge the most cruel and heterodox – though not admittedly blasphemous or sexually frank – opinions while at the same time making it quite clear that he didn't hold them himself. In other words, it completed the revolution in sensibility of the Romantic movement while at the same time preventing the subversion of English society.

If the iconoclasm of Byron and Shelley had been taken up and carried further by the early Victorians, the moral disorder of the later Georgian period would have been boosted – or so many people believed – into social chaos. There was a tide of revulsion against the lax behaviour of the Regency, partly, of course, fostered by the rise of the middle classes, with their dislike of the aristocratic callousness of the class they had seen oppressing their fathers. If Byron and Shelley had lived, they might have carried their standards into the 1840s and created a resistance movement to the new orthodoxy: on the other hand, they might have fossilized or died away, as Wordsworth and Leigh Hunt did, into an unproductive old age. Either way, very little could have altered the changed spirit of the times, which was demanding a new poetry to match a new taste, a desire for adventure within order, for excitement within bounds, and for imaginative exploration within moral conformity.

So far as Browning himself was concerned, the dramatic monologue released a whole range of attitudes – from spite to heroism – which lay far beyond the bounds of his surface social personality. Nobody, of course, could have got away with a poem like *Soliloquy of The Spanish Cloister* in the early Victorian period, if he had presented it as his own personal attitude. The envy would have seemed too vicious, too reminiscent of the worst excesses of Hood in his *Whims and Oddities*. (Significantly, Hood himself was turning into a conventional poet of sentimental social protest in his later work, notably in *The Song of The Shirt*.) Even today, we might find the condemnation of Brother Lawrence too harsh if we thought the poem was a sort of Lowellian Life Study. As an obviously *imaginary* diatribe, however, it falls into a perfectly acceptable category. The question of whether Browning is indulging wicked or cruel impulses can be dismissed as irrelevant. The poem is a piece of fiction.

Of course, it isn't always quite so easy to be sure. Browning's *Prospice*, for example, has often been taken as an expression of personal opinion, and not a monologue, and its shallow optimism has been deservedly attacked. Its noble sentiments, critics have claimed, chime ill with the available details about the pressures bearing on Browning in real life. Its up-beat, they say, hasn't been earned. The bitter pessimism of Eugene Lee-Hamilton, for example, when he cries out against his paralysis in the *Sonnets of The Wingless Hours* obviously springs from a more felt experience and so, the argument runs, we listen to him with more respect. In fact *Prospice* is not an autobiographical poem. It first appeared in a volume of monologues plainly titled *Dramatis Personae*, and the real case against it is the aesthetic one that, as a dramatic monologue, it fails to give adequate richness of placing detail and argument. It isn't nearly fictional *enough*. A much deeper optimistic poem about heroism in the face of approaching death is *Childe Rolande To The Dark Tower Came*, where the speaker is clearly an imaginary character, and the landscape through which he moves is vividly conveyed as a medieval one totally different from Browning's surroundings in real life.

Moreover, to return to Lee-Hamilton, good though some of his autobiographical sonnets are, his best work is in his monologues. The savage anti-Catholic satire of *Ipsissimus* is a far stronger expression of his bitterness at his physical plight than any of his directly agnostic outpourings. The distance of the emotion gives it edge. The strength of Browning and Lee-Hamilton is that both were powerful imaginative writers, as Shakespeare and Webster were. Their fiction extends the range of heard tones, and it makes no difference to a poem like *My Last Duchess* that Browning didn't 'know' what he was talking about, or 'mean' what he was saying. The poem gives us the feel of a way of life entirely beyond the scope of the liberal-humanist tradition.

Apart from Browning and Lee-Hamilton, the poets who made extensive use of the dramatic monologue include Tennyson, Kipling, Hardy, Evans, de Tabley, Augusta Webster, Symons, Morris, Rossetti, Locker-Lampson, Austin, Thornbury, Dobson, Barnes and Brown. It makes an impressive list. In the case of Dobson, the poise of Praed and Moore was fused with the savagery of *My Last Duchess* to produce the elegant satire of *A Virtuoso*. In the case of Brown, the dialect of Barnes was fused with the garrulous envy of the *Soliloquy of The Spanish Cloister* to produce the genial irritability of *Conjergal Rights*. The possibilities of development were endless. In the twentieth century they were taken up (irony of ironies!) by Eliot himself in his development of the dramatic consciousness in *The Waste Land* and *Gerontion*, as pointed out by Hugh Kenner. They were directly exploited in America by Lowell and Jarrell and have recently taken on a new lease of life in England.

The narrative developments of Tennyson were in their own way almost as influential, though their direct connexion with the work of other poets is less easy to trace. In the case of *The Defence of Guenevere*, of course, there seems little doubt that Morris had profited considerably from a reading of the *Morte d'Arthur* and *The Lady of Shalott*. It may be, however, that the sharp cinematic openings of some of his Arthurian poems were an influence on later Tennyson rather than the other way about. Certainly, the driving interest in painting as a metaphor for the narrative content of fiction came to both of them through Rossetti, though he himself never effectively exploited this intuition. Perhaps the most apt pupil of early Tennyson was Matthew Arnold, a poet whose merger of eighteenth-century classicism with nineteenth-century doubt has never fully had its due.

The problem for Arnold was how to reconcile his recurrent pessimism with his intellectual conviction that poetry must be an organized and reasonable response to the question of how to live. A century earlier Arnold would have solved the problem in the same way as Pope. He would have been happy in the luxurious manipulation of the classical genres, reflecting the ordered structure of the world in the structure of his verse. Religious doubt – the syndrome often referred to as the Death of God – had made this impossible. The Death of God is a key theme in later nineteenth-century poetry, and Arnold was one of its pioneers. The most useful cause to allege for it would be the publication of Darwin's *Origin of Species* in 1858, but in fact the symptoms had been widely prevalent long before this. I suspect the central cause to be the Industrial Revolution which led to the breakdown of the clockwork universe of the eighteenth century before Darwin was even born. As factories and railways began to replace farms and stage coaches as the central features of the English landscape, the possibility of treating God as a country squire began to seem less available. A new God was needed, and extensive attempts were made by the mass of the early Victorian poets to find one. The fascinating complex of changing faiths which confront the eye in the Oxford of the 1840s provides one symptom of the search. Not all the seekers, however, were able to find what they sought.

As the century advanced, agnosticism began to gain ground more quickly than a superficial glance at the surface of society would suggest. It was very much a repetition of the situation in Imperial Rome. Public lip service to religion had to be regularly paid, but private disbelief was common and respectable. In poetry, the tension revealed itself regularly – and fruitfully – in the best fiction of Arnold and Meredith. A poem like *Balder Dead*, though written as early as 1855, already expresses the theme of *Dover Beach* (1865) with a more extensive and moving richness. Its preservation of the eighteenth-century harmonies in its construction only serves to underline the deep-seated agony of a mind wrestling with the tragedy of spiritual doubt. In its way, *Balder Dead* is *The Waste Land* of the nineteenth century, the first subjective epic: it advances the Satanism of *Paradise Lost* to a point where *all* the props of the religious life are threatened, and the death of Balder only presages the total götterdämmerung of the gods. The great advantage of the Nordic myth is that it enables Arnold to treat the theme with an explicitness that would have been impossible within the framework of an autobiographical – or even a fictional Christian – narrative. By comparison, the directly personal elegiac poems of Arnold – like *Thyrsis* and *The Scholar Gypsy* – relapse into a pale shadow of the tough classicism of Gray in the *Elegy In a Country Church-yard*.

In the case of Meredith, the Death of God is a background theme in his greatest narrative poem *The Nuptials of Attila*. The foreground theme, however, is Meredith's frustration at his marital problems. These had already been tackled more directly – and less effectively – twenty years earlier in his contemporary verse novel *Modern Love*. This poem is an excellent example of how a single layer of fiction was sometimes less useful to a Victorian poet than a double one. In writing about Attila or King Harald Meredith had the advantage of a remote and appropriately savage period of history to hand. He could write quite naturally about the expression of physical frustration in violent action. In dealing with the contemporary – though thinly disguised – situation of *Modern Love* he had to give his characters the appropriately mixed and uneasy feelings of his own day, the very feelings that the poem was probably written to exorcise, but which it could only suppress and help to foster. As with *In Memoriam* and *Thyrsis*, one sees the whole awkward hesitant frightened unease of Victorian society working through the poet's sincerity – his truth to his 'real', or surface, feelings – to prevent the full expression of rich emotions which lay underneath them. In Meredith's case these eventually obtained their release in the surging, hammering trochees of the later dramatic poems, working out the frustrated husband's inner tensions with the motion of a piston or a battle-axe. For Tennyson, they found their outlet in *The Idylls of The King*, for Arnold in *Balder Dead* and *Sohrab and Rustum*.

For many smaller poets, the problem was never solved at all. Of course, there are good individual poems affirming personal feeling and traditional faith, and there is one group of poets – the Roman Catholics – who devoted much of their output to this. Nevertheless, even the work of Patmore and Thompson is damaged by large tracts of rainbow assertion and misty wrestling. The most available religious poet of the period – after Hopkins – is Richard Watson Dixon, and his best poems depend on an inventive use of dreams in the manner of Blake, not on an honest unpacking of personal opinions.

Dixon, of course, is one of the few poets whose reputation has mildly profited from the re-ordering of the Victorian Age in the wake of Eliot. The same could be said for Arthur Symons. In the past both suffered from the indiscriminate herding-together methods of what one might call the old-boy-net view of the period. This was long fostered by some of the old boys themselves, particularly those who went into the business of public-school-mastering. Hence we find an irritating tendency in critics of the pre-Eliot period to concentrate attention on who was at school – or college – with whom, and – in annoying consequence – what faith he decided to switch to there. On this analysis of the period, the deficiencies of a classical education are mated with those of a Christian upbringing, and the result is a false elevation of quite negligible figures like Cory and Calverley. It also leads – perhaps by little more than the play on words – to an excessive concern with 'schools'. There is a school of Bridges (this is the one Dixon went to), a school of Rossetti, even – by a bit of juggling with the 1890s – a school of Wilde. This kind of discrimination and labelling need not be entirely vicious if the members of the school are legitimately enrolled by similarity of theme and style, as those in my own favourite, the school of Browning, would be. However, the failure of older critics to notice or create a school of Browning illustrates the illegitimate tendency to call groups or movements schools only when the members were *literally* at school or college together, or at least friends and associates. Browning was never at school with anyone. Even a competent survey like Ifor Evans's *English Poetry in The Later 19th Century*, published as late as 1933, is marred by this Edwardian distortion: poets are still being herded together as specimens of their 'class' or as members of a larger poet's 'circle'. The virtues of this method include its genuine comprehensiveness and, in the case of the seventeenth century, it could be argued that the passage of time has left more to be learnt from the sympathetic fullness of Saintsbury than the stringent exclusiveness of Helen Gardner. Nevertheless, in the case of the Victorians, the time is still ripe for the axe rather than the lassoo. The question is only at what points in the joint the cuts should be made.

In Sir Arthur Quiller-Couch's *Oxford Book of Victorian Verse*, there are 273 poets, including such eminent Trojan horses as Ezra Pound and James Joyce. Q was using 'Victorian' as a term of praise rather than time, and as late as 1922 this evidently still made sense. In John Hayward's

31

Oxford Book of 19th Century Verse, published in 1964, there are only eighty-five poets, of whom ten were dead before the reign began. My own object has been to limit the number to about one poet for every year of the reign. If this is felt to be too inclusive, I can only suggest that the *Penguin Book of Elizabethan Verse*, for example, has fifty-three poets for a reign of only forty-five years. The poets I have included are those who seem to me, by and large, the best. In the case of very minor writers there is obviously room for dispute about a number of exclusions. In the case of better known names, I can only think of two deliberately excluded, and this was only after much heart-searching. However, the relative importance of the poets is not always indicated either by the number of poems or the number of pages they get. For example, Arnold is easy to cut, and is under-represented. Evans is difficult to cut, and is over-represented. Moreover, some poets – like Kipling – need more space to demonstrate their quality than others. Nevertheless, I have worked hard to make room for a sensible and just representation of each poet according to his strongest talent, and I have therefore not been afraid to quote a handful of very long poems, and a fairly large number of extracts. The important thing, ultimately, is not a man's poems but his poetry.

Finally, a word about the terminal figures. None of the poets included had established his or her reputation much before 1837. This accounts for the absence of later work by Wordsworth, Landor, Peacock, Leigh Hunt, Clare and Hood, who were all already widely known as far back as the 1820s. Some of the earliest writers included – Macaulay, Tennyson and the Brownings for example – were beginning to come to the fore in the early 1830s, but none was really well known until after 1840. Hence, where to begin is fairly easy to decide. At the other end of the reign the problems of inclusion are more difficult. My youngest poets – Johnson and Dowson – scarcely outlived Victoria herself: those of their generation who survived as men – like

Housman or Symons – often fossilized or died as poets. The great exception is Yeats, whom I have salved my conscience by representing only as a nineties poet. (The same applies to Gray, whose twentieth-century work is quite different from his earlier writings.) The other great exception – though of a much older generation – is Hardy. Although all his best verse was written in the twentieth century it seems to me indisputably late Victorian. As a man of sixty-one when Victoria died, his mind was entirely of the nineteenth century, though the poems he wrote with it were delayed until the twentieth. In a curious way, he is a case – like Hopkins – of delayed publication: the poems were already in existence, but remained locked up in Hardy's brain awaiting a favourable moment to appear before the public.

Like Symons and Stevenson, Hardy is part of the late nineteenth-century autobiographical tradition to which the central Victorian taste for fiction was gradually yielding. His early work, like that of Symons, contains a good proportion of obvious monologues. His later poetry, like that of middle Yeats, is becoming more personal. This drive towards greater sincerity has been the dominant movement of the twentieth century. In the novel it started with the draining away of purely fictional elements by Joyce, Proust and Hemingway, and in our own time it has reached its climax in the theatre of fact and the poetry of confession. The novel itself has begun to yield ground increasingly to the slanted autobiography. The drive for science has led to a drive for the truth. Unless we can escape from this fascination with the thing itself – a process with its analogues in painting and music – the achievement of the Victorian Age will remain unclear and inaccessible. In architecture we shall continue to elevate the Crystal Palace – with its 'honest' expression of structure in glass and iron – above the courteous deceit of St Pancras Station, where iron girders are tucked away under brick arches. In painting we shall continue to prefer the insipid truth to life of

Whistler to the spectacular inventiveness of Watts and Alma-Tadema. In poetry we shall prefer the opium dream of Francis Thompson to the fictive riches of *Brother Fabian's Manuscript*.

GEORGE MACBETH

NOTE ON TEXT AND DATING

THE text of the poems is usually that of the first edition. Victorian spelling and punctuation have been retained as their authors employed them. As far as dating is concerned, I have thought it most convenient to place the date of first publication in book form below each poem quoted. However, this is not always a guide as to when the poem was written. In the case of a poet like Hopkins, not published till long after his death, this is obvious. In the case of a poet like Rossetti, whom I represent by posthumously printed poems, it may be less obvious. The chronological list of books from which poems are quoted (see p. 431) adds some further information in cases of known discrepancy between composition and publication when this exceeds five years.

THOMAS BABINGTON,
LORD MACAULAY
1800–1859

THOMAS BABINGTON MACAULAY was born at Rothley
Temple in Leicestershire. His verse expresses the vigorous
amateur talent of a professional historian. Poems like *The
Armada* and *The Lays of Ancient Rome* form a vital link in
the long chain of English battle poetry going back to Camp-
bell (and eventually Bishop Still) and on to Kipling. Possibly
for sexual reasons, almost all Victorian poets wrote spirited
battle poetry: frustrated desire found its release in the urgent
music of trumpet and drum.

From *The Armada*

Night sank upon the dusky beach, and on the purple sea,
Such night in England ne'er had been, nor e'er again shall
be.
From Eddystone to Berwick bounds, from Lynn to Milford
Bay.
That time of slumber was as bright and busy as the day;
For swift to east and swift to west the ghastly war-flame
spread.
High on St Michael's Mount it shone: it shone on Beachy
Head.
Far on the deep the Spaniard saw, along each southern
shire,
Cape beyond cape, in endless range, those twinkling points
of fire.
The fisher left his skiff to rock on Tamar's glittering waves:
The rugged miners poured to war from Mendip's sunless
caves:
O'er Longleat's towers, o'er Cranbourne's oaks, the fiery
herald flew:
He roused the shepherds of Stonehenge, the rangers of
Beaulieu.

Right sharp and quick the bells all night rang out from
  Bristol town,
And ere the day three hundred horse had met on Clifton
  down;
The sentinel on Whitehall gate looked forth into the night,
And saw o'erhanging Richmond Hill the streak of blood-
  red light.
Then bugle's note and cannon's roar the deathlike silence
  broke,
And with one start, and with one cry, the royal city woke.
At once on all her stately gates arose the answering fires;
At once the wild alarum clashed from all her reeling spires;
From all the batteries of the Tower pealed loud the voice of
  fear;
And all the thousand masts of Thames sent back a louder
  cheer:
And from the furthest wards was heard the rush of hurrying
  feet,
And the broad streams of pikes and flags rushed down each
  roaring street;
And broader still became the blaze, and louder still the
  din,
As fast from every village round the horse came spurring in:
And eastward straight from wild Blackheath the warlike
  errand went,
And roused in many an ancient hall the gallant squires of
  Kent.
Southward from Surrey's pleasant hills flew those bright
  couriers forth;
High on bleak Hampstead's swarthy moor they started for
  the north;
And on, and on, without a pause, untired they bounded
  still:
All night from tower to tower they sprang; they sprang
  from hill to hill:
Till the proud peak unfurled the flag o'er Darwin's rocky
  dales,

Till like volcanoes flared to heaven the stormy hills of
 Wales,
Till twelve fair counties saw the blaze on Malvern's lonely
 height,
Till streamed in crimson on the wind the Wrekin's crest of
 light,
Till broad and fierce the star came forth on Ely's stately
 fane,
And tower and hamlet rose in arms o'er all the boundless
 plain;
Till Belvoir's lordly terraces the sign to Lincoln sent,
And Lincoln sped the message on o'er the wide vale of
 Trent;
Till Skiddaw saw the fire that burned on Gaunt's embattled
 pile,
And the red glare on Skiddaw roused the burghers of
 Carlisle.

[1842]

WILLIAM BARNES
1801–1886

WILLIAM BARNES was born at Sturminster in Dorset. At the age of twenty-three he became the headmaster of a Dorsetshire school. His failure to interest London managements in his plays seems to have been the making of his poetry, since it caused a fusion of his dramatic and metrical talent. The value to Barnes of the Dorsetshire dialect, in which he soon began to write exclusively, was its power to release him from the bondage of a genteel Regency poetic personality. When he wrote in dialect he easily ceased to be himself: the pedantic classicism of a duller Arnold, to which he might have gravitated, freshened into the taut poise of an English Hesiod.

The Best Man in the Vield
(*Eclogue*)

SAM AND BOB

Sam

That's slowish work, Bob. What'st a-been about?
Thy pooken don't goo on not over sprack.
Why I've a-pook'd my weale, lo'k zee, clear out,
An' here I be agean a-turnen back.

Bob

I'll work wi' thee then, Sammy, any day,
At any work dost like to teake me at,
Vor any money thou dost like to lay.
Now, Mister Sammy, what dost think o' that?
My weale is nearly twice so big as thine,
Or else, I warnt, I shouldden be behin'.

Sam

Ah! hang thee, Bob! don't tell sich whoppen lies.
My weale's the biggest, if do come to size.

'Tis jist the seame whatever bist about;
Why, when dost goo a-tedden grass, you sloth,
Another hand's a-fwoc'd to teake thy zwath,
An' ted a half way back to help thee out;
An' then a-reaken rollers, bist so slack,
Dost keep the very bwoys an' women back.
An' if dost think that thou canst challenge I
At any thing, – then, Bob, we'll teake a pick a-piece,
An' woonce thease zummer, goo an' try
To meake a rick a-piece.
A rick o' thine wull look a little funny,
When thou'st a-done en, I'll bet any money.

Bob

You noggerhead! last year thou mead'st a rick,
An' then we had to trig en wi' a stick.
An' what did John that tipp'd en zay? Why zaid
He stood a-top o'en all the while in dread,
A-thinken that avore he should a-done en
He'd tumble over slap wi' him upon en.

Sam

You yoppen dog! I warnt I meade my rick
So well's thou mead'st thy lwoad o' hay last week.
They hadden got a hundred yards to haul en,
An' then they vound 'twer best to have en boun',
Vor if they hadden, 'twould a-tumbl'd down;
An' after that I zeed en all but vallen,
An' trigg'd en up wi' woone o'm's pitchen pick,
To zee if I could meake en ride to rick;
An' when they had the dumpy heap unboun',
He vell to pieces flat upon the groun'.

Bob

Do shut thy lyen chops! What dosten mind
Thy pitchen to me out in Gully-plot,
A-meaken o' me wait (wast zoo behind)

41

A half an hour vor ev'ry pitch I got?
An' how didst groun' thy pick? an' how didst quirk
To get en up on end? Why hadst hard work
To rise a pitch that wer about so big
'S a goodish crow's nest, or a wold man's wig!
Why bist so weak, dost know, as any roller:
Zome o' the women vo'k will beat thee hollor.

Sam

You snub-nos'd flopperchops! I pitch'd so quick,
That thou dost know thou hadst a hardish job
To teake in all the pitches off my pick;
An' dissen zee me groun' en, nother, Bob.
An' thou bist stronger, thou dost think, than I?
Girt bandy-lags! I jist should like to try.
We'll goo, if thou dost like, an' jist zee which
Can heave the mwost, or car the biggest nitch.

Bob

There, Sam, do meake me zick to hear thy braggen!
Why bissen strong enough to car a flagon.

Sam

You grinnen fool! why I'd zet thee a-blowen,
If thou wast wi' me vor a day a-mowen.
I'd wear my cwoat, an' thou midst pull thy rags off,
An' then in half a zwath I'd mow thy lags off.

Bob

Thee mow wi' me! Why coosen keep up wi' me:
Why bissen fit to goo a-vield to skimmy,
Or mow down docks an' thistles! Why I'll bet
A shillen, Samuel, that thou cassen whet.

Sam

Now don't thee zay much mwore than what'st a-zaid,
Or else I'll knock thee down, heels over head.

Bob

Thou knock me down, indeed! Why cassen gi'e
A blow half hard enough to kill a bee.

Sam

Well, thou shalt veel upon thy chops and snout.

Bob

Come on, then Samuel; jist let's have woone bout.

[1844]

The Bachelor

No! I don't begrudge en his life,
　　Nor his goold, nor his housen, nor lands;
Teake all o't, an' gi'e me my wife,
　　A wife's be the cheapest ov hands.
　　　　Lie alwone! sigh alwone! die alwone!
　　　　　　Then be vorgot.
　　　　No! I be content wi' my lot.

Ah! where be the vingers so feair,
　　Vor to pat en so soft on the feace,
To mend ev'ry stitch that do tear,
　　An' keep ev'ry button in pleace?
　　　　Crack a-tore! brack a-tore! back a-tore!
　　　　　　Buttons a-vled!
　　　　Vor want ov a wife wi' her thread.

Ah! where is the sweet-perty head
　　That do nod till he's gone out o' zight?
An' where be the two earms a-spread,
　　To show en he's welcome at night?
　　　　Dine alwone! pine alwone! whine alwone!
　　　　　　Oh! what a life!
　　　　I'll have a friend in a wife.

43

An' when vrom a meeten o' me'th
  Each husban'd do lead hwome his bride,
Then he do slink hwome to his he'th,
  Wi' his earm a-hung down his cwold zide.
    Slinken on! blinken on! thinken on!
        Gloomy an' glum;
    Nothen but dullness to come.

An' when he do onlock his door,
  Do rumble as hollow's a drum,
An' the vearies a-hid roun' the vloor,
  Do grin vor to see en so glum.
    Keep alwone! sleep alwone! weep alwone!
        There let en bide,
    I'll have a wife at my zide.

But when he's a-laid on his bed
  In a zickness, O, what wull he do!
Vor the hands that would lift up his head,
  An' sheake up his pillor anew.
    Ills to come! pills to come! bills to come!
        Noo soul to sheare
    The trials the poor wratch must bear.

[1859]

Sam'el Down vrom Lon'on

When Cousin Sam come down vrom Lon'on,
Along at vu'st I wer' so mad wi'n,
He though hizzelf so very cunnen;
But eet, vor all, what fun we had wi'n!
Why, if a goose did only wag her tail,
An' come a-hissen at his lags, she'd zet en
A-meaken off behine a wall or rail
A-waken, but as vast as shame would let en.
Or if a zow did nod her lop-ear'd head,
A-trotten an' a-grunten wi' her litter,

44

Sh'd put the little chap in zich a twitter,
His vaice did quiver in his droat wi' dread,
An' if a bull did screape the ground an' bleare,
His dizzy head did poke up every heair.
An' eet he thought hizzell a goodish rider,
An' we all thought there werden many woo'se;
'E zot upon the meare so scram's a spider,
A-holden on the web o'n, when 'tis loose.
Oone day, when we wer' all a little idle,
He zaid he'd have a ride upon the hoss a bit.
An' Sorrell when she vound en pull the bridle
In his queer way, begun to prance an' toss a bit.
An' he did knit his brows, an' scwold the meare,
An' she agean did trample back an' rear,
A-woonderen who 'twer' she had to zit zoo,
An' what queer han' di tuggy at her bit zoo.
But when she got her head a little rightish,
She carr'd en off, while we did nearly split
Our zides a-laefen, vor to zee en zit,
If zit he did, an' that did meake en spitish.
Zoo on 'e rod so fine, a poken out
His two splay veet avore en, all astrout,
A-flappen up his elbows, lik' two wings,
To match the hosses steps, wi' timely springs.
But there, poor Sam'el hadded gone
Droo Hwomegroun' when wold Sorrel shied
At zome 'hat there, an' sprung azide
An' shot off Sam'el lik' a bag o' bron.
'E vell, 'tis true, upon a grassy hump,
But nearly squilch'd his breath out wi' the thump,
An' squot the sheenen hat 'e wore,
An' laid wi' all his lim's a-spread,
An' seemenly so loose an' dead,
'S a doll a-cast upon a vloor.
When Cousin Sam come down vrom Lon'on,
He thought hizzell so very cunnen.

[1879]

45

JAMES CLARENCE MANGAN

1803–1849

JAMES CLARENCE MANGAN was born in Dublin of poor parents. His life is a record of privation succeeded by addiction to drugs and alcohol ending in insanity. His *Poems On Oriental Subjects*, of which *The Karamanian Exile* is the most vigorous, were imaginary translations aimed to give the name of Mangan the aura of Hafiz.

The Karamanian Exile

I see thee ever in my dreams,
Karaman!
Thy hundred hills, thy thousand streams,
Karaman, O Karaman!
As when thy gold-bright morning gleams,
As when the deepening sunset seams
With lines of light thy hills and streams,
Karaman!
So thou loomest on my dreams,
Karaman!
On all my dreams, my homesick dreams,
Karaman, O Karaman!

The hot bright plains, the sun, the skies,
Karaman!
Seem death-black marble to mine eyes,
Karaman, O Karaman!
I turn from summer's blooms and dyes;
Yet in my dreams thou dost arise
In welcome glory to mine eyes,
Karaman!
In thee my life of life yet lies,
Karaman!

Thou still art holy in mine eyes,
Karaman, O Karaman!

Ere my fighting years were come,
Karaman!
Troops were few in Erzerome,
Karaman, O Karaman!
Their fiercest came from Erzerome,
They came from Ukhbar's palace dome,
They dragg'd me forth from thee, my home,
Karaman!
Thee, my own, my mountain home,
Karaman!
In life and death, my spirit's home,
Karaman, O Karaman!

O none of all my sisters ten,
Karaman!
Loved like me my fellow-men,
Karaman, O Karaman!
I was mild as milk till then,
I was soft as silk till then;
Now my breast is as a den,
Karaman!
Foul with blood and bones of men,
Karaman!
With blood and bones of slaughter'd men,
Karaman, O Karaman!

My boyhood's feelings newly born,
Karaman!
Wither'd like young flowers uptorn,
Karaman, O Karaman!
And in their stead sprang weed and thorn;
What once I loved now moves my scorn;
My burning eyes are dried to horn,
Karaman!

I hate the blessed light of morn,
Karaman!
It maddens me, the face of morn,
Karaman, O Karaman!

The Spahi wears a tyrant's chains,
Karaman!
But bondage worse than this remains,
Karaman, O Karaman!
His heart is black with million stains:
Thereon, as on Kaf's blasted plains,
Shall nevermore fall dews and rains,
Karaman!
Save poison-dews and bloody rains,
Karaman!
Hell's poison-dews and bloody rains,
Karaman, O Karaman!

But life at worst must end ere long,
Karaman!
Azrael avengeth every wrong,
Karaman, O Karaman!
Of late my thoughts rove more among
Thy fields; o'ershadowing fancies throng
My mind, and texts of bodeful song,
Karaman!
Azrael is terrible and strong,
Karaman!
His lightning sword smites all ere long,
Karaman, O Karaman!

There's care to-night in Ukhbar's halls,
Karaman!
There's hope, too, for his trodden thralls,
Karaman, O Karaman!
What lights flash red along yon walls?
Hark! hark, the muster-trumpet calls!

I see the sheen of spears and shawls,
Karaman!
The foe! the foe! – they scale the walls,
Karaman!
To-night Muràd or Ukhbar falls,
Karaman, O Karaman!

[1832]

GEORGE OUTRAM
1805–1851

GEORGE OUTRAM was born at Clyde Ironworks, of which his father was manager. He died at Rosemore on the Holy Loch. In 1837 he became editor of *The Glasgow Herald*. Many of his poems were casually dashed off for dinners and social occasions. *The Annuity* vividly demonstrates the effectiveness of Scots as a vehicle for robust humour.

The Annuity

I gaed to spend a week in Fife –
 An unco week it proved to be –
For there I met a waesome wife
 Lamentin' her viduity.
Her grief brak out sae fierce and fell,
I thought her heart wad burst the shell;
And – I was sae left to mysel' –
 I sell't her an annuity.

The bargain lookit fair eneugh –
 She just was turned o' saxty-three –
I couldna guessed she'd prove sae teugh
 By human ingenuity.
But years have come, and years have gane
And there she's yet as stieve's a stane –
The limmer's growin' young again,
 Since she got her annuity.

She's crined awa' to bane an' skin;
 But that it seems is naught to me;
She's like to live – although she's in
 The last stage o' tenuity.
She munches wi' her wizened gums,
An' stumps about on legs o' thrums,
But comes – as sure as Christmas comes –
 To ca' for her annuity.

She jokes her joke, an' cracks her crack,
    As spunkie as a growin' flea –
An' there she sits upon my back,
    A livin' perpetuity.
She hurkles by the ingle side,
An' toasts an' tans her wrunkled hide –
Lord kens how lang she yet may bide
    To ca' for her annuity.

I read the tables drawn wi' care
    For an Insurance Company,
Her chance o' life was stated there,
    Wi' perfect perspicuity.
But tables here or tables there,
She's lived ten years beyond her share,
An's like to live a dozen mair,
    To ca' for her annuity.

I got the loon that drew the deed –
    We spelled it o'er right carefully; –
In vain he yerked his souple head,
    To find an ambiguity:
It's dated – tested – a' complete –
The proper stamp – nae word delete –
And diligence, as on decreet,
    May pass for her annuity.

Last Yule she had a fearfu' hoast –
    I thought a kink might set me free;
I led her out, 'mang snaw and frost,
    Wi' constant assiduity.
But Deil ma' care! – the blast gaed by,
An' missed the auld anatomy;
It just cost me a tooth, forbye
    Discharging her annuity.

I thought the grief might gar her quit -
    Her only son was lost at sea –
But aff her wits behuved to flit,
    An' leave her in fatuity!
She threeps, an' threeps, he's livin' yet,
For a' the tellin' she can get;
But catch the doited runt forget
    To ca' for her annuity!

If there's a sough o' cholera
    Or typhus – wha sae gleg as she?
She buys up baths, an' drugs, an' a',
    In siccan superfluity!
She doesna need – she's fever proof –
The pest gaed o'er her very roof;
She tauld me sae – an' then her loof
    Held out for her annuity.

Ae day she fell – her arm she brak, –
    A compound fracture as could be;
Nae Leech the cure wad undertak,
    Whate'er was the gratuity.
It's cured! – She handles't like a flail –
It does as weel in bits as hale;
But I'm a broken man mysel'
    Wi' her and her annuity.

Her broozled flesh an' broken banes,
    Are weel as flesh an' banes can be.
She beats the taeds that live in stanes,
    An' fatten in vacuity.
They die when they're exposed to air –
They canna thole the atmosphere;
But her! – expose her onywhere, –
    She lives for her annuity.

If mortal means could nick her thread,
    Sma' crime it wad appear to me;
Ca't murder – or ca't homicide –
    I'd justify't – an' do it tae.
But how to fell a wither'd wife
That's carved out o' the tree o' life –
The timmer limmer daurs the knife
    To settle her annuity.

I'd try a shot. – But whar's the mark? –
    Her vital parts are hid frae me;
Her backbane wanders through her sark,
    In an unkenn'd corkscrewity.
She's palsified – and shakes her head
Sae fast about, yet scarce can see't;
It's past the power o' steel or lead
    To settle her annuity.

She might be drowned; but go she'll not
    Within a mile o' loch or sea; –
Or hanged – if cord could grip a throat
    O' siccan exiguity.
It's fitter far to hang the rope –
It draws out like a telescope;
'Twad tak a dreadfu' length o' drop
    To settle her annuity.

Will puzion do't? – It has been tried;
    But, be't in hash or fricassee,
That's just the dish she can't abide,
    Whatever kind o' *goût* it hae.
It's needless to assail her doubts, –
She gangs by instinct – like the brutes –
An' only eats and drinks what suits
    Hersel' an' her annuity.

The Bible says the age o' man
    Threescore an' ten perchance may be;
She's ninety-four; – let them wha can
    Explain the incongruity.
She should hae lived afore the Flood –
She's come o' Patriarchal blood –
She's some auld Pagan mummified,
    Alive for her annuity.

She's been embalm'd inside and out –
    She's sauted to the last degree –
There's pickle in her very snout,
    Sae caper-like an' cruety;
Lot's wife was fresh compared to her;
They've Kayanized the useless knir;
She canna decompose – nae mair
    Than her accursed annuity.

The water-drap wears out the rock
    As this eternal jaud wears me;
I could withstand the single shock,
    But no the continuity.
It's pay me here – an' pay me there –
And pay me, pay me, evermair;
I'll gang demented wi' despair –
    I'm *charged* for her annuity.

[1851]

knir: witch.

54

ELIZABETH BARRETT BROWNING
1806–1861

ELIZABETH BARRETT BROWNING was born in County
Durham and died in Italy. She was an invalid from the age
of fifteen, and a precocious writer of verse. In 1846 she
married Robert Browning, and thereafter both her health and
her poetry improved. Her surviving claim to literary fame
(though a considerable one) is the book-length poem *Aurora
Leigh* published when she was fifty-one. This dissolves into
a series of energetic fragments, but these demonstrate a
striking power to argue in rhythm, and to support reasons
with original images.

From *Aurora Leigh*

(Book V)

The critics say that epics have died out
With Agamemnon and the goat-nursed gods;
I'll not believe it. I could never deem
As Payne Knight did, (the mythic mountaineer
Who travelled higher than he was born to live,
And showed sometimes the goitre in his throat
Discoursing of an image seen through fog,)
That Homer's heroes measured twelve feet high.
They were but men: – his Helen's hair turned gray
Like any plain Miss Smith's who wears a front;
And Hector's infant whimpered at a plume
As yours last Friday at a turkey-cock.
All actual heroes are essential men,
And all men possible heroes: every age,
Heroic in proportions, double-faced,
Looks backward and before, expects a morn
And claims an epos.
                              Ay, but every age
Appears to souls who live in't (ask Carlyle)
Most unheroic. Ours, for instance, ours:

The thinkers scout it, and the poets abound
Who scorn to touch it with a finger-tip:
A pewter age, – mixed metal, silver-washed;
An age of scum, spooned off the richer past,
An age of patches for old gaberdines,
An age of mere transition, meaning nought
Except that what succeeds must shame it quite
If God please. That's wrong thinking, to my mind,
And wrong thoughts make poor poems.

       Every age,
Through being beheld too close, is ill-discerned
By those who have not lived past it. We'll suppose
Mount Athos carved, as Alexander schemed,
To some colossal statue of a man.
The peasants, gathering brushwood in his ear,
Had guessed as little as the browsing goats
Of form or feature of humanity
Up there, – in fact, had travelled five miles off
Or ere the giant image broke on them,
Full human profile, nose and chin distinct,
Mouth, muttering rhythms of silence up the sky
And fed at evening with the blood of suns;
Grand torso, – hand, that flung perpetually
The largesse of a silver river down
To all the country pastures. 'T is even thus
With times we live in, – evermore too great
To be apprehended near.

       But poets should
Exert a double vision; should have eyes
To see near things as comprehensively
As if afar they took their point of sight,
And distant things as intimately deep
As if they touched them. Let us strive for this.
I do distrust the poet who discerns
No character or glory in his times,
And trundles back his soul five hundred years,
Past moat and drawbridge, into a castle-court,

To sing – oh, not of lizard or of toad
Alive i' the ditch there, – 't were excusable,
But of some black chief, half knight, half sheep-lifter,
Some beauteous dame, half chattel and half queen,
As dead as must be, for the greater part,
The poems made on their chivalric bones;
And that's no wonder: death inherits death.

Nay, if there 's room for poets in this world
A little overgrown, (I think there is)
Their sole work is to represent the age,
Their age, not Charlemagne's, – this live, throbbing age
That brawls, cheats, maddens, calculates, aspires,
And spends more passion, more heroic heat,
Betwixt the mirrors of its drawing-rooms,
Than Roland with his knights at Roncesvalles.
To flinch from modern varnish, coat or flounce,
Cry out for togas and the picturesque,
Is fatal, – foolish too. King Arthur's self
Was commonplace to Lady Guenever;
And Camelot to minstrels seemed as flat
As Fleet Street to our poets.

[1857]

From *Aurora Leigh*

(Book VII)

I just knew it when we swept
Above the old roofs of Dijon: Lyons dropped
A spark into the night, half trodden out
Unseen. But presently the winding Rhone
Washed out the moonlight large along his banks
Which strained their yielding curves out clear and clean
To hold it, – shadow of town and castle blurred
Upon the hurrying river. Such an air
Blew thence upon the forehead, – half an air

And half a water, – that I leaned and looked,
Then, turning back on Marian, smiled to mark
That she looked only on her child, who slept,
His face toward the moon too.
                              So we passed
The liberal open country and the close,
And shot through tunnels, like a lightning-wedge
By great Thor-hammers driven through the rock,
Which, quivering through the intestine blackness, splits,
And lets it in at once: the train swept in
Athrob with effort, trembling with resolve,
The fierce denouncing whistle wailing on
And dying off smothered in the shuddering dark,
While we, self-awed, drew troubled breath, oppressed
As other Titans underneath the pile
And nightmare of the mountains. Out, at last,
To catch the dawn afloat upon the land!
– Hills, slung forth broadly and gauntly everywhere,
Not crampt in their foundations, pushing wide
Rich outspreads of the vineyards and the corn,
(As if they entertained i' the name of France)
While, down their straining sides, streamed manifest
A soil as red as Charlemagne's knightly blood,
To consecrate the verdure. Some one said,
'Marseilles!' And lo, the city of Marseilles,
With all her ships behind her, and beyond,
The scimitar of ever-shining sea
For right-hand use, bared blue against the sky!

[1857]

CHARLES TENNYSON TURNER
1808–1879

CHARLES TENNYSON TURNER, an elder brother of Alfred
Tennyson, was also born in Lincolnshire. He died in
Cheltenham after a life spent as a country clergyman.
Almost all his poems are sonnets, though the Victorians –
keen critics in this area – debated whether they were all in
acceptable sonnet form. Nowadays, his relaxed naturalness
at the expense of traditional structure is unlikely to be an
obstacle. Read in bulk his work bores, despite its attractive
variety of subject-matter: there is too often a tendency to
moralize. The earlier – and worse – sonnets (published in
a joint collection of poems with his brother Alfred) were
admired and annotated by Coleridge.

The Buoy-Bell

How like the leper, with his own sad cry
Enforcing his own solitude, it tolls!
That lonely bell set in the rushing shoals,
To warn us from the place of jeopardy!
O friend of man! sore-vext by ocean's power,
The changing tides wash o'er thee day by day;
Thy trembling mouth is fill'd with bitter spray,
Yet still thou ringest on from hour to hour;
High is thy mission, though thy lot is wild –
To be in danger's realm a guardian sound;
In seamen's dreams a pleasant part to bear,
And earn their blessing as the year goes round;
And strike the key-note of each grateful prayer,
Breathed in their distant homes by wife or child!

[1864]

The White Horse of Westbury

As from the Dorset shore I travell'd home,
I saw the charger of the Wiltshire wold;
A far-seen figure, stately to behold,
Whose groom the shepherd is, the hoe his comb;
His wizard-spell even sober daylight own'd;
That night I dream'd him into living will;
He neigh'd – and, straight, the chalk pour'd down the hill;
He shook himself, and all beneath was stoned;
Hengist and Horsa shouted o'er my sleep,
Like fierce Achilles; while that storm-blanch'd horse
Sprang to the van of all the Saxon force,
And push'd the Britons to the Western deep;
Then, dream-wise, as it were a thing of course,
He floated upwards, and regain'd the steep.

[1868]

Letty's Globe

When Letty had scarce pass'd her third glad year,
And her young, artless words began to flow,
One day we gave the child a colour'd sphere
Of the wide earth, that she might mark and know,
By tint and outline, all its sea and land.
She patted all the world; old empires peep'd
Between her baby fingers; her soft hand
Was welcome at all frontiers. How she leap'd,
And laugh'd, and prattled in her world-wide bliss;
But when we turned her sweet unlearned eye
On our own isle, she raised a joyous cry,
'Oh! yes, I see it, Letty's home is there!'
And, while she hid all England with a kiss,
Bright over Europe fell her golden hair.

[1880]

The Drowned Spaniel

The day-long bluster of the storm was o'er:
The sands were bright; the winds had fallen asleep:
And, from the far horizon, o'er the deep
The sunset swam unshadow'd to the shore.
High up the rainbow had not pass'd away,
When roving o'er the shingly beach I found
A little waif, a spaniel newly drown'd;
The shining waters kiss'd him as he lay.
In some kind heart thy gentle memory dwells,
I said, and, though thy latest aspect tells
Of drowning pains and mortal agony,
Thy master's self might weep and smile to see
His little dog stretch'd on these rosy shells,
Betwixt the rainbow and the golden sea.

[1880]

EDWARD FITZGERALD
1809–1883

EDWARD FITZGERALD was born in Suffolk. His version of
the Rubáiyát of Omar Khayyám – much criticized for in-
accuracy, and much revised – was one of the most widely
read poems of the late nineteenth and early twentieth
centuries. Its 'philosophy' offered a crude hedonism to
replace the homely Christianity put out of court for many
people by the supposed Death of God. The earliest and
most Romantic text is still the best.

From *The Rubáiyát of Omar Khayyám*

I

Awake! for Morning in the Bowl of Night
Has flung the Stone that puts the Stars to Flight:
  And Lo! the Hunter of the East has caught
The Sultán's Turret in a Noose of Light.

II

Dreaming when Dawn's Left Hand was in the Sky
I heard a Voice within the Tavern cry,
  'Awake, my Little ones, and fill the Cup
Before Life's Liquor in its Cup be dry.'

III

And, as the Cock crew, those who stood before
The Tavern shouted – 'Open then the Door!
  You know how little while we have to stay,
And, once departed, may return no more.'

IV

Now the New Year reviving old Desires,
The thoughful Soul to Solitude retires,
  Where the WHITE HAND OF MOSES on the bough
Puts out, and Jesus from the Ground suspires.

V

Irám indeed is gone with all its Rose,
And Jamshýd's Sev'n-ring'd Cup where no one knows;
   But still the Vine her ancient Ruby yields,
And still a Garden by the Water blows.

VI

And David's Lips are lock't; but in divine
High piping Pehleví, with 'Wine! Wine! Wine!
   Red Wine!' – the Nightingale cries to the Rose
That yellow Cheek of her's to incarnadine.

VII

Come, fill the Cup, and in the Fire of Spring
The Winter Garment of Repentance fling:
   The Bird of Time has but a little way
To fly – and Lo! the Bird is on the Wing.

VIII

And look – a thousand Blossoms with the Day
Woke – and a thousand scatter'd into Clay:
   And this first Summer Month that brings the Rose
Shall take Jamshýd and Kaikobád away.

IX

But come with old Khayyám, and leave the Lot
Of Kaikobád and Kaikhosrú forgot:
   Let Rustum lay about him as he will,
Or Hátim Tai cry Supper – heed them not.

X

With me along some Strip of Herbage strown
That just divides the desert from the sown,
   Where name of Slave and Sultán scarce is known,
And pity Sultán Máhmúd on his Throne.

XI

Here with a Loaf of Bread beneath the Bough,
A Flask of Wine, a Book of Verse – and Thou
    Beside me singing in the Wilderness –
And Wilderness is Paradise enow.

XII

'How sweet is mortal Sovranty!' – think some:
Others – 'How blest the Paradise to come!'
    Ah, take the Cash in hand and waive the Rest;
Oh, the brave Music of a *distant* Drum!

[1859]

ALFRED, LORD TENNYSON
1809–1892

ALFRED TENNYSON was born at Somersby in Lincoln-shire. In the course of his long life he travelled widely and settled in various parts of England including Twickenham, the Isle of Wight and Sussex. After his appointment as Poet Laureate in 1850, Tennyson began to speak and write with more public authority than any other English poet except Kipling. His was the true voice of Victorian England, ex-pressing with richness, grace and variety the central attitudes of his age. This public success has worked very strongly against the survival of Tennyson's reputation. Older twentieth-century critics began to emphasize the more per-sonal poetry of his early period culminating in the (to me) dully abstract elegy *In Memoriam*. There are now many signs, however, that the neglected power of later Tennyson is beginning to make its mark. Dowse and Palmer have stressed the importance of *Maud* as an anticipation of the frustration-aggression complex: Philip Drew has drawn attention to the cinematic narrative structure of the *Idylls of the Hearth*, particularly *Aylmer's Field*: I myself would want to stress the hallucinatory vividness of *The Idylls of The King* as evidence that Tennyson anticipated the Sur-realists (see the Introduction, p. 24). The full re-instatement of his talent has yet to come. His ability to compete with, and learn from, his juniors marks out Tennyson as a genuine professional who never allowed his work to fossilize and who could still in his seventies produce one of his best poems, *Rizpah*.

Mariana

'Mariana in the moated grange' – *Measure for Measure*

With blackest moss the flower-plots
 Were thickly crusted, one and all:
The rusted nails fell from the knots
 That held the peach to the garden-wall.

The broken sheds look'd sad and strange:
   Unlifted was the clinking latch;
   Weeded and worn the ancient thatch
Upon the lonely moated grange.
      She only said, 'My life is dreary,
        He cometh not,' she said;
      She said, 'I am aweary, aweary,
        I would that I were dead!'

Her tears fell with the dews at even;
   Her tears fell ere the dews were dried;
She could not look on the sweet heaven,
   Either at morn or eventide.
After the flitting of the bats,
   When thickest dark did trance the sky,
   She drew her casement-curtain by,
And glanced athwart the glooming flats.
      She only said, 'The night is dreary,
        He cometh not,' she said;
      She said, 'I am aweary, aweary,
        I would that I were dead!'

Upon the middle of the night,
   Waking she heard the night-fowl crow:
The cock sung out an hour ere light:
   From the dark fen the oxen's low
Came to her: without hope of change,
   In sleep she seem'd to walk forlorn,
   Till cold winds woke the gray-eyed morn
About the lonely moated-grange.
      She only said, 'The day is dreary,
        He cometh not,' she said;
      She said, 'I am aweary, aweary,
        I would that I were dead!'

About a stone-cast from the wall
   A sluice with blacken'd waters slept,

And o'er it many, round and small,
   The cluster'd marish-mosses crept.
Hard by a poplar shook alway,
   All silver-green with gnarled bark:
For leagues no other tree did mark
The level waste, the rounding gray.
      She only said, 'My life is dreary,
         He cometh not,' she said;
      She said, 'I am aweary, aweary,
         I would that I were dead!'

And ever when the moon was low,
   And the shrill winds were up and away,
In the white curtain, to and fro,
   She saw the gusty shadow sway.
But when the moon was very low,
   And wild winds bound within their cell,
   The shadow of the poplar fell
Upon her bed, across her brow.
      She only said, 'The night is dreary,
         He cometh not,' she said;
      She said, 'I am aweary, aweary,
         I would that I were dead!'

All day within the dreamy house,
   The doors upon their hinges creak'd;
The blue fly sung in the pane; the mouse
   Behind the mouldering wainscot shriek'd,
Or from the crevice peer'd about.
   Old faces glimmer'd through the doors,
   Old footsteps trod the upper floors,
Old voices called her from without.
      She only said, 'My life is dreary,
         He cometh not,' she said;
      She said, 'I am aweary, aweary,
         I would that I were dead!'

The sparrow's chirrup on the roof,
    The slow clock ticking, and the sound
Which to the wooing wind aloof
    The poplar made, did all confound
Her sense; but most she loathed the hour
    When the thick-moted sunbeam lay
    Athwart the chambers, and the day
Was sloping toward his western bower.
        Then, said she, 'I am very dreary,
            He will not come,' she said;
        She wept, 'I am aweary, aweary,
            Oh God, that I were dead!'

                                        [1830]

Audley Court

'The Bull, the Fleece are cramm'd, and not a room
For love or money. Let us picnic there
At Audley Court.'
                    I spoke, while Audley feast
Humm'd like a hive all round the narrow quay,
To Francis, with a basket on his arm,
To Francis just alighted from the boat,
And breathing of the sea. 'With all my heart,'
Said Francis. Then we shoulder'd through the swarm,
And rounded by the stillness of the beach
To where the bay runs up its latest horn.
    We left the dying ebb that faintly lipp'd
The flat red granite; so by many a sweep
Of meadow smooth from aftermath we reach'd
The griffin-guarded gates, and pass'd thro' all
The pillar'd dusk of sounding sycamores,
And cross'd the garden to the gardener's lodge,
With all its casements bedded, and its walls
And chimneys muffled in the leafy vine.
    There, on a slope of orchard, Francis laid

A damask napkin wrought with horse and hound,
Brought out a dusky loaf that smelt of home,
And, half-cut-down, a pasty costly-made,
Where quail and pigeon, lark and leveret lay,
Like fossils of the rock, with golden yolks
Imbedded and injellied; last, with these,
A flask of cider from his father's vats,
Prime, which I knew; and so we sat and eat
And talk'd old matters over: who was dead,
Who married, who was like to be, and how
The races went, and who would rent the hall:
Then touch'd upon the game, how scarce it was
This season; glancing thence, discuss'd the farm,
The fourfield system, and the price of grain;
And struck upon the corn-laws, where we split,
And came again together on the king
With heated faces; till he laugh'd aloud;
And, while the blackbird on the pippin hung
To hear him, clapt his hand in mine and sang –

  'Oh! who would fight and march and countermarch,
Be shot for sixpence in a battle-field,
And shovell'd up into a bloody trench
Where no one knows? but let me live my life.

  'Oh! who would cast and balance at a desk,
Perch'd like a crow upon a three-legg'd stool,
Till all his juice is dried, and all his joints
Are full of chalk? but let me live my life.

  'Who'd serve the state? for if I carved my name
Upon the cliffs that guard my native land,
I might as well have traced it in the sands;
The sea wastes all: but let me live my life.

  'Oh! who would love? I woo'd a woman once,
But she was sharper than an eastern wind,
And all my heart turn'd from her, as a thorn
Turns from the sea: but let me live my life.'

  He sang his song, and I replied with mine:
I found it in a volume, all of songs,

Knock'd down to me, when old Sir Robert's pride,
His books – the more the pity, so I said –
Came to the hammer here in March – and this –
I set the words, and added names I knew.
  'Sleep, Ellen Aubrey, sleep, and dream of me:
Sleep, Ellen, folded in thy sister's arm,
And sleeping, haply dream her arm is mine.
  'Sleep, Ellen, folded in Emilia's arm;
Emilia, fairer than all else but thou,
For thou art fairer than all else that is.
  'Sleep, breathing health and peace upon her breast:
Sleep, breathing love and trust against her lip:
I go to-night: I come to-morrow morn.
  'I go, but I return: I would I were
The pilot of the darkness and the dream.
Sleep, Ellen Aubrey, love, and dream of me.'
  So sang we each to either, Francis Hale,
The farmer's son who lived across the bay,
My friend; and I, that having wherewithal,
And in the fallow leisure of my life,
Did what I would; but ere the night we rose
And saunter'd home beneath a moon, that, just
In crescent, dimly rain'd about the leaf
Twilights of airy silver, till we reach'd
The limit of the hills; and as we sank
From rock to rock upon the glooming quay,
The town was hush'd beneath us: lower down
The bay was oily-calm; the harbour-buoy
With one green sparkle ever and anon
Dipt by itself, and we were glad at heart.

[1842]

'Come not, when I am dead'

Come not, when I am dead,
   To drop thy foolish tears upon my grave,
To trample round my fallen head,
   And vex the unhappy dust thou would'st not save.
There let the wind sweep and the plover cry;
     But thou, go by.

Child, if it were thine error or thy crime
   I care no longer, being all unblest:
Wed whom thou wilt, but I am sick of Time,
   And I desire to rest.
Pass on, weak heart, and leave me where I lie:
     Go by, go by.

[1842]

From *The Princess*

The splendour falls on castle walls
   And snowy summits old in story:
The long light shakes across the lakes,
   And the wild cataract leaps in glory.
Blow, bugle, blow, set the wild echoes flying,
Blow, bugle; answer, echoes, dying, dying, dying.

O hark, O hear! how thin and clear,
   And thinner, clearer, farther going!
O sweet and far from cliff and scar
   The horns of Elfland faintly blowing!
Blow, let us hear the purple glens replying:
Blow, bugle; answer, echoes, dying, dying, dying.

O love, they die in yon rich sky,
　　They faint on hill or field or river:
Our echoes roll from soul to soul,
　　And grow for ever and for ever.
Blow, bugle, blow, set the wild echoes flying,
And answer, echoes, answer, dying, dying, dying.

[1847]

From *Maud*

XII

I

Birds in the high Hall-garden
　　When twilight was falling,
Maud, Maud, Maud, Maud,
　　They were crying and calling.

2

Where was Maud? in our wood;
　　And I, who else, was with her,
Gathering woodland lilies,
　　Myriads blow together.

3

Birds in our wood sang
　　Ringing thro' the vallies,
Maud is here, here, here
　　In among the lilies.

4

I kiss'd her slender hand,
　　She took the kiss sedately;
Maud is not seventeen,
　　But she is tall and stately.

5

I to cry out on pride
    Who have won her favour!
O Maud were sure of Heaven
    If lowliness could save her.

6

I know the way she went
    Home with her maiden posy,
For her feet have touch'd the meadows
    And left the daisies rosy.

7

Birds in the high Hall-garden
    Were crying and calling to her,
Where is Maud, Maud, Maud,
    One is come to woo her.

8

Look, a horse at the door,
    And little King Charles is snarling,
Go back, my lord, across the moor,
    You are not her darling.

[1855]

The Charge of The Light Brigade

Half a league, half a league,
    Half a league onward,
All in the valley of Death
    Rode the six hundred.
'Charge,' was the captain's cry;
Their's not to reason why,
Their's not to make reply,
Their's but to do and die,
Into the valley of Death
    Rode the six hundred.

Cannon to right of them,
Cannon to left of them,
Cannon in front of them
  Volley'd and thunder'd;
Storm'd at with shot and shell,
Boldly they rode and well;
Into the jaws of Death,
Into the mouth of Hell,
  Rode the six hundred.

Flash'd all their sabres bare,
Flash'd all at once in air,
Sabring the gunners there,
Charging an army, while
  All the world wonder'd:
Plunged in the battery-smoke
Fiercely the line they broke;
Strong was the sabre-stroke;
Making an army reel
  Shaken and sunder'd.
Then they rode back, but not,
  Not the six hundred.

Cannon to right of them,
Cannon to left of them,
Cannon behind them
  Volley'd and thunder'd;
Storm'd at with shot and shell,
They that had struck so well
Rode thro' the jaws of Death,
Half a league back again,
Up from the mouth of Hell,
All that was left of them,
  Left of six hundred.

Honour the brave and bold!
Long shall the tale be told,
Yea, when our babes are old –
How they rode onward.

[1855]

From *The Holy Grail*

'When the hermit made an end,
In silver armour suddenly Galahad shone
Before us, and against the chapel door
Laid lance, and enter'd, and we knelt in prayer.
And there the hermit slaked my burning thirst
And at the sacring of the mass I saw
The holy elements alone; but he:
"Saw ye no more? I, Galahad, saw the Grail,
The Holy Grail, descend upon the shrine:
I saw the fiery face as of a child
That smote itself into the bread, and went;
And hither am I come; and never yet
Hath what thy sister taught me first to see,
This Holy Thing, fail'd from my side, nor come
Cover'd, but moving with me night and day,
Fainter by day, but always in the night
Blood-red, and sliding down the blacken'd marsh
Blood-red, and on the naked mountain top
Blood-red, and in the sleeping mere below
Blood-red. And in the strength of this I rode,
Shattering all evil customs everywhere,
And past thro' Pagan realms, and made them mine,
And clash'd with Pagan hordes, and bore them down,
And broke thro' all, and in the strength of this
Come victor. But my time is hard at hand,
And hence I go; and one will crown me king
Far in the spiritual city; and come thou, too,
For thou shalt see the vision when I go."

75

'While thus he spake, his eye, dwelling on mine,
Drew me, with power upon me, till I grew
One with him, to believe as he believed.
Then, when the day began to wane, we went.

'There rose a hill that none but man could climb,
Scarr'd with a hundred wintry watercourses –
Storm at the top, and when we gain'd it, storm
Round us and death; for every moment glanced
His silver arms and gloom'd: so quick and thick
The lightnings here and there to left and right
Struck, till the dry old trunks about us, dead,
Yea, rotten with a hundred years of death,
Sprang into fire: and at the base we found
On either hand, as far as eye could see,
A great black swamp and of an evil smell,
Part black, part whiten'd with the bones of men,
Not to be crost, save that some ancient king
Had built a way, where, link'd with many a bridge,
A thousand piers ran into the great Sea.
And Galahad fled along them bridge by bridge,
And every bridge as quickly as he crost
Sprang into fire and vanish'd, tho' I yearn'd
To follow; and thrice above him all the heavens
Open'd and blazed with thunder such as seem'd
Shoutings of all the sons of God: and first
At once I saw him far on the great Sea,
In silver-shining armour starry-clear;
And o'er his head the holy vessel hung
Clothed in white samite or a luminous cloud.
And with exceeding swiftness ran the boat
If boat it were – I saw not whence it came.
And when the heavens open'd and blazed again
Roaring, I saw him like a silver star –
And had he set the sail, or had the boat
Become a living creature clad with wings?
And o'er his head the holy vessel hung

Redder than any rose, a joy to me,
For now I knew the veil had been withdrawn.
Then in a moment when they blazed again
Opening, I saw the least of little stars
Down on the waste, and straight beyond the star
I saw the spiritual city and all her spires
And gateways in a glory like one pearl –
No larger, tho' the goal of all the saints –
Strike from the sea; and from the star there shot
A rose-red sparkle to the city, and there
Dwelt, and I knew it was the Holy Grail,
Which never eyes on earth again shall see.
Then fell the flood of heaven drowning the deep.
And how my feet recross'd the deathful ridge
No memory in me lives; but that I touch'd
The chapel-doors at dawn I know; and thence
Taking my war-horse from the holy man,
Glad that no phantom vext me more, return'd
To whence I came, the gate of Arthur's wars.'

* * *

'Then there remain'd but Lancelot, for the rest
Spake but of sundry perils in the storm;
Perhaps, like him of Cana in Holy Writ,
Our Arthur kept his best until the last;
"Thou, too, my Lancelot," ask'd the King, "my friend,
Our mightiest, hath this Quest avail'd for thee?"

'"Our mightiest!" answer'd Lancelot, with a groan;
"O King!" – and when he paused, methought I spied
A dying fire of madness in his eyes –
"O King, my friend, if friend of thine I be,
Happier are those that welter in their sin,
Swine in the mud, that cannot see for slime,
Slime of the ditch: but in me lived a sin
So strange, of such a kind, that all of pure,
Noble, and knightly in me twined and clung

Round that one sin, until the wholesome flower
And poisonous grew together, each as each,
Not to be pluck'd asunder; and when thy knights
Sware, I sware with them only in the hope
That could I touch or see the Holy Grail
They might be pluck'd asunder. Then I spake
To one most holy saint, who wept and said,
That save they could be pluck'd asunder, all
My quest were but in vain; to whom I vow'd
That I would work according as he will'd.
And forth I went, and while I yearn'd and strove
To tear the twain asunder in my heart,
My madness came upon me as of old,
And whipt me into waste fields far away;
There was I beaten down by little men,
Mean knights, to whom the moving of my sword
And shadow of my spear had been enow
To scare them from me once; and then I came
All in my folly to the naked shore,
Wide flats, where nothing but coarse grasses grew;
But such a blast, my King, began to blow,
So loud a blast along the shore and sea,
Ye could not hear the waters for the blast,
Tho' heapt in mounds and ridges all the sea
Drove like a cataract, and all the sand
Swept like a river, and the clouded heavens
Were shaken with the motion and the sound.
And blackening in the sea-foam sway'd a boat,
Half-swallow'd in it, anchor'd with a chain;
And in my madness to myself I said,
'I will embark and I will lose myself,
And in the great sea wash away my sin.'
I burst the chain, I sprang into the boat.
Seven days I drove along the dreary deep,
And with me drove the moon and all the stars;
And the wind fell, and on the seventh night
I heard the shingle grinding in the surge,

And felt the boat shock earth, and looking up,
Behold, the enchanted towers of Carbonek,
A castle like a rock upon a rock,
With chasm-like portals open to the sea,
And steps that met the breaker! there was none
Stood near it but a lion on each side
That kept the entry, and the moon was full.
Then from the boat I leapt, and up the stairs.
There drew my sword. With sudden-flaring manes
Those two great beasts rose upright like a man,
Each gript a shoulder, and I stood between;
And, when I would have smitten them, heard a voice,
'Doubt not, go forward; if thou doubt, the beasts
Will tear thee piecemeal.' Then with violence
The sword was dash'd from out my hand, and fell.
And up into the sounding hall I past;
But nothing in the sounding hall I saw
No bench nor table, painting on the wall
Or shield of knight; only the rounded moon
Thro' the tall oriel on the rolling sea.
But always in the quiet house I heard,
Clear as a lark, high o'er me as a lark,
A sweet voice singing in the topmost tower
To the eastward: up I climb'd a thousand steps
With pain: as in a dream I seem'd to climb
For ever: at the last I reached a door,
A light was in the crannies, and I heard,
'Glory and joy and honour to our Lord
And to the Holy Vessel of the Grail.'
Then in my madness I essay'd the door;
It gave; and thro' a stormy glare, a heat
As from a seventimes-heated furnace, I,
Blasted and burnt, and blinded as I was,
With such a fierceness that I swoon'd away –
O, yet methought I saw the Holy Grail,
All pall'd in crimson samite, and around
Great angels, awful shapes, and wings and eyes.

And but for all my madness and my sin,
And then my swooning, I had sworn I saw
That which I saw; but what I saw was veil'd
And cover'd; and this quest was not for me.'''

[1869]

From *The Passing of Arthur*

Then rose the King and moved his host by night,
And ever push'd Sir Modred, league by league,
Back to the sunset bound of Lyonnesse –
A land of old upheaven from the abyss
By fire, to sink into the abyss again;
Where fragments of forgotten peoples dwelt,
And the long mountains ended in a coast
Of ever-shifting sand, and far away
The phantom circle of a moaning sea.
There the pursuer could pursue no more,
And he that fled no further fly the King;
And there, that day when the great light of heaven
Burn'd at his lowest in the rolling year,
On the waste sand by the waste sea they closed.
Nor ever yet had Arthur fought a fight
Like this last, dim, weird battle of the west.
A deathwhite mist slept over sand and sea:
Whereof the chill, to him who breathed it, drew
Down with his blood, till all his heart was cold
With formless fear; and ev'n on Arthur fell
Confusion, since he saw not whom he fought,
For friend and foe were shadows in the mist,
And friend slew friend not knowing whom he slew;
And some had visions out of golden youth,
And some beheld the faces of old ghosts
Look in upon the battle; and in the mist
Was many a noble deed, many a base,

And chance and craft and strength in single fights,
And ever and anon with host to host
Shocks, and the splintering spear, the hard mail hewn,
Shield-breakings, and the clash of brands, the crash
Of battleaxes on shatter'd helms, and shrieks
After the Christ, of those who falling down
Looked up for heaven, and only saw the mist;
And shouts of heathen and the traitor knights,
Oaths, insult, filth, and monstrous blasphemies,
Sweat, writhings, anguish, labouring of the lungs
In that close mist, and cryings for the light,
Moans of the dying, and voices of the dead.

   Last, as by some one deathbed after wail
Of suffering, silence follows, or thro' death
Or deathlike swoon, thus over all that shore,
Save for some whisper of the seething seas,
A dead hush fell; but when the dolorous day
Grew drearier toward twilight falling, came
A bitter wind, clear from the North, and blew
The mist aside, and with that wind the tide
Rose, and the pale king glanced across the field
Of battle: but no man was moving there;
Nor any cry of Christian heard thereon,
Nor yet of heathen; only the wan wave
Brake in among dead faces, to and fro
Swaying the helpless hands, and up and down
Tumbling the hollow helmets, of the fallen,
And shiver'd brands that once had fought with Rome,
And rolling far along the gloomy shores
The voice of days of old and days to be.

[1869]

Northern Farmer

NEW STYLE

Dosn't thou 'ear my 'erse's legs, as they canters awaäy?
Proputty, proputty, proputty – that's what I 'ears 'em saäy.
Proputty, proputty, proputty – Sam, thou's an ass for thy
paaïns:
Theer's moor sense i' one o' 'is legs nor in all thy braaïns.

Woä – theer's a craw to pluck wi' tha, Sam: yon's parson's
'ouse –
Dosn't thou knaw that a man mun be eäther a man or a
mouse?
Time to think on it then; for thou'll be twenty to weeäk.
Proputty, proputty – woä then woä – let ma 'ear mysén
speäk.

Me an' thy muther, Sammy, 'as beän a-talkin' o' thee;
Thou's been talkin' to muther, an' she beän a tellin' it me.
Thou'll not marry for munny – thou's sweet upo' parson's
lass –
Noä – thou'll marry fur luvv – an' we boäth on us thinks
tha an ass.

Seeä'd her todaäy goä by – Saäint's-daäy – they was ringing
the bells.
She's a beauty thou thinks – an' soä is scoors o' gells,
Them as 'as munny an' all – wots a beauty? – the flower as
blaws.
But proputty, proputty sticks, an' proputty, proputty graws.

Do'ant be stunt: taäke time: I knaws what maäkes tha sa
mad.
Warn't I craäzed fur the lasses mysén when I wur a lad?
But I knaw'd a Quaäker feller as often 'as towd ma this:
'Doänt thou marry for munny, but goä wheer munny is!'

to weeäk: this week.   *stunt:* obstinate.

An' I went wheer munny war: an' thy muther coom to
'and,
Wi' lots o' munny laaïd by, an' a nicetish bit o' land.
Maäybe she warn't a beauty: – I niver giv it a thowt –
But warn't she as good to cuddle an' kiss as a lass as 'ant
nowt?

Parson's lass 'ant nowt, an' she weänt 'a nowt when 'e's
deäd,
Mun be a guvness, lad, or summut, and addle her breäd:
Why? fur 'e's nobbut a curate, an' weänt nivir git naw
'igher;
An' 'e maäde the bed as 'e ligs on afoor 'e coom'd to the
shire.

And thin 'e coom'd to the parish wi' lots o' Varsity debt,
Stook to his taaïl they did, an' 'e 'ant got shut on 'em yet.
An' 'e ligs on 'is back i' the grip, wi' noän to lend 'im a
shove,
Woorse nor a far-welter'd yowe: fur, Sammy, 'e married
fur luvv.

Luvv? what's luvv? thou can luvv thy lass an' 'er munny
too,
Maakin' 'em goä togither as they've good right to do.
Could'n I luvv thy muther by cause o' 'er munny laaïd by?
Naäy – for I luvv'd 'er a vast sight moor fur it: reäson why.

Ay an' thy muther says thou wants to marry the lass,
Cooms of a gentleman burn: an' we boäth on us thinks tha
an ass.
Woä then, proputty, wiltha? – an ass as near as mays nowt –
Woä then, wiltha? dangtha? – the bees is as fell as owt.

addle: earn.
far-welter'd: or *fow-welter'd* – said of a sheep lying on its back in
the furrow.
mays nowt: makes nothing.
the bees is as fell as owt: the flies are as fierce as anything.

Breäk me a bit 'o the esh for his 'eäd, lad, out o' the fence!
Gentleman burn! what's gentleman burn? is it shillins an'
    pence?
Proputty, proputty's ivrything 'ere, an', Sammy, I'm blest
If it isn't the saäme oop yonder, fur them as 'as it's the best.

Tis'n them as 'as munny as breäks into 'ouses an' steäls,
Them as 'as coäts to their backs an' taäkes their regular
    meäls.
Noä, but it's them as niver knaws wheer a meäl's to be 'ad.
Taäke my word for it, Sammy, the poor in a loomp is bad.

Them or thir feythers, tha sees, mun 'a beän a laäzy lot,
Fur work mun a' gone to the gittin' whiniver munny was
    got.
Feyther 'ad ammost nowt; leästwaays 'is munny was 'id.
But 'e tued an' moil'd 'issén deäd, an 'e died a good un, 'e
    did.

Look thou theer wheer Wrigglesby beck comes out by the
    'ill!
Feyther run up to the farm, an' I runs up to the mill;
An' I'll run up to the brig, an' that thou'll live to see;
And if thou marries a good un I'll leäve the land to thee.

Thim's my noätions, Sammy, wheerby I means to stick;
But if thou marries a bad un, I'll leäve the land to Dick –
Coom oop, proputty, proputty – that's what I 'ears 'im
    saäy –
Proputty, proputty, proputty – canter an' canter awaäy.

[1869]

Rizpah

Wailing, wailing, wailing, the wind over land and sea –
And Willy's voice in the wind, 'O mother, come out to me.'
Why should he call me to-night, when he knows that I
 cannot go?
For the downs are as bright as day, and the full moon stares
 at the snow.

We should be seen, my dear; they would spy us out of the
 town.
The loud black nights for us, and the storm rushing over the
 down,
When I cannot see my own hand, but am led by the creak
 of the chain,
And grovel and grope for my son till I find myself drenched
 with the rain.

Anything fallen again? nay – what was there left to fall?
I have taken them home, I have number'd the bones, I
 have hidden them all.
What am I saying? and what are *you*? do you come as a
 spy?
Falls? what falls? who knows? As the tree falls so must it lie.
Who let her in? how long has she been? you – what have
 you heard?
Why did you sit so quiet? you never have spoken a word.
O – to pray with me – yes – a lady – none of their spies –
But the night has crept into my heart, and begun to darken
 my eyes.

Ah – you, that have lived so soft, what should *you* know
 of the night,
The blast and the burning shame and the bitter frost and
 the fright?

I have done it, while you were asleep – you were only made
 for the day.
I have gather'd my baby together – and now you may go
 your way.

Nay – for it's kind of you, Madam, to sit by an old dying
 wife.
But say nothing hard of my boy, I have only an hour of life.
I kiss'd my boy in the prison, before he went out to die.
'They dared me to do it,' he said, and he never has told me
 a lie.
I whipt him for robbing an orchard once when he was but
 a child –
'The farmer dared me to do it,' he said; he was always so
 wild –
And idle – and couldn't be idle – my Willy – he never
 could rest.
The King should have made him a soldier, he would have
 been one of his best.

But he lived with a lot of wild mates, and they never would
 let him be good;
They swore that he dare not rob the mail, and he swore that
 he would;
And he took no life, but he took one purse, and when all
 was done
He flung it among his fellows – I'll none of it, said my son.

I came into court to the Judge and the lawyers. I told them
 my tale,
God's own truth – but they kill'd him, they kill'd him for
 robbing the mail.
They hang'd him in chains for a show – we had always
 borne a good name –
To be hang'd for a thief – and then put away – isn't that
 enough shame?

Dust to dust – low down – let us hide! but they set him so
  high
That all the ships of the world could stare at him, passing
  by.
God 'ill pardon the hell-black raven and horrible fowls of
  the air,
But not the black heart of the lawyer who kill'd him and
  hang'd him there.

And the jailer forced me away. I had bid him my last
  goodbye;
They had fasten'd the door of his cell. 'O mother!' I heard
  him cry.
I couldn't get back tho' I tried, he had something further
  to say,
And now I never shall know it. The jailer forced me away.

Then since I couldn't but hear that cry of my boy that was
  dead,
They seized me and shut me up: they fasten'd me down
  on my bed.
'Mother, O mother!' – he call'd in the dark to me year
  after year –
They beat me for that, they beat me – you know that I
  couldn't but hear;
And then at the last they found I had grown so stupid and
  still
They let me abroad again – but the creatures had worked
  their will.

Flesh of my flesh was gone, but bone of my bone was left –
I stole them all from the lawyers – and you, will you call it
  a theft? –
My baby, the bones that had suck'd me, the bones that
  had laughed and had cried –
Theirs? O no! they are mine – not theirs – they had moved
  in my side.

Do you think I was scared by the bones? I kiss'd 'em, I
  buried 'em all –
I can't dig deep, I am old – in the night by the churchyard
  wall.
My Willy 'ill rise up whole when the trumpet of judgment
  'ill sound,
But I charge you never to say that I laid him in holy ground.

They would scratch him up – they would hang him again
  on the cursed tree.
Sin? O yes – we are sinners, I know – let all that be,
And read me a Bible verse of the Lord's good will toward
  men –
'Full of compassion and mercy, the Lord' – let me hear it
  again;
'Full of compassion and mercy – long-suffering.' Yes, O
  yes!
For the lawyer is born but to murder – the Saviour lives
  but to bless.
He'll never put on the black cap except for the worst of the
  worst,
And the first may be last – I have heard it in church – and
  the last may be first.
Suffering – O long-suffering – yes, as the Lord must know,
Year after year in the mist and the wind and the shower
  and the snow.

Heard, have you? what? they have told you he never
  repented his sin.
How do they know it? are *they* his mother? are *you* of his
  kin?
Heard! have you ever heard, when the storm on the downs
  began,
The wind that 'ill wail like a child and the sea that 'ill moan
  like a man?

Election, Election and Reprobation – it's all very well.
But I go to-night to my boy, and I shall not find him in
Hell.
For I cared so much for my boy that the Lord has look'd
into my care,
And he means me I'm sure to be happy with Willy, I know
not where.

And if *he* be lost – but to save *my* soul, that is all your
desire:
Do you think that I care for *my* soul if my boy be gone to
the fire?
I have been with God in the dark – go, go, you may leave
me alone –
You never have borne a child – you are just as hard as a
stone.

Madam, I beg your pardon! I think that you mean to be
kind,
But I cannot hear what you say for my Willy's voice in the
wind –
The snow and the sky so bright – he used but to call in the
dark,
And he calls to me now from the church and not from the
gibbet – for hark!
Nay – you can hear it yourself – it is coming – shaking the
walls –
Willy – the moon's in a cloud – Good night. I am going.
He calls.

[1880]

Battle of Brunanburh

Constantinus, King of the Scots, after having sworn allegiance to Athelstan, allied himself with the Danes of Ireland under Anlaf, and invading England, was defeated by Athelstan and his brother Edmund with great slaughter at Brunanburh in the year 937.

Athelstan King,
Lord among Earls,
Bracelet-bestower and
Baron of Barons,
He with his brother,
Edmund Atheling,
Gaining a lifelong
Glory in battle,
Slew with the sword-edge
There by Brunanburh,
Brake the shield-wall,
Hew'd the lindenwood,
Hack'd the battleshield,
Sons of Edward with hammer'd brands.

Theirs was a greatness
Got from their Grandsires –
Theirs that so often in
Strife with their enemies
Struck for their hoards and their hearths and their homes.

Bow'd the spoiler,
Bent the Scotsman,
Fell the shipcrews
Doom'd to the death.
All the field with blood of the fighters
Flow'd, from when first the great
Sun-star of morningtide,
Lamp of the Lord God
Lord everlasting,

Glode over earth till the glorious creature
    Sunk to his setting.

    There lay many a man
    Marr'd by the javelin,
    Men of the Northland
    Shot over shield.
    There was the Scotsman
    Weary of war.

    We the West-Saxons,
    Long as the daylight
    Lasted, in companies
Troubled the track of the host that we hated,
Grimly with swords that were sharp from the grindstone,
Fiercely we hack'd at the flyers before us.

    Mighty the Mercian,
    Hard was his hand-play,
    Sparing not any of
    Those that with Anlaf,
    Warriors over the
    Weltering waters
    Borne in the bark's-bosom,
    Drew to this island,
    Doom'd to the death.

Five young kings put asleep by the sword-stroke,
Seven strong Earls of the army of Anlaf
Fell on the war-field, numberless numbers,
Shipmen and Scotsmen.

    Then the Norse leader,
    Dire was his need of it,
    Few were his following,
    Fled to his warship:
Fleeted his vessel to sea with the king in it,
Saving his life on the fallow flood.

Also the crafty one,
Constantinus,
Crept to his North again,
Hoar-headed hero!

Slender reason had
He to be proud of
The welcome of war-knives –
He that was reft of his
Folk and his friends that had
Fallen in conflict,
Leaving his son too
Lost in the carnage,
Mangled to morsels,
A youngster in war!

Slender reason had
He to be glad of
The clash of the war-glaive –
Traitor and trickster
And spurner of treaties –
He nor had Anlaf
With armies so broken
A reason for bragging
That they had the better
In perils of battle
On places of slaughter –
The struggle of standards,
The rush of the javelins,
The crash of the charges,
The wielding of weapons –
The play that they play'd with
The children of Edward.

Then with their nail'd prows
Parted the Norsemen, a
Blood-redden'd relic of

Javelins over
The jarring breaker, the deepsea billow,
Shaping their way toward Dyflen again,
Shamed in their souls.

Also the brethren,
King and Atheling,
Each in his glory,
Went to his own in his own West-Saxonland,
Glad of the war.

Many a carcase they left to be carrion,
Many a livid one, many a sallow-skin –
Left for the white-tail'd eagle to tear it, and
Left for the horny-nibb'd raven to rend it, and
Gave to the garbaging war-hawk to gorge it, and
That gray beast, the wolf of the weald.

Never had huger
Slaughter of heroes
Slain by the sword-edge –
Such as old writers
Have writ of in histories –
Hapt in this isle, since
Up from the East hither
Saxon and Angle from
Over the broad billow
Broke into Britain with
Haughty war-workers who
Harried the Welshman, when
Earls that were lured by the
Hunger of glory gat
Hold of the land.

[1880]

WILLIAM MAKEPEACE THACKERAY

1811–1863

WILLIAM MAKEPEACE THACKERAY was born at Calcutta
and died at Palace Green. Thackeray is, of course, best
known for his novels but much of his social verse is elegant
and biting in a rare combination. The mock Irish of poems
like *Mr Molony's Account of the Crystal Palace* gives the
satire a likeably farcical quality.

Mr Molony's Account of the Crystal Palace

WITH ganial foire
Thransfuse me loyre,
Ye sacred nympths of Pindus,
The whoile I sing
That wondthrous thing,
The Palace made o' windows!
Say, PAXTON, truth,
Thou wondthrous youth,
What sthroke of art celistial,
What power was lint
You to invint
This combineetion cristial.

O would before
That THOMAS MOORE,
Likewise the late LORD BOYRON,
Thim aigles sthrong
Of godlike song,
Cast oi on that cast oiron!

And saw thim walls,
And glittering halls,
Thim rising slendther columns,
Which I, poor pote,
Could not denote,
No, not in twinty vollums.

My Muse's words
Is like the birds
That roosts beneath the panes there;
Her wings she spoils
'Gainst them bright iles,
And cracks her silly brains there.

This Palace tall,
This Cristial Hall,
Which Imperors might covet,
Stands in High Park
Like Noah's Ark,
A rainbow bint above it.

The towers and fanes,
In other scaynes,
The fame of this will undo,
Saint Paul's big doom,
Saint Payther's Room,
And Dublin's proud Rotundo.

'Tis here that roams,
As well becomes
Her dignitee and stations,
VICTORIA Great,
And houlds in state
The Congress of the Nations.

Her subjects pours
From distant shores,
Her Injians and Canajians;
And also we,
Her kingdoms three,
Attind with our allagiance.

Here come likewise
Her bould allies,
Both Asian and Europian;
From East and West
They send their best
To fill her Coornucopean.

I seen (thank Grace!)
This wondthrous place
(His Noble Honour MISTHER
H. COLE it was
That gave the pass
And let me see what is there).

With conscious proide
I stud insoide
And looked the World's Great Fair in,
Until me sight
Was dazzled quite,
And couldn't see for staring.

There's holy saints
And window paints,
By Maydiayval Pugin;
Alhamborough JONES
Did paint the tones
Of yellow and gambouge in.

There's fountains there
And crosses fair;
There's water-gods with urrns;
There's organs three
To play, d'ye see,
'God save the QUEEN,' by turrns.

There's Statues bright
Of marble white,
Of silver, and of copper;
And some in zinc,
And some, I think,
That isn't over proper.

There's staym Ingynes,
That stands in lines,
Enormous and amazing,
That squeal and snort
Like whales in sport,
Or elephants a-grazing.

There's carts and gigs,
And pins for pigs;
There's dibblers and there's harrows,
And ploughs like toys
For little boys,
And elegant wheel-barrows.

For them genteels
Who ride on wheels,
There's plenty to indulge 'em;
There's Droskys snug
From Paytersbug
And vayhcles from Bulgium.

There's Cabs on Stands
And Shandthry-danns;
There's Waggons from New York here;
There's Lapland Sleighs
Have crossed the seas,
And Jaunting Cyars from Cork here.

Amazed I pass
From glass to glass
Deloigted I survey 'em;
Fresh wondthers grows
Before me nose
In this sublime Musayum!

Look, here's a fan
From far Japan,
A sabre from Damasco;
There's shawls ye get
From far Thibet,
And cotton prints from Glasgow.

There's German flutes,
Marocky boots,
And Naples Macaronies;
Bohaymia
Has sent Bohay;
Polonia her polonies.

There's granite flints
That's quite imminse,
There's sacks of coals and fuels,
There's swords and guns,
And soap in tuns,
And Ginger-bread and Jewels.

There's taypots there,
And cannons rare;
There's coffins filled with roses;
There's canvass tints,
Teeth insthrumints,
And shuits of clothes by MOSES.

There's lashins more
Of things in store,
But thim I don't remimber;
Nor could disclose
Did I compose
From May time to Novimber!

Ah, JUDY thrue!
With eyes so blue,
That you were here to view it! –
And could I screw
But tu pound tu,
'Tis I would thrait you to it!

So let us raise
VICTORIA'S praise,
And ALBERT'S proud condition,
That takes his ayse
As he surveys
This Cristial Exhibition.

[*Punch*, 1851]

ROBERT BROWNING
1812–1889

ROBERT BROWNING was born in Camberwell and died in Venice. In 1846 he married Elizabeth Barrett and, until her death fifteen years later, lived in devoted happiness with her in Florence. After her death he returned for a time to London, but spent much of the latter part of his life again in Italy, whose history and art form the central inspiration of his uniquely original work. As suggested in the Introduction, the outward events of Browning's life do little to explain the power and richness of his verse: his was the life of the mind. Equipped with an exceptionally fertile and original imagination, Browning was fortunate in finding, early in his career, an adequately novel form – the dramatic monologue – for the expression of his ideas (see the Introduction, p. 24). His contemporaries sometimes found him difficult and speculated about whether he would be read by their grandsons. In fact, in the mid twentieth century, he has become the most accessible of the great Victorians, directly imitated by younger poets in England as he once was by Lowell and Jarrell in America. From *Bells and Pomegranates* in 1841 until *The Ring and The Book* in 1868 – more than a quarter of a century – Browning maintained a consistent and brilliant level. In his later work there is a sharp falling-off into prolixity, and his earlier writing (despite the crabbed allure of *Sordello*) exaggerates his forced diction. Nevertheless there are hundreds of pages in his *Collected Works* which will be read as long as the English language has meaning.

My Last Duchess

FERRARA

That's my last Duchess painted on the wall,
Looking as if she were alive; I call
That piece a wonder, now: Frà Pandolf's hands
Worked busily a day, and there she stands.
Will't please you sit and look at her? I said
'Frà Pandolf' by design, for never read

Strangers like you that pictured countenance,
The depth and passion of its earnest glance,
But to myself they turned (since none puts by
The curtain I have drawn for you, but I)
And seemed as they would ask me, if they durst,
How such a glance came there; so, not the first
Are you to turn and ask thus. Sir, 'twas not
Her husband's presence only, called that spot
Of joy into the Duchess' cheek: perhaps
Frà Pandolf chanced to say 'Her mantle laps
'Over my Lady's wrist too much,' or 'Paint
'Must never hope to reproduce the faint
'Half-flush that dies along her throat;' such stuff
Was courtesy, she thought, and cause enough
For calling up that spot of joy. She had
A heart . . . how shall I say? . . . too soon made glad,
Too easily impressed; she liked whate'er
She looked on, and her looks went everywhere.
Sir, 'twas all one! My favour at her breast,
The drooping of the daylight in the West,
The bough of cherries some officious fool
Broke in the orchard for her, the white mule
She rode with round the terrace – all and each
Would draw from her alike the approving speech,
Or blush, at least. She thanked men, – good; but thanked
Somehow . . . I know not how . . . as if she ranked
My gift of a nine hundred years old name
With anybody's gift. Who'd stoop to blame
This sort of trifling? Even had you skill
In speech – (which I have not) – to make your will
Quite clear to such an one, and say 'Just this
'Or that in you disgusts me; here you miss,
'Or there exceed the mark' – and if she let
Herself be lessoned so, nor plainly set
Her wits to yours, forsooth, and made excuse,
– E'en then would be some stooping, and I chuse
Never to stoop. Oh, Sir, she smiled, no doubt,

Whene'er I passed her; but who passed without
Much the same smile? This grew; I gave commands;
Then all smiles stopped together. There she stands
As if alive. Will't please you rise? We'll meet
The company below, then. I repeat,
The Count your Master's known munificence
Is ample warrant that no just pretence
Of mine for dowry will be disallowed;
Though his fair daughter's self, as I avowed
At starting, is my object. Nay, we'll go
Together down, Sir! Notice Neptune, tho',
Taming a sea-horse, thought a rarity,
Which Claus of Innsbruck cast in bronze for me.

[1842]

Soliloquy of the Spanish Cloister

Gr-r-r – there go, my heart's abhorrence!
    Water your damned flower-pots, do!
If hate killed men, Brother Lawrence,
    God's blood, would not mine kill you!
What? your myrtle-bush wants trimming?
    Oh, that rose has prior claims –
Needs its leaden vase filled brimming?
    Hell dry you up with its flames!

At the meal we sit together:
    Salve tibi! I must hear
Wise talk of the kind of weather,
    Sort of season, time of year:
Not a plenteous cork-crop: scarcely
    Dare we hope oak-galls, I doubt:
What's the Latin name for 'parsley'?
    What's the Greek name for Swine's Snout?

Whew! We'll have our platter burnished,
  Laid with care on our own shelf!
With a fire-new spoon we're furnished,
  And a goblet for ourself,
Rinsed like something sacrificial
  Ere 'tis fit to touch our chaps –
Marked with L. for our initial!
  (He, he! There his lily snaps!)

Saint, forsooth! While brown Dolores
  Squats outside the Convent bank,
With Sanchicha, telling stories,
  Steeping tresses in the tank,
Blue-black, lustrous, thick like horsehairs,
  – Can't I see his dead eye glow
Bright, as 'twere a Barbary corsair's?
  (That is, if he'd let it show!)

When he finishes refection,
  Knife and fork he never lays
Cross-wise, to my recollection,
  As do I, in Jesu's praise.
I, the Trinity illustrate,
  Drinking watered orange-pulp –
In three sips the Arian frustrate;
  While he drains his at one gulp!

Oh, those melons! If he's able
  We're to have a feast; so nice!
One goes to the Abbot's table,
  All of us get each a slice.
How go on your flowers? None double?
  Not one fruit-sort can you spy?
Strange! – And I, too, at such trouble,
  Keep 'em close-nipped on the sly!

There's a great text in Galatians,
　　Once you trip on it, entails
Twenty-nine distinct damnations,
　　One sure, if another fails.
If I trip him just a-dying,
　　Sure of Heaven as sure can be,
Spin him round and send him flying
　　Off to Hell, a Manichee?

Or, my scrofulous French novel,
　　On grey paper with blunt type!
Simply glance at it, you grovel
　　Hand and foot in Belial's gripe:
If I double down its pages
　　At the woeful sixteenth print,
When he gathers his greengages,
　　Ope a sieve and slip it in't?

Or, there's Satan! – one might venture
　　Pledge one's soul to him, yet leave
Such a flaw in the indenture
　　As he'd miss till, past retrieve,
Blasted lay that rose-acacia
　　We're so proud of! *Hy, Zy, Hine* . . .
'St, there's Vespers! *Plena gratiâ*
　　Ave, Virgo! Gr-r-r – you swine!

[1842]

'How They Brought the Good News
from Ghent to Aix'

I sprang to the stirrup, and Joris, and he;
I galloped, Dirck galloped, we galloped all three;
'Good speed!' cried the watch, as the gate-bolts undrew;
'Speed!' echoed the wall to us galloping through;
Behind shut the postern, the lights sank to rest,
And into the midnight we galloped abreast.

Not a word to each other; we kept the great pace
Neck by neck, stride by stride, never changing our place;
I turned in my saddle and made its girths tight,
Then shortened each stirrup, and set the pique right,
Rebuckled the cheek-strap, chained slacker the bit,
Nor galloped less steadily Roland a whit.

'Twas moonset at starting; but while we drew near
Lokern, the cocks crew and twilight dawned clear;
At Boom, a great yellow star came out to see;
At Düffield, 'twas morning as plain as could be;
And from Mecheln church-steeple we heard the half-chime,
So Joris broke silence with, 'Yet there is time!'

At Aerschot, up leaped of a sudden the sun,
And against him the cattle stood black every one,
To stare thro' the mist at us galloping past,
And I saw my stout galloper Roland at last,
With resolute shoulders, each butting away
The haze, as some bluff river headland its spray.

And his low head and crest, just one sharp ear bent back
For my voice, and the other pricked out on his track;
And one eye's black intelligence, – ever that glance
O'er its white edge at me, his own master, askance!
And the thick heavy spume-flakes which aye and anon
His fierce lips shook upwards in galloping on.

By Hasselt, Dirck groaned; and cried Joris, 'Stay spur!
'Your Roos galloped bravely, the fault's not in her,
'We'll remember at Aix' – for one heard the quick wheeze
Of her chest, saw the stretched neck and staggering knees,
And sunk tail, and horrible heave of the flank,
As down on her haunches she shuddered and sank.

So we were left galloping, Joris and I,
Past Looz and past Tongres, no cloud in the sky;
The broad sun above laughed a pitiless laugh,
'Neath our feet broke the brittle bright stubble like chaff;
Till over by Dalhem a dome-spire sprang white,
And 'Gallop,' gasped Joris, 'for Aix is in sight!'

'How they'll greet us!' – and all in a moment his roan
Rolled neck and croup over, lay dead as a stone;
And there was my Roland to bear the whole weight
Of the news which alone could save Aix from her fate,
With his nostrils like pits full of blood to the brim,
And with circles of red for his eye-sockets' rim.

Then I cast loose my buffcoat, each holster let fall,
Shook off both my jack-boots, let go belt and all,
Stood up in the stirrup, leaned, patted his ear,
Called my Roland his pet-name, my horse without peer;
Clapped my hands, laughed and sang, any noise, bad or
    good,
Till at length into Aix Roland galloped and stood.

And all I remember is, friends flocking round
As I sate with his head 'twixt my knees on the ground,
And no voice but was praising this Roland of mine,
As I poured down his throat our last measure of wine,
Which (the burgesses voted by common consent)
Was no more than his due who brought good news from
    Ghent.

[1845]

Meeting at Night

The grey sea and the long black land;
And the yellow half-moon large and low;
And the startled little waves that leap
In fiery ringlets from their sleep,
As I gain the cove with pushing prow,
And quench its speed in the slushy sand.

Then a mile of warm sea-scented beach;
Three fields to cross till a farm appears;
A tap at the pane, the quick sharp scratch
And blue spurt of a lighted match,
And a voice less loud, thro' its joys and fears,
Than the two hearts beating each to each!

[1845]

'Childe Roland to the Dark Tower came'

(See Edgar's Song in 'Lear')

My first thought was, he lied in every word,
   That hoary cripple, with malicious eye
   Askance to watch the working of his lie
On mine, and mouth scarce able to afford
Suppression of the glee that pursed and scored
   Its edge at one more victim gained thereby.

What else should he be set for, with his staff?
   What, save to waylay with his lies, ensnare
   All travellers that might find him posted there,
And ask the road? I guessed what skull-like laugh
Would break, what crutch 'gin write my epitaph
   For pastime in the dusty thoroughfare,

If at his counsel I should turn aside
   Into that ominous tract which, all agree,
   Hides the Dark Tower.   Yet acquiescingly
I did turn as he pointed; neither pride
Nor hope rekindling at the end descried,
   So much as gladness that some end should be.

For, what with my whole world-wide wandering,
   What with my search drawn out thro' years, my hope
   Dwindled into a ghost, not fit to cope
With that obstreperous joy success would bring, –
I hardly tried now to rebuke the spring
   My heart made, finding failure in its scope.

As when a sick man very near to death
   Seems dead indeed, and feels begin and end
   The tears and takes the farewell of each friend,
And hears one bid the other go, draw breath
Freelier outside ('since all is o'er,' he saith,
   'And the blow fall'n no grieving can amend;')

While some discuss if near the other graves
   Be room enough for this, and when a day
   Suits best for carrying the corpse away,
With care about the banners, scarves and staves, –
And still the man hears all, and only craves
   He may not shame such tender love and stay.

Thus, I had so long suffered in this quest,
   Heard failure prophesied so oft, been writ
   So many times among 'The Band' – to wit,
The knights who to the Dark Tower's search addressed
Their steps – that just to fail as they, seemed best,
   And all the doubt was now – should I be fit.

So, quiet as despair, I turned from him,
   That hateful cripple, out of his highway
   Into the path he pointed. All the day
Had been a dreary one at best, and dim
Was settling to its close, yet shot one grim
   Red leer to see the plain catch its estray.

For mark! no sooner was I fairly found
   Pledged to the plain, after a pace or two,
   Than pausing to throw backward a last view
To the safe road, 'twas gone! grey plain all round!
Nothing but plain to the horizon's bound.
   I might go on; nought else remained to do.

So on I went. I think I never saw
   Such starved ignoble nature; nothing throve:
   For flowers – as well expect a cedar grove!
But cockle, spurge, according to their law
Might propagate their kind, with none to awe,
   You'd think: a burr had been a treasure-trove.

No! penury, inertness, and grimace,
   In some strange sort, were the land's portion. 'See
   Or shut your eyes' – said Nature peevishly –
'It nothing skills: I cannot help my case:
The Judgment's fire alone can cure this place,
   Calcine its clods and set my prisoners free.'

If there pushed any ragged thistle-stalk
   Above its mates, the head was chopped – the bents
   Were jealous else. What made those holes and rents
In the dock's harsh swarth leaves – bruised as to baulk
All hope of greenness? 'tis a brute must walk
   Pushing their life out, with a brute's intents.

As for the grass, it grew as scant as hair
  In leprosy – thin dry blades pricked the mud
  Which underneath looked kneaded up with blood,
One stiff blind horse, his every bone a-stare,
Stood stupified, however he came there–
  Thrust out past service from the devil's stud!

Alive? he might be dead for all I know,
  With that red gaunt and colloped neck a-strain,
  And shut eyes underneath the rusty mane.
Seldom went such grotesqueness with such woe:
I never saw a brute I hated so –
  He must be wicked to deserve such pain.

I shut my eyes and turned them on my heart.
  As a man calls for wine before he fights,
  I asked one draught of earlier, happier sights
Ere fitly I could hope to play my part.
Think first, fight afterwards – the soldier's art:
  One taste of the old times sets all to rights!

Not it! I fancied Cuthbert's reddening face
  Beneath its garniture of curly gold,
  Dear fellow, till I almost felt him fold
An arm in mine to fix me to the place,
That way he used. Alas! one night's disgrace!
  Out went my heart's new fire and left it cold.

Giles, then, the soul of honour – there he stands
  Frank as ten years ago when knighted first.
  What honest men should dare (he said) he durst.
Good – but the scene shifts – faugh! what hangman's hands
Pin to his breast a parchment? his own bands
  Read it. Poor traitor, spit upon and curst!

Better this present than a past like that –
    Back therefore to my darkening path again.
    No sound, no sight as far as eye could strain.
Will the night send a howlet or a bat?
I asked: when something on the dismal flat
    Came to arrest my thoughts and change their train.

A sudden little river crossed my path
    As unexpected as a serpent comes.
    No sluggish tide congenial to the glooms –
This, as it frothed by, might have been a bath
For the field's glowing hoof – to see the wrath
    Of its black eddy bespate with flakes and spumes.

So petty yet so spiteful! all along,
    Low scrubby alders kneeled down over it;
    Drenched willows flung them headlong in a fit
Of mute despair, a suicidal throng:
The river which had done them all the wrong,
    Whate'er that was, rolled by, deterred no whit.

Which, while I forded, – good saints, how I feared
    To set my foot upon a dead man's cheek,
    Each step, or feel the spear I thrust to seek
For hollows, tangled in his hair or beard!
– It may have been a water-rat I speared,
    But, ugh; it sounded like a baby's shriek.

Glad was I when I reached the other bank.
    Now for a better country. Vain presage!
    Who were the strugglers, what war did they wage
Whose savage trample thus could pad the dank
Soil to a plash? toads in a poisoned tank,
    Or wild cats in a red-hot iron cage –

The fight must so have seemed in that fell cirque.
  What kept them there, with all the plain to choose?
  No foot-print leading to that horrid mews,
None out of it: mad brewage set to work
Their brains, no doubt, like galley-slaves the Turk
  Pits for his pastime, Christians against Jews.

And more than that – a furlong on – why, there!
  What bad use was that engine for, that wheel,
  Or brake, no wheel – that harrow fit to reel
Men's bodies out like silk? with all the air
Of Tophet's tool, on earth left unaware,
  Or brought to sharpen its rusty teeth of steel.

Then came a bit of stubbed ground, once a wood,
  Next a marsh, it would seem, and now mere earth
  Desperate and done with; (so a fool finds mirth,
Makes a thing and then mars it, till his mood
Changes and off he goes!) within a rood
  Bog, clay and rubble, sand and stark black dearth.

Now blotches rankling, coloured gay and grim,
  Now patches where some leanness of the soil's
  Broke into moss or substances like boils;
Then came some palsied oak, a cleft in him
Like a distorted mouth that splits its rim
  Gaping at death, and dies while it recoils.

And just as far as ever from the end!
  Nought in the distance but the evening, nought
  To point my footstep further! At the thought,
A great black bird, Apollyon's bosom-friend,
Sailed past, nor beat his wide wing dragon-penned
  That brushed my cap – perchance the guide I sought.

For looking up, aware I somehow grew,
  'Spite of the dusk, the plain had given place
  All round to mountains – with such name to grace
Mere ugly heights and heaps now stol'n in view.
How thus they had surprised me, – solve it, you!
  How to get from them was no plainer case.

Yet half I seemed to recognise some trick
  Of mischief happened to me, God knows when –
  In a bad dream perhaps. Here ended, then,
Progress this way. When, in the very nick
Of giving up, one time more, came a click
  As when a trap shuts – you're inside the den!

Burningly it came on me all at once,
  This was the place! those two hills on the right
  Crouched like two bulls locked horn in horn in fight –
While to the left, a tall scalped mountain . . . Dunce,
Fool, to be dozing at the very nonce,
  After a life spent training for the sight!

What in the midst lay but the Tower itself?
  The round squat turret, blind as the fool's heart,
  Built of brown stone, without a counterpart
In the whole world. The tempest's mocking elf
Points to the shipman thus the unseen shelf
  He strikes on, only when the timbers start.

Not see? because of night perhaps? – Why, day
  Came back again for that! before it left,
  The dying sunset kindled through a cleft:
The hills, like giants at a hunting, lay –
Chin upon hand, to see the game at bay, –
  'Now stab and end the creature – to the heft!'

Not hear? when noise was everywhere? it tolled
  Increasing like a bell. Names in my ears,
  Of all the lost adventurers my peers, –
How such a one was strong, and such was bold,
And such was fortunate, yet each of old
  Lost, lost! one moment knelled the woe of years.

There they stood, ranged along the hill-sides – met
  To view the last of me, a living frame
  For one more picture; in a sheet of flame
I saw them and I knew them all. And yet
Dauntless the slug-horn to my lips I set
  And blew. '*Childe Roland to the Dark Tower came.*'

[1855]

Caliban upon Setebos;
or Natural Theology in the Island

'Thou thoughtest that I was altogether such a one as thyself'

['Will sprawl, now that the heat of day is best,
Flat on his belly in the pit's much mire,
With elbows wide, fists clenched to prop his chin.
And, while he kicks both feet in the cool slush,
And feels about his spine small eft-things course,
Run in and out each arm, and make him laugh:
And while above his head a pompion-plant,
Coating the cave-top as a brow its eye,
Creeps down to touch and tickle hair and beard,
And now a flower drops with a bee inside,
And now a fruit to snap at, catch and crunch, –
He looks out o'er yon sea which sunbeams cross
And recross till they weave a spider-web
(Meshes of fire, some great fish breaks at times)
And talks to his own self, howe'er he please,
Touching that other, whom his dam called God.

Because to talk about Him, vexes – ha,
Could He but know! and time to vex is now,
When talk is safer than in winter-time.
Moreover Prosper and Miranda sleep
In confidence he drudges at their task,
And it is good to cheat the pair, and gibe,
Letting the rank tongue blossom into speech.]

Setebos, Setebos, and Setebos!
'Thinketh, He dwelleth i' the cold o' the moon.
'Thinketh He made it, with the sun to match,
But not the stars; the stars came otherwise;
Only made clouds, winds, meteors, such as that:
Also this isle, what lives and grows thereon,
And snaky sea which rounds and ends the same.

'Thinketh, it came of being ill at ease:
He hated that He cannot change His cold,
Nor cure its ache. 'Hath spied an icy fish
That longed to 'scape the rock-stream where she lived,
And thaw herself within the lukewarm brine
O' the lazy sea her stream thrusts far amid,
A crystal spike 'twixt two warm walls of wave;
Only, she ever sickened, found repulse
At the other kind of water, not her life,
(Green-dense and dim-delicious, bred o' the sun)
Flounced back from bliss she was not born to breathe,
And in her old bounds buried her despair,
Hating and loving warmth alike: so He.

'Thinketh, He made thereat the sun, this isle,
Trees and the fowls here, beast and creeping thing.
Yon otter, sleek-wet, black, lithe as a leech;
Yon auk, one fire-eye in a ball of foam,
That floats and feeds; a certain badger brown
He hath watched hunt with that slant white-wedge eye
By moonlight; and the pie with the long tongue

115

That pricks deep into oakwarts for a worm,
And says a plain word when she finds her prize,
But will not eat the ants; the ants themselves
That build a wall of seeds and settled stalks
About their hole – He made all these and more,
Made all we see, and us, in spite: how else?
He could not, Himself, make a second self
To be His mate: as well have made Himself:
He would not make what he mislikes or slights,
An eyesore to Him, or not worth His pains:
But did, in envy, listlessness or sport,
Make what Himself would fain, in a manner, be –
Weaker in most points, stronger in a few,
Worthy, and yet mere playthings all the while,
Things He admires and mocks too, – that is it.
Because, so brave, so better though they be,
It nothing skills if He begin to plague.
Look now, I melt a gourd-fruit into mash,
Add honeycomb and pods, I have perceived,
Which bite like finches when they bill and kiss, –
Then, when froth rises bladdery, drink up all,
Quick, quick, till maggots scamper through my brain;
Last, throw me on my back i' the seeded thyme,
And wanton, wishing I were born a bird.
Put case, unable to be what I wish,
I yet could make a live bird out of clay:
Would not I take clay, pinch my Caliban
Able to fly? – for, there, see, he hath wings,
And great comb like the hoopoe's to admire,
And there, a sting to do his foes offence,
There, and I will that he begin to live,
Fly to yon rock-top, nip me off the horns
Of grigs high up that make the merry din,
Saucy through their veined wings, and mind me not.
In which feat, if his leg snapped, brittle clay,
And he lay stupid-like, – why, I should laugh;
And if he, spying me, should fall to weep,

Beseech me to be good, repair his wrong,
Bid his poor leg smart less or grow again, –
Well, as the chance were, this might take or else
Not take my fancy: I might hear his cry,
And give the mankin three sound legs for one,
Or pluck the other off, leave him like an egg,
And lessoned he was mine and merely clay.
Were this no pleasure, lying in the thyme,
Drinking the mash, with brain become alive,
Making and marring clay at will? So He.

'Thinketh, such shows nor right nor wrong in Him,
Nor kind, nor cruel: He is strong and Lord.
'Am strong myself compared to yonder crabs
That march now from the mountain to the sea;
'Let twenty pass, and stone the twenty-first,
Loving not, hating not, just choosing so.
'Say, the first straggler that boasts purple spots
Shall join the file, one pincer twisted off;
'Say, this bruised fellow shall receive a worm,
And two worms he whose nippers end in red;
As it likes me each time, I do: so He.

Well then, 'supposeth He is good i' the main,
Placable if His mind and ways were guessed,
But rougher than His handiwork, be sure!
Oh, He hath made things worthier than Himself,
And envieth that, so helped, such things do more
Than He who made them! What consoles but this?
That they, unless through Him, do nought at all,
And must submit: what other use in things?
'Hath cut a pipe of pithless elder joint
That, blown through, gives exact the scream o' the jay
When from her wing you twitch the feathers blue:
Sound this, and little birds that hate the jay
Flock within stone's throw, glad their foe is hurt:
Put case such pipe could prattle and boast forsooth

'I catch the birds, I am the crafty thing,
'I make the cry my maker cannot make
'With his great round mouth; he must blow through mine!'
Would not I smash it with my foot? So He.

But wherefore rough, why cold and ill at ease?
Aha, that is a question! Ask, for that,
What knows, – the something over Setebos
That made Him, or He, may be, found and fought,
Worsted, drove off and did to nothing, perchance.
There may be something quiet o'er His head,
Out of His reach, that feels nor joy nor grief,
Since both derive from weakness in some way.
I joy because the quails come; would not joy
Could I bring quails here when I have a mind:
This Quiet, all it hath a mind to, doth.
'Esteemeth stars the outposts of its couch,
But never spends much thought nor care that way.
It may look up, work up, – the worse for those
It works on! 'Careth but for Setebos
The many-handed as a cuttle-fish,
Who, making Himself feared through what He does,
Looks up, first, and perceives he cannot soar
To what is quiet and hath happy life;
Next looks down here, and out of very spite
Makes this a bauble-world to ape yon real,
These good things to match those as hips do grapes.
'Tis solace making baubles, ay, and sport.
Himself peeped late, eyed Prosper at his books
Careless and lofty, lord now of the isle:
Vexed, 'stitched a book of broad leaves, arrow-shaped,
Wrote thereon, he knows what, prodigious words;
Has peeled a wand and called it by a name;
Weareth at whiles for an enchanter's robe
The eyed skin of a supple oncelot;
And hath an ounce sleeker than youngling mole,
A four-legged serpent he makes cower and couch,

Now snarl, now hold its breath and mind his eye,
And saith she is Miranda and my wife:
'Keeps for his Ariel a tall pouch-bill crane
He bids go wade for fish and straight disgorge;
Also a sea-beast, lumpish, which he snared,
Blinded the eyes of, and brought somewhat tame,
And split its toe-webs, and now pens the drudge
In a hole 'o the rock and calls him Caliban;
A bitter heart that bides its time and bites.
'Plays thus at being Prosper in a way,
Taketh his mirth with make-believes: so He.

His dam held that the Quiet made all things
Which Setebos vexed only: 'holds not so.
Who made them weak, meant weakness He might vex.
Had He meant other, while His hand was in,
Why not make horny eyes no thorn could prick,
Or plate my scalp with bone against the snow,
Or overscale my flesh 'neath joint and joint,
Like an orc's armour? Ay, – so spoil His sport!
He is the One now: only He doth all.

'Saith, He may like, perchance, what profits Him.
Ay, himself loves what does him good; but why?
'Gets good no otherwise. This blinded beast
Loves whoso places flesh-meat on his nose,
But, had he eyes, would want no help, but hate
Or love, just as it liked him: He hath eyes.
Also it pleaseth Setebos to work,
Use all His hands, and exercise much craft,
By no means for the love of what is worked.
'Tasteth, himself, no finer good i' the world
When all goes right, in this safe summer-time,
And he wants little, hungers, aches not much,
Than trying what to do with wit and strength.
'Falls to make something: 'piled yon pile of turfs,
And squared and stuck there squares of soft white chalk,

And, with a fish-tooth, scratched a moon on each,
And set up endwise certain spikes of tree,
And crowned the whole with a sloth's skull a-top,
Found dead i' the woods, too hard for one to kill.
No use at all i' the work, for work's sole sake;
'Shall some day knock it down again: so He.

'Saith He is terrible: watch His feats in proof!
One hurricane will spoil six good months' hope.
He hath a spite against me, that I know,
Just as He favours Prosper, who knows why?
So it is, all the same, as well I find.
'Wove wattles half the winter, fenced them firm
With stone and stake to stop she-tortoises
Crawling to lay their eggs here: well, one wave,
Feeling the foot of Him upon its neck,
Gaped as a snake does, lolled out its large tongue,
And licked the whole labour flat: so much for spite.
'Saw a ball flame down late (yonder it lies)
Where, half an hour before, I slept i' the shade:
Often they scatter sparkles: there is force!
'Dug up a newt He may have envied once
And turned to stone, shut up inside a stone.
Please Him and hinder this? – What Prosper does?
Aha, if He would tell me how! Not He!
There is the sport: discover how or die!
All need not die, for of the things o' the isle
Some flee afar, some dive, some run up trees;
Those at His mercy, – why, they please Him most
When . . . when . . . well, never try the same way twice!
Repeat what act has pleased, He may grow wroth.
You must not know His ways, and play Him off,
Sure of the issue. 'Doth the like himself:
'Spareth a squirrel that it nothing fears
But steals the nut from underneath my thumb,
And when I threat, bites stoutly in defence:
'Spareth an urchin that contrariwise,

Curls up into a ball, pretending death
For fright at my approach: the two ways please.
But what would move my choler more than this,
That either creature counted on its life
To-morrow and next day and all days to come,
Saying, forsooth, in the inmost of its heart,
'Because he did so yesterday with me,
'And otherwise with such another brute,
'So must he do henceforth and always.' – Ay?
Would teach the reasoning couple what 'must' means!
'Doth as he likes, or wherefore Lord? So He.

'Conceiveth all things will continue thus,
And we shall have to live in fear of Him
So long as He lives, keeps His strength: no change,
If He have done His best, make no new world
To please Him more, so leave off watching this, –
If He surprise not even the Quiet's self
Some strange day, – or, suppose, grow into it
As grubs grow butterfiies: else, here are we,
And there is He, and nowhere help at all.

'Believeth with the life, the pain shall stop.
His dam held different, that after death
He both plagued enemies and feasted friends:
Idly! He doth His worst in this our life,
Giving just respite lest we die through pain,
Saving last pain for worst, – with which, an end.
Meanwhile, the best way to escape His ire
Is, not to seem too happy. 'Sees, himself,
Yonder two flies, with purple films and pink,
Bask on the pompion-bell above; kills both.
'Sees two black painful beetles roll their ball
On head and tail as if to save their lives:
Moves them the stick away they strive to clear.

Even so, 'would have Him misconceive, suppose
This Caliban strives hard and ails no less,
And always, above all else, envies Him;
Wherefore he mainly dances on dark nights,
Moans in the sun, gets under holes to laugh,
And never speaks his mind save housed as now:
Outside, 'groans, curses. If He caught me here,
O'erheard this speech, and asked 'What chucklest at?'
'Would, to appease Him, cut a finger off,
Or of my three kid yearlings burn the best,
Or let the toothsome apples rot on tree,
Or push my tame beast for the orc to taste:
While myself lit a fire, and made a song
And sung it, *'What I hate, be consecrate*
'To celebrate Thee and Thy state, no mate
'For Thee; what see for envy in poor me?'
Hoping the while, since evils sometimes mend,
Warts rub away and sores are cured with slime,
That some strange day, will either the Quiet catch
And conquer Setebos, or likelier He
Decrepit may doze, doze, as good as die.

[What, what? A curtain o'er the world at once!
Crickets stop hissing; not a bird – or, yes,
There scuds His raven that has told Him all!
It was fool's play, this prattling! Ha! The wind
Shoulders the pillared dust, death's house o' the move,
And fast invading fires being! White blaze –
A tree's head snaps – and there, there, there, there, there,
His thunder follows! Fool to gibe at Him!
Lo! 'Lieth flat and loveth Setebos!
'Maketh his teeth meet through his upper lip,
Will let those quails fly, will not eat this month
One little mess of whelks, so he may 'scape!]

[1864]

EDWARD LEAR

1812–1888

EDWARD LEAR was born in Lancashire and died in San Remo. While sketching one day in the London zoo, he caught the attention of the Earl of Derby, who invited him to his house at Knowsley to draw the birds. In 1846 he published *A Book of Nonsense* containing limericks he had written to amuse the Earl's grandchildren. In later life he travelled widely in Europe and the Far East, and the landscape paintings recording the scenes he visited sold well. Lear's poetry has always enjoyed a high reputation – Ruskin placed him first amongst his 100 authors – but the depth and subtlety of his appeal has perhaps never been fully analysed. Compared with Carroll, Lear is a Romantic poet: his world is more of the imagination than the intelligence. Nevertheless, when writing for purely lyric effect, he seems to have freshened a number of devices which others had exploited more coldly, in particular by his use of parody and his revival of the limerick.

'There was a Young Lady of Sweden'

There was a Young Lady of Sweden,
Who went by the slow train to Weedon;
When they cried, 'Weedon Station!' she made no observa-
tion,
But she thought she should go back to Sweden.

[1846]

The Jumblies

They went to sea in a Sieve, they did,
   In a Sieve they went to sea:
In spite of all their friends could say,
  On a winter's morn, on a stormy day,
    In a Sieve they went to sea!

And when the Sieve turned round and round,
And every one cried, 'You'll all be drowned!'
They called aloud, 'Our Sieve ain't big,
But we don't care a button! we don't care a fig!
  In a Sieve we'll go to sea!'
    Far and few, far and few,
      Are the lands where the Jumblies live;
      Their heads are green, and their hands are blue,
      And they went to sea in a Sieve.

They sailed away in a Sieve, they did,
  In a Sieve they sailed so fast,
With only a beautiful pea-green veil
Tied with a riband by way of a sail,
  To a small tobacco-pipe mast;
And every one said, who saw them go,
'O won't they be soon upset, you know!
For the sky is dark, and the voyage is long,
And happen what may, it's extremely wrong
  In a Sieve to sail so fast!'
    Far and few, far and few,
      Are the lands where the Jumblies live,
      Their heads are green, and their hands are blue,
      And they went to sea in a Sieve.

The water it soon came in, it did,
  The water it soon came in;
So to keep them dry, they wrapped their feet
In a pinky paper all folded neat,
  And they fastened it down with a pin.
And they passed the night in a crockery-jar,
And each of them said, 'How wise we are!
Though the sky be dark, and the voyage be long,
Yet we never can think we were rash or wrong,
  While round in our Sieve we spin!'

Far and few, far and few,
  Are the lands where the Jumblies live;
Their heads are green, and their hands are blue,
  And they went to sea in a Sieve.

And all night long they sailed away;
  And when the sun went down,
They whistled and warbled a moony song
To the echoing sound of a coppery gong,
  In the shade of the mountains brown.
'O Timballo! How happy we are,
When we live in a sieve and a crockery-jar,
And all night long in the moonlight pale,
We sail away with a pea-green sail,
  In the shade of the mountains brown!'
    Far and few, far and few,
      Are the lands where the Jumblies live;
    Their heads are green, and their hands are blue,
      And they went to sea in a Sieve.

They sailed to the Western Sea, they did,
  To a land all covered with trees,
And they bought an Owl, and a useful Cart,
And a pound of Rice, and a Cranberry Tart,
  And a hive of silvery Bees.
And they bought a Pig, and some green Jack-daws,
And a lovely Monkey with lollipop paws,
And forty bottles of Ring-Bo-Ree,
  And no end of Stilton Cheese.
  Far and few, far and few,
    Are the lands where the Jumblies live;
    Their heads are green, and their hands are blue,
      And they went to sea in a Sieve.

[1871]

The Quangle Wangle's Hat

On the top of the Crumpetty Tree
   The Quangle Wangle sat,
But his face you could not see,
   On account of his Beaver Hat.
For his Hat was a hundred and two feet wide,
With ribbons and bibbons on every side
And bells, and buttons, and loops, and lace,
So that nobody ever could see the face
     Of the Quangle Wangle Quee.

The Quangle Wangle said
   To himself on the Crumpetty Tree, –
'Jam; and jelly; and bread;
   'Are the best food for me!
'But the longer I live on this Crumpetty Tree
'The plainer than ever it seems to me
'That very few people come this way
'And that life on the whole is far from gay!'
    Said the Quangle Wangle Quee.

But there came to the Crumpetty Tree,
   Mr and Mrs Canary;
And they said, – 'Did you ever see
   'Any spot so charmingly airy?
'May we build a nest on your lovely Hat?
'Mr Quangle Wangle, grant us that!
'O please let us come and build a nest
'Of whatever material suits you best,
    'Mr Quangle Wangle Quee!'

And besides, to the Crumpetty Tree
   Came the Stork, the Duck, and the Owl;
The Snail, and the Bumble-Bee,
   The Frog, and the Fimble Fowl;
(The Fimble Fowl, with a Corkscrew leg;)

And all of them said, – 'We humbly beg,
  'We may build our homes on your lovely Hat, –
'Mr Quangle Wangle, grant us that!
    'Mr Quangle Wangle Quee!'

And the Golden Grouse came there,
  And the Pobble who has no toes, –
And the small Olympian bear, –
  And the Dong with a luminous nose.
And the Blue Baboon, who played the flute, –
And the Orient Calf from the Land of Tute, –
And the Attery Squash, and the Bisky Bat, –
All came and built on the lovely Hat
    Of the Quangle Wangle Quee.

And the Quangle Wangle said
  To himself on the Crumpetty Tree, –
'When all these creatures move
  'What a wonderful noise there'll be!'
And at night by the light of the Mulberry moon
They danced to the Flute of the Blue Baboon,
On the broad green leaves of the Crumpetty Tree,
And all were as happy as happy could be,
    With the Quangle Wangle Quee.

[1877]

WILLIAM BELL SCOTT

1812–1890

WILLIAM BELL SCOTT was born in Edinburgh and died at Penkill Castle in Ayrshire, the seat of his friend Miss Boyd, for whom he designed a medieval hall and painted murals. His friendship with Christina Rossetti (see p. 220) has not yet been fully documented. *The Witch's Ballad* mixes a fey, Scottish gaiety and grimness with a Pre-Raphaelite love of ornament.

The Witch's Ballad

O, I hae come from far away,
　From a warm land far away,
A southern land across the sea,
With sailor-lads about the mast,
Merry and canny, and kind to me.

And I hae been to yon town
　To try my luck in yon town;
Nort, and Mysie, Elspie too.
Right braw we were to pass the gate,
Wi' gowden clasps on girdles blue.

Mysie smiled wi' miminy mouth,
　Innocent mouth, miminy mouth;
Elspie wore a scarlet gown,
Nort's grey eyes were unco' gleg.
My Castile comb was like a crown.

We walked abreast all up the street,
　Into the market up the street;
Our hair with marigolds was wound,
Our bodices with love-knots laced,
Our merchandise with tansy bound.

Nort had chickens, I had cocks,
  Gamesome cocks, loud-crowing cocks;
Mysie ducks, and Elspie drakes, –
For a wee groat or a pound,
We lost nae time wi' gives and takes.

Lost nae time, for well we knew,
  In our sleeves full well we knew
When the gloaming came that night,
Duck nor drake, nor hen nor cock
Would be found by candle-light.

And when our chaffering all was done,
  All was paid for, sold and done,
We drew a glove on ilka hand,
We sweetly curtsied each to each,
And deftly danced a saraband.

The market-lassies looked and laughed
  Left their gear, and looked and laughed;
They made as they would join the game,
But soon their mithers, wild and wud,
With whack and screech they stopped the same.

Sae loud the tongues o' randies grew,
  The flytin' and the skirlin' grew,
At all the windows in the place,
Wi' spoons or knives, wi' needle or awl,
Was thrust out every hand and face.

And down each stair they thronged anon,
  Gentle, semple, thronged anon;
Souter and tailor, frowsy Nan,
The ancient widow young again,
Simpering behind her fan.

Without a choice, against their will,
　Doited, dazed, against their will,
The market lassie and her mither,
The farmer and his husbandman,
Hand in hand dance a' thegither.

Slow at first, but faster soon,
　Still increasing, wild and fast,
Hoods and mantles, hats and hose,
Blindly doffed and cast away,
Left them naked, heads and toes.

They would have torn us limb from limb,
　Dainty limb from dainty limb;
But never one of them could win
Across the line that I had drawn
With bleeding thumb a-widdershin.

But there was Jeff the provost's son,
　Jeff the provost's only son;
There was Father Auld himsel',
The Lombard frae the hostelry,
And the lawyer Peter Fell.

All goodly men we singled out,
　Waled them well, and singled out,
And drew them by the left hand in;
Mysie the priest, and Elspie won
The Lombard, Nort the lawyer carle,
I mysel' the provost's son.

Then, with cantrip kisses seven,
　Three times round with kisses seven
Warped and woven there spun we
Arms and legs and flaming hair,
Like a whirlwind on the sea.

Like a wind that sucks the sea,
    Over and in and on the sea,
Good sooth it was a mad delight;
And every man of all the four
Shut his eyes and laughed outright.

Laughed as long as they had breath,
    Laughed while they had sense or breath;
And close about us coiled a mist
Of gnats and midges, wasps and flies,
Like the whirlwind shaft it rist.

Drawn up I was right off my feet;
    Into the mist and off my feet;
And, dancing on each chimney-top,
I saw a thousand darling imps
Keeping time with skip and hop.

And on the provost's brave ridge-tile,
    On the provost's grand ridge-tile,
The Blackamoor first to master me
I saw, I saw that winsome smile,
The mouth that did my heart beguile,
And spoke the great Word over me,
In the land beyond the sea.

I called his name, I called aloud,
    Alas! I called on him aloud;
And then he filled his hand with stour
And threw it towards me in the air;
My mouse flew out, I lost my pow'r!

My lusty strength, my power were gone;
    Power was gone, and all was gone.
He will not let me love him more!
Of bell and whip and horse's tail
He cares not if I find a store.

But I am proud if he is fierce!
   I am as proud as he is fierce;
I'll turn about and backward go,
If I meet again that Blackamoor,
And he'll help us then, for he shall know
I seek another paramour.

And we'll gang once more to yon town,
   Wi' better luck to yon town;
We'll walk in silk and cramoisie,
And I shall wed the provost's son;
My lady of the town I'll be!

For I was born a crownèd king's child,
   Born and nursed a king's child,
King o' a land ayont the sea,
Where the Blackamoor kissed me first,
And taught me art and glamourie.

Each one in her wame shall hide
   Her hairy mouse, her wary mouse,
Fed on madwort and agramie, –
Wear amber beads between her breasts,
And blind-worm's skin about her knee.

The Lombard shall be Elspie's man,
   Elspie's gowden husband-man;
Nort shall take the lawyer's hand;
The priest shall swear another vow
We'll dance again the saraband!

[1875]

132

THOMAS WESTWOOD
1814–1888

THOMAS WESTWOOD was born at Enfield. Much of his life was spent in Belgium as director and secretary of the Tournay and Jurbise railway. *The Quest of the Sancgreall* was published before Tennyson's treatment of the same theme. It has intermittent stretches of dense clotted energy, and is superior, I think, to Hawker's poem on the same subject.

From *The Quest of the Sancgreall*

Motionless sat the shadow at the helm –
And steered them on, through fen and fallow tract,
Pasture and plain and limitless expanse
Of windy waste, till, widening to the main,
The river ran in shallows, or was caught
In weedy pools, and swerving from its course,
The shallop shuddered with a grating keel.
Then seemed it to Sir Galahad, in his dream,
A woman's cry crept curdling o'er the wave,
Wild, inarticulate – crept o'er pool and bay,
And winding creek, and gully of the shore;
Sobbed 'mid the sedges – round the boulders wailed
And whimpered, wandering up and wandering down.
And ere it ceased, the stagnant stream began
To plash and whirl and dimple; – now an arm,
And now a dripping head, and now a foot,
Flashed up and frisked and flirted in the moon;
The water grew alive with elfin fry,
Quaint atomies, with fins and flapping tails,
That piped a reedy music, out of tune;
Kelpy and Neck, and all their kith and kin,
Came at the summons, and a shimmering throng
Of creatures, lissom-limbed and lithe, that shed
A sea-green glory round them as they swam.

All these swarmed round the shallop, and at a sign
From her that steered, made plain a path through beds
Of osiers, and the tangled undergrowth,
And drove it o'er the shallows and the sands. . . .

And seaward, like an arrow, shot the bark;
The seething water rustled round its prow;
The silver water glittered in its wake;
The stars spun round and round; the chalky flats
Broke, gradual, into beetling cliff and crag,
And soon Sir Galahad, in his drowse, was 'ware
Dim headlands loomed majestical through mist,
And the salt billows flecked him with their foam.
Then rose that mystic moan anew, and swept,
Shrill, o'er the shuddering waves and through the depths –
Till, from the under-world, surged up the brood
Of ocean, the great sea-snake, coil on coil,
The kraken, demon-eyed, and hundred-armed,
The sea-wolf and narwhal, mermaids and men –
A ghastly crew of scaled and slimy things –
With hiss, and whoop, and hollo, swift they came, –
Dashing the spray in moon-bows overhead, –
And huddled, interlaced, with one combined
Impulsion, snout and fin and fold and tail,
They sent the shallop skimming through the foam,
Into the distance, fleet as shooting star. . . .

A haze slid down the headlands o'er the main –
A blinding haze, that blotted out the stars;
The shallop clove it, as a kestrel cleaves
The gloaming, hieing homeward to its nest.
A whirlwind wrenched the air, and swooping, made
Mad havoc of the sea; but wind and wave
The shallop stemmed, as stems an angry swan
The blasts and billows of its native tarn.
From out the foam, a jagged and hideous reef
Rose horrent – range on range of splintered crag.

With serpentine, swift motion, in and out,
And to and fro, betwixt the deadly saws,
The shallop flitted, and the reef was past –
But in its rear, a mighty mountain wall
Towered absolute – no outlet – on its brow
A blackness – smooth its shining front as steel.
Then roared the kraken, and the great sea-snake,
Uncoiling, clanked his jaws and hissed in ire.
Bubbled the thick shoal-water with the plunge
Of furious limb – with swish of tail and fin
And the swart merman yelled beneath the moon.

But at the helm, the shadow, swaying, sung
A song of glamour, stern, that pierced through rock,
And water, to the deep root of the world.
A shiver shook the air – the sea leaped up;
And tossed its crest and shrieked in mad affright;
Shuddered the mighty mountain wall; its front
Grew blurred with cracks and ruinous fissures, rent
From base to battlement, and the loathly crew,
Cheered by the din and downfall and dismay,
Renewed their toil; – with sharp, impetuous stroke,
The shallop smit the rock – a narrow cleft
Opened, grew wider, gaped – the bark shot through –
And lo! the roseate morning in the heavens
Flushing the splendours of the syren seas!

[1868]

CHARLES KINGSLEY

1819–1875

CHARLES KINGSLEY was born in Devonshire. His poetry has been overshadowed by the success of his novels and his preaching. His personality expresses much of what is meant by muscular Christianity, a kind of healthy extrovert blend of team games, love of country and strenuous family relations. The underlying force of *Andromeda* – his best poem – can now be seen as powerfully sexual, anticipating some of the speed and resonance of Swinburne, but the poem was rightly admired in its own day for narrative flow and accuracy of observation.

From *Andromeda*

Whelming the dwellings of men, and the toils of the slow-
footed oxen,
Drowning the barley and flax, and the hard-earned gold of
the harvest,
Up to the hillside vines, and the pastures skirting the wood-
land,
Inland the floods came yearly; and after the waters a
monster,
Bred of the slime, like the worms which are bred from the
muds of the Nile-bank,
Shapeless, a terror to see; and by night it swam out to the
seaward,
Daily returning to feed with the dawn, and devoured of the
fairest,
Cattle, and children, and maids, till the terrified people fled
inland.
Fasting in sackcloth and ashes they came, both the king
and his people,
Came to the mountain of oaks, to the house of the terrible
sea-gods,

Hard by the gulf in the rocks, where of old the world-wide
  deluge
Sank to the inner abyss; and the lake where the fish of the
  goddess
Holy, undying, abide; whom the priests feed daily with
  dainties.
There to the mystical fish, high-throned in her chamber of
  cedar,
Burnt they the fat of the flock; till the flame shone far to
  the seaward.
Three days fasting they prayed: but the fourth day the
  priests of the goddess
Cunning in spells, cast lots, to discover the crime of the
  people.
All day long they cast, till the house of the monarch was
  taken,
Cepheus, king of the land; and the faces of all gathered
  blackness.

*　　*　　*

Loosing his arms from her waist he flew upward, await-
  ing the sea-beast.
Onward it came from the southward, as bulky and black as
  a galley,
Lazily coasting along, as the fish fled leaping before it;
Lazily breasting the ripple, and watching by sandbar and
  headland,
Listening for laughter of maidens at bleaching, or song of
  the fisher,
Children at play on the pebbles, or cattle that pawed on the
  sandhills.
Rolling and dripping it came, where bedded in glistening
  purple
Cold on the cold sea-weeds lay the long white sides of the
  maiden,
Trembling, her face in her hands, and her tresses afloat on
  the water.

As when an osprey aloft, dark-eyebrowed, royally crested,
Flags on by creek and by cove, and in the scorn of the anger
of Nereus
Ranges, the king of the shore; if he see on a glittering shallow,
Chasing the bass and the mullet, the fin of a wallowing
dolphin,
Halting, he wheels round slowly, in doubt at the weight of
his quarry,
Whether to clutch it alive, or to fall on the wretch like a
plummet,
Stunning with terrible talon the life of the brain in the
hindhead:
Then rushes up with a scream, and stooping the wrath of
his eyebrows
Falls from the sky like a star, while the wind rattles hoarse
in his pinions.
Over him closes the foam for a moment; then from the
sand-bed
Rolls up the great fish, dead, and his side gleams white in
the sunshine.
Thus fell the boy on the beast, unveiling the face of the
Gorgon;
Thus fell the boy on the beast; thus rolled up the beast in
his horror,
Once, as the dead eyes glared into his; then his sides, death-
sharpened,
Stiffened and stood, brown rock, in the wash of the wander-
ing water.

[1858]

CHARLES KINGSLEY

The Last Buccanier

Oh England is a pleasant place for them that's rich and high,
But England is a cruel place for such poor folks as I;
And such a port for mariners I ne'er shall see again
As the pleasant Isle of Avès, beside the Spanish main.

There were forty craft in Avès that were both swift and
  stout,
All furnished well with small arms and cannons round
  about;
And a thousand men in Avès made laws so fair and free
To choose their valiant captains and obey them loyally.

Thence we sailed against the Spaniard with his hoards of
  plate and gold,
Which he wrung with cruel tortures from Indian folk of old;
Likewise the merchant captains, with hearts as hard as
  stone,
Who flog men and keel-haul them, and starve them to the
  bone.

Oh the palms grew high in Avès, and fruits that shone like
  gold,
And the colibris and parrots they were gorgeous to behold;
And the negro maids to Avès from bondage fast did flee,
To welcome gallant sailors, a-sweeping in from sea.

Oh sweet it was in Avès to hear the landward breeze
A-swing with good tobacco in a net between the trees,
With a negro lass to fan you, while you listened to the roar
Of the breakers on the reef outside, that never touched the
  shore.

But Scripture saith, an ending to all fine things must be;
So the King's ships sailed on Avès, and quite put down
    were we.
All day we fought like bulldogs, but they burst the booms
    at night;
And I fled in a piragua, sore wounded, from the fight.

Nine days I floated starving, and a negro lass beside,
Till for all I tried to cheer her, the poor young thing she
    died;
But as I lay a gasping, a Bristol sail came by,
And brought me home to England here, to beg until I die.

And now I'm old and going – I'm sure I can't tell where;
One comfort is, this world's so hard, I can't be worse off
    there:
If I might but be a sea-dove, I'd fly across the main,
To the pleasant Isle of Avès, to look at it once again.

[1858]

ARTHUR HUGH CLOUGH
1819–1861

ARTHUR HUGH CLOUGH was born in Liverpool, where he later wrote his first long poem in hexameters, the *Bothie of Tober-na-Vuelich*. He died in Florence. His reputation has risen sharply since the Oxford edition of his work appeared in 1951. The colloquial tone and attractively unstuffy personality of his great hexameter poem *Amours de Voyage* are the supreme achievement of the *vers de société* tradition in the nineteenth century. Metrically, Clough's hexameters may owe something to Longfellow's in *Evangeline* but their flexibility and grace of tone go back to the Regency poise of Thomas Moore's epistolary sequence *The Fudge Family in Paris*. Clough was one of the few nineteenth-century poets who had first hand experience of warfare, which may account for his unheroic note. In *Dipsychus*, the Faustian dilemma is ingeniously re-run through the mind-searching of a pompous young don in Venice: despite its unfinished state, this is the most interesting closet-drama of the century, pointing forward by its sudden shifts of tone to the cinematic cutting of *The Waste Land*.

From *Amours de Voyage*

V. CLAUDE TO EUSTACE

Yes, we are fighting at last, it appears. This morning as usual,
Murray, as usual, in hand, I enter the Caffè Nuovo;
Seating myself with a sense as it were of a change in the weather,
Not understanding, however, but thinking mostly of Murray,
And, for to-day is their day, of the Campidoglio Marbles,
Caffè-latte! I call to the waiter, – and *Non c' è latte*,
This is the answer he makes me, and this the sign of a battle.

So I sit; and truly they seem to think anyone else more
Worthy than me of attention. I wait for my milkless *nero*,
Free to observe undistracted all sorts and sizes of persons,
Blending civilian and soldier in strangest costume, coming
    in, and
Gulping in hottest haste, still standing, their coffee, – with-
    drawing
Eagerly, jangling a sword on the steps, or jogging a musket
Slung to the shoulder behind. They are fewer, moreover,
    than usual,
Much, and silenter far; and so I begin to imagine
Something is really afloat. Ere I leave, the Caffè is empty,
Empty too the streets, in all its length the Corso
Empty, and empty I see to my right and left the Condotti.
    Twelve o'clock, on the Pincian Hill, with lots of English,
Germans, Americans, French, – the Frenchmen, too, are
    protected, –
So we stand in the sun, but afraid of a probable shower;
So we stand and stare, and see, to the left of St Peter's,
Smoke, from the cannon, white, – but that is at intervals
    only, –
Black, from a burning house, we suppose, by the Caval-
    leggieri;
And we believe we discern some lines of men descending
Down through the vineyard-slopes, and catch a bayonet
    gleaming.
Every ten minutes, however, – in this there is no miscon-
    ception, –
Comes a great white puff from behind Michael Angelo's
    dome, and
After a space the report of a real big gun, – not the French-
    man's? –
That must be doing some work. And so we watch and
    conjecture.
    Shortly, an Englishman comes, who says he has been to
        St Peter's,
Seen the Piazza and troops, but that is all he can tell us;

So we watch and sit, and, indeed, it begins to be tiresome. –
All this smoke is outside; when it has come to the inside,
It will be time, perhaps, to descend and retreat to our houses.
  Half-past one, or two. The report of small arms frequent,
Sharp and savage indeed; that cannot all be for nothing:
So we watch and wonder; but guessing is tiresome, very.
Weary of wondering, watching, and guessing, and gossiping
  idly,
Down I go, and pass through the quiet streets with the
  knots of
National Guards patrolling, and flags hanging out at the
  windows,
English, American, Danish, – and, after offering to help an
Irish family moving *en masse* to the Maison Serny,
After endeavouring idly to minister balm to the trembling
Quinquagenarian fears of two lone British spinsters,
Go to make sure of my dinner before the enemy enter.
But by this there are signs of stragglers returning; and
  voices
Talk, though you don't believe it, of guns and prisoners
  taken;
And on the walls you read the first bulletin of the morning. –
This is all that I saw, and all I know of the battle.

VII. CLAUDE TO EUSTACE

So, I have seen a man killed! An experience that, among
  others!
Yes, I suppose I have; although I can hardly be certain,
And in a court of justice could never declare I had seen it.
But a man was killed, I am told, in a place where I saw
Something; a man was killed, I am told, and I saw some-
  thing.
  I was returning home from St Peter's; Murray, as usual,
Under my arm, I remember; had crossed the St Angelo
  bridge; and

Moving towards the Condotti, had got to the first barricade,
    when
Gradually, thinking still of St Peter's, I became conscious
Of a sensation of movement opposing me, – tendency this
    way
(Such as one fancies may be in a stream when the wave of
    the tide is
Coming and not yet come, – a sort of poise and retention);
So I turned, and, before I turned, caught sight of stragglers
Heading a crowd, it is plain, that is coming behind that
    corner.
Looking up, I see windows filled with heads; the Piazza,
Into which you remember the Ponte St Angelo enters,
Since I passed, has thickened with curious groups; and now
    the
Crowd is coming, has turned, has crossed that last barricade,
    is
Here at my side. In the middle they drag at something.
    What is it?
Ha! bare swords in the air, held up! There seem to be
    voices
Pleading and hands putting back; official, perhaps; but the
    swords are
Many, and bare in the air. In the air? They descend; they
    are smiting,
Hewing, chopping – At what? In the air once more up-
    stretched! And
Is it blood that's on them? Yes, certainly blood! Of whom,
    then?
Over whom is the cry of this furor of exultation?
    While they are skipping and screaming, and dancing
        their caps on the points of
Swords and bayonets, I to the outskirts back, and ask a
Mercantile-seeming bystander, 'What is it?' and he, looking
    always
That way, makes me answer, 'A Priest, who was trying to
    fly to

The Neapolitan army,' – and thus explains the proceeding.
  You didn't see the dead man? No; – I began to be
  doubtful;
I was in black myself, and didn't know what mightn't
  happen; –
But a National Guard close by me, outside of the hubbub,
Broke his sword with slashing a broad hat covered with
  dust, – and
Passing away from the place with Murray under my arm,
  and
Stooping, I saw through the legs of the people the legs of
  a body.
  You are the first, do you know, to whom I have mentioned
  the matter.
Whom should I tell it to, else? – these girls? – the Heavens
  forbid it? –
Quidnuncs at Monaldini's? – idlers upon the Pincian?
  If I rightly remember, it happened on that afternoon
  when
Word of the nearer approach of a new Neapolitan army
First was spread. I began to bethink me of Paris Septembers,
Thought I could fancy the look of the old 'Ninety-two. On
  that evening
Three or four, or, it may be, five, of these people were
  slaughtered.
Some declare they had, one of them, fired on a sentinel;
  others
Say they were only escaping; a Priest, it is currently stated,
Stabbed a National Guard on the very Piazza Colonna:
History, Rumour of Rumours, I leave it to thee to deter-
  mine!
  But I am thankful to say the government seems to have
  strength to
Put it down; it has vanished, at least; the place is most
  peaceful.
Through the Trastevere walking last night, at nine of the
  clock, I

Found no sort of disorder; I crossed by the Island-bridges,
So by the narrow streets to the Ponte Rotto, and onwards
Thence by the Temple of Vesta, away to the great Coliseum,
Which at the full of the moon is an object worthy a visit.

[1862]

Spectator Ab Extra

I

As I sat at the Café I said to myself,
They may talk as they please about what they call pelf,
They may sneer as they like about eating and drinking,
But help it I cannot, I cannot help thinking
　　How pleasant it is to have money, heigh-ho!
　　How pleasant it is to have money.

I sit at my table *en grand seigneur*,
And when I have done, throw a crust to the poor;
Not only the pleasure itself of good living,
But also the pleasure of now and then giving:
　　So pleasant it is to have money, heigh-ho!
　　So pleasant it is to have money.

They may talk as they please about what they call pelf,
And how one ought never to think of one's self,
How pleasures of thought surpass eating and drinking, –
My pleasure of thought is the pleasure of thinking
　　How pleasant it is to have money, heigh-ho!
　　How pleasant it is to have money.

II

LE DINER

Come along, 'tis time, ten or more minutes past,
And he who came first had to wait for the last;
The oysters ere this had been in and been out;
Whilst I have been sitting and thinking about
　　How pleasant it is to have money, heigh-ho!
　　How pleasant it is to have money.

A clear soup with eggs; *voilà tout*; of the fish
The *filets de sole* are a moderate dish
À la Orly, but you're for red mullet, you say:
By the gods of good fare, who can question to-day
  How pleasant it is to have money, heigh-ho!
  How pleasant it is to have money.

After oysters, sauterne; then sherry; champagne,
Ere one bottle goes, comes another again;
Fly up, thou bold cork, to the ceiling above,
And tell to our ears in the sound that they love
  How pleasant it is to have money, heigh-ho!
  How pleasant it is to have money.

I've the simplest of palates; absurd it may be,
But I almost could dine on a *poulet-au-riz*,
Fish and soup and omelette and that – but the deuce –
There were to be woodcocks, and not *Charlotte Russe*!
  So pleasant it is to have money, heigh-ho!
  So pleasant it is to have money.

Your chablis is acid, away with the hock,
Give me the pure juice of the purple médoc:
St Péray is exquisite; but, if you please,
Some burgundy just before tasting the cheese.
  So pleasant it is to have money, heigh-ho!
  So pleasant it is to have money.

As for that, pass the bottle, and d——n the expense,
I've seen it observed by a writer of sense,
That the labouring classes could scarce live a day,
If people like us didn't eat, drink, and pay.
  So useful it is to have money, heigh-ho!
  So useful it is to have money.

One ought to be grateful, I quite apprehend,
Having dinners and suppers and plenty to spend,
And so suppose now, while the things go away,
By way of a grace we all stand up and say
  How pleasant it is to have money, heigh-ho!
  How pleasant it is to have money.

III

PARVENANT

I cannot but ask, in the park and the streets
When I look at the number of faces one meets,
What e'er in the world the poor devils can do
Whose fathers and mothers can't give them a *sou*.
  So needful it is to have money, heigh-ho!
  So needful it is to have money.

I ride, and I drive, and I care not a d——n,
The people look up and they ask who I am;
And if I should chance to run over a cad,
I can pay for the damage, if ever so bad.
  So useful it is to have money, heigh-ho!
  So useful it is to have money.

It was but this winter I came up to town,
And already I'm gaining a sort of renown;
Find my way to good houses without much ado,
Am beginning to see the nobility too.
  So useful it is to have money, heigh-ho!
  So useful it is to have money.

O dear what a pity they ever should lose it,
Since they are the people that know how to use it;
So easy, so stately, such manners, such dinners,
And yet, after all, it is we are the winners.
  So needful it is to have money, heigh-ho!
  So needful it is to have money.

It's all very well to be handsome and tall,
Which certainly makes you look well at a ball;
It's all very fine to be clever and witty,
But if you are poor, why it's only a pity.
  So needful it is to have money, heigh-ho!
  So needful it is to have money.

There's something undoubtedly in a fine air,
To know how to smile and be able to stare,
High breeding is something, but well-bred or not,
In the end the one question is, what have you got.
  So needful it is to have money, heigh-ho!
  So needful it is to have money.

And the angels in pink and the angels in blue,
In muslins and moirés so lovely and new,
What is it they want, and so wish you to guess,
But if you have money, the answer is Yes.
  So needful, they tell you, is money, heigh-ho!
  So needful it is to have money.

[1862/1863]

From *Dipsychus*

SCENE I

VENICE. THE PIAZZA. SUNDAY, 9 P.M.

Dipsychus

The scene is different, and the place; the air
Tastes of the nearer North: the people too
Not perfect southern lightness. Wherefore then
Should these old verses come into my mind
I made last year at Naples? O poor fool,
Still nesting on thyself!

149

'Through the great sinful streets of Naples as I past,
With fiercer heat than flamed above my head
My heart was hot within; the fire burnt, and at last
My brain was lightened when my tongue had said,
    Christ is not risen!'

Spirit

Christ is not risen? Oh indeed!
Wasn't aware that was your creed.

Dipsychus

So it goes on. Too lengthy to repeat—
    'Christ is not risen.'

Spirit

    Dear, how odd!
He'll tell us next there is no God.
I thought 'twas in the Bible plain,
On the third day he rose again.

Dipsychus

Ashes to Ashes, Dust to Dust;
As of the Unjust also of the Just –
    Yea, of that Just One too!
Is He not risen, and shall we not rise?
    O we unwise!

Spirit

H'm! and the tone then after all
Something of the ironical?
Sarcastic, say; or were it fitter
To style it the religious bitter?

Dipsychus

Interpret it I cannot. I but wrote it –
At Naples, truly, as the preface tells,
Last year in the Toledo; it came on me,

And did me good at once. At Naples then,
At Venice now. Ah! and I think at Venice
Christ is not risen either.

Spirit

           Nay –
T'was well enough once in a way;
Such things don't fall out every day.
Having once happened, as we know,
In Palestine so long ago,
How should it now at Venice here?
Where people, true enough, appear
To appreciate more and understand
Their ices, and their Austrian band,
And dark-eyed girls –

Dipsychus

      The whole great square they fill,
From the red flaunting streamers on the staffs,
And that barbaric portal of St Mark's,
To where, unnoticed, at the darker end,
I sit upon my step. One great gay crowd.
The Campanile to the silent stars
Goes up, above – its apex lost in air.
While these – do what?

Spirit

         Enjoy the minute,
And the substantial blessings in it;
Ices, *par exemple*; evening air;
Company, and this handsome square;
Some pretty faces here and there;
Music! Up, up; it isn't fit
With beggars here on steps to sit.
Up – to the café! Take a chair
And join the wiser idlers there.
Aye! what a crowd! and what a noise!

With all these screaming half-breeched boys.
Partout dogs, boys, and women wander –
And see, a fellow singing yonder;
Singing, ye gods, and dancing too –
Tooraloo, tooraloo, tooraloo, loo;
Fiddle di, diddle di, diddle di da
Figaro sù, Figaro giù –
Figaro quà, Figaro là!
How he likes doing it! Ah, ha, ha!

Dipsychus

While these do what – ah heaven!

Spirit

If you want to pray
I'll step aside a little way.
Eh? But I will not be far gone;
You may be wanting me anon.
Our lonely pious altitudes
Are followed quick by prettier moods.
Who knows not with what ease devotion
Slips into earthlier emotion?

Dipsychus

While these do what? Ah, heaven, too true, at Venice
Christ is not risen either!

[1865]

EBENEZER JONES
1820–1860

EBENEZER JONES was born in Canonbury Square, Islington, and died at Brentwood. He was born into a family of strict Calvinists, and went through a brutal schooling. John Betjeman has versified the touching story of his attempt to stop a vicious usher killing a dog. His book, *Studies of Sensation and Event*, was paid for out of his earnings as a clerk. He sympathized with the Chartists but had no leisure to take part in their activities. He seems to have been a man of consistent courage and reasonableness in the face of bad health, marital problems, lack of money and critical neglect. *A Development of Idiotcy* has the urgency of Emily Brontë's prose combined with the rough strength of Wordsworth: it also presages the twentieth-century break-up of the iambic pentameter in its sudden surges of anapaests.

A Development of Idiotcy

Fearful the chamber's quiet; the veiled windows
Admit no breath of the out-door throbbing sunshine;
She moans in the bed's dusk; – some sharp revulsion
Shuddereth her lips as though she strives to cry,
But finds no voice: she draweth up her limbs,
They flutter fast and shake their covering.
Seven watch her, as might men a noonday sun,
Who vanishing backward in the top of heaven,
Leaves them all blindly staring through the dark; –
Physicians and servitors; – pryingly they bend,
While by her head kneels one in agony.
A gloom seems passing o'er her countenance,
As the shadow of a cloud across a field;
Perchance the ghastly expression of the horror
With which life ends: it darkened but a moment;
Now she turns white as stone, as fixed, as dead.
God! ten days hence she laughed out in thy sunshine!
Her filmed eyes looked, gestured happiness! –
They have no look at all.

The seven shuffle from the bed which hides
Her clutching fingers, and her doubled limbs,
So stiffening 'twixt its sheets; and one by one,
They coweringly glance towards her fallen mouth,
And all together hurry from out the room,
Not caring to leave it singly. All is still;
He rises from the ground, fast locks the door,
Breaks through her couch-clothes, feels about her heart; –
All there is motionless: he lifts her hand; –
There is nothing but dead form, it moves not, warms not,
It weighs, it slides away, it drops like lead,
Lies where it dropped: recoiling, the man gasps,
As though by ocean seized: his jaws contract,
He bounds, he rends the window; savagely
Looking right up into the broad blue sky,
No congruous curses aid him, – he is silent,
Save with his clenched hands, his writhing face,
His heaving chest.

                He was a force-filled man,
Whom the wise envy not; his passionate soul,
Being mighty to detect life's secret beauty,
Detecting, would display; and in his youth,
When first visions unveiled before his gaze
Their moral loveliness and physical grace,
With the sweet melody of affectionate clamour
He sang them to the world, and bade it worship:
But the world unrecognized his visions of goodness,
Or recognizing, hated them and him.
As some full cloud foregoes his native country
Of sublime hills, where bask'd he near to heaven,
And descends gently on his shadowy wings
Through the hot sunshine to refresh all creatures;
So came he to the world; – as the same cloud
Might slowly wend back to his Alpine home,
Unwatering the plain, – so left he men
Who knew not of their loss.

Yet sad was loneliness, and never beheld he
Aught beautiful amidst our world of beauty –
From sunsets flushing heaven with sudden crimson,
To the moth's wing that spots the poplar leaf;
Never developed he fact, or dreamed he glory,
Without being faint for sympathy, – that one
Might share with him his blissful adoration,
Loving even as he loved. This holy want
Wasted him unto sickness: then she came;
And while he hung above death's gloomy gulf,
Sternly considering its maddening stillness,
Measuring the plunge; – her soft voice called to him:
He turned; he saw her eyes his soul acquiring;
He saw her look of woman's infinite giving;
He saw her arms of eloquent entreaty,
Praying indeed to clasp him: yea, she saved;
And Oh! but he was happy, for her being
Loved all things as he loved, and thence to him
Came hope and rapturous quiet. Then no more
Lamented he the wingless minds of men,
Than pines the swan, – who down the midnight river,
Moves on considering the reflected stars –
Because dark reptiles burrowing in the ooze,
Care not for starry glories.

She is dead within that bed; and never more
Will she hearken to his dreams of paradise,
And wind her arms around him, sweetly paling
With excess of happiness.
Three days and nights he haunted a near mountain;
The sky was cloudless, and the sunshine strong,
And not one mournful breeze ever stole to him,
Loosening his tears. High on its top he stood;
His voice rose solemn, and loud, and fearlessly: –
The angels watching him midway in the air,
Rushed swift to heaven, and all heaven's shining group
Weepingly pleaded against his blasphemy; –

'Roll back! thou lying robe of halcyon blue!
And let me speak unto thy cowering Lord,
The slayer of my love, that I may tell him
My infinite hate, that he may slaughter me:
He has killed her: I will not have his life; –
Thou lying robe of halcyon blue! roll back!'
The peaks prolonged with echoings his defiance;
Still the sky stirred not – still the sunshine smiled,
And beneath the smile low rose a low wild sound: –
'And then my breast will be as cold as hers, –
My face as white – as signless.'

The fourth day, back he rushed into the chamber,
Where she lay coffined. None dared speak to him;
Great grief is majesty; he is alone.
Oh! is that she, or can it all be dreaming?
Fine lace is plaited round her countenance;
Her eyes are closed, as they would seem to say,
'My last farewell is taken.' Round her lips
Is fixed a sweet smile; her shrunken hands
Are clasped upon her bosom, their dark fingers
Cunningly hidden. Can it all be dreaming?
Striving to stare the mistiness from his eyes,
Griping his throat, he lightly presses her hand, –
The pressure of his fingers doth not vanish; –
Senseless he falls.
This singer of the beautiful, who retreated
Back from a scowling world; this force-filled man,
Who finding nothing whereunto he might sing,
Of power unuttered, and of passion unshared,
Nigh died; this gentle minister of love,
Who, hailed by loving sympathy, thrice lived
In singing his deities, and seeing them loved,
And loving their lover, and forgetting all else; –
Is now a thing that hideth most fair weathers,
Outwandering in most glooms, – after whose path
The village boys shout 'idiot', that some sport

His face may make them, when it turns enraged
With idiot rage, that slinks to empty smiles,
And tears, and laughter, empty. His chief habit
Is secretly rending piecemeal beauteous flowers; –
He ever shows when the groaning thunder toils,
And when the lightnings flash! and they who meet
His shrinking, shuddering, blank countenance,
Wonder to heaven with somewhat shaken trust.

[1843]

FREDERICK LOCKER-LAMPSON

1821–1895

FREDERICK LOCKER-LAMPSON was born at Greenwich
Hospital. He was admired and praised by his pupil (and
superior) Austin Dobson. Most of his pieces fall far short of
the patrician grace he noted in his model Praed. His style is
frequently awkward and sentimental, but *Mr Placid's Flirta-
tion* sustains the delightful tradition of middle-aged infatu-
ation which reached its climax a century later in Betjeman.

Mr Placid's Flirtation

*Jemima was cross, and I lost my umbrella
That day at the tomb of Cecilia Metella.*
LETTERS FROM ROME

Miss Tristram's *poulet* ended thus: 'Nota bene,
We meet for croquet in the Aldobrandini.'
Says my wife, 'Then I'll drive, and you'll ride with Selina'
(Jones's fair spouse, of the Via Sistina).

We started: I'll own that my family deem
I'm an ass, but I'm not such an ass as I seem;
As we cross'd the stones gently a nursemaid said 'La –
There goes Mrs Jones with Miss Placid's papa!'

Our friends, one or two may be mention'd anon,
Had arranged *rendezvous* at the Gate of St John:
That pass'd, off we spun over turf that's not green there,
And soon were all met at the villa. You've been there?

I'll try and describe, or I won't, if you please,
The cheer that was set for us under the trees:
You have read the *menu*, may you read it again;
Champagne, perigord, galantine, and – champagne.

Suffice it to say, I got seated between
Mrs Jones and old Brown – to the latter's chagrin.
Poor Brown, who believes in himself, and – another thing,
Whose talk is so bald, but whose cheeks are so – t'other
    thing.

She sang, her sweet voice fill'd the gay garden alleys;
I jested, but Brown would not smile at my sallies; –
Selina remark'd that a swell met at Rome
Is not always a swell when you meet him at home.

The luncheon despatch'd, we adjourn'd to croquet,
A dainty, but difficult sport in its way.
Thus I counsel the sage, who to play at it stoops,
Belabour thy neighbour, and spoon through thy hoops.

Then we stroll'd, and discourse found its kindest of tones:
'Oh, how charming were solitude and – Mrs Jones!'
'Indeed, Mr Placid, I dote on the sheeny
And shadowy paths of the Aldobrandini!'

A girl came with violet posies, and two
Gentle eyes, like her violets, freshen'd with dew,
And a kind of an indolent, fine-lady air, –
As if she by accident found herself there.

I bought one. Selina was pleased to accept it;
She gave me a rosebud to keep – and I've kept it
Then twilight was near, and I think, in my heart,
When she vow'd she must go, she was loth to depart.

Cattivo momento! we dare not delay:
The steeds are remounted, and wheels roll away:
The ladies *condemn* Mrs Jones, as the phrase is,
But vie with each other in chanting my praises.

'He has so much to say!' cries the fair Mrs Legge;
'How amusing he was about missing the peg!'
'What a beautiful smile!' says the plainest Miss Gunn.
All echo, 'He's charming! delightful! – What fun!'

This sounds rather *nice*, and it's perfectly clear it
Had sounded more *nice* had I happen'd to hear it;
The men were less civil, and gave me a rub,
So I happen'd to hear when I went to the Club.

Says Brown, 'I shall drop Mr Placid's society;'
(Brown is a prig of improper propriety;)
'Hang him,' said Smith (who from cant's not exempt)
'Why he'll bring immorality into contempt.'

Says I (to myself) when I found me alone,
'My dear wife has my heart, is it always her own?'
And further, says I (to myself) 'I'll be shot
If I know if Selina adores me or not.'

Says Jones, 'I've just come from the *scavi*, at Veii,
And I've bought some remarkably fine scarabæi!'

[1857]

160

MATTHEW ARNOLD
1822–1888

MATTHEW ARNOLD was born at Laleham on the Thames.
His father was Thomas Arnold, the famous headmaster
of Rugby. Arnold himself spent his life as an Inspector
of Schools. More than any other great Victorian writer
he sought to integrate practice with theory: his criticism,
with its concept of poetry as a substitute for religion,
sprang from the same heroic attempt to grapple with
loss of faith as his major poems. By far the most sus-
tained of these is *Balder Dead*, where the distancing power of
the Nordic myth about the death of a god enables Arnold
both to release and to control his deepest feelings about the
Death of God (see the Introduction p. 28). In an ideal
anthology of Victorian poetry *Balder Dead* would appear
entire: as a ritual celebration of the tears of things it comes
nearer to the true note of Virgil than anything in Tennyson,
and it has no rival as the third English epic. The direct treat-
ment of the same subject-matter in Arnold's most admired
lyric, *Dover Beach*, makes a fascinating contrast. Arnold's
remaining narrative poems, particularly *Sohrab and Rustum*
and *Tristram and Iseult*, excel his two much-praised odes,
The Scholar Gypsy and *Thyrsis*, in evading the mummifying
classicism which was his besetting weakness. Like Coleridge,
he will continue to be read for a handful of masterpieces
which transcend the general level of his work.

From *Sohrab and Rustum*

So, on the bloody sand, Sohrab lay dead;
And the great Rustum drew his horseman's cloak
Down o'er his face, and sate by his dead son.
As those black granite pillars, once high-rear'd
By Jemshid in Persepolis, to bear
His house, now 'mid their broken flights of steps
Lie prone, enormous, down the mountain side –
So in the sand lay Rustum by his son.
   And night came down over the solemn waste,
And the two gazing hosts, and that sole pair,

And darken'd all; and a cold fog, with night,
Crept from the Oxus. Soon a hum arose,
As of a great assembly loosed, and fires
Began to twinkle through the fog; for now
Both armies moved to camp and took their meal:
The Persians took it on the open sands
Southward, the Tartars by the river marge;
And Rustum and his son were left alone.

But the majestic river floated on,
Out of the mist and hum of that low land,
Into the frostly starlight, and there moved,
Rejoicing, through the hush'd Chorasmian waste,
Under the solitary moon; – he flow'd
Right for the polar star, past Orgunjè,
Brimming, and bright, and large; then sands begin
To hem his watery march, and dam his streams,
And split his currents; that for many a league
The shorn and parcell'd Oxus strains along
Through beds of sand and matted rushy isles –
Oxus, forgetting the bright speed he had
In his high mountain-cradle in Pamere,
A foil'd circuitous wanderer – till at last
The long'd-for dash of waves is heard, and wide
His luminous home of waters opens, bright
And tranquil, from whose floor the new-bathed stars
Emerge, and shine upon the Aral Sea.

[1853]

From *Balder Dead*

(Book II)

Forth from the east, up the ascent of Heaven,
Day drove his courser with the shining mane;
And in Valhalla, from his gable-perch,
The golden-crested cock began to crow.
Hereafter, in the blackest dead of night,

With shrill and dismal cries that bird shall crow,
Warning the Gods that foes draw nigh to Heaven;
But now he crew at dawn, a cheerful note,
To wake the Gods and Heroes to their tasks.
And all the Gods, and all the Heroes, woke.
And from their beds the Heroes rose, and donn'd
Their arms, and led their horses from the stall,
And mounted them, and in Valhalla's court
Were ranged; and then the daily fray began.
And all day long they there are hack'd and hewn,
'Mid dust, and groans, and limbs lopp'd off, and blood;
But all at night return to Odin's hall,
Woundless and fresh; such lot is theirs in Heaven.
And the Valkyries on their steeds went forth
Tow'rd earth and fights of men; and at their side
Skulda, the youngest of the Nornies, rode;
And over Bifrost, where is Heimdall's watch,
Past Migdard fortress, down to earth they came;
There through some battle-field, where men fall fast,
Their horses fetlock-deep in blood, they ride,
And pick the bravest warriors out for death,
Whom they bring back with them at night to Heaven
To glad the Gods, and feast in Odin's hall.
  But the Gods went not now, as otherwhile,
Into the tilt-yard, where the Heroes fought,
To feast their eyes with looking on the fray;
Nor did they to their judgment-place repair
By the ash Igdrasil, in Ida's plain,
Where they hold council, and give laws for men.
But they went, Odin first, the rest behind,
To the hall Gladheim, which is built of gold;
Where are in circle ranged twelve golden chairs,
And in the midst one higher, Odin's throne.
There all the Gods in silence sate them down;
And thus the Father of the ages spake: –
  'Go quickly, Gods, bring wood to the seashore,
With all, which it beseems the dead to have,

And make a funeral-pile on Balder's ship;
On the twelfth day the Gods shall burn his corpse.
But Hermod, thou take Sleipner, and ride down
To Hela's kingdom, to ask Balder back.'
So said he; and the Gods arose, and took
Axes and ropes, and at their head came Thor,
Shouldering his hammer, which the giants know.
Forth wended they, and drave their steeds before.
And up the dewy mountain-tracks they fared
To the dark forests, in the early dawn;
And up and down, and side and slant they roam'd.
And from the glens all day an echo came
Of crashing falls; for with his hammer Thor
Smote 'mid the rocks the lichen-bearded pines,
And burst their roots, while to their tops the Gods
Made fast the woven ropes, and haled them down,
And lopp'd their boughs; and clove them on the sward,
And bound the logs behind their steeds to draw,
And drave them homeward; and the snorting steeds
Went straining through the crackling brushwood down,
And by the darkling forest-paths the Gods
Follow'd and on their shoulders carried boughs.
And they came out upon the plain, and pass'd
Asgard, and led their horses to the beach,
And loosed them of their loads on the seashore,
And ranged the wood in stacks by Balder's ship;
And every God went home to his own house.

From *Balder Dead*

(Book III)

But when the Gods and Heroes heard, they brought
The wood to Balder's ship, and built a pile,
Full the deck's breadth, and lofty; then the corpse
Of Balder on the highest top they laid,
With Nanna on his right, and on his left

Hoder, his brother, whom his own hand slew.
And they set jars of wine and oil to lean
Against the bodies, and stuck torches near,
Splinters of pine-wood, soak'd with turpentine;
And brought his arms and gold, and all his stuff,
And slew the dogs who at his table fed,
And his horse, Balder's horse, whom most he loved,
And placed them on the pyre, and Odin threw
A last choice gift thereon, his golden ring.
The mast they fixt, and hoisted up the sails,
Then they put fire to the wood; and Thor
Set his stout shoulder hard against the stern
To push the ship through the thick sand; – sparks flew
From the deep trench she plough'd, so strong a God
Furrow'd it; and the water gurgled in.
And the ship floated on the waves, and rock'd.
But in the hills a strong east-wind arose,
And came down moaning to the sea; first squalls
Ran black o'er the sea's face, then steady rush'd
The breeze, and fill'd the sails, and blew the fire.
And wreathed in smoke the ship stood out to sea.
Soon with a roaring rose the mighty fire,
And the pile crackled; and between the logs
Sharp quivering tongues of flame shot out, and leapt,
Curling and darting, higher, until they lick'd
The summit of the pile, the dead, the mast,
And ate the shrivelling sails; but still the ship
Drove on, ablaze above her hull with fire.
And the Gods stood upon the beach, and gazed.
And while they gazed, the sun went lurid down
Into the smoke-wrapt sea, and night came on.
Then the wind fell, with night, and there was calm;
But through the dark they watch'd the burning ship
Still carried o'er the distant waters on,
Farther and farther, like an eye of fire.
And long, in the far dark, blazed Balder's pile;
But fainter, as the stars rose high, it flared,

The bodies were consumed, ash choked the pile.
And as, in a decaying winter-fire,
A charr'd log, falling, makes a shower of sparks –
So with a shower of sparks the pile fell in,
Reddening the sea around; and all was dark.

[1855]

Dover Beach

The sea is calm to-night.
The tide is full, the moon lies fair
Upon the straits; – on the French coast the light
Gleams and is gone; the cliffs of England stand,
Glimmering and vast, out in the tranquil bay.
Come to the window, sweet is the night-air!
Only, from the long line of spray
Where the sea meets the moon-blanch'd land,
Listen! you hear the grating roar
Of pebbles which the waves draw back, and fling,
At their return, up the high strand,
Begin, and cease, and then again begin,
With tremulous cadence slow, and bring
The eternal note of sadness in.
Sophocles long ago
Heard it on the Ægæan, and it brought
Into his mind the turbid ebb and flow
Of human misery; we
Find also in the sound a thought,
Hearing it by this distant northern sea.

The Sea of Faith
Was once, too, at the full, and round earth's shore
Lay like the folds of a bright girdle furl'd.
But now I only hear
Its melancholy, long, withdrawing roar,
Retreating, to the breath
Of the night-wind, down the vast edges drear
And naked shingles of the world.

Ah, love, let us be true
To one another! for the world, which seems
To lie before us like a land of dreams,
So various, so beautiful, so new,
Hath really neither joy, nor love, nor light,
Nor certitude, nor peace, nor help for pain;
And we are here as on a darkling plain
Swept with confused alarms of struggle and flight,
Where ignorant armies clash by night.

[1867]

COVENTRY PATMORE
1823–1896

COVENTRY KERSAY DIGHTON PATMORE was born at Woodford in Essex. After the death of his first wife in 1862 he was converted to Roman Catholicism and married a Catholic. After his second wife's death in 1880 he married a third time. When nearly seventy he met Alice Meynell and is said to have experienced a strong physical attraction for her which she rejected. The interest roused by these marital and emotional tragedies, however, is largely frustrated by Patmore's discreetly marmoreal verse which veers from the sweet reticence of *The Angel In The House* to the knotted Pindarics of *The Unknown Eros*. Neither collection – despite Patmore's keen interest in prosody – seems rich enough in specifically poetic resources to achieve its purposes. It may be that a modern taste for originality is acting as a temporary block to a proper appreciation of Patmore's quality. Certainly some critics – notably John Heath-Stubbs – have made very high claims for him. Yet in an age of widespread agnosticism Patmore emerges as the most serious casualty among ambitious Victorian poets, often seeming to achieve most – as in *A London Fete* – when at his least characteristic.

From *The Angel in the House*

GOING TO CHURCH

I woke at three; for I was bid
    To breakfast with the Dean at nine,
And thence to Church. My curtain slid,
    I found the dawning Sunday fine,
And could not rest, so rose. The air
    Was dark and sharp; the roosted birds
Cheep'd, 'Here am I, Sweet; are you there?'
    On Avon's misty flats the herds
Expected, comfortless, the day,
    Which slowly fired the clouds above;

The cock scream'd, somewhere far away;
   In sleep the matrimonial dove
Was brooding; no wind waked the wood,
   Nor moved the midnight river-damps,
Nor thrill'd the poplar; quiet stood
   The chestnut with its thousand lamps;
The moon shone yet, but weak and drear,
   And seem'd to watch, with bated breath,
The landscape, all made sharp and clear
   By stillness, as a face by death.

[1854]

Arbor Vitae

With honeysuckle, over-sweet, festooned;
With bitter ivy bound;
Terraced with funguses unsound;
Deformed with many a boss
And closèd scar, o'ercushioned deep with moss;
Bunched all about with pagan mistletoe;
And thick with nests of the hoarse bird
That talks, but understands not his own word;
Stands, and so stood a thousand years ago,
A single tree.
Thunder has done its worst among its twigs,
Where the great crest yet blackens, never pruned,
But in its heart, alway
Ready to push new verdurous boughs, whene'er
The rotting saplings near it fall and leave it air,
Is all antiquity and no decay.
Rich, though rejected by the forest pigs,
Its fruit, beneath whose rough, concealing rind
They that will it break find
Heart-succouring savor of each several meat,
And kernelled drink of brain-renewing power,
With bitter condiment and sour,

And sweet economy of sweet,
And odors that remind
Of haunts of childhood and a different day.
Beside this tree,
Praising no Gods nor blaming, sans a wish,
Sits, Tartar-like, the Time's civility,
And eats its dead-dog off a golden dish.

[1878]

A London Fete

All night fell hammers, shock on shock;
With echoes Newgate's granite clanged:
The scaffold built, at eight o'clock
They brought the man out to be hanged.
Then came from all the people there
A single cry, that shook the air;
Mothers held up their babes to see,
Who spread their hands, and crowed with glee;
Here a girl from her vesture tore
A rag to wave with, and joined the roar;
There a man, with yelling tired,
Stopped, and the culprit's crime inquired;
A sot, below the doomed man dumb,
Bawled his health in the world to come;
These blasphemed and fought for places;
These, half-crushed, with frantic faces,
To windows, where, in freedom sweet,
Others enjoyed the wicked treat.
At last, the show's black crisis pended;
Struggles for better standings ended;
The rabble's lips no longer cursed,
But stood agape with horrid thirst;
Thousands of breasts beat horrid hope;
Thousands of eyeballs, lit with hell,
Burnt one way all, to see the rope

Unslacken as the platform fell.
The rope flew tight; and then the roar
Burst forth afresh; less loud, but more
Confused and affrighting than before.
A few harsh tongues for ever led
The common din, the chaos of noises,
But ear could not catch what they said.
As when the realm of the damned rejoices
At winning a soul to its will,
That clatter and clangour of hateful voices
Sickened and stunned the air, until
The dangling corpse hung straight and still.
The show complete, the pleasure past,
The solid masses loosened fast:
A thief slunk off, with ample spoil,
To ply elsewhere his daily toil;
A baby strung its doll to a stick;
A mother praised the pretty trick;
Two children caught and hanged a cat;
Two friends walked on, in lively chat;
And two, who had disputed places,
Went forth to fight, with murderous faces.

[1890]

SYDNEY DOBELL

1824–1874

SYDNEY DOBELL was born in Kent. He was, with Alexander Smith, whose lifelong friend he became, the leading figure in the movement satirized by Aytoun as the Spasmodics. His verse, particularly in the long unfinished poem *Balder*, is less spasmodic than soporific in effect. The sequence *England in Time of War* does contain one or two moving poems, of which the best is perhaps *Tommy's Dead*.

Tommy's Dead

You may give over plough, boys,
You may take the gear to the stead;
All the sweat o' your brow, boys,
Will never get beer and bread.
The seed's waste, I know, boys;
There's not a blade will grow, boys;
'Tis cropped out, I trow, boys,
And Tommy's dead.

Send the colt to the fair, boys –
He's going blind, as I said,
My old eyes can't bear, boys,
To see him in the shed;
The cow's dry and spare, boys,
She's neither here nor there, boys,
I doubt she's badly bred;
Stop the mill to-morn, boys,
There'll be no more corn, boys,
Neither white nor red;
There's no sign of grass, boys,
You may sell the goat and the ass, boys,
The land's not what it was, boys,
And the beasts must be fed;
You may turn Peg away, boys,

You may pay off old Ned,
We've had a dull day, boys,
And Tommy's dead.

Move my chair on the floor, boys,
Let me turn my head:
She's standing there in the door, boys,
Your sister Winifred!
Take her away from me, boys,
Your sister Winifred!
Move me round in my place, boys,
Let me turn my head,
Take her away from me, boys,
As she lay on her death-bed –
The bones of her thin face, boys,
As she lay on her death-bed!
I don't know how it be, boys,
When all's done and said,
But I see her looking at me, boys,
Wherever I turn my head;
Out of the big oak-tree, boys,
Out of the garden-bed,
And the lily as pale as she, boys,
And the rose that used to be red.

There's something not right, boys,
But I think it's not in my head;
I've kept my precious sight, boys,
The Lord be hallowèd.
Outside and in,
The ground is cold to my tread,
The hills are wizen and thin,
The sky is shrivelled and shred;
The hedges down by the loan
I can count them bone by bone,
The leaves are open and spread.
But I see the teeth of the land,

And hands like a dead man's hand,
And the eyes of a dead man's head.
There's nothing but cinders and sand,
The rat and the mouse have fled,
And the summer's empty and cold;
Over valley and wold,
Wherever I turn my head,
There's a mildew and a mould;
The sun's going out overhead,
And I'm very old,
And Tommy's dead.

What am I staying for, boys?
You're all born and bred –
'Tis fifty years and more, boys,
Since wife and I were wed;
And she's gone before, boys,
And Tommy's dead.

She was always sweet, boys,
Upon his curly head,
She knew she'd never see't, boys,
And she stole off to bed;
I've been sitting up alone, boys,
For he'd come home, he said,
But it's time I was gone, boys,
For Tommy's dead.

Put the shutters up, boys,
Bring out the beer and bread,
Make haste and sup, boys,
For my eyes are heavy as lead;
There's something wrong i' the cup, boys,
There's something ill wi' the bread;
I don't care to sup, boys,
And Tommy's dead.

I'm not right, I doubt, boys,
I've such a sleepy head;
I shall never more be stout, boys,
You may carry me to bed.
What are you about, boys?
The prayers are all said,
The fire's raked out, boys,
And Tommy's dead.

The stairs are too steep, boys,
You may carry me to the head,
The night's dark and deep, boys,
Your mother's long in bed;
'Tis time to go to sleep, boys,
And Tommy's dead.

I'm not used to kiss, boys;
You may shake my hand instead.
All things go amiss, boys,
You may lay me where she is, boys,
And I'll rest my old head;
'Tis a poor world, this, boys,
And Tommy's dead.

[1856]

WALTER C. SMITH

1824–1908

WALTER CHALMERS SMITH was born at Aberdeen. He spent his life as a minister and, though by no means an orthodox one, rose to be moderator of the General Assembly of the Free Church of Scotland. *Glenaradale* turns bitterness at the Highland clearances into tragedy. The form of the poem, with its relaxed metre and mixture of loose and absent rhyme, is in advance of its time. Most of Smith's work, alas, is more conventional.

Glenaradale

There is no fire of the crackling boughs
    On the hearth of our fathers,
There is no lowing of brown-eyed cows
    On the green meadows,
Nor do the maidens whisper vows
    In the still gloaming,
      Glenaradale.

There is no bleating of sheep on the hill
    Where the mists linger,
There is no sound of the low hand-mill
    Ground by the women,
And the smith's hammer is lying still
    By the brown anvil,
      Glenaradale.

Ah! we must leave thee and go away
    Far from Ben Luibh,
Far from the graves where we hoped to lay
    Our bones with our fathers',
Far from the kirk where we used to pray
    Lowly together,
      Glenaradale.

We are not going for hunger of wealth,
    For the gold and silver,
We are not going to seek for health
    On the flat prairies,
Nor yet for the lack of fruitful tilth
    On thy green pastures,
        Glenaradale.

Content with the croft and the hill were we,
    As all our fathers,
Content with the fish in the lake to be
    Carefully netted,
And garments spun of the wool from thee,
    O black-faced wether
        Of Glenaradale!

No father here but would give a son
    For the old country,
And his mother the sword would have girded on
    To fight her battles:
Many's the battle that has been won
    By the brave tartans,
        Glenaradale.

But the big-horn'd stag and his hinds, we know,
    In the high corries,
And the salmon that swirls in the pool below
    Where the stream rushes
Are more than the hearts of men, and so
    We leave thy green valley,
        Glenaradale.

[1912]

177

GEORGE MEREDITH
1828–1909

GEORGE MEREDITH was born in Hampshire. His family
were naval outfitters in Portsmouth. The painter Thomas
Wallis used Meredith for his model in his most famous work
The Death of Chatterton and then ran away with his wife.
Meredith's sequence *Modern Love*, which deals with some of
the background to this, and which introduced the sixteen
line sonnet to the language, is highly regarded as a
verse novel. Despite its lyrical fervour and ingenious
architecture, however, its absence of situating décor weakens
its poetic impact (see the Introduction p. 29). Meredith's best
work is in his dramatic pieces such as *The Nuptials of Attila*
where he robustly indicates the connexions between passion
and violence as Tennyson had done in *Maud*. This insight is
vividly conveyed at shorter length in *King Harald's Trance*,
where the truncated syntax and trochaic rhythm underline
the primitive emotions of the story.

A Ballad of Past Meridian

Last night returning from my twilight walk
I met the grey mist Death, whose eyeless brow
Was bent on me, and from his hand of chalk
He reached me flowers as from a withered bough:
O Death, what bitter nosegays givest thou!

Death said, I gather, and pursued his way.
Another stood by me, a shape in stone,
Sword-hacked and iron-stained, with breasts of clay,
And metal veins that sometimes fiery shone:
O Life, how naked and how hard when known!

Life said, As thou hast carved me, such am I.
Then memory, like the nightjar on the pine,
And sightless hope, a woodlark in night sky,
Joined notes of Death and Life till night's decline:
Of Death, of Life, those inwound notes are mine.

[1883]

From *The Nuptials of Attila*

I

Flat as to an eagle's eye,
    Earth hung under Attila.
Sign for carnage gave he none.
In the peace of his disdain,
Sun and rain, and rain and sun,
Cherished men to wax again,
Crawl, and in their manner die.
On his people stood a frost.
Like the charger cut in stone,
Rearing stiff, the warrior host,
Which had life from him alone,
Craved the trumpet's eager note,
As the bridled earth the Spring.
Rusty was the trumpet's throat.
He let chief and prophet rave;
Venturous earth around him string
Threads of grass and slender rye,
Wave them, and untrampled wave.
O for the time when God did cry,
    Eye and have, my Attila!

II

Scorn of conquest filled like sleep
Him that drank of havoc deep
When the Green Cat pawed the globe:
When the horsemen from his bow
Shot in sheaves and made the foe
Crimson fringes of a robe,
Trailed o'er towns and fields in woe;
When they streaked the rivers red,
When the saddle was the bed.
    Attila, my Attila!

III

He breathed peace and pulled a flower.
    Eye and have, my Attila!
This was the damsel Ildico,
Rich in bloom until that hour:
Shyer than the forest doe
Twinkling slim through branches green.
Yet the shyest shall be seen.
    Make the bed for Attila!

IV

Seen of Attila, desired,
She was led to him straightway:
Radiantly was she attired;
Rifled lands were her array,
Jewels bled from weeping crowns,
Gold of woeful fields and towns.
She stood pallid in the light.
How she walked, how withered white,
From the blessing to the board,
She who should have proudly blushed,
Women whispered, asking why,
Hinting of a youth, and hushed.
Was it terror of her lord?
Was she childish? was she sly?
Was it the bright mantle's dye
Drained her blood to hues of grief
Like the ash that shoots the spark?
See the green tree all in leaf:
See the green tree stripped of bark! –
    Make the bed for Attila!

V

Round the banquet-table's load
Scores of iron horsemen rode;
Chosen warriors, keen and hard;

Grain of threshing battle-dints;
Attila's fierce body-guard,
Smelling war like fire in flints.
Grant them peace be fugitive!
Iron-capped and iron-heeled,
Each against his fellow's shield
Smote the spear-head, shouting, Live,
    Attila! my Attila!
Eagle, eagle of our breed,
Eagle, beak the lamb, and feed!
Have her, and unleash us! live,
    Attila! my Attila!

VI

He was of the blood to shine
Bronze in joy, like skies that scorch.
Beaming with the goblet wine
In the wavering of the torch,
Looked he backward on his bride.
    Eye and have, my Attila!
Fair in her wide robe was she:
Where the robe and vest divide,
Fair she seemed surpassingly:
Soft, yet vivid as the stream
Danube rolls in the moonbeam
Through rock-barriers: but she smiled
Never, she sat cold as salt:
Open-mouthed as a young child
Wondering with a mind at fault.
    Make the bed for Attila!

* * *

XXII

Square along the couch, and stark,
Like the sea-rejected thing
Sea-sucked white, behold their King.
    Attila, my Attila!

Beams that panted black and bright,
Scornful lightnings danced their sight:
Him they see an oak in bud,
Him an oaklog stripped of bark:
Him, their lord of day and night,
White, and lifting up his blood
Dumb for vengeance. Name us that,
Huddled in the corner dark,
Humped and grinning like a cat,
Teeth for lips! – 'tis she! she stares,
Glittering through her bristled hairs.
Rend her! Pierce her to the hilt!
She is Murder: have her out!
What! this little fist, as big
As the southern summer fig!
She is Madness, none may doubt.
Death, who dares deny her guilt!
Death, who says his blood she spilt!
    Make the bed for Attila!

XXIII

Torch and lamp and sunset-red
Fell three-fingered on the bed.
In the torch the beard-hair scant
With the great breast seemed to pant:
In the yellow lamp the limbs
Wavered, as the lake-flower swims:
In the sunset red the dead
Dead avowed him, dry blood-red.

XXIV

Hatred of that abject slave,
Earth, was in each chieftain's heart.
Earth has got him, whom God gave,
Earth may sing, and earth shall smart!
    Attila, my Attila!

XXV

Thus their prayer was raved and ceased.
Then had Vengeance of her feast
Scent in their quick pang to smite
Which they knew not, but huge pain
Urged them for some victim slain
Swift, and blotted from the sight.
Each at each, a crouching beast,
Glared, and quivered for the word.
Each at each, and all on that,
Humped and grinning like a cat,
Head-bound with its bridal-wreath.
Then the bitter chamber heard
Vengeance in a cauldron seethe.
Hurried counsel rage and craft
Yelped to hungry men, whose teeth
Hard the grey lip-ringlet gnawed,
Gleaming till their fury laughed.
With the steel-hilt in the clutch,
Eyes were shot on her that froze
In their blood-thirst overawed;
Burned to rend, yet feared to touch.
She that was his nuptial rose,
She was of his heart's blood clad:
Oh! the last of him she had! –
Could a little fist as big
As the southern summer fig
Push a dagger's point to pierce
Ribs like those? Who else! They glared
Each at each. Suspicion fierce
Many a black remembrance bared.
       Attila, my Attila!
Death, who dares deny her guilt!
Death, who says his blood she spilt!
Traitor he, who stands between!
Swift to hell, who harms the Queen!

She, the wild contention's cause,
Combed her hair with quiet paws.
    Make the bed for Attila!

XXVI

Night was on the host in arms.
Night, as never night before,
Hearkened to an army's roar
Breaking up in snaky swarms:
Torch and steel and snorting steed,
Hunted by the cry of blood,
Cursed with blindness, mad for day.
Where the torches ran a flood,
Tales of him and of the deed
Showered like a torrent spray.
Fear of silence made them strive
Loud in warrior-hymns that grew
Hoarse for slaughter yet unwreaked.
Ghostly Night across the hive
With a crimson finger drew
Letters on her breast and shrieked.
Night was on them like the mould
On the buried half alive.
Night, their bloody Queen, her fold
Wound on them and struck them through.
    Make the bed for Attila!

XXVII

Earth has got him whom God gave,
Earth may sing, and earth shall smart!
None of earth shall know his grave.
They that dig with Death depart.
    Attila, my Attila!

XXVIII

Thus their prayer was raved and passed:
Passed in peace their red sunset:

Hewn and earthed those men of sweat
Who had housed him in the vast,
Where no mortal might declare,
There lies he – his end was there!
    Attila, my Attila!

XXIX

Kingless was the army left:
Of its head the race bereft.
Every fury of the pit
Tortured and dismembered it.
Lo, upon a silent hour,
When the pitch of frost subsides,
Danube with a shout of power
Loosens his imprisoned tides:
Wide around the frighted plains
Shake to hear his riven chains,
Dreadfuller than heaven in wrath,
As he makes himself a path:
High leap the ice-cracks, towering pile
Floes to bergs, and giant peers
Wrestle on a drifted isle;
Island on ice-island rears;
Dissolution battles fast:
Big the senseless Titans loom,
Through a mist of common doom
Striving which shall die the last:
Till a gentle-breathing morn
Frees the stream from bank to bank
So the Empire built of scorn
Agonized, dissolved and sank.
Of the Queen no more was told
Than of leaf on Danube rolled.
    Make the bed for Attila!

[1887]

185

King Harald's Trance

Sword in length a reaping-hook amain
Harald sheared his field, blood up to shank:
    'Mid the swathes of slain,
    First at moonrise drank.

Thereof hunger, as for meats the knife,
Pricked his ribs, in one sharp spur to reach
    Home and his young wife,
    Nigh the sea-ford beach.

After battle keen to feed was he:
Smoking flesh the thresher washed down fast,
    Like an angry sea
    Ships from keel to mast.

Name us glory, singer, name us pride
Matching Harald's in his deeds of strength;
    Chiefs, wife, sword by side,
    Foemen stretched their length!

Half a winter night the toasts hurrahed,
Crowned him, clothed him, trumpeted him high,
    Till awink he bade
    Wife to chamber fly.

Twice the sun had mounted, twice had sunk,
Ere his ears took sound; he lay for dead;
    Mountain on his trunk,
    Ocean on his head.

Clamped to couch, his fiery hearing sucked
Whispers that at heart made iron-clang:
    Here fool-women clucked,
    There men held harangue.

Burial to fit their lord of war
They decreed him: hailed the kingling: ha!
    Hateful! but this Thor
    Failed a weak lamb's baa.

King they hailed a branchlet, shaped to fare,
Weighted so, like quaking shingle spume,
    When his blood's own heir
    Ripened in the womb!

Still he heard, and doglike, hoglike, ran
Nose of hearing till his blind sight saw:
    Woman stood with man
    Mouthing low, at paw.

Woman, man, they mouthed; they spake a thing
Armed to split a mountain, sunder seas:
    Still the frozen king
    Lay and felt him freeze.

Doglike, hoglike, horselike now he raced,
Riderless, in ghost across a ground
    Flint of breast, blank-faced,
    Past the fleshly bound.

Smell of brine his nostrils filled with might:
Nostrils quickened eyelids, eyelids hand:
    Hand for sword at right
    Groped, the great haft spanned.

Wonder struck to ice his people's eyes:
Him they saw, the prone upon the bier,
    Sheer from backbone rise,
    Sword uplifting peer.

Sitting did he breathe against the blade,
Standing kiss it for that proof of life:
    Strode, as netters wade,
    Straightway to his wife.

Her he eyed: his judgement was one word,
Foulbed! and she fell: the blow clove two.
    Fearful for the third,
    All their breath indrew.

Morning danced along the waves to beach;
Dumb his chiefs fetched breath for what might hap:
    Glassily on each
    Stared the iron cap.

Sudden, as it were a monster oak
Split to yield a limb by stress of heat,
    Strained he, staggered, broke
    Doubled at their feet.

                              [1887]

DANTE GABRIEL ROSSETTI
1828–1882

DANTE GABRIEL ROSSETTI was born in London, of
Italian parents, and died near Margate. He was the moving
spirit of the Pre-Raphaelite movement, and the influence of
his ideas and personality both in the visual and literary arts
of the nineteenth century was profound. His own art is weak
in technical resource: Burne-Jones surpassed him as a
draughtsman and colourist in painting, Swinburne as a
verse musician. His best verse remained unpublished until
after his death. The early verse letters to his brother William,
collected as *A Trip To Paris And Belgium*, reveal a gift for
spontaneous impressionism which he never cultivated. *The
Orchard Pit* is evocative as a fragment. Both poems suggest
that Rossetti's obsession with planning and revision may have
dimmed his flair.

A Trip to Paris and Belgium

I.

LONDON TO FOLKESTONE

A constant keeping-past of shaken trees,
And a bewildered glitter of loose road;
Banks of bright growth, with single blades atop
Against white sky: and wires – a constant chain –
That seem to draw the clouds along with them
(Things which one stoops against the light to see
Through the low window; shaking by at rest,
Or fierce like water as the swiftness grows);
And, seen through fences or a bridge far off,
Trees that in moving keep their intervals
Still one 'twixt bar and bar; and then at times
Long reaches of green level, where one cow,
Feeding among her fellows that feed on,
Lifts her slow neck, and gazes for the sound.

Fields mown in ridges; and close garden-crops
Of the earth's increase; and a constant sky
Still with clear trees that let you see the wind;
And snatches of the engine-smoke, by fits
Tossed to the wind against the landscape, where
Rooks stooping heave their wings upon the day.

Brick walls we pass between, passed so at once
That for the suddenness I cannot know
Or what, or where begun, or where at end.
Sometimes a station in grey quiet; whence,
With a short gathered champing of pent sound,
We are let out upon the air again.
Pauses of water soon, at intervals,
That has the sky in it; – the reflexes
O' the trees move towards the bank as we go by,
Leaving the water's surface plain. I now
Lie back and close my eyes a space; for they
Smart from the open forwardness of thought
Fronting the wind.

*　　*　　*

I did not scribble more,
Be certain, after this; but yawned, and read,
And nearly dozed a little, I believe;
Till, stretching up against the carriage-back,
I was roused altogether, and looked out
To where the pale sea brooded murmuring.

II.
BOULOGNE TO AMIENS AND PARIS

Strong extreme speed, that the brain hurries with,
Further than trees, and hedges, and green grass
Whitened by distance, – further than small pools
Held among fields and gardens, further than
Haystacks, and wind-mill-sails, and roofs and herds, –
The sea's last margin ceases at the sun.

The sea has left us, but the sun remains.
Sometimes the country spreads aloof in tracts
Smooth from the harvest; sometimes sky and land
Are shut from the square space the window leaves
By a dense crowd of trees, stem behind stem
Passing across each other as we pass:
Sometimes tall poplar-wands stand white, their heads
Outmeasuring the distant hills. Sometimes
The ground has a deep greenness; sometimes brown
In stubble; and sometimes no ground at all,
For the close strength of crops that stand unreaped.
The water-plots are sometimes all the sun's, –
Sometimes quite green through shadows filling them,
Or islanded with growths of reeds, – or else
Masked in green dust like the wide face o' the fields.
And still the swiftness lasts; that to our speed
The trees seem shaken like a press of spears.

There is some count of us: – folks travelling capped,
Priesthood, and lank hard-featured soldiery,
Females (no women), blouses, Hunt, and I.

We are relayed to Amiens. The steam
Snorts, chafes, and bridles, like three hundred horse,
And flings its dusky mane upon the air.
Our company is thinned, and lamps alight.
But still there are the folks in travelling-caps,
No priesthood now, but always soldiery.
And babies to make up for show in noise;
Females (no women), blouses, Hunt, and I.

Our windows at one side are shut for warmth;
Upon the other side, a leaden sky,
Hung in blank glare, makes all the country dim,
Which too seems bald and meagre, – be it truth,

Or of the waxing darkness. Here and there
The shade takes light, where in thin patches stand
The unstirred dregs of water.

* * *

V.

ANTWERP TO GHENT

We are upon the Scheldt. We know we move
Because there is a floating at our eyes
Whatso they seek; and because all the things
Which on our outset were distinct and large
Are smaller and much weaker and quite grey,
And at last gone from us. No motion else.

We are upon the road. The thin swift moon
Runs with the running clouds that are the sky,
And with the running water runs – at whiles
Weak 'neath the film and heavy growth of reeds.
The country swims with motion. Time itself
Is consciously beside us, and perceived.
Our speed is such the sparks our engine leaves
Are burning after the whole train has passed.
The darkness is a tumult. We tear on,
The roll behind us and the cry before,
Constantly, in a lull of intense speed
And thunder. Any other sound is known
Merely by sight. The shrubs, the trees your eye
Scans for their growth, are far along in haze.
The sky has lost its clouds, and lies away
Oppressively at calm: the moon has failed:
Our speed has set the wind against us. Now
Our engine's heat is fiercer, and flings up
Great glares alongside. Wind and steam and speed
And clamour and the night. We are in Ghent.

[1886]

The Orchard-pit

Piled deep below the screening apple-branch
   They lie with bitter apples in their hands:
And some are only ancient bones that blanch,
And some had ships that last year's wind did launch,
   And some were yesterday the lords of lands.

In the soft dell, among the apple-trees,
   High up above the hidden pit she stands,
And there for ever sings, who gave to these,
That lie below, her magic hour of ease,
   And those her apples holden in their hands.

This in my dream is shown me; and her hair
   Crosses my lips and draws my burning breath;
Her song spreads golden wings upon the air,
Life's eyes are gleaming from her forehead fair,
   And from her breasts the ravishing eyes of Death.

Men say to me that sleep hath many dreams,
   Yet I knew never but this dream alone:
There, from a dried-up channel, once the stream's,
The glen slopes up; even such in sleep it seems
   As to my waking sight the place well known.

* * *

My love I call her, and she loves me well:
   But I love her as in the maelstrom's cup
The whirled stone loves the leaf inseparable
That clings to it round all the circling swell,
   And that the same last eddy swallows up.

[1886]

193

A Fragment

And the Sibyl, you know. I saw her with my own eyes at
Cumæ, hanging in a jar; and, when the boys asked her,
'What would you, Sibyl?' she answered, 'I would die.' –
PETRONIUS.

'I saw the Sibyl at Cumæ'
   (One said) 'with mine own eye.
She hung in a cage, and read her rune
   To all the passers-by.
Said the boys, "What wouldst thou, Sibyl?"
   She answered, "I would die."'

[1886]

WALTER THORNBURY
1828–1876

GEORGE WALTER THORNBURY was born in London.
His *Songs of The Cavaliers and Roundheads* expressed the
Imperialist mood of the mid-1850s with a convenient his-
torical dressing. The extrovert violence of these poems in
swinging lyric metre was giving way towards the end of
Thornbury's life to a more ironic and subtle treatment fore-
shadowing (in *Smith of Maudlin*) the tone of Lee-Hamilton
and even (in *The Court Historian*, where the refrain is used
to counterpoint the narrative) the later work of Yeats.

The Court Historian

LOWER EMPIRE. CIRCA 700 A.D.

The Monk Arnulphus uncorked his ink
   That shone with a blood-red light,
Just as the sun began to sink;
   His vellum was pumiced a silvery white.
'The Basileus' – for so he began –
'Is a royal sagacious Mars of a man,
   Than the very lion bolder;
He has married the stately widow of Thrace' –
   'Hush!' cried a voice at his shoulder.

His palette gleamed with a burnished green,
   Bright as a dragon-fly's skin;
His gold-leaf shone like the robe of a queen,
   His azure glowed as a cloud worn thin,
Deep as the blue of the king-whale's lair:
'The Porphyrogenita Zoe the fair
   Is about to wed with a prince much older,
Of an unpropitious mien and look' –
   'Hush!' cried a voice at his shoulder.

The red flowers trellised the parchment page,
　　The birds leaped up on the spray,
The yellow fruit swayed and drooped and swung,
　　It was Autumn mixed up with May
(O but his cheek was shrivelled and shrunk!)
'The child of the Basileus,' wrote the Monk,
　　'Is golden-haired, tender the queen's arms fold her
Her step-mother Zoe doth love her so' –
　　'Hush!' cried a voice at his shoulder.

The kings and martyrs and saints and priests
　　All gathered to guard the text:
There was Daniel snug in the lions' den,
　　Singing no whit perplexed;
Brazen Samson with spear and helm: –
'The Queen,' wrote the Monk, 'rules firm the realm,
　　For the King gets older and older;
The Norseman Thorkill is brave and fair' –
　　'Hush!' cried a voice at his shoulder.

[1875]

Smith of Maudlin

My chums will burn their Indian weeds
　　The very night I pass away,
And cloud-propelling puff and puff
　　As white the thin smoke melts away;
Then Jones of Wadham, eyes half-closed,
　　Rubbing the ten hairs on his chin,
Will say, 'This very pipe I use
　　Was poor old Smith's of Maudlin.'

That night in High Street there will walk
　　The ruffling gownsmen three abreast,
The stiff-necked proctors, wary-eyed,
　　The dons, the coaches, and the rest;

Sly 'Cherub Sims' will then propose
  Billiards, or some sweet ivory sin;
Tom cries, 'He played a pretty game –
  Did honest Smith of Maudlin.'

The boats are out! – the arrowy rush,
  The mad bull's jerk, the tiger's strength;
The Balliol men have wopped the Queen's –
  Hurrah! but only by a length.
Dig on ye muffs, ye cripples dig!
  Pull blind, till crimson sweats the skin; –
The man who bobs and steers cries, 'Oh
  For plucky Smith of Maudlin.'

Wine parties met – a noisy night,
  Red sparks are breaking through the cloud;
The man who won the silver cup
  Is in the chair erect and proud;
Three are asleep – one to himself
  Sings 'Yellow jacket's sure to win.'
A silence: – 'Men, the memory
  Of poor old Smith of Maudlin!'

The boxing-rooms – with solemn air
  A freshman dons the swollen glove;
With slicing strokes the lapping sticks
  Work out a rubber – three and love;
With rasping jar the padded man
  Whips Thompson's foil so square and thin,
And cries, 'Why zur, you've not the wrist
  Of Muster Smith of Maudlin.'

But all this time beneath the sheet
  I shall lie still, and free from pain,
Hearing the bed-makers sluff in
  To gossip round the blinded pane;

Try on my rings, sniff up my scent,
   Feel in my pockets for my tin;
While one hag says, 'We all must die,
   Just like this Smith of Maudlin.'

Ah! then a dreadful hush will come,
   And all I hear will be the fly
Buzzing impatient round the wall,
   And on the sheet where I must lie;
Next day a jostling of feet –
   The men who bring the coffin in:
'This is the door – the third pair back,
   Here's Mr Smith of Maudlin.'

[1875]

ALEXANDER SMITH

1829–1867

ALEXANDER SMITH was born in Kilmarnock. His verse in
A Life Drama is genuinely spasmodic, veering from imagistic
brilliance to contortion. The city poems *Glasgow* and
Edinburgh have good things in them, but his best piece is
A Boy's Poem, which effectively conveys the rigours and
occasional treats of his own working-class childhood.

From *A Boy's Poem*

The steamer left the black and oozy wharves,
And floated down between dark ranks of masts.
We heard the swarming streets, the noisy mills;
Saw sooty foundries full of glare and gloom,
Great bellied chimneys tipped by tongues of flame,
Quiver in smoky heat. We slowly passed
Loud building-yards, where every ship contained
A mighty vessel with a hundred men
Battering its iron sides. A cheer! a ship
In a gay flutter of innumerous flags
Slid gaily to her home. At length the stream
Broadened 'tween banks of daisies, and afar
The shadows flew upon the sunny hills;
And down the river, 'gainst the pale blue sky,
A town sat in its smoke. Look backward now!
Distance has stilled three hundred thousand hearts,
Drowned the loud roar of commerce, changed the proud
Metropolis which turns all things to gold,
To a thick vapour o'er which stands a staff
With smoky pennon streaming on the air.
Blotting the azure too, we floated on,
Leaving a long and weltering wake behind.
And now the grand and solitary hills
That never knew the toil and stress of man,

Dappled with sun and cloud, rose far away.
My heart stood up to greet the distant land
Within the hollows of whose mountains lochs
Moan in their restless sleep; around whose peaks,
And scraggy islands ever dim with rain,
The lonely eagle flies. The ample stream
Widened into a sea. The boundless day
Was full of sunshine and divinest light,
And far above the region of the wind
The barred and rippled cirrus slept serene,
With combed and winnowed streaks of faintest cloud
Melting into the blue. A sudden veil
Of rain dimmed all; and when the shade drew off,
Before us, out toward the mighty sun,
The firth was throbbing with glad flakes of light.
The mountains from their solitary pines
Ran down in bleating pastures to the sea;
And round and round the yellow coasts I saw
Each curve and bend of the delightful shore
Hemmed with a line of villas white as foam.
Far off, the village smiled amid the light;
And on the level sands, the merriest troops
Of children sported with the laughing waves,
The sunshine glancing on their naked limbs.
White cottages, half smothered in rose blooms,
Peeped at us as we passed. We reached the pier,
Whence girls in fluttering dresses, shady hats,
Smiled rosy welcome. An impatient roar
Of hasty steam; from the broad paddles rushed
A flood of pale green foam, that hissed and freathed
Ere it subsided in the quiet sea.
With a glad foot I leapt upon the shore,
And, as I went, the frank and lavish winds
Told me about the lilac's mass of bloom,
The slim laburnum showering golden tears,
The roses of the gardens where they played.

[1857]

SEBASTIAN EVANS
1830–1909

SEBASTIAN EVANS was born at Market Bosworth in
Leicestershire. In a particularly energetic and varied career
he was active as journalist, politician, barrister, painter,
factory manager and poet. He published three collections of
verse: *Brother Fabian's Manuscript*, *Songs and Etchings* and
In the Studio. The title poem of the first collection, here
re-printed in its entirety, is the most important forgotten
masterpiece of the Victorian period. In richness of detail,
homogeneity of tone, vividness of imagery and variety of
rhythm it matches any monologue of comparable length by
Browning. Its structure – development by digression – is
both unique and in character. The skill with which the
narrative is constructed may be best appreciated by trying to
cut the poem.

How the Abbey of Saint Werewulf Juxta Slingsby Came by Brother Fabian's Manuscript

Scene – Saint Werewulf's Cloisters. A.D. 1497. *Time* – Afternoon
PRIOR HUGO *speaks.*

You know Saint Wigbald's, – yonder nunnery cell
Out there, due South, some fourteen furlongs hence? –
Well, five years since, – five? – six, come Michaelmas,
While old Dame Chesslyn, bless her pious soul,
Still Prioress, tended that good Saint's ewe-lambs,
This tome you speak of, then itself a nun,
Fruitlessly holy, waxing year by year
Yellow and yellower in virginity,
Graced the refectory lettern. Truth to tell,
Of all the sisters, six besides the dame,
Was only Margery who could read at all.

Now, John the Archbishop, (some four years it was
Since Bourchier peradventure went to Heaven,
And John, translated to the archbishopric
From Ely, himself as slippery as an eel,
Wriggled right busily in the Church's mud,)
Just then, to clinch his pastoral on the wear
Of broidered girdles, silken liripoops,
Swords, daggers and such vanities, thought meet
To swinge Saint Werewulf's with a special charge,
A rasping monitory, five skins long;
Four and nine-tenths a schedule of our sins
Item on item, bearing each the name
Of some delinquent brother fairly engrossed,
And, these recited, stinglike in the tail,
Came threats of visitation, Heaven knows what,
All ills on this side Purgatory and Hell,
Unless we all in three-score days exact
Abjured the nether trinity, world, flesh, fiend,
And donned the radiant nimbus of the Saints.

Straight, Blaize, our Abbot, red with saintly wrath,
Summons us all to meet him; reads the charge,
And bids us all digest it; storms and fumes,
Dubs us all liars, hypocrites, and fools; –
Swears he foretold the issue. There was one,
A lurching, lean-lipped, lollardizing loon,
Whom we all hated: 'Brother Joce,' quoth Blaize,
'Some blatant lollard slanderer of the faith
'No doubt hath played the spy on us, and blabbed.
'My lord Archbishop sneaps us for our sloth;
''T is time I startled some of ye! Suppose
'I take and roast you for a heretic?
'Pitch you like Prophet Jonas to the whale,
'And still the storm you had raised about our ears
'Take rede, Sir Lollard!' So he frowned and left,
And hastened to Saint Wigbald's through the fields.
'Gramercy, Abbot,' quoth the Dame, 'what ails?

'Gout? No, it can't be gout, you have walked too quick.
'Anything wrong at Malton with the Grange?
'Or Ralph among the deer again? What, – no?
'Well, then 'tis Joce! – I'll swear an oath 'tis Joce!'
'Peace, wench!' says he, 'his grace of Canterbury
'Has heard your doings at Saint Wigbald's here,
'And swears to scourge ye with a whip of steel!
'What! Is your house in order? I must see
'And make report!' – Lord, how the poor soul cried
And cursed the lollards!
                              What, you marvel how
I know she cursed them? Thus; – I heard her curse. –
You see, the Abbot walked across the fields; –
I, skirting by the fence along the lane.
I knew of course that, like the holy oil
On Aaron's head, which trickled to his beard,
And thence dropped fatness on his garment's hem,
The precious balm with which the Archbishop broke
Dan Blaize's pate would fall irriguous down
And reach Saint Wigbald's first unless I sped;
So, lest the sweet inunction, oozing forth,
Should chance to anoint the sisters unawares,
I thought I'd just let Margery hear the news,
And——

   Well, in short, Blaize tramped Saint Wigbald's through,
Chapel and chamber, cellar, dortour, all;
The Dame behind him: not a kinder soul
E'er lived than Dame Aylse Chesslyn. As they passed
Through the refectory to the strangers' hall,
Blaize caught a glimpse of something on the desk;
And knowing how bare Saint Werewulf's was of books,
Stept up to inspect the volume: 'Ha, what's this? –
'H'm, – sermons, – Fabian, – 'tis a clerkly hand; –
'You don't much use them, mother!' Here he wiped
The dust from thumb and finger on her hood.
'We are short of books up there. Suppose we say
'I take the book and send you a brace of trout

'On Fridays every year the season through?
'Come, is't a bargain?'
                                    'Nay,' says she, 'you know,
'Abbot, where Abel snares you all your trout.
'There's never a scale of trout in Slingsby brook,
'And though I bid Ben Gogolai not keep count
'How many Abel poaches, every fish,
'If all had right alike, belongs to me.
'Besides, that book, – the Archdeacon said himself
''T was worth St Wigbald's whole year's rent twice told;
'And more, I would not part with it – '
                                    'Well, well,
'No matter!' quoth the Abbot, but the Dame
Felt that he meant to have the book, and would.

But how? Well, maybe you remember him,
Young Randal, nephew of the Prioress?
A scholar here at the Abbey, where he learnt
At least how not to learn the sciences:
For what with our abundant lack of clerks,
Our liking for the lad and his for play,
The schooling, trivial and quadrivial, all
Fared at the best but evil. Doctrinal,
Donat and Æsop, Cato, small and great,
At seven years' end, I take it, still for him
Were dark as Daniel or the Apocalypse.
No less he found books useful. Once, indeed,
He sent a poet soaring through the skies
Who never else had reached them, Theodule,
With his *Æthiopum terras* torn to strips
And twisted in a kite-tail. More, he learnt
To play at knucklebone with augrim stones,
And found his abacus expressly scored
For nine-men's morris on an indoor scale.
So that, you see, all told, he might have trussed
His sum of scholarship in one round O,

Had it been worth the trussing. Blaize himself,
Not being poet Marcian, who contrived
That wondrous wedding of Dan Mercury
Once on a time to Dame Philology,
Could find no foil to fix his quicksilver.

'Curst knave!' says he, 'why learn ye not to read?
'There's nought but gallows in your gait and eye, –
'Gallows from boot to birret, top to toe,
'Yet ye dare scoff at clergy! Come the day
'When ye're caught tripping in your pranks, how then?
'What, can't even spell a neckverse? Learn, I say!
'For of all knaves that ever God let live,
'Unless all promises fail and saws prove false,
'Thou'lt most rue lack of clergy!'
                                         'Nay, no fear,'
Quoth Randal, 'You are surety for my life!
'No judge will bid you live that bids me hang!'
Faith, had you bought knave Randal for a fool,
Knave Randal soon had sold you for the same!
You should have seen him on Saint Nicholas' day,
When he was Abbot of Misrule, and shaved
Dickon Precentor clean on half his face,
And tonsured half the bristles of his scalp:
'My son,' quoth he, 'Thou'rt drunk but thrice a week,
'I cannot make thee more than half a monk!'
Once, too, on Innocents' eve, the day we showed
Hell Harrowed in the chancel every year
Before we turned the pageants out of church,
He read us such a gibe! – Our stage, you know,
Rested upon the roodloft, just above
My stall and Blaize's, all the screed below
Hid by the arras of the Amazons: –
Randal presented Belzebub that year:
But when Saint Peter on his bugle horn
Had blown tantivy for the final soul,

And locked the elect within the golden gates,
Lo, on a sudden, forth leaps Belzebub,
Vaults from the roodloft with a sobresault
Into the pulpit.

               'What care I?' quoth he;
'Well robbed, well rid! Yon feeless Janitor
'Up there, I ween, hath weightier cause than I
'To howl a *De Profundis!* Saw ye e'er
'Such lenten lozels as these saintly souls?
'Prime booty, be they not, for Heaven to steal?
'Poor skulking lazars, bare of cross and pile
'As toads of fur or feather! Ragman's Roll
'Would take precedence of their calendar!
'Bah! let the churls live happy! I am content!
  'But you, my gallant masters, fear ye not!
'Mine own dear muttons of Saint Werewulf's fold!
'Ye claim no kindred with these babes of grace!
'In yonder kingdom ye nor sow nor mow!
'No, ye are mine, sweet souls, for ever mine!
'O, ere ye schooled me, I was dunce as dull
'As Santanas or Lucifer, – unskilled
'Even to hold yon souls of right mine own, –
'A mere untutored prentice in my craft!
'But now, accepted brother of your guild,
'And master in all mysteries of sin,
'Shall I forget, nor quite ye for the boon?
'Nay, my seraphic doctors! Never yet
'Was Belzebub ungrateful to his peers!
'O, ye shall feast with cardinals and kings
'And all the purpled demi-gods of fame
'At Hell's high table, Dives in the midst,
'Where nevermore shall thief break in and steal
'*In sæcula sæculorum!* Lo, even now
'I go to spread the banquet for my guests!'
With that, my knave louts low and wags his tail,
Clambers from desk to roodloft like a cat,
And skips again into the jaws of Hell!

Well, 't was one Thursday, just on Michaelmas,
At daydawn, Randal starts him off to fish
Down at Saint Wigbald's; – Whether he knew no trout
Were in the brook, or whether he hoped for sport
More to his mind in the Dame's private pond
Behind the cell, – or whether as I surmise,
Diabolo instigante, – God best knows;
But down he walked to the triangular stew
Sacred to poor Dame Aylse's favourite luce.
The Dame, – she had some wry whimsies in her skull, –
Had wont each morn and even, rain or shine,
To cross the croft to this triangular pool
And ring her silver sanctus on the marge, –
The bell, by the way, – a gift from Ulverscroft,
Rang oftener far at mass for Sir John Pike
Than for the sisters, and Sir John, who lurked
Plotting his raids among the chestnut roots
That weave a wattled rampart round the bank
Against the lower floodgate, – when he heard,
Would dart from out his hiding with a swirl,
And shoal on shoal of startled sticklebacks
Leap silver-sided, flash on flash before,
Like sprays of osier when the summer wind
Toys with their upturned leaves, while to and fro,
All proud at heart of argent-damasked mail
And glistening hinges of his golden fins,
The knightly vassal of the pool glanced by
To claim his sovereign's largess. If to-day
She brought a full-fed frog, (she docked the feet
Before she gave him frogs,) to-morrow came
A brace of gudgeon or a slice of beef;
Except indeed on Fridays, when the fare
Was only rye-bread manchet, soaked in milk.
She had her faults, good dame, – for who is free?
But none can say she ever gave her fish
Flesh on a Friday. Once in every year
Moreover, at Saint-John's-tide, after mass,

The Prioress marched with all the sisterhood
And Abel and Ben Gogolai to the pool
And weighed her darling. 'T was a sight to see
Ben Gogolai wheedling with a landing-net,
And Abel with the steel-yard, Michael-like,
Waiting, till spooned out on the shaven turf
Ben clutched the brute adroitly by the eyes
And coiled him gasping in the scale; – that year
I well remember, he just turned nine pounds.

Well, down steps Randal to the pool, when, lo,
Just as he pinned his gudgeon on the hook,
A herd of fat geese from the grange-yard gate
Marched cackling through the meadow. Quick as thought,
Randal was in among them, gripped the neck
Of him who gabbled loudest, held him tight,
Bore him, a fluttering prisoner to the pool,
Made fast his line, – the gudgeon on the hook,
About the fowl's left leg and let him swim.
Dame Juliana Berners, by the way,
Had taught this double treatment in her tract
Then lately printed with new-fangled types
By Caxton at Saint Alban's, which discourse
Being sent, a gift from Sopwell to my Dame,
Was read to Randal through by Margery,
Not without profit, – as the gander felt.

Meanwhile, Ben Gogolai, – What? – You don't know Ben?
The curst old Hebrew with the wooden leg?
Why, he was half the income of the cell!
'T was Blaize, – of course, first saw the man's true worth,
Transmuted him by alchemy to gold,
And minted him. You see, when first he came,
Ben stumped on errands for the Prioress,
Tended the geese, fetched water, piled the logs,
Did all that none else would, got cuffs and kicks,
Victualled on orts, – if ever he got the bones

Before the greyhound, he fared sumptuously.
Blaize came, saw, christened! – Why, the noise it made
Was worth a farm in fee. A Hebrew Jew
Christened at Easter in Saint Werewulf's font!
Never a hallow in five counties round
Was half so holy! Blaize and Ben were saints,
And the whole house a pattern to the world!
Alas! so warm a piety, zeal so true
Found such sweet favour with the Cherubim
That soon 't was all translated to the skies!
At least, none lingered here below. Ere long
Blaize was again but Blaize, and Ben was Ben,
Not saints, nor one nor 't other. Still, our fame
Bruited abroad, pricked other Abbots' souls
To achieve the like, and Blaize, who deemed it shame
To waste such wealth of glory on himself,
Farmed the old Jew to others. Twenty marks
In gold the Abbot of St Alban's gave
To rebaptize Ben Gogolai, – twenty-five
The Abbot of St Edmund's, so throughout,
As each in turn converted and baptized,
Called the lost sheep of Judah to the fold,
And showed the world an Israelite indeed.

Ben's single leg was a sore cross to Blaize:
Had he had two, Ben might have dyed his beard,
Filched a new suit, and been another Jew,
Aaron or Levi, Solomon or Saul,
Fit for a fresh conversion. As it was,
'T was hardly politic to baptize him twice
Within a lifetime in the self-same font.
Failing more baptism, Blaize, who ever sought
The glory of God, next thought of miracle.
Could Heaven restore the Hebrew's missing shank,
We, too, might walk more firmly, and support
Fresh fame on that new pillar of the Church.
Deaf brother Cradock was a skilful leech

And mainly cunning in chirurgery.
All that Salerno, all that Oxford taught
Of medicine, magic and astrology
From Galen, Haly or Averröes,
Gilbert or Gatsden, Gordon, Glatisaunt,
Was Cradock skilled in. Marry, if e'er a leech
By leechcraft could work miracle, 'twas he!
But though the leg he fashioned was a leg
As natural as a Christian's, for indeed
'T was shaped in willow on Saint Luke's day hewn,
The planets all propitious, save perhaps
That envious Saturn stood just one degree
Too nigh the ascendant, – though the Hebrew's stump
To fit it featly had been seared again
With actual cautery when the moon was full,
Though the fair childlike skin, right cheveril, shamed
Its fellow's true Jew leather, – still, the knee,
Perversely unmiraculous, eschewed
All offices of kneeship; first too lax, –
Then, when the thews were braced, as much too stiff,
Then, when the happy medium seemed just hit,
Lax when 't was wanted stiff, and stiff when lax.
Maugre all Cradock's art, apostate still,
Ben without crutch could only at best achieve
Good-fellow's gait, two stumbles and a fall;
And though Saint Werewulf, doubtless, at a pinch
Would have wrought fifty miracles at once,
Had each one single leg to stand upon,
'T was clear the leg that foundered with a Jew
Could never bear both Jew and miracle.

'Yea, brother Cradock, 't is a goodly leg,'
Quoth Blaize, 'a marvel! Avicen himself
'Ne'er wrought more artificial counterfeit!
'Yet, for we live not in the good old days,
'And these New-Learning firebrands of the faith
'Singe us so closely, that 't were well to fling

'No touchwood nigh them, – 't were improvident
'For Providence to interpose herein!
''T were best, I think, to drop the miracle:
'The leg will give us a name for works of alms.'
And so the miracle dropped, and Ben dropped too,
Into a mere Jew menial of my Dame's,
A mongrel cowherd, verdurer, messenger,
Lord Paramount of Saint Wigbald's geese and fish.

Well, as I said before you snapped my web
Of chronicle, Randal scarce had turned adrift
His gander with the gudgeon tied to his leg,
When down limps Ben, blaspheming through the croft,
The Avenging Fate of goose-rape, halt but dread,
Breathing out scourge and cudgel, foam on beard: –
'Thief, thief! – The goose, the goose! – Thou Nazarene
    hound,
'Come thou within the circle of my crutch
'I'll score a charm on thy Barabbas hide
'Shall teach thee chant *Peccavi* for a month
'To the tune of *Os fregisti!*' Down he bears
Like a lop-sided pirate caravel
Banging his mangonels as he rolls and nears.

Just as he skirts the pool, up Randal leaps,
Butts at his ribs full-tilt without a word,
Rolls him plump backwards, sprawling on the turf,
Clutches his timber peg, and with a wrench
Unscrews it from the stump and leaves him flat,
An Israelite spread-eagle, one leg couped. –
Then, fiddler-like, while low the Avenger lies,
The leg for viol, and the crutch for bow,
Rattles a *Jubilate* in his ears.
'So-ho!' he chuckles, 'have I drawn your sting,
'Old hornet Judas? Will you teach me chant,
'My bird of Paradise? Come, suppose you try
'*Adhesit pavimento,* – *Ecce nunc,*

'Or *Vir beatus qui non abiit*,
'Eh, my heraldic martlet?'
                                    But, meanwhile,
Sir John the pike, who has not yet broke his fast,
Eyes greedily Randal's gudgeon as it trails
Behind the gander, tempting, silvery sweet,
Darts out and gulps it bodily, hooks and all;
Not waiting, graceless infidel, to mark
That still unblessed, the perilous morsel lacks
The matins-tinkle of the silver bell.

Now clangs the din of battle! – Gander, pike,
Pike, gander, tugging, wrestling for the life!
'Hooked, by Saint Wigbald, hooked!' – Off Randal skips,
Flinging Ben's leg and crutch with dexterous aim
Athwart the feathered fisher's mid career;
Clapping his hands and dancing on the marge
As though Saint Vitus kicked him. Ben the while,
Dumb-struck at first, incredulous of the crime,
Sits up and stares bewildered: then, the truth
Through the eyes brainward filtering drop by drop,
'Gins howl 'Thieves! – murder! – help! my leg! the pike!'
Till, as the royal fray 'fwixt fowl and fish
Still fiercer waxes, he forgets to howl,
And watches – eye, mouth, nostril all agape.

Gabbling and plashing half across the pool,
A fleet of goose-down scudding in his wake,
Wrestles the gander, straining web and wing. –
Suddenly halts, – a charm-wrecked argosy
Dreamily foundering in enchanted deeps,
The feathery poop half tugged beneath the waves
By a live anchor. Up he flaps again,
Like a mad trampler in a vintage-vat,
Churning the ripples into foam, his head
Now ducking fruitlessly beneath the surge,

Now lifted cackling his despair to Heaven!
A lull! – Sir John fights sulky. Randal's bird
Now prematurely jubilant, as before
Despairing prematurely, wags his tail
And prunes his ruffled pinions, gabbling low
The while a ditty of gracious self-applause.

Again the poop bobs under! – Off he starts,
The craziest he of biped lunatics,
A gander desperate! Universal earth,
Itself fast shuddering into chaos, holds
But one thing certain, that the pool's bewitched!
Within the unhallowed banks weird sorcery lurks
Fatal to goose-kind! With a spooming plunge
That rails his torturer victim in his wake
He wrestles shoreward, paddling piteously
With impotent neck outstretched beyond the marge,
So freely near, so inaccessible,
With that lithe fiend still jerking at his leg:
Till Randal, conscious of the coming Dame,
Clutching the chance and outstretched neck at once
With his right hand, falls flat, and with his left
Gropes for his pike-line in the muddy ooze,
Unmoors the hapless proxy of his rod,
And lands Sir John in triumph. – Ben, the while,
Weary of shouting, emptied of his oaths,
Turns his grey muzzle to the grass and groans.

But what about this volume? Nay, no haste! –
You laymen are impatient, – live too quick!
Albertus, in the unfathomable gloss
Which moats his version of the Apocalypse
Against the siege of modern heretics,
'T is true, interpreted beyond a doubt
The world to verge on Antichrist and Doom
More than two centuries since: – still here we are!

And, say these lollard Doctors speak sheer truth
About the Scarlet Woman in the sun
And other like conundrums, here we are,
Walking Saint Werewulf's cloisters. Two hours hence
We sup with Blaize in the refectory:
Till then, what matter how we slay the time?
Granted your science and philosophy
Divine and human are momentous things: –
I am loath to cavil: – still, my tale's of geese!
Patience! The tale will end before we sup.

Now, so Saint Werewulf or the devil ordained,
As Randal, flushed with guilt and triumph, sneaked
In at Saint Werewulf's orchard-gate, prize-fraught,
Full front he met the Abbot: 'Ha, sir Knave,
'What mischief now! – By'r lady, a noble luce! –
'Where gat ye such?' He lifts Sir John by the eyes,
And weighs him by the scale of arm and eye:
'Within five ounces of ten pound,' quoth he,
'Where gat ye –' Then the treacherous secret flashed
Across his brain. 'Saint Wigbald! 'T is my Dame's!
'Dame Aylse's darling! Why, thou Judas imp!
'Unnatural varlet! – Sirrah, to my cell!
'I'll teach ye how to angle with a rod,
'Poaching your – aunt's pet luce!'
                                    Off Randal slinks:
'Stop!' thunders Blaize, the grin about his mouth
As like the pike's he held as egg to egg, –
'I have spared the rod too long and spoilt the child:
'Hanging's the only heal for neck so stiff!
'Mark me, – hie straightway to my Solomon room
'And creep behind the arras! If one soul
'Catch sight of one-ninth part of a hair of thine
'Till I release thee, 't were as good to dance
'At high noon, honied, on a hornet's nest
'Naked, as meet me after! Quick, be off!'

Back strides the Abbot to the buttery hatch,
Leaves the Dame's pike in charge of pantler John:
'Mark, – stuffed, and sodden with sweet herbs and wine,
'And, mind, no hint of garlic!' – starts once more
Down to Saint Wigbald's sorely vexed at heart.

Meanwhile, the Dame and Margery, hearing Ben
Bawling for help, steered Jewry-ward full sail,
Almost ere Randal's heels were out of sight.
Ben, who till now had ever known the Dame
Tender and pitiful-hearted as a Saint,
Whined out his grief with groans that might have wrung
A crab-tree with compassion; but the Dame,
No crab-tree, certes, – toward the martyred Jew
Was more than crab-tree callous! When she heard
'T was Randal's hand had widowed her, 'Take that!'
Says she, and flings three minnows in his face,
Meant for the breakfast of the late Sir John, –
'Judas! and that!' – here spits upon his beard
And kicks him; 'Marry, a dastard Hebrew dog!
'Randal!' – another kick, but Margery here
Catches and holds her back by sleeve and hood:
'May all the lies that gender in thy heart
'Be turned to weevils, fiery canker-worms
'To fret thy vitals, ere they reach thy lips!
'Randal, forsooth! And thou, thou polecat Jew,
'Sittest and watchest, waitest patiently,
'Heedless and helpless, scarecrow as thou art!
'And Randal – Randal,' here the wrath broke down
Into a pitiful whimper, 'killed my pike!
'Killed! – Margery, Margery! Randal killed my pike!'

Well, Margery led the Dame across the croft,
Fetched spice and comfits, milk and peppermint,
Then found and sent old Abel to the Jew.
Blaize in the meantime enters, finds the Dame: –
'Lord, Abbot, here so soon? – You've heard our news?'

She whimpered, 'take a draught of peppermint;
''T is sovereign to corroborate the heart!'
A sniff – 'That Judas, Ben!' another sniff:
''T is my belief Ben helped him!' – 'H'm!' quoth Blaize,
'I have baulked Dan Randal's poaching, anyway!
'Why, let such tales get wind about the court,
'And Heaven knows what might happen!' 'True,' says she,
'But, Abbot, what do you mean about the boy?'
'Oh, he, – the thief? I packed him off at once
'With Joce,' – now mark ye, Joce had angered Blaize
Again the night before, rebuking him
The brethren by, for swearing at the dice
When Cradock won the dagger and silver sheath,
And Blaize, five cups of Rhenish in his brain,
Vowed that he'd roast him at the stake ere Yule
In Slingsby bull-ring for a heretic:
So Joce ere morrow morning took the hint,
His books and his departure. Blaize, you see,
In lying, always built his lies on truth; –
'Joce hates me, as you know, and I hate Joce;
'So when I knew 't was Randal killed your pike,
'I packed the brace of traitors off at once
'To Grimleysdyke, to try our penitent cell.'

'Gramercy, Blaize, – why Joce will kill the lad!'
Breaks in the Prioress. 'Kill the lad! Not he!
'I scarce suppose he loves him overmuch,
'But kill, – – Besides, I bade on no account
'To keep him fasting more than twice a week,
'Nor scourge him more than twice, nor then with knots
'Bigger than beans.' The Prioress stared and paled. –
'Good Lord, Blaize Archer!' – then she clutched his arm,
Glared straight into his eyes, nor breathed, nor winked,
Then loosed her fingers on his arm, and sighed, –
'You're a hard man, Blaize Archer, hard and false!
'What is 't you want? God knows I am poor enough!'

Blaize gulped a dose of peppermint and coughed.
'Nay, Dame, 'tis I should ask what is't you want,
'I – I want nothing!' – 'This, forgive the lad!
' 'Twas but a madcap frolic!' – 'Yea,' quoth he,
'But madcap tricks are rank as murder now!
'Hath he not brought our holy faith to shame,
'And jeoparded our houses? Still, perchance; –
'Well, Dame, I'll think about it!' Then, as one
Who knows he has lied to one who knows he lies,
With brazen courtesy bids good day, and parts.

Returned, he had scarce dispatched three larded quails
With a half-stoup of egg-whip hypocras,
When lo, my Dame rides ambling on her mule
Up to Saint Werewulf's, Abel close behind,
Puffing and staggering under half a buck.
Blaize lifts the Prioress from the selle; – 'Why, Dame,
'What cheer? How fresh thou'rt looking! By my hand,
'This evil time hath been so busy of late
'Vexing the souls of statesmen and of clerks,
'He clean forgets you quiet godly dames;
'Withers us doctors, – leaves you fair and young!'
So kisses her and enters, hand in hand,
And leads her, fluttered, to the Solomon-room.

'Abbot,' says she, 'I have brought ye half a buck:
' 'Twas killed – our Lady's octave – why, let's see,
'To-morrow will be the fortnight. Come, the lad!
'Say you forgive him!' – Randal, who the while
Behind the arras – 'twas a Flanders piece
Of the Wise King's just judgment – watched the twain
Through a small rent whose dog's-ear lid curled wide
Just where the right hand of the doomsman grasps
The huge gold-hilted falchion, heaved to halve
The live child 'twixt the mothers, pricked his ears.
'Tell me, at least, he's safe!' 'Yea, safe enow,'

Quoth Blaize, 'I'll warrant Joce will see him safe!
'They are safe enough at Grimleysdyke ere now:
'As to the penance, maybe – –' 'Blaize,' says she,
'I swear thou'rt lying by thy naughty smile!
' 'Twas just that smile was ever on the lips
'Of my poor darling' – Here she wiped her eyes
And fell to whimpering: 'Tell me where he is!
'Look, here's the silver bell from Ulverscroft:
'Now my pike's gone, I want no silver bells,
'And you, perhaps, may value it! Nay, come,
'Tell me where Randal is, and take the bell!'

'I tell thee, Dame, he's gone to Grimleysdyke
'With Joce, to do strict penance in the cell.
'Still, since thou plead'st for him so urgently,
'Suppose I say three months instead of twelve,
'And take him back at Christmas? Art content?'

'Randal three months with Joce at Grimleysdyke,
'And I content? Blaize Archer, body and soul
'Have I been none but yours this thirty years,
'Come Whitsun, and though false ye've been and are,
'God knows I am true to you as false to Him!
'Jesu forgive me! – 'Tis a cruel thing
'A father to set ransom on his child
'And bid the mother pay to the utmost mite!
'Once was a time you loved the lad and me;
'Him for my sake you loved, and me for his!
'Blaize! Where's my boy and thine, thou kindless man!
'Unnatural father! – Here, is't this you crave?'
With that, she draws from out her purfled sleeve
This book you speak of, Fabian's Manuscript,
Dusted and furbished up, with clasps like gold,
A bait to snare an emperor or pope, –
'I knew you meant to have it!' Blaize sat mute.
'Speak, Blaize, 'a God's name!' Smiling, up he rose
And kissed her. 'Bless thee, thou'rt a kindly soul!

'Randal, thou knave, come hither!'
                                   Sore abashed
The culprit creeps from under Solomon's throne: –
'Down on thy marrowbones, thou graceless imp,
'And sue forgiveness!' – 'Randal, mine own boy!'
The Dame could say no more, but hugged the lad
As if he had saved her soul, not killed her pike!

'Bless thee, my son!' quoth Blaize: 'Man's life's a span!
'Why make that span unhappy? Here, you see,
'We all are happy! Thou, thou hast caught thy luce,
'And a fine brace of parents! This good Dame
'Finds, for the nonce, a sweetheart and a son!
'And I, – thus ever virtue reaps reward, –
'I, too, achieve my guerdon: – first, the fish,
'Item, a side of venison, nearly ripe,
'Item, a silver sanctus, – item, this,
'This goodly volume, useless to my Dame,
'And last, a conscience void of all offence!'

Incipiunt multi, non perficiunt bona stulti.

                                        [1865]

CHRISTINA ROSSETTI

1830–1894

CHRISTINA GEORGINA ROSSETTI, sister of Dante Gabriel
Rossetti, was born and died in London. She was the youngest
in a family of four. She was deeply attached to her mother,
and a devout high Anglican. It has also been suggested that,
after rejecting two suitors on religious grounds, she formed
a close emotional attachment to the poet William Bell Scott.
Her poetry has been praised for its delicacy and intensity of
feeling but much of it is thin and repetitive. Its reticence
would have been enriched by a stronger indulgence in the
dream-world of *The Convent Threshold* and *Despised and
Rejected* with their hints of bloodier passion than the pale
renunciation of the much-anthologized *Remember*.

A Birthday

My heart is like a singing bird
    Whose nest is in a watered shoot;
My heart is like an apple-tree
    Whose boughs are bent with thickset fruit;
My heart is like a rainbow shell
    That paddles in a halcyon sea;
My heart is gladder than all these
    Because my love is come to me.

Raise me a dais of silk and down;
    Hang it with vair and purple dyes;
Carve it in doves, and pomegranates,
    And peacocks with a hundred eyes;
Work it in gold and silver grapes,
    In leaves, and silver fleurs-de-lys;
Because the birthday of my life
    Is come, my love is come to me.

[1862]

From *The Convent Threshold*

'I tell you what I dreamed last night:
It was not dark, it was not light,
Cold dews had drenched my plenteous hair
Through clay; you came to seek me there,
And "Do you dream of me?" you said.
My heart was dust that used to leap
To you; I answered half asleep;
"My pillow is damp, my sheets are red,
There's a leaden tester to my bed:
Find you a warmer playfellow,
A warmer pillow for your head,
A kinder love to love than mine."
You wrung your hands; while I, like lead,
Crushed downwards through the sodden earth:
You smote your hands but not in mirth,
And reeled but were not drunk with wine.

For all night long I dreamed of you:
I woke and prayed against my will,
Then slept to dream of you again.
At length I rose and knelt and prayed;
I cannot write the words I said,
My words were slow my tears were few
But through the dark my silence spoke
Like thunder. When this morning broke,
My face was pinched, my hair was grey,
And frozen blood was on the sill
Where stifling in my struggle I lay.'

[1862]

The Queen of Hearts

How comes it, Flora, that, whenever we
Play cards together, you invariably,
    However pack the parts,
    Still hold the Queen of Hearts?

I've scanned you with a scrutinizing gaze,
Resolved to fathom these your secret ways:
    But, sift them as I will,
    Your ways are secret still.

I cut and shuffle, shuffle, cut again;
But all my cutting, shuffling, proves in vain:
    Vain hope, vain forethought too;
    That Queen still falls to you.

I dropped her once, prepense; but, ere the deal
Was dealt, your instinct seemed her loss to feel:
    'There should be one card more,'
    You said, and searched the floor.

I cheated once; I made a private notch
In Heart-Queen's back, and kept a lynx-eyed watch;
    Yet such another back
    Deceived me in the pack:

The Queen of Clubs assumed by arts unknown
An imitative dint that seemed my own;
    This notch, not of my doing,
    Misled me to my ruin.

It baffles me to puzzle out the clue,
Which must be skill, or craft, or luck in you:
    Unless, indeed, it be
    Natural affinity.

                [*Collected Poems*, 1904]

From *Despised and Rejected*

'Then I cried out upon him: Cease,
Leave me in peace;
Fear not that I should crave
Aught thou mayst have.
Leave me in peace, yea trouble me no more,
Lest I arise and chase thee from my door.
What, shall I not be let
Alone, that thou dost vex me yet?

But all night long that voice spake urgently:
"Open to Me."
Still harping in mine ears:
"Rise, let Me in."
Pleading with tears:
"Open to Me, that I may come to thee."
While the dew dropped, while the dark hours were cold:
"My Feet bleed, see My Face,
See My Hands bleed that bring thee grace,
My Heart doth bleed for thee,
Open to Me."

So till the break of day:
Then died away
That voice, in silence as of sorrow;
Then footsteps echoing like a sigh
Passed me by,
Lingering footsteps slow to pass.
On the morrow
I saw upon the grass
Each footprint marked in blood, and on my door
The mark of blood for evermore.'

[*Collected Poems,* 1904]

T. E. BROWN

1830–1897

THOMAS EDWARD BROWN was born at Douglas in the
Isle of Man. His life as a schoolmaster at Clifton is engag-
ingly at odds with the (superficially) unlettered rusticism of
his verse: in fact, his handling of Manx dialect for every
mood from tear-jerking sentiment to rough humour (for
example, in *Betsy Lee*) is a product of technique subdued by
intelligence. Like Outram and Barnes, by writing in dialect
he was able to avoid many of the common Victorian pitfalls
of sentimentality and coyness while enlarging his power to
speak with a coarse warmth far from his natural tone of voice.
In The Coach has a freedom of movement and a sense of
drama which can only be fully appreciated in public per-
formance, as, for example, by John Bielby-Wright.

From *In The Coach*

NO. III.—CONJERGAL RIGHTS

Conjergal rights! conjergal rights!
I don't care for the jink of her and I don't care for the jaw
    of her,
But I'll have the law of her.
Conjergal rights! yis, yis, I know what I'm sayin'
Fuss-rate, Misthress Corkhill, fuss-rate, Misther Cain,
And all the people in the coach – is there a man or a
    woman of the lot of ye –
Well now, that's what I wudn' have thought of ye,
I wudn' raelly – No, *I haven' got a little sup*,
Not me – is there one of ye that wudn' stand up
For conjergal rights?
No, ma'am, *tight's*
Not the word, not a drop since yesterday. But lizzen, good
    people, lizzen!
I'll have her in the coorts, I'll have her in prison –

It's the most scandalous thing you ever – What! this
    woman and her daughter –
It's clane murder, it's abslit manslaughter,
Aye, and I wudn'i trus' but beggamy, that's what it is –
    Married yesterday mornin'
In Kirk Breddhan Church, and not the smallest taste of
    warnin',
Takes her to her house in Castletown,
And jus' for I axed a quashtin – and I'll be boun'
It's a quashtin any one of you wud have axed – picks a
    quarrel, makes a row,
The two of them, aye, the two of them – bow-wow!
Hammer and tungs! sends for a pleeceman, puts me to the
    door –
But I'll owe her! I'll owe her!
Aisy, Mr Cretney? No, I'll not be aisy;
It's enough to make a body crazy,
That's what it is, and the supper on the table,
And the hoss in the stable.
And I said nothin', nor I done nothin'. Aw, if there's law
    in the land,
Law or justice, I'll have it, d'ye understand?
Do ye see the thing? My grayshurs! married is married,
Isn' it? what? and me that carried
The woman's box. And that isn' all; what raison? what
    sense?
Think of the expense! think of the expense!
Don't ye know? God bless me! The certif'cake, that's
    hafe-a-crown,
And the licence, that's five shillin', money down, money
    down!
And not a farlin' off for cash, these Pazons, not a farlin';
And said she was my darlin'
And all to that, guy heng! it's thrue! it's thrue!
And look at me now! boo-hoo-oo-oo!

    quashtin: question.   *tungs:* tongs.
        guy heng: go hang!

Yis, cryin' I am, and no wondher –
You don't see me it's that dark in the coach. By the livin'
    thundher
I'm kilt mos'ly, that's what I am, almos' kilt
With throuble and disthress and all. *A jilt*,
You say, *a jilt?* But married, married, married, d'ye hear?
Married, Misthress Creer,
Married afore twelve at Kirk Breddhan,
Married, a reg'lar proper weddin'
And no mistake,
And this woman . . . O my gough! don't spake of her!
    don't spake!
It's me that's spakin'? Yis, and I will! I will!
Who's to spake if I amn'? But still –
It's lek you don't see, the coach is so dark, and no light
    from these houses,
But feel of this new coat, and the pair of new trousis,
Bought o' puppose, o' puppose! what else?
Bran new; and the shirt and the frells,
And the cuffs and the collar, every d— thing
As bran and as new as a gull's wing –
And all to plaze her, and to look accordin'
To the occasion, and to do her credit, and ho'rdin'
The teens of months. And O, if I'd only borrowed them
    from a neighbour!
That's the thing, but bought them, bought them! and even
    so they might ha' been chaber,
Yis, they might, at another shop. But you don' see the way
    I'm goin',
No, no, you don' –
But I'd lek you to – the tears! I'm jus' slushin' the sthraw
With the tears, makin' the coach all damp for the people –
    yis, I know I am, but I'll have the law, I'll have the law.
Just a quashtin about a bit of proppity,
The house, in fac', the very house we come into, d'ye see?

o'*puppose*: on purpose.   *chaber*: cheaper.

The house, her house! Of coorse! Of coorse! But goodness
   grayshurs!
Who doesn' know the law about a thing like that? the
   iggorant! the ordashurs!
If ever there was a thing on God's earth
That was mine, it was yandhar house! But it isn' worth
Talkin' – no! There's people that'll go against anything.
   But what! no suttlement goin' a-makin',
Nor nothin', jus' everything goin' a-takin'
Undher the common law of matrimony theer –
At my massy! at my massy! With your lave, Mr Tear,
At my massy, sir. You'll 'scuse me.
But you know the law. Married – my chree! my chree!
What *iss* 'married', if that isn'? it's as plain as a dus'bin –
Your own dear lovin' husin'
As kind as kind!
See the beauty of it! And 'all that's thine is mine',
Isn' it sayin' that in the Bible?
And surely the woman is li'ble
As well as the man; and to 'love, honour, and obey',
Isn' that what they say?
But it's my heart, that's it! my poor broken heart! aw dear!
   aw dear!
And my feelin's! my feelin's! and that son of mine girnin'
   from ear to ear,
And his lip, and his imprince, and his disrespeck,
And the waste and the neglec' –
O, it's awful! it's awful! O, the wounds that there's no
   healin's!
O' my feelin's! my feelin's!
But I'll see aburt, I will, I'll see aburt –
The dirt!
The wife of my bosom! Don't be mockin'!
I heard a woman laughing: it's shockin'

> *no suttlement goin' a-makin'*: settlement to be made.
>   *massy*: mercy.   *aburt*: about it.

That a woman'd laugh at the lek of such doin's, yis, it is,
Downright wickedness –
A woman that I could name –
Fie for shame! fie for shame!
But I'll have law. Look here! Is James Gell a lawyer? You'll
    hardly uphould me
He isn', will ye? James Gell – the Attorney-Gineral: well,
    that's the man that tould me.
Did I spake to him about it? was I axin' him afore
I was anything to her?
Sartinly! my gough! was I goin' to run my neck into a
    noose,
And navar no 'pinion nor . . . I'm not such a goose
As yandhar ither, I've gorrit in writin', yis, I have,
I've gorrit here – aw, you'll get lave! you'll get lave!
Not aisy to read, but God bless me! where's my specs?
    But lar't! lar't!
It's my feelin's: O my heart! my heart!
My poor heart! my poor heart! boo-hoo-oo-oo! Aye, and
    you'd think there'd be
Some semperthy,
Some . . . Crow, open this door and let me out! there's no
    regard with ye
For a man's . . . I'll not ride another yard with ye . . .
Theer then! theer! No, I'll have none of your goodnights . . .
Conjergal rights! conjergal rights!

                                     [1893]

        gorrit: got it.   *lar't:* let it be.

LEWIS CARROLL
1832–1898

CHARLES LUTWIDGE DODGSON, better known by his pseudonym, was a brilliant mathematician and pioneer of modern logic. His prose fantasy *Alice's Adventures in Wonderland* has fascinated philosophers and psychologists even more than children. With Lear, Carroll is the only Victorian poet admired in his own day whose reputation has never declined. I suspect the reason may lie in their joint ability to suppress all personal feeling and commitment. In the case of Carroll, this was the result of deliberate policy: one could term him a writer of *classical* nonsense, irrational yet rigidly logical. *The Hunting of The Snark* was an episode of Darwinian care, undertaken, like the voyage of the Beagle, with every preparation. Lear, on the other hand, achieves his effects by an appearance of unconscious accident, and this is mirrored in the fortunes of his characters. Why the Jumblies went to sea nobody knows. Despite their differences Lear and Carroll have a world in common, and Carroll seems to have caught a tone from Lear as Pope did from Dryden.

Rules and Regulations

A short direction
To avoid dejection,
By variations
In occupations,
And prolongation
Of relaxation,
And combinations
Of recreations,
And disputation
On the state of the nation
In adaptation
To your station,
By invitations

To friends and relations,
By evitation
Of amputation,
By permutation
In conversation,
And deep reflection
You'll avoid dejection.

Learn well your grammar,
And never stammer,
Write well and neatly,
And sing most sweetly,
Be enterprising,
Love early rising,
Go walk of six miles,
Have ready quick smiles,
With lightsome laughter,
Soft flowing after.
Drink tea, not coffee;
Never eat toffy.
Eat bread with butter.
Once more, don't stutter.
Don't waste your money,
Abstain from honey.
Shut doors behind you,
(Don't slam them, mind you.)
Drink beer, not porter.
Don't enter the water
Till to swim you are able.
Sit close to the table.
Take care of a candle.
Shut a door by the handle,
Don't push with your shoulder
Until you are older.
Lose not a button.
Refuse cold mutton.
Starve your canaries.

Believe in fairies.
If you are able,
Don't have a stable
With any mangers.
Be rude to strangers.

Moral: Behave.

[1845]

Jabberwocky

'Twas brillig, and the slithy toves
    Did gyre and gimble in the wabe;
All mimsy were the borogoves,
    And the mome raths outgrabe.

'Beware the Jabberwock, my son!
    The jaws that bite, the claws that catch!
Beware the Jubjub bird, and shun
    The frumious Bandersnatch!'

He took his vorpal sword in hand:
    Long time the manxome foe he sought –
So rested he by the Tumtum tree,
    And stood awhile in thought.

And as in uffish thought he stood,
    The Jabberwock, with eyes of flame,
Came whiffling through the tulgey wood,
    And burbled as it came!

One, two! One, two! And through and through
    The vorpal blade went snicker-snack!
He left it dead, and with its head
    He went galumphing back.

231

'And hast thou slain the Jabberwock?
  Come to my arms, my beamish boy!
O frabjous day! Callooh! Callay!'
  He chortled in his joy.

'Twas brillig, and the slithy toves
  Did gyre and gimble in the wabe;
All mimsy were the borogoves,
  And the mome raths outgrabe.

[1871]

Humpty Dumpty's Recitation

In winter, when the fields are white,
I sing this song for your delight –

In Spring, when woods are getting green,
I'll try and tell you what I mean.

In summer, when the days are long,
Perhaps you'll understand the song:

In autumn, when the leaves are brown,
Take pen and ink, and write it down.

I sent a message to the fish:
I told them 'This is what I wish.'

The little fishes of the sea,
They sent an answer back to me.

The little fishes' answer was
'We cannot do it, Sir, because –'

I sent to them again to say
'It will be better to obey.'

The fishes answered with a grin,
'Why, what a temper you are in!'

I told them once, I told them twice:
They would not listen to advice.

I took a kettle large and new,
Fit for the deed I had to do.

My heart went hop, my heart went thump;
I filled the kettle at the pump.

Then someone came to me and said
'The little fishes are in bed.'

I said to him, I said it plain,
'Then you must wake them up again.'

I said it very loud and clear;
I went and shouted in his ear.

But he was very stiff and proud;
He said 'You needn't shout so loud!'

And he was very proud and stiff;
He said 'I'd go and wake them, if – '

I took a corkscrew from the shelf:
I went to wake them up myself.

And when I found the door was locked,
I pulled and pushed and kicked and knocked.

And when I found the door was shut,
I tried to turn the handle, but –

[1871]

ADAM LINDSAY GORDON
1833–1870

ADAM LINDSAY GORDON was born in the Azores, the son
of an officer in the Indian army. In 1853 he emigrated to
Australia, where he became famous as a gentleman jockey.
Broken, however, by debt and riding accidents, he fell a
victim to melancholy. In 1870, on the morning following the
publication of his third book, he was found dead in the scrub
with a bullet wound in his head. Gordon anticipates Kipling
in adapting the lightness of society verse to the depiction of
scenes of outdoor life.

How We Beat the Favourite

A LAY OF THE LOAMSHIRE HUNT CUP

'Aye, squire,' said Stevens, 'they back him at evens;
    The race is all over, bar shouting, they say;
The Clown ought to beat her; Dick Neville is sweeter
    Than ever – he swears he can win all the way.

'A gentleman rider – well, I'm an outsider,
    But if he's a gent who the mischief's a jock?
You swells mostly blunder, Dick rides for the plunder,
    He rides, too, like thunder – he sits like a rock.

'He calls "hunted fairly" a horse that has barely
    Been stripped for a trot within sight of the hounds,
A horse that at Warwick beat Birdlime and Yorick,
    And gave Abdelkader at Aintree nine pounds.

'They say we have no test to warrant a protest;
    Dick rides for a lord and stands in with a steward;
The light of their faces they show him – his case is
    Prejudged and his verdict already secured.

'But none can outlast her, and few travel faster,
  She strides in her work clean away from The Drag;
You hold her and sit her, she couldn't be fitter,
  Whenever you hit her she'll spring like a stag.

'And perhaps the green jacket, at odds though they back it,
  May fall, or there's no knowing what may turn up.
The mare is quite ready, sit still and ride steady,
  Keep cool; and I think you may just win the Cup.'

Dark-brown with tan muzzle, just stripped for the tussle,
  Stood Iseult, arching her neck to the curb,
A lean head and fiery, strong quarters and wiry,
  A loin rather light, but a shoulder superb.

Some parting injunction, bestowed with great unction,
  I tried to recall, but forgot like a dunce,
When Reginald Murray, full tilt on White Surrey,
  Came down in a hurry to start us at once.

'Keep back in the yellow! Come up on Othello!
  Hold hard on the chestnut! Turn round on the Drag!
Keep back there on Spartan! Back you, sir, in tartan!
  So, steady there, easy,' and down went the flag.

We started, and Kerr made strong running on Mermaid,
  Through furrows that led to the first stake-and-bound,
The crack, half extended, looked bloodlike and splendid,
  Held wide on the right where the headland was sound.

I pulled hard to baffle her rush with the snaffle,
  Before her two-thirds of the field got away,
All through the wet pasture where floods of the last year
  Still loitered, they clotted my crimson with clay.

The fourth fence, a wattle, floored Monk and Bluebottle;
  The Drag came to grief at the blackthorn and ditch,
The rails toppled over Redoubt and Red Rover,
  The lane stopped Lycurgus and Leicestershire Witch.

She passed like an arrow Kildare and Cock Sparrow,
  And Mantrap and Mermaid refused the stone wall;
And Giles on The Greyling came down at the paling,
  And I was left sailing in front of them all.

I took them a burster, nor eased her nor nursed her
  Until the Black Bullfinch led into the plough,
And through the strong bramble we bored with a scramble –
  My cap was knocked off by the hazel-tree bough.

Where furrows looked lighter, I drew the rein tighter –
  Her dark chest all dappled with flakes of white foam,
Her flanks mud-bespattered, a weak rail she shattered –
  We landed on turf with our heads turned for home.

Then crashed a low binder, and then close behind her
  The sward to the strokes of the favourite shook;
His rush roused her mettle, yet ever so little
  She shortened her stride as we raced at the brook.

She rose when I hit her. I saw the stream glitter,
  A wide scarlet nostril flashed close to my knee,
Between sky and water The Clown came and caught her,
  The space that he cleared was a caution to see.

And forcing the running, discarding all cunning,
  A length to the front went the rider in green;
A long strip of stubble, and then the big double,
  Two stiff flights of rails with a quickset between.

She raced at the rasper, I felt my knees grasp her,
  I found my hands give to her strain on the bit,
She rose when The Clown did – our silks as we bounded
  Brushed lightly, our stirrups clashed loud as we lit.

A rise steeply sloping, a fence with stone coping –
  The last – we diverged round the base of the hill;
His path was the nearer, his leap was the clearer,
  I flogged up the straight, and he led sitting still.

She came to his quarter, and on still I brought her,
  And up to his girth, to his breast-plate she drew;
A short prayer from Neville just reached me, 'The Devil,'
  He muttered – locked level the hurdles we flew.

A hum of hoarse cheering, a dense crowd careering,
  All sights seen obscurely, all shouts vaguely heard;
'The green wins!' 'The crimson!' The multitude swims
  on,
    And figures are blended and features are blurred.

'The horse is her master!' 'The green forges past her!'
  'The Clown will outlast her!' 'The Clown wins!' 'The
  Clown!'
The white railing races with all the white faces,
  The chestnut outpaces, outstretches the brown.

On still past the gateway she strains in the straightway,
  Still struggles, 'The Clown by a short neck at most,'
He swerves, the green scourges, the stand rocks and surges,
  And flashes, and verges, and flits the white post.

Aye! so ends the tussle, – I knew the tan muzzle
  Was first, though the ring-men were yelling 'Dead heat!'
A nose I could swear by, but Clarke said 'The mare by
  A short head.' And that's how the favourite was beat.

                                              [1870]

RICHARD WATSON DIXON
1833–1900

RICHARD WATSON DIXON was born at Islington. The son of a Wesleyan minister, he was ordained as an Anglican curate in 1858. The best of his poetry has a visionary intensity surpassed in Victorian religious writing only by Hopkins. Dixon is able (in *Dream*, for example) to reveal and control other-worldly images in a way Blake had done, and later Yeats does, but his successes are rare.

Dream

(i)

With camel's hair I clothed my skin,
  I fed my mouth with honey wild;
And set me scarlet wool to spin,
  And all my breast with hyssop filled;
Upon my brow and cheeks and chin
  A bird's blood spilled.

I took a broken reed to hold,
  I took a sponge of gall to press;
I took weak water-weeds to fold
  About my sacrificial dress.

I took the grasses of the field,
  The flax was bolled upon my crine;
And ivy thorn and wild grapes healed
  To make good wine.

I took my scrip of manna sweet,
  My cruse of water did I bless;
I took the white dove by the feet,
  And flew into the wilderness.

(ii)

The tiger came and played;
Uprose the lion in his mane;
The jackal's tawny nose
And sanguine dripping tongue
Out of the desert rose
And plunged its sands among;
The bear came striding o'er the desert plain.

Uprose the horn and eyes
And quivering flank of the great unicorn,
And galloped round and round;
Uprose the gleaming claw
Of the leviathan, and wound
In steadfast march did draw
Its course away beyond the desert's bourn.

I stood within a maze
Woven round about me by a magic art,
And ordered circle-wise:
The bear more near did tread,
And with two fiery eyes,
And with a wolfish head,
Did close the circle round in every part.

(iii)

With scarlet corded horn,
With frail wrecked knees and stumbling pace,
The scapegoat came:
His eyes took flesh and spirit dread in flame
At once, and he died looking toward my face.

[1861]

The Wizard's Funeral

For me, for me, two horses wait,
Two horses stand before my gate:
Their vast black plumes on high are cast,
Their black manes swing in the midnight blast,
Red sparkles from their eyes fly fast.
But can they drag the hearse behind,
Whose black plumes mystify the wind?
What a thing for this heap of bones and hair!
Despair, despair!
Yet think of half the world's winged shapes
Which have come to thee wondering:
At thee the terrible idiot gapes,
At thee the running devil japes,
And angels stoop to thee and sing
From the soft midnight that enwraps
Their limbs, so gently, sadly fair; –
Thou seest the stars shine through their hair.
I go to a mansion that shall outlast;
And the stoled priest that steps before
Shall turn and welcome me at the door.

[1861]

WILLIAM MORRIS
(1834-1896)

WILLIAM MORRIS was born at Walthamstow and died at Hammersmith. His career as a pioneer Socialist and founder of the Arts and Crafts movement expressed the dynamism of a strongly extrovert personality. The absence of personal comment or bias gives bone-hard strength to Morris's early poetry in *The Defence of Guenevere*. For a man of twenty-four, this book was a remarkable achievement, surpassing the grip and bite of the other Pre-Raphaelite poets, and introducing a new tone of moral neutrality into the treatment of Arthurian themes before the organized symbolism of Tennyson's *Idylls*. Morris's later poetry is prolix and sadly dull. After his friend Rossetti's affair with his wife Janey, he seems (perhaps not surprisingly) to have lost his taste for the portrayal of crime and passion.

Shameful Death

There were four of us about that bed;
    The mass-priest knelt at the side,
I and his mother stood at the head,
    Over his feet lay the bride;
We were quite sure that he was dead,
    Though his eyes were open wide.

He did not die in the night,
    He did not die in the day,
But in the morning twilight
    His spirit pass'd away,
When neither sun nor moon was bright,
    And the trees were merely grey.

He was not slain with the sword,
    Knight's axe, or the knightly spear,
Yet spoke he never a word
    After he came in here;

I cut away the cord
  From the neck of my brother dear.

He did not strike one blow,
  For the recreants came behind,
In a place where the hornbeams grow,
  A path right hard to find,
For the hornbeam boughs swing so,
  That the twilight makes it blind.

They lighted a great torch then,
  When his arms were pinion'd fast,
Sir John the night of the Fen,
  Sir Guy of the Dolorous Blast,
With knights threescore and ten,
  Hung brave Lord Hugh at last.

I am threescore and ten,
  And my hair is all turn'd grey,
But I met Sir John of the Fen
  Long ago on a summer day,
And am glad to think of the moment when
  I took his life away.

I am threescore and ten,
  And my strength is mostly pass'd,
But long ago I and my men,
  When the sky was overcast,
And the smoke roll'd over the reeds of the fen,
  Slew Guy of the Dolorous Blast.

And now, knights all of you,
  I pray you pray for Sir Hugh,
A good knight and a true,
  And for Alice, his wife, pray too.

[1858]

The Judgment of God

Swerve to the left, son Roger, he said,
  When you catch his eyes through the helmet-slit,
Swerve to the left, then out at his head,
  And the Lord God give you joy of it.

The blue owls on my father's hood
  Were a little dimm'd as I turn'd away;
This giving up of blood for blood
  Will finish here somehow to-day.

So, when I walk'd out from the tent,
  Their howling almost blinded me;
Yet for all that I was not bent
  By any shame. Hard by, the sea

Made a noise like the aspens where
  We did that wrong, but now the place
Is very pleasant, and the air
  Blows cool on any passer's face.

And all the wrong is gather'd now
  Into the circle of these lists:
Yea, howl out, butchers! tell me how
  His hands were cut off at the wrists;

And how Lord Roger bore his face
  A league above his spear-point, high
Above the owls, to that strong place
  Among the waters; yea, yea, cry:

What a brave champion we have got!
  Sir Oliver, the flower of all
The Hainault knights! The day being hot,
  He sat beneath a broad white pall,

White linen over all his steel;
    What a good knight he look'd! his sword
Laid thwart his knees; he liked to feel
    Its steadfast edge clear as his word.

And he look'd solemn; how his love
    Smiled whitely on him, sick with fear!
How all the ladies up above
    Twisted their pretty hands! so near

The fighting was: Ellayne! Ellayne!
    They cannot love like you can, who
Would burn your hands off, if that pain
    Could win a kiss; am I not true

To you for ever? therefore I
    Do not fear death or anything;
If I should limp home wounded, why,
    While I lay sick you would but sing,

And soothe me into quiet sleep.
    If they spat on the recreant knight,
Threw stones at him, and cursed him deep,
    Why then: what then? your hand would light

So gently on his drawn-up face,
    And you would kiss him, and in soft
Cool scented clothes would lap him, pace
    The quiet room and weep oft, oft

Would turn and smile, and brush his cheek
    With your sweet chin and mouth; and in
The order'd garden you would seek
    The biggest roses: any sin.

And these say: No more now my knight,
  Or God's knight any longer: you,
Being than they so much more white,
  So much more pure and good and true,

Will cling to me for ever; there,
  Is not that wrong turn'd right at last
Through all these years, and I wash'd clean?
  Say, yea, Ellayne; the time is past,

Since on that Christmas-day last year
  Up to your feet the fire crept,
And the smoke through the brown leaves sere
  Blinded your dear eyes that you wept;

Was it not I that caught you then,
  And kiss'd you on the saddle-bow?
Did not the blue owl mark the men
  Whose spears stood like the corn a-row?

This Oliver is a right good knight,
  And must needs beat me, as I fear,
Unless I catch him in the fight,
  My father's crafty way: John, here!

Bring up the men from the south gate,
  To help me if I fall or win,
For even if I beat, their hate
  Will grow to more than this mere grin.

                                    [1858]

245

The Haystack in the Floods

Had she come all the way for this,
To part at last without a kiss?
Yea, had she borne the dirt and rain
That her own eyes might see him slain
Beside the haystack in the floods?

Along the dripping leafless woods,
The stirrup touching either shoe,
She rode astride as troopers do;
With kirtle kilted to her knee,
To which the mud splash'd wretchedly;
And the wet dripp'd from every tree
Upon her head and heavy hair,
And on her eyelids broad and fair;
The tears and rain ran down her face.
By fits and starts they rode apace,
And very often was his place
Far off from her; he had to ride
Ahead, to see what might betide
When the roads cross'd; and sometimes, when
There rose a murmuring from his men,
Had to turn back with promises.
Ah me! she had but little ease;
And often for pure doubt and dread
She sobb'd, made giddy in the head
By the swift riding; while, for cold,
Her slender fingers scarce could hold
The wet reins; yea, and scarcely, too,
She felt the foot within her shoe
Against the stirrup: all for this,
To part at last without a kiss
Beside the haystack in the floods.

For when they near'd that old soak'd hay,
They saw across the only way
That Judas, Godmar, and the three
Red running lions dismally
Grinn'd from his pennon, under which
In one straight line along the ditch,
They counted thirty heads.

          So then,
While Robert turn'd round to his men,
She saw at once the wretched end,
And, stooping down, tried hard to rend
Her coif the wrong way from her head,
And hid her eyes; while Robert said:
'Nay, love, 'tis scarcely two to one,
At Poictiers where we made them run
So fast: why, sweet my love, good cheer,
The Gascon frontier is so near,
Nought after this.

          But: O! she said,
The long way back without you; then
The court at Paris; those six men;
The gratings of the Chatelet;
The swift Seine on some rainy day
Like this, and people standing by,
And laughing, while my weak hands try
To recollect how strong men swim.
All this, or else a life with him,
For which I should be damned at last,
Would God that this next hour were past!

He answer'd not, but cried his cry,
St George for Marny! cheerily;
And laid his hand upon her rein.
Alas! no man of all his train
Gave back that cheery cry again;

And, while for rage his thumb beat fast
Upon his sword-hilt, some one cast
About his neck a kerchief long,
And bound him.

             Then they went along
To Godmar; who said: Now, Jehane,
Your lover's life is on the wane
So fast, that, if this very hour
You yield not as my paramour,
He will not see the rain leave off:
Nay, keep your tongue from gibe and scoff
Sir Robert, or I slay you now.

She laid her hand upon her brow,
Then gazed upon the palm, as though
She thought her forehead bled, and: No!
She said, and turn'd her head away,
As there were nothing else to say,
And everything were settled: red
Grew Godmar's face from chin to head:
Jehane, on yonder hill there stands
My castle, guarding well my lands;
What hinders me from taking you,
And doing that I list to do
To your fair wilful body, while
Your knight lies dead?

             A wicked smile
Wrinkled her face, her lips grew thin,
A long way out she thrust her chin:
You know that I should strangle you
While you were sleeping; or bite through
Your throat, by God's help: ah! she said,
Lord Jesus, pity your poor maid!
For in such wise they hem me in,
I cannot choose but sin and sin,

Whatever happens: yet I think
They could not make me eat or drink,
And so should I just reach my rest.
Nay, if you do not my behest,
O Jehane! though I love you well,
Said Godmar, would I fail to tell
All that I know? Foul lies, she said.
Eh? lies, my Jehane? by God's head,
At Paris folks would deem them true!
Do you know, Jehane, they cry for you:
Jehane the brown! Jehane the brown!
Give us Jehane to burn or drown!
Eh! gag me Robert! Sweet my friend,
This were indeed a piteous end
For those long fingers, and long feet,
And long neck, and smooth shoulders sweet;
An end that few men would forget
That saw it. So, an hour yet:
Consider, Jehane, which to take
Of life or death!

        So, scarce awake,
Dismounting, did she leave that place,
And totter some yards: with her face
Turn'd upward to the sky she lay,
Her head on a wet heap of hay,
And fell asleep: and while she slept,
And did not dream, the minutes crept
Round to the twelve again; but she,
Being waked at last, sigh'd quietly,
And strangely childlike came, and said:
I will not. Straightway Godmar's head,
As though it hung on strong wires, turn'd
Most sharply round, and his face burn'd.

For Robert, both his eyes were dry,
He could not weep, but gloomily

He seem'd to watch the rain; yea, too,
His lips were firm; he tried once more
To touch her lips; she reach'd out, sore
And vain desire so tortured them,
The poor grey lips, and now the hem
Of his sleeve brush'd them.

               With a start
Up Godmar rose, thrust them apart;
From Robert's throat he loosed the bands
Of silk and mail; with empty hands
Held out, she stood and gazed, and saw,
The long bright blade without a flaw
Glide out from Godmar's sheath, his hand
In Robert's hair; she saw him bend
Back Robert's head; she saw him send
The thin steel down; the blow told well,
Right backward the knight Robert fell,
And moaned as dogs do, being half dead,
Unwitting, as I deem: so then
Godmar turn'd grinning to his men,
Who ran, some five or six, and beat
His head to pieces at their feet.

Then Godmar turn'd again and said:
So, Jehane, the first fitte is read!
Take note, my lady, that your way
Lies backward to the Chatelet!
She shook her head and gazed awhile
At her cold hands with a rueful smile,
As though this thing had made her mad.

This was the parting that they had
Beside the haystack in the floods.

                                 [1858]

In Prison

Wearily, drearily,
Half the day long,
Flap the great banners
High over the stone;
Strangely and eerily
Sounds the wind's song,
Bending the banner-poles.

While, all alone,
Watching the loophole's spark,
Lie I, with life all dark,
Feet tether'd, hands fetter'd
Fast to the stone,
The grim walls, square letter'd
With prison'd men's groan.
Still strain the banner-poles
Through the wind's song,
Westward the banner rolls
Over my wrong.

[1858]

JAMES THOMSON
1834–1882

JAMES THOMSON was born at Port Glasgow. He died, broken by drink and melancholy, in University College Hospital. *The City of Dreadful Night* is often regarded as one of the major long poems of the century: however, its attempt to infect a real London of the 1870s with the symbolic gloom of Thomson's private hell is marred by inadequate concrete detail and by heaviness of rhythm. *In The Room*, though morbid, is more sustained in style.

In the Room
(1867/68)

The sun was down, and twilight grey
   Fill'd half the air; but in the room,
Whose curtain had been drawn all day,
   The twilight was a dusky gloom:
Which seem'd at first as still as death,
   And void; but was indeed all rife
With subtle thrills, the pulse and breath
   Of multitudinous lower life.

In their abrupt and headlong way
   Bewilder'd flies for light had dash'd
Against the curtain all the day,
   And now slept wintrily abash'd,
And nimble mice slept, wearied out
   With such a double night's uproar;
But solid beetles crawl'd about
   The chilly hearth and naked floor.

And so throughout the twilight hour
   That vaguely murmurous hush and rest
There brooded; and beneath its power
   Life throbbing held its throbs supprest:

Until the thin-voiced mirror sigh'd,
   I am all blurr'd with dust and damp,
So long ago the clear day died,
   So long has gleamed nor fire nor lamp.

Whereon the curtain murmur'd back,
   Some change is on us, good or ill;
Behind me and before is black
   As when those human things lie still:
But I have seen the darkness grow
   As grows the daylight every morn;
Have felt out there long shine and glow,
   In here long chilly dusk forlorn.

The cupboard grumbled with a groan,
   Each new day worse starvation brings:
Since *he* came here I have not known
   Or sweets or cates or wholesome things:
But now! a pinch of meal, a crust,
   Throughout the week is all I get.
I am so empty; it is just
   As when they said we were to let.

What is become, then, of our Man?
   The petulant old glass exclaim'd;
If all this time he slumber can,
   He really ought to be ashamed.
I wish we had our Girl again,
   So gay and busy, bright and fair:
The girls are better than these men,
   Who only for their dull selves care.

It is so many hours ago –
   The lamp and fire were both alight –
I saw him pacing to and fro,
   Perturbing restlessly the night.

His face was pale to give one fear,
  His eyes when lifted looked too bright;
He mutter'd; what, I could not hear:
  Bad words though; something was not right.

The table said, He wrote so long
  That I grew weary of his weight;
The pen kept up a cricket song,
  It ran and ran at such a rate:
And in the longer pauses he
  With both his folded arms downpress'd
And stared as one who does not see,
  Or sank his head upon his breast.

The fire-grate said, I am as cold
  As if I never had a blaze;
The few dead cinders here I hold,
  I held unburn'd for days and days.
Last night he made them flare; but still
  What good did all his writing do?
Among my ashes curl and thrill
  Thin ghosts of all those papers too.

The table answer'd, Not quite all;
  He saved and folded up one sheet,
And seal'd it fast, and let it fall;
  And here it lies now white and neat.
Whereon the letter's whisper came,
  My writing is closed up too well;
Outside there's not a single name,
  And who should read me I can't tell.

The mirror sneer'd with scornful spite,
  (That ancient crack which spoil'd her looks
Had marr'd her temper), Write and write!
  And read those stupid, worn-out books!

That's all he does, – read, write, and read,
   And smoke that nasty pipe which stinks:
He never takes the slightest heed
   How any of us feels or thinks.

But Lucy fifty times a day
   Would come and smile here in my face,
Adjust a tress that curl'd astray,
   Or tie a ribbon with more grace:
She look'd so young and fresh and fair,
   She blush'd with such a charming bloom,
It did one good to see her there,
   And brighten'd all things in the room.

She did not sit hours stark and dumb
   As pale as moonshine by the lamp;
To lie in bed when day was come,
   And leave us curtain'd chill and damp.
She slept away the dreary dark,
   And rose to greet the pleasant morn;
And sang as gaily as a lark
   While busy as the flies sun-born.

And how she loved us every one;
   And dusted this and mended that,
With trills and laughs and freaks of fun,
   And tender scoldings in her chat!
And then her bird, that sang as shrill
   As she sang sweet; her darling flowers
That grew there in the window-sill,
   Where she would sit at work for hours.

It was not much she ever wrote;
   Her fingers had good work to do;
Say, once a week a pretty note;
   And very long it took her too.

And little more she read, I wis;
　　Just now and then a pictured sheet,
Besides those letters she would kiss
　　And croon for hours, they were so sweet.

She had her friends too, blithe young girls,
　　Who whisper'd, babbled, laugh'd, caress'd,
And romp'd and danced with dancing curls,
　　And gave our life a joyous zest.
But with this dullard, glum and sour,
　　Not one of all his fellow-men
Has ever pass'd a social hour;
　　We might be in some wild beast's den.

This long tirade aroused the bed,
　　Who spoke in deep and ponderous bass,
Befitting that calm life he led,
　　As if firm-rooted in his place:
In broad majestic bulk alone,
　　As in thrice venerable age,
He stood at once the royal throne,
　　The monarch, the experienced sage:

I know what is and what has been;
　　Not anything to me comes strange,
Who in so many years have seen
　　And lived through every kind of change.
I know when men are good or bad,
　　When well or ill, he slowly said;
When sad or glad, when sane or mad,
　　And when they sleep alive or dead.

At this last word of solemn lore
　　A tremor circled through the gloom,
As if a crash upon the floor
　　Had jarr'd and shaken all the room:

For nearly all the listening things
    Were old and worn, and knew what curse
Of violent change death often brings,
    From good to bad, from bad to worse;

They get to know each other well,
    To feel at home and settled down;
Death bursts among them like a shell,
    And strews them over all the town.
The bed went on, This man who lies
    Upon me now is stark and cold;
He will not any more arise,
    And do the things he did of old.

But we shall have short peace or rest;
    For soon up here will come a rout,
And nail him in a queer long chest,
    And carry him like luggage out.
They will be muffled all in black,
    And whisper much, and sigh and weep:
But he will never more come back,
    And some one else in me must sleep.

Thereon a little phial shrill'd,
    Here empty on the chair I lie:
I heard one say, as I was fill'd,
    With half of this a man would die.
The man there drank me with slow breath,
    And murmur'd, Thus ends barren strife:
O sweeter, thou cold wine of death,
    Than ever sweet warm wine of life!

One of my cousins long ago,
    A little thing, the mirror said,
Was carried to a couch to show,
    Whether a man was really dead.

Two great improvements marked the case:
    He did not blur her with his breath,
His many-wrinkled, twitching face
    Was smooth old ivory: verdict, Death. –

It lay, the lowest thing there, lull'd
    Sweet-sleep-like in corruption's truce;
The form whose purpose was annull'd,
    While all the other shapes meant use.
It lay, the *he* become now *it*,
    Unconscious of the deep disgrace,
Unanxious how its parts might flit
    Through what new forms in time and space.

It lay and preach'd, as dumb things do,
    More powerfully than tongues can prate;
Though life be torture through and through,
    Man is but weak to plain of fate:
The drear path crawls on drearier still
    To wounded feet and hopeless breast?
Well, he can lie down when he will,
    And straight all ends in endless rest.

And while the black night nothing saw,
    And till the cold morn came at last,
That old bed held the room in awe
    With tales of its experience vast.
It thrill'd the gloom; it told such tales
    Of human sorrows and delights,
Of fever moans and infant wails,
    Of births and deaths and bridal nights.

[1880]

LORD DE TABLEY

1835-1895

JOHN BYRNE LEICESTER WARREN, LORD DE TABLEY,
was born at Tabley House in Cheshire. Like Thackeray and
Austin, he made an unsuccessful bid to enter politics. His
interests included numismatics on which he published two
papers. His poetry—and editors keep saying so—has never
quite had its due. The reason may be its lack of direct con-
nexion with the various trends and movements of his age,
though if there were agreed to be a school of Browning his
best work could fit neatly enough into that. His lyrical poems
are sometimes heavy in movement, and earth-bound in tone,
as Lee-Hamilton's can be: but these vices go with a weight
and compactness often missing in more dynamic poets of
the reign.

The Count of Senlis at His Toilet

What scrap is this, you thrust upon me now?
Some grievance-bill; I'm sick of seeing such.
What can these burghers always want with me?
I am weary of petitions, yet they pour.
This is a brave word, liberty, indeed;
And now-a-days each lean and mongrel whelp
Littered about these streets chimes in his voice
For liberty. I loathe the letters' sound.
How dare you bring this in at tiring time,
Fretting my soul? This chain is dull as brass,
Lean down, you caitiff, lacquer up the gold;
Rub for your life, rub. There's another stone
Flawed in the centre droplet, where it shows,
Cracked like a nut; why, man, it was a gem,
An amethyst as clear as a girl's eye.
And you must crash my chain about like sacks
Of Kathern pears; there are no servants, none,
As I remember service, in these days;

A new time pestilent; each clown must ride,
And nobles trudge behind him in the dirt –
Lay out my murrey-coloured velvet suit;
How you detain me fumbling; knave and fool,
Don't ruffle back the pile of Genoa's looms
With your rank sweating fingers the wrong way.
Do you suppose I wear a wild cat's fur
For your amusement? You must play these tricks,
With only half-an-hour to banquet time;
And when I rail, stand helpless, gibbering there,
As if a nobleman could tire himself
Like a field scare-crow against time and grain,
You'd have me round my shoulders toss a sack,
And give my hair one shake, and make an end,
And so stride in among the grey-green eyes,
And dainty hands, and little perfumed arms,
And white smooth laughing kittens at their play;
Dear hearts, I think they call it love-making,
A purr begins it and a scratching ends,
Or each succeeds alternate; bless them all:
You, with these darlings waiting, prove a snail,
Your careless hands would send me to the feast
Much as a diver from the castle moat,
Slimed in disorder. You've the mind, it seems,
And leisure to disgrace me. Try, my knave.
You that are born upon my liberties,
And I've the right of gibbet on my lands,
At least my fathers had it; that's the same;
If time is able to filch lawful rights
Away from any man without his leave,
Then let time void the ducats from my pouch,
When I refuse to spend them. Have then heed;
And now this gentle rabble, that I own,
Have bribed you here, my thrall, to bring me in
A string of rank seditions on a rag
Of calfskin, at the very time and hour,
You know, it chiefly sets me out of gear

To find thus rudely thrust beneath my nose
The wrongs of carrion butchers, the sweet sighs
Of carters, longing after equal laws.
To push these in, of all the hours of the day,
To vex me here half-dressed, is shameless deed.
Consider only, certain moments hence
The banquet summons finds me, pest of heaven!
With my mind ruffled, half my clothes awry;
I'm sent among the damsels at the board,
With a sour taste of serfdom in my mouth;
I am put from my whole amenity;
My pleasing power and courteous manner lost;
For such light sunny ways will not beam out,
Unless I can forget, ignore, abolish,
The sweating boors penned in their styes below.

Man, man, is this a time for wrong and right?
The doublet bulges, the ruff hangs awry,
Limp as the wool of some damp wether's fleece.
The feast is ready – they are going down, –
I hear Count Edmund, coxcomb, on the stairs –
You loiter, varlet, and I'm late; your deed;
You thrust your charters when I ought to dress;
Charters indeed. I, that have known it long,
Have never seen this precious burgh of mine
Save on the eve of starving thro' my dues,
At least their song has run so all these years.
And yet they are fed enough to roar out loud,
'Behold, we starve!' – My ruffles; that's the left,
You idiot – And they breed too, breed like rats;
So much the better for my toll per head.
They will not starve; I'd like to see it done.
They can cheat hunger in a hundred ways;
They rob my saw-pits clean of bran for bread;
There never were such greedy knaves as these.
They clear my outer court of nettles next;
They boil them, so I'm told, I hope they sting.

Well, I shall not complain, it saves the scythe,
And we great lords must wink and let ourselves
Be pilfered by the small fry halter-ripe.
It is the doom and meed of noble blood,
To be a prey to clowns; and God, He knows,
I am not one of those who grudge the poor.
And so my kindness fills them full of corn,
And rains this plague down in petitions thus.
I am soft-hearted, they presume on this –
And I will singe clean out your fishy eyes
With white-hot tongs, unless you make that cloak
Fall smoother on the carriage of my sword.
Why, you lean hound, whom mange will soon destroy,
And save your hanging, where's the scabbard brace?
See, you have made it stick right out behind,
Like Satan's sister's broom-stick. And the cooks
Are at it dishing up. You fumble there,
As if the precious minutes stood like sheep,
And you'd the day to lie upon the grass
And count the crows. There, that goes better – Come,
I'll glance on this petition – What is here?
'That our starvation is no idle tale,
Of his own seeing our liege lord must know;
Since his own noble and peculiar pack,
In tufted sedges at the mort o' th' deer,
Lately unearthed a lean white woman dead –
Confound the knaves; and granting this were so,
This is a delicate and savoury thing
Just before dinner to remind me of.
This shall spoil all I meant to do for them;
How dare they? Why this same wan rigid face,
Must thrust itself upon my grounds and die,
And sicken several pretty damsels found,
And spoil the hunting of a score of lords;
And damp the show. No wonder; I myself
Felt rather squeamish half a dial's turn,
And found strong waters needful to reset

The impassive mettle of high breeding's ways.
And then my Kate, who'll laugh a lawyer dumb,
Was all that evening dull as a town clock;
And later on – here catch this trash – a word
More and I clap a double impost on,
And make them starve in earnest. Tell them so,
Sir thief, my varlet, their ambassador –
Enough of this, why drivel we on these?
Get, for Saint Job's sake, forward with my beard.
You push this trivial business in my jowl,
And make me dawdle over urgent cares,
And tice me to peruse, while your rough hands
Will turn me out a Scythian for the feast,
In barbarous disorder. Is that all?
My ring and gloves; – Count Edmund, there he goes;
How that fool brags about his pedigree.
His veins must run pure ichor, ours mere blood.
I'd gladly try my rapier on his ribs,
And bleed him much as any plough-boy bleeds.
How can a man speak any such vain words? –
I hear him swinging down the corridor,
With all his plumage and bedizened hide
As clean as a cobswan's – trust him for that –
He has no thought above his skin and gloves,
Or at what angle his trim beard should grow:
Despatch, thou slave; complete me, or indeed
He'll be before me with the duchess yet.

[1893]

A Song of Faith Forsworn

Take back your suit.
It came when I was weary and distraught
With hunger. Could I guess the fruit you brought?
I ate in mere desire of any food,
Nibbled its edge and nowhere found it good.
Take back your suit.

Take back your love,
It is a bird poached from my neighbour's wood:
Its wings are wet with tears, its beak with blood.
'Tis a strange fowl with feathers like a crow:
Death's raven, it may be, for all we know.
Take back your love.

Take back your gifts.
False is the hand that gave them; and the mind
That planned them, as a hawk spread in the wind
To poise and snatch the trembling mouse below.
To ruin where it dares – and then to go.
Take back your gifts.

Take back your vows.
Elsewhere you trimmed and taught these lamps to burn;
You bring them stale and dim to serve my turn.
You lit those candles in another shrine,
Guttered and cold you offer them on mine.
Take back your vows.

Take back your words.
What is your love? Leaves on a woodland plain,
Where some are running and where some remain:
What is your faith? Straws on a mountain height,
Dancing like demons on Walpurgis night.
Take back your words.

Take back your lies.
Have them again: they wore a rainbow face,
Hollow with sin and leprous with disgrace;
Their tongue was like a mellow turret bell
To toll hearts burning into wide-lipped hell.
Take back your lies.

Take back your kiss.
Shall I be meek, and lend my lips again
To let this adder daub them with his stain?
Shall I turn cheek to answer, when I hate?
You kiss like Judas in the garden gate!
Take back your kiss.

Take back delight,
A paper boat launched on a heaving pool
To please a child, and folded by a fool;
The wild elms roared: it sailed – a yard or more.
Out went our ship but never came to shore.
Take back delight.

Take back your wreath.
Has it done service on a fairer brow?
Fresh, was it folded round her bosom snow?
Her cast-off weed my breast will never wear:
Your word is 'love me.' My reply 'despair!'
Take back your wreath.

[1893]

Nuptial Song
'Sigh, heart, break not'

Sigh, heart, and break not; rest, lark, and wake not!
   Day I hear coming to draw my Love away.
As mere-waves whisper, and clouds grow crisper,
   Ah, like a rose he will waken up with day.

In moon-light lonely, he is my Love only,
   I share with none when Luna rides in grey.
As dawn-beams quicken, my rivals thicken,
   The light and deed and turmoil of the day.

To watch my sleeper to me is sweeter,
    Than any waking words my love can say:
In dream he finds me and closer winds me!
    Let him rest by me a little more and stay.

Ah, mine eyes, close not: and, tho' he knows not,
    My lips, on his be tender while you may;
Ere leaves are shaken, and ring-doves waken,
    And infant buds begin to scent new day.

Fair Darkness, measure thine hours, as treasure
    Shed each one slowly from thine urn, I pray;
Hoard in and cover each from my lover;
    I cannot lose him yet; dear night, delay.

Each moment dearer, true-love, lie nearer,
    My hair shall blind thee lest thou see the ray;
My locks encumber thine ears in slumber,
    Lest any bird dare give thee note of day.

He rests so calmly; we lie so warmly;
    Hand within hand, as children after play; –
In shafted amber on roof and chamber
    Dawn enters; my Love wakens; here is day.

                                                    [1893]

The Knight in the Wood

The thing itself was rough and crudely done,
Cut in coarse stone, spitefully placed aside
As merest lumber, where the light was worst
On a back staircase. Overlooked it lay
In a great Roman palace crammed with art.
It had no number in the list of gems,
Weeded away long since, pushed out and banished,
Before insipid Guidos over-sweet

266

And Dolce's rose sensationalities,
And curly chirping angels spruce as birds.
And yet the motive of this thing ill-hewn
And hardly seen *did* touch me. O, indeed,
The skill-less hand that carved it had belonged
To a most yearning and bewildered brain:
There was such desolation in the work;
And through its utter failure the thing spoke
With more of human message, heart to heart,
Than all these faultless, smirking, skin-deep saints,
In artificial troubles picturesque,
And martyred sweetly, not one curl awry –
Listen; a clumsy knight, who rode alone
Upon a stumbling jade in a great wood
Belated. The poor beast with head low-bowed
Snuffing the treacherous ground. The rider leant
Forward to sound the marish with his lance.
You saw the place was deadly; that doomed pair,
The wretched rider and the hide-bound steed,
Feared to advance, feared to return – That's all!

[1893]

ALFRED AUSTIN

1835-1913

ALFRED AUSTIN was born at Headingley, near Leeds. He
was created Poet Laureate in 1896. His work covers a wide
range even for a Victorian, taking in both satire in heroic
couplets and Elizabethan lyrics. Unfortunately, he is
usually competent but unoriginal. In *The Last Night* he
gives moving expression to some of the attitudes of the
Victorian right, which he defended vigorously elsewhere in
his political pamphlets.

The Last Night

Sister, come to the chestnut toll,
And sit with me on the dear old bole,
Where we oft have sate in the snow and the rain,
And perhaps I never shall sit again.
Longer and darker the shadows grow:
'Tis my last night, dear. With the dawn I go.

Oh the times, and times, we two have played
Alone, alone, in its nursing shade.
When once we the breadth of the park had crossed,
We fancied ourselves to be hid and lost
In a secret world that seemed to be
As vast as the forests I soon shall see.

Do you remember the winter days
When we piled up the leaves and made them blaze,
While the blue smoke curled in the frosty air,
Up the great wan trunks that rose gaunt and bare,
And we clapped our hands, and the rotten bough
Came crackling down to our feet, as now?

But dearer than all was the April weather,
When off we set to the woods together,
And piled up the lap of your clean white frock
With primrose, and bluebell, and ladysmock,
And notched the pith of the sycamore stem
Into whistles. Do you remember them?

And in summer you followed me fast and far –
How cruel and selfish brothers are! –
With tottering legs, and with cheeks aflame,
Till back to the chestnut toll we came,
And rested and watched the long tassels swing
That seemed with their scent to prolong the Spring.

And in Autumn 'twas still our favourite spot,
When school was over and tasks forgot,
And we scampered away and searched till dusk
For the smooth bright nuts in the prickly husk,
And carried them home, by the shepherd's star,
Then roasted them on the nursery bar.

O, Winnie, I do not want to go
From the dear old home; I love it so.
Why should I follow the sad sea-mew
To a land where everything is new,
Where we never bird-nested, you and I,
Where I was not born, but perhaps shall die?

No; I did not mean that. Come, dry your tears,
You may want them all in the coming years.
There's nothing to cry for, Win: be brave.
I will work like a horse, like a dog, like a slave,
And will come back long ere we both are old,
The clods of my clearing turned to gold.

But could I not stay and work at home,
Clear English woods, turn up English loam?
I shall have to work with my hands out there,
Shear sheep, shoe horses, put edge on share,
Dress scab, drive bullocks, trim hedge, clean ditch,
Put in here a rivet and there a stitch.

It were sweeter to moil in the dear old land,
And sooth, why not? Have we grown so grand?
So grand! When the rear becomes the van,
Rich idleness makes the gentleman.
Gentleman! What is a gentleman now?
A swordless hand and a helmless brow.

Would you blush for me, Win, if you saw me there
With my sleeves turned up and my sinews bare,
And the axe on the log come ringing down
Like a battering-ram on a high-walled town,
And my temples beaded with diamond sweat,
As bright as a wealth-earned coronet?

And, pray, if not there, why here? Does crime
Depend upon distance, or shame on clime?
Will your sleek-skinned plutocrats cease to scoff
At a workman's hands, if he works far off?
And is theirs the conscience men born to sway
Must accept for their own in this latter day?

I could be Harry's woodreeve. Who should scorn
To work for his House, and the eldest-born?
I know every trunk, and bough, and stick,
Much better than Glebe, and as well as Dick.
Loving service seems banned in a monied age,
Or a brother's trust might be all my wage.

Or his keeper, Win? Do you think I'd mind
Being out in all weathers, wet, frost, or wind?
Because I have got a finer coat,
Do I shrink from a weasel or dread a stoat?
Have I not nailed them by tens and scores
To the pheasant-hutch and the granary doors?

Don't I know where the partridge love to hatch,
And wouldn't the poachers meet their match?
A hearty word has a wondrous charm,
And, if not – well, there's always the stalwart arm.
Thank Heaven! spite pillows and counterpanes,
The blood of the savage still haunts my veins.

They may boast as they will of our moral days,
Our mincing manners and softer ways,
And our money value for everything,
But he who will fight should alone be king;
And when gentlemen go, unless I'm wrong,
Men, too, will grow scarce before very long.

There, enough! let us back. I'm a fool, I know;
But I *must* see Gladys before I go.
Good bye, old toll. In my log-hut bleak,
I shall hear your leaves whisper, your branches creak,
Your wood-quests brood, your wood-peckers call,
And the shells of your ripened chestnuts fall.

Harry never must let the dear old place
To a stranger foot and a stranger's face.
He may live as our fathers lived before,
With a homely table and open door.
But out on the pomp the upstart hires,
And that drives a man from the roof of his sires!

I never can understand why they,
Who founded thrones in a braver day,
Should cope with the heroes of 'change and mart,
Whose splendour puts rulers and ruled apart,
Insults the lowly and saps the State,
Makes the servile cringe, and the manly hate.

You will write to me often, dear, when I'm gone,
And tell me how everything goes on;
If the trout spawn well, where the beagles meet,
Who is married or dies in the village street;
And mind you send me the likeliest pup
Of Fan's next litter. There, Win, cheer up!

[1885]

SIR ALFRED LYALL

1835-1911

SIR ALFRED COMYNS LYALL was born in Surrey. He was educated at Eton, and enjoyed a distinguished career in the Indian Civil Service. His short poem demonstrates how the expertise of a lifetime spent in public affairs can crystallize into a penetrating insight.

From *Studies at Delhi, 1876*

II.—BADMINTON

Hardly a shot from the gate we stormed,
  Under the Moree battlement's shade;
Close to the glacis our game was formed,
  There had the fight been, and there we played.

Lightly the demoiselles tittered and leapt,
  Merrily capered the players all;
North, was the garden where Nicholson slept,
  South, was the sweep of a battered wall.

Near me a Musalmán, civil and mild,
  Watched as the shuttlecocks rose and fell;
And he said, as he counted his beads and smiled,
  'God smite their souls to the depths of hell.'

[1889]

ELLICE HOPKINS
1836–1904

ELLICE HOPKINS was born in Cambridge. As a social reformer she worked among navvies. She wrote a number of pamphlets – one *On True Manliness* sold 300,000 copies – and these helped to achieve social reforms, notably for children working in factories. In the midst of her busy life she found time for only one book of verse, though this is rich in absorbed metaphysical echoes. *Life In Death* has a kinship with the more dream-like poems of Vaughan.

Life In Death

I heard him in the autumn winds,
I felt him in the cadent star,
And in the shattered mirror of the wave,
That still in death a rapture finds,
I caught his image faint and far;
And musing in the twilight on the grave,
I heard his footsteps stealing by,
Where the long churchyard grasses sigh.

But never might I see his face,
Though everywhere I found Death's hand,
And his large language all things living spake;
And ever heavy with the grace
Of bygone things through all the land
The song of birds or distant church-bells brake.
'I will arise and seek his face,'
I said, 'ere wrapped in his embrace.'

'For Death is king of life,' I cried;
'Beauty is but his pomp and state;
His kiss is on the apple's crimson cheek,
And with the grape his feet are dyed,

Treading at noon the purple vat;
And flowers, more radiant hued, more quickly seek
His face betraying in disguise,
Their young blooms are but autumn dyes!'

Then I arose ere dawn, and found
A faded lily. 'Lo, 'tis He!
I will surprise him in his golden bed,
Where, muffled close from light and sound,
He sleeps the day up.' Noiselessly
I drew the faded curtains from his head,
And, peeping, found, not Death below,
But fairly life set all arow.

A chrysalis next I chanced upon:
'Death in this dusty shroud has dwelt!'
But stooping saw a wingèd Thing, sun-kist,
Crusted with jewels Life had won
From Death's dim dust; and as I knelt,
Some passion shook the jewels into mist,
Some ecstasy of coming flight,
And lo, he passed in morning light.

And as I paced, still questioning,
Behold, a dead bird at my feet;
The faded violets of his filmy eyes,
And tender loosened throat to sing
No more to us his nocturns sweet,
Told me that death at length before me lies.
But gazing, quick I turned in fear,
Not Death, but teeming Life was there.

Then haply Death keeps house within?
And with the scalpel of keen thought
I traced the chemic travail of the brain,
The throb and pulse of Life's machine,

And mystic force with force still caught
In the embrace that maketh one of twain;
　　And all the beating, swift and slow,
　　Of Life's vibrations to and fro.

　　And still I found the downward swing,
　　Decay, but ere I cried, 'Lo, here!'
The upward stroke rang out glad life and breath
　　And still dead winters changed with spring,
　　And graves the new birth's cradle were;
And still I grasped the flying skirts of Death,
　　And still he turned, and, beaming fair,
　　The radiant face of Life was there.

[1883]

AUGUSTA WEBSTER
1837–1894

AUGUSTA WEBSTER was born at Poole in Dorsetshire. Her
father was an admiral. After her marriage in 1863 to a lecturer
in Law at Cambridge, she took a keen interest in social
matters and published a number of essays later collected as
A Housewife's Opinions. Her poetry is largely flawed by too
slavish an addiction to the faults of later Browning – arbit-
rary use of dramatic monologue, densely prosaic argument,
and great length. *Circe*, however, with a little cutting, remains
alive and readable and spells out an effective moral about
feminine prurience and boredom in the England of the 1860s.

From *Circe*

The sun drops luridly into the west;
Darkness has raised her arms to draw him down
Before the time, not waiting as of wont
Till he has come to her behind the sea;
And the smooth waves grow sullen in the gloom
And wear their threatening purple; more and more
The plain of waters sways and seems to rise
Convexly from its level of the shores;
And low dull thunder rolls along the beach:
There will be storm at last, storm, glorious storm.

Oh welcome, welcome, though it rend my bowers,
Scattering my blossomed roses like the dust,
Splitting the shrieking branches, tossing down
My riotous vines with their young half-tinged grapes
Like small round amethysts or beryls strung
Tumultuously in clusters, though it sate
Its ravenous spite among my goodliest pines
Standing there round and still against the sky
That makes blue lakes between their sombre tufts,
Or harry from my silvery olive slopes

277

Some hoary king whose gnarled fantastic limbs
Wear rugged armour of a thousand years;
Though it will hurl high on my flowery shores
The hostile wave that rives at the poor sward
And drags it down the slants, that swirls its foam
Over my terraces, shakes their firm blocks
Of great bright marbles into tumbled heaps,
And makes my pleached and mossy labyrinths,
Where the small odorous blossoms grow like stars
Strewn in the milky way, a briny marsh.
What matter? let it come and bring me change,
Breaking the sickly sweet monotony.

*　　*　　*

Oh, look! a speck on this side of the sun,
Coming – yes, coming with the rising wind
That frays the darkening cloud-wrack on the verge
And in a little while will leap abroad,
Spattering the sky with rushing blacknesses,
Dashing the hissing mountainous waves at the stars.
'Twill drive me that black speck a shuddering hulk
Caught in the buffeting waves, dashed impotent
From ridge to ridge, will drive it in the night
With that dull jarring crash upon the beach,
And the cries for help and the cries of fear and hope.
　　And then to-morrow they will thoughtfully,
With grave low voices, count their perils up,
And thank the gods for having let them live,
And tell of wives or mothers in their homes,
And children, who would have such loss in them
That they must weep (and may be I weep too)
With fancy of the weepings had they died.
And the next morrow they will feel their ease
And sigh with sleek content, or laugh elate,
Tasting delights of rest and revelling,
Music and perfumes, joyaunce for the eyes
Of rosy faces and luxurious pomps,

The savour of the banquet and the glow
And fragrance of the wine-cup; and they'll talk
How good it is to house in palaces
Out of the storms and struggles, and what luck
Strewed their good ship on our accessless coast.
Then the next day the beast in them will wake,
And one will strike and bicker, and one swell
With puffed up greatness, and one gibe and strut
In apish pranks, and one will line his sleeve
With pilfered booties, and one snatch the gems
Out of the carven goblets as they pass,
One will grow mad with fever of the wine,
And one will sluggishly besot himself,
And one be lewd, and one be gluttonous;
And I shall sickly look, and loathe them all.

Oh my rare cup! my pure and crystal cup
With not one speck of colour to make false
The entering lights, or flaw to make them swerve!
My cup of Truth! How the lost fools will laugh
And thank me for my boon, as if I gave
Some momentary flash of the gods' joy,
To drink where *I* have drunk and touch the touch
Of *my* lips with their own! Aye, let them touch.

Too cruel am I? And the silly beasts,
Crowding around me when I pass their way,
Glower on me and, although they love me still,
(With their poor sorts of love such as they could)
Call wrath and vengeance to their humid eyes
To scare me into mercy, or creep near
With piteous fawnings, supplicating bleats.
Too cruel? Did I choose them what they are?
Or change them from themselves by poisonous charms?
But any draught, pure water, natural wine,
Out of my cup, revealed them to themselves
And to each other. Change? there was no change;

Only disguise gone from them unawares:
And had there been one true right man of them
He would have drunk the draught as I had drunk,
And stood unharmed and looked me in the eyes,
Abashing me before him. But these things –
Why, which of them has even shown the kind
Of some one nobler beast? Pah! yapping wolves
And pitiless stealthy wild-cats, curs and apes
And gorging swine and slinking venomous snakes,
All false and ravenous and sensual brutes
That shame the Earth that bore them, these they are.

Lo, lo! the shivering blueness darting forth
On half the heaven, and the forked thin fire
Strikes to the sea, and hark, the sudden voice
That rushes through the trees before the storm,
And shuddering of the branches. Yet the sky
Is blue against them still, and early stars
Sparkle above the pine-tops; and the air
Clings faint and motionless around me here.

Another burst of flame – and the black speck
Shows in the glare, lashed onwards. It were well
I bade make ready for our guests to-night.

[1870]

ALGERNON CHARLES SWINBURNE
1837–1909

ALGERNON CHARLES SWINBURNE was born and died in London. Perhaps no other nineteenth-century poet has enjoyed such enormous fashionable success followed by such total eclipse. This is largely due to the vice of prolixity, which afflicted Swinburne more than any of his contemporaries. Like Beckett in our own day, he invented a style which was fluid and cool, and it froze into a compound he could easily mass-produce. Fortunately for his initial success, and unfortunately for his lasting reputation, the rainbow mist of the style obscured the full shock-effect of the content: Swinburne was the raw Scotch of Baudelaire with a strong dash of soda. Today, favouring or faulting his content depends on finding it, and this is often hard: the meaning is *in* the music, and the music moves. After Swinburne's discovery of his masochistic tendencies, however, and his physical satisfaction of them with prostitutes the resonant (albeit blurred) algolagnia of *Poems And Ballads* fades through the strident idealism of *Songs Before Sunrise* into the tail-swallowing technique for technique's sake of the *Century of Roundels*. There are good later poems, including some of the parodies, and the poems about the sea, such as *Ex-voto*, but the energy was whipped out (quite literally) in the 1860s. Nevertheless the initial decade produced a score of masterpieces – a new poetry of frustrated cruelty. Moreover, the variety of Swinburne's effects is greater than adverse criticism has supposed. He could be funny, bawdy and grim, and he could laugh at his own vices.

Satia Te Sanguine

If you loved me ever so little,
   I could bear the bonds that gall,
I could dream the bonds were brittle;
   You do not love me at all.

O beautiful lips, O bosom
   More white than the moon's and warm,
A sterile, a ruinous blossom
   Is blown your way in a storm.

As the lost white feverish limbs
　Of the Lesbian Sappho, adrift
In foam where the sea-weed swims,
　Swam loose for the streams to lift,

My heart swims blind in a sea
　That stuns me; swims to and fro,
And gathers to windward and lee
　Lamentation, and mourning, and woe.

A broken, an emptied boat,
　Sea saps it, winds blow apart,
Sick and adrift and afloat,
　The barren waif of a heart.

Where, when the gods would be cruel,
　Do they go for a torture? where
Plant thorns, set pain like a jewel?
　Ah, not in the flesh, not there!

The racks of earth and the rods
　Are weak as foam on the sands;
In the heart is the prey for gods,
　Who crucify hearts, not hands.

Mere pangs corrode and consume,
　Dead when life dies in the brain;
In the infinite spirit is room
　For the pulse of an infinite pain.

I wish you were dead, my dear;
　I would give you, had I to give,
Some death too bitter to fear;
　It is better to die than live.

I wish you were stricken of thunder
    And burnt with a bright flame through,
Consumed and cloven in sunder,
    I dead at your feet like you.

If I could but know after all,
    I might cease to hunger and ache,
Though your heart were ever so small,
    If it were not a stone or a snake.

You are crueller, you that we love,
    Than hatred, hunger, or death;
You have eyes and breasts like a dove,
    And you kill men's hearts with a breath.

As plague in a poisonous city
    Insults and exults on her dead,
So you, when pallid for pity
    Comes love, and fawns to be fed.

As a tame beast writhes and wheedles,
    He fawns to be fed with wiles;
You carve him a cross of needles,
    And whet them sharp as your smiles.

He is patient of thorn and whip,
    He is dumb under axe or dart;
You suck with a sleepy red lip
    The wet red wounds in his heart.

You thrill as his pulses dwindle,
    You brighten and warm as he bleeds,
With insatiable eyes that kindle
    And insatiable mouth that feeds.

Your hands nailed love to the tree,
　　You stript him, scourged him with rods,
And drowned him deep in the sea
　　That hides the dead and their gods.

And for all this, die will he not;
　　There is no man sees him but I;
You came and went and forgot;
　　I hope he will some day die.

[1866]

The Garden of Proserpine

Here, where the world is quiet;
　　Here, where all trouble seems
Dead winds' and spent waves' riot
　　In doubtful dreams of dreams;
I watch the green field growing
For reaping folk and sowing,
For harvest-time and mowing,
　　A sleepy world of streams.

I am tired of tears and laughter,
　　And men that laugh and weep;
Of what may come hereafter
　　For men that sow to reap:
I am weary of days and hours,
Blown buds of barren flowers,
Desires and dreams and powers
　　And everything but sleep.

284

Here life has death for neighbour,
  And far from eye or ear
Wan waves and wet winds labour,
  Weak ships and spirits steer;
They drive adrift, and whither
They wot not who make thither;
But no such winds blow hither,
  And no such things grow here.

No growth of moor or coppice,
  No heather-flower or vine,
But bloomless buds of poppies,
  Green grapes of Proserpine,
Pale beds of blowing rushes
Where no leaf blooms or blushes
Save this whereout she crushes
  For dead men deadly wine.

Pale, without name or number,
  In fruitless fields of corn,
They bow themselves and slumber
  All night till light is born;
And like a soul belated,
In hell and heaven unmated,
By cloud and mist abated
  Comes out of darkness morn.

Though one were strong as seven
  He too with death shall dwell,
Nor wake with wings in heaven,
  Nor weep for pains in hell;
Though one were fair as roses,
His beauty clouds and closes;
And well though love reposes,
  In the end it is not well.

Pale, beyond porch and portal,
  Crowned with calm leaves, she stands
Who gathers all things mortal
  With cold immortal hands;
Her languid lips are sweeter
Than love's who fears to greet her
To men· that mix and meet her
  From many times and lands.

She waits for each and other,
  She waits for all men born;
Forgets the earth her mother,
  The life of fruits and corn;
And spring and seed and swallow
Take wing for her and follow
Where summer song rings hollow
  And flowers are put to scorn.

There go the loves that wither,
  The old loves with wearier wings;
And all dead years draw thither,
  And all disastrous things;
Dead dreams of days forsaken,
Blind buds that snows have shaken,
Wild leaves that winds have taken,
  Red strays of ruined springs.

We are not sure of sorrow,
  And joy was never sure;
To-day will die to-morrow;
  Time stoops to no man's lure;
And love, grown faint and fretful,
With lips but half regretful
Sighs, and with eyes forgetful
  Weeps that no loves endure.

From too much love of living,
From hope and fear set free,
We thank with brief thanksgiving
Whatever gods may be
That no life lives for ever;
That dead men rise up never;
That even the weariest river
Winds somewhere safe to sea.

Then star nor sun shall waken,
Nor any change of light:
Nor sound of waters shaken,
Nor any sound or sight:
Nor wintry leaves nor vernal,
Nor days nor things diurnal;
Only the sleep eternal
In an eternal night.

[1866]

The Sundew

A little marsh-plant, yellow green
And pricked at lip with tender red.
Tread close, and either way you tread
Some faint black water jets between
Lest you should bruise the curious head.

A live thing maybe; who shall know?
The summer knows and suffers it;
For the cool moss is thick and sweet
Each side, and saves the blossom so
That it lives out the long June heat.

The deep scent of the heather burns
About it; breathless though it be,
Bow down and worship; more than we
Is the least flower whose life returns,
Least weed renascent in the sea.

We are vexed and cumbered in earth's sight
With wants, with many memories;
These see their mother what she is,
Glad-growing, till August leave more bright
The apple-coloured cranberries.

Wind blows and bleaches the strong grass,
Blown all one way to shelter it
From trample of strayed kine, with feet
Felt heavier than the moorhen was,
Strayed up past patches of wild wheat.

You call it sundew: how it grows,
If with its colour it have breath,
If life taste sweet to it, if death
Pain its soft petal, no man knows:
Man has no sight or sense that saith.

My sundew, grown of gentle days,
In these green miles the spring begun
Thy growth ere April had half done
With the soft secret of her ways
Or June made ready for the sun.

O red-lipped mouth of marsh-flower,
I have a secret halved with thee.
The name that is love's name to me
Thou knowest, and the face of her
Who is my festival to see.

The hard sun, as thy petals knew,
Coloured the heavy moss-water:
Thou wert not worth green midsummer
Nor fit to live to August blue,
O sundew, not remembering her.

[1866]

After Death

The four boards of the coffin lid
Heard all the dead man did.

The first curse was in his mouth,
Made of grave's mould and deadly drouth.

The next curse was in his head,
Made of God's work discomfited.

The next curse was in his hands,
Made out of two grave-bands.

The next curse was in his feet,
Made out of a grave-sheet.

'I had fair coins red and white,
And my name was as great light;

I had fair clothes green and red,
And strong gold bound round my head.

But no meat comes in my mouth,
Now I fare as the worm doth;

And no gold binds in my hair,
Now I fare as the blind fare.

My live thews were of great strength,
Now am I waxen a span's length;

My live sides were full of lust,
Now are they dried with dust.'

The first board spake and said:
'Is it best eating flesh or bread?'

The second answered it:
'Is wine or honey the more sweet?'

The third board spake and said:
'Is red gold worth a girl's gold head?'

The fourth made answer thus:
'All these things are as one with us.'

The dead man asked of them:
'Is the green land stained brown with flame?

Have they hewn my son for beasts to eat,
And my wife's body for beasts' meat?

Have they boiled my maid in a brass pan,
And built a gallows to hang my man?'

The boards said to him:
'This is a lewd thing that ye deem.

Your wife has gotten a golden bed,
All the sheets are sewn with red.

Your son has gotten a coat of silk,
The sleeves are soft as curded milk.

Your maid has gotten a kirtle new,
All the skirt has braids of blue.

Your man has gotten both ring and glove,
Wrought well for eyes to love.'

The dead man answered thus:
'What good gift shall God give us?'

The boards answered him anon:
'Flesh to feed hell's worm upon.'

[1866]

Fragment on Death

And Paris be it or Helen dying,
    Who dies soever, dies with pain.
He that lacks breath and wind for sighing,
    His gall bursts on his heart; and then
    He sweats, God knows what sweat! again,
No man may ease him of his grief;
    Child, brother, sister, none were fain
To bail him thence for his relief.

Death makes him shudder, swoon, wax pale,
    Nose bend, veins stretch, and breath surrender,
Neck swell, flesh soften, joints that fail
    Crack their strained nerves and arteries slender.
    O woman's body found so tender,
Smooth, sweet, so precious in men's eyes,
    Must thou too bear such count to render?
Yes; or pass quick into the skies.

[1878]

Ballad of the Lords of Old Time
(after the former argument)

What more? Where is the third Calixt,
    Last of that name now dead and gone,
Who held four years the Papalist?
    Alfonso king of Aragon,
    The gracious lord, duke of Bourbon,
And Arthur, duke of old Britaine?
    And Charles the Seventh, that worthy one?
Even with the good knight Charlemain.

The Scot too, king of mount and mist,
    With half his face vermilion,
Men tell us, like an amethyst
    From brow to chin that blazed and shone;
    The Cypriote king of old renown,
Alas! and that good king of Spain,
    Whose name I cannot think upon?
Even with the good knight Charlemain.

No more to say of them I list;
    'Tis all but vain, all dead and done:
For death may no man born resist,
    Nor make appeal when death comes on.
    I make yet one more question;
Where's Lancelot, king of far Bohain?
    Where's he whose grandson called him son?
Even with the good knight Charlemain.

Where is Guesclin, the good Breton?
    The lord of the eastern mountain-chain
And the good late duke of Alençon?
    Even with the good knight Charlemain.

[1878]

The Higher Pantheism
in a Nutshell

One, who is not, we see: but one, whom we see not, is:
Surely this is not that: but that is assuredly this.

What, and wherefore, and whence? for under is over and
under:
If thunder could be without lightning, lightning could be
without thunder.

Doubt is faith in the main: but faith, on the whole, is
doubt:
We cannot believe by proof: but could we believe without?

Why, and whither, and how? for barley and rye are not
clover:
Neither are straight lines curves: yet over is under and over.

Two and two may be four: but four and four are not eight:
Fate and God may be twain: but God is the same thing as
fate.

Ask a man what he thinks, and get from a man what he
feels:
God, once caught in the fact, shows you a fair pair of heels.

Body and spirit are twins: God only knows which is which:
The soul squats down in the flesh, like a tinker drunk in a
ditch.

More is the whole than a part: but half is more than the
whole:
Clearly, the soul is the body: but is not the body the soul?

One and two are not one: but one and nothing is two:
Truth can hardly be false, if falsehood cannot be true.

Once the mastodon was: pterodactyls were common as
    cocks:
Then the mammoth was God: now is He a prize ox.

Parallels all things are: yet many of these are askew:
You are certainly I: but certainly I am not you.

Springs the rock from the plain, shoots the stream from the
    rock:
Cocks exist for the hen: but hens exist for the cock.

God, whom we see not, is: and God, who is not we see:
Fiddle, we know, is diddle: and diddle, we take it, is dee.

[1880]

Nephelidia

From the depth of the dreamy decline of the dawn through
    a notable nimbus of nebulous noonshine,
    Pallid and pink as the palm of the flag-flower that flickers
        with fear of the flies as they float,
Are they looks of our lovers that lustrously lean from a
    marvel of mystic miraculous moonshine,
    These that we feel in the blood of our blushes that
        thicken and threaten with throbs through the throat?
Thicken and thrill as a theatre thronged at appeal of an
    actor's appalled agitation,
    Fainter with fear of the fires of the future than pale with
        the promise of pride in the past;
Flushed with the famishing fullness of fever that reddens
    with radiance of rathe recreation,
    Gaunt as the ghastliest of glimpses that gleam through
        the gloom of the gloaming when ghosts go aghast?
Nay, for the nick of the tick of the time is a tremulous
    touch on the temples of terror,
    Strained as the sinews yet strenuous with strife of the
        dead who is dumb as the dust-heap of death:

Surely no soul is it, sweet as the spasm of erotic emotional
    exquisite error,
  Bathed in the balms of beatified bliss, beatific itself by
    beatitude's breath.
Surely no spirit or sense of a soul that was soft to the spirit
    and soul of our senses
  Sweetens the stress of suspiring suspicion that sobs in
    the semblance and sound of a sigh;
Only this oracle opens Olympian, in mystical moods and
    triangular tenses –
  'Life is the lust of a lamp for the light that is dark till
    the dawn of the day when we die.'
Mild is the mirk and monotonous music of memory,
    melodiously mute as it may be,
  While the hope in the heart of a hero is bruised by the
    breach of men's rapiers, resigned to the rod;
Made meek as a mother whose bosom-beats bound with
    the bliss-bringing bulk of a balm-breathing baby,
  As they grope through the grave-yard of creeds, under
    skies growing green at a groan for the grimness of God.
Blank is the book of his bounty beholden of old, and its
    binding is blacker than bluer:
  Out of blue into black is the scheme of the skies, and
    their dews are the wine of the bloodshed of things;
Till the darkling desire of delight shall be free as a fawn
    that is freed from the fangs that pursue her,
  Till the heart-beats of hell shall be hushed by a hymn
    from the hunt that has harried the kennel of kings.

                                              [1880]

Oscar Wilde

When Oscar came to join his God,
Not earth to earth, but sod to sod,
It was for sinners such as this
Hell was created bottomless.

                                            [1957]

AUSTIN DOBSON
1840–1921

AUSTIN DOBSON was born at Plymouth and died in Ealing.
The run of his verse expresses an oddly rococo sensibility,
poised between yearning for the eighteenth century and
alertness to the surface *mores* of his own age. To the addict
of the slight, this can be a rich pleasure: few poets have
written more lovingly of emotive bric-a-brac, the décor of
a bookish conservative nostalgia. However, Dobson is best
represented by less vulnerable poems. *Before Sedan* has real
compassion, and *A Virtuoso* real indignation: here the
butterfly delicacy becomes the play of the rapier.

Before Sedan

'*The dead hand clasped a letter*' SPECIAL CORRESPONDENCE

Here in this leafy place
　　Quiet he lies,
Cold, with his sightless face
　　Turned to the skies.
'Tis but another dead;
All you can say is said.

Carry his body hence, –
　　Kings must have slaves;
Kings climb to eminence
　　Over men's graves:
So this man's eye is dim; –
Throw the earth over him.

What was the white you touched,
　　There, at his side?
Paper his hand had clutched
　　Tight ere he died; –
Message or wish, may be; –
Smooth the folds out and see.

Hardly the worst of us
    Here could have smiled! –
Only the tremulous
    Words of a child; –
Prattle, that has for stops
Just a few ruddy drops.

Look. She is sad to miss,
    Morning and night,
His – her dead father's – kiss;
    Tries to be bright,
Good to mamma, and sweet.
That is all. 'Marguerite.'

Ah, if beside the dead
    Slumbered the pain!
Ah, if the hearts that bled
    Slept with the slain!
If the grief died; – But no; –
Death will not have it so.

[1873]

A Virtuoso

Be seated, pray. 'A grave appeal'?
    The sufferers by the war, of course;
Ah, what a sight for us who feel, –
    This monstrous *mélodrame* of Force!
We, Sir, we connoisseurs, should know,
    On whom its heaviest burden falls;
Collections shattered at a blow,
    Museums turned to hospitals!

'And worse,' you say; 'the wide distress!'
   Alas, 'tis true distress exists,
Though, let me add, our worthy Press
   Have no mean skill as colourists;
Speaking of colour, next your seat
   There hangs a sketch from Vernet's hand;
Some Moscow fancy, incomplete,
   Yet not indifferently planned;

Note specially the gray old guard,
   Who tears his tattered coat to wrap
A closer bandage round the scarred
   And frozen comrade in his lap; –
But, as regards the present war, –
   Now don't you think our pride of pence
Goes – may I say it? – somewhat far
   For objects of benevolence?

You hesitate. For my part, I –
   Though ranking Paris next to Rome,
Aesthetically – still reply
   That 'Charity begins at Home.'
The words remind me. Did you catch
   My so-named 'Hunt'? The girl's a gem;
And look how those lean rascals snatch
   The pile of scraps she brings to them!

'But your appeal's for home,' – you say, –
   For home, and English poor! Indeed!
I thought Philanthropy to-day
   Was blind to mere domestic need –
However sore – Yet though one grants
   That home should have the foremost claims,
At least these Continental wants
   Assume intelligible names;

While here with us – Ah! who could hope
　　To verify the varied pleas,
Or from his private means to cope
　　With all our shrill necessities!
Impossible! One might as well
　　Attempt comparison of creeds;
Or fill that huge Malayan shell
　　With these half-dozen Indian beads.

Moreover, add that every one
　　So well exalts his pet distress,
'Tis – Give to all, or give to none,
　　If you'd avoid invidiousness.
Your case, I feel, is sad as A.'s,
　　The same applies to B.'s and C.'s;
By my selection I should raise
　　An alphabet of rivalries;

And life is short, – I see you look
　　At yonder dish, a priceless bit;
You'll find it etched in Jacquemart's book,
　　They say that Raphael painted it; –
And life is short, you understand;
　　So, if I only hold you out
An open though an empty hand,
　　Why, you'll forgive me, I've no doubt.

Nay, do not rise. You seem amused;
　　One can but be consistent, Sir!
'Twas on these grounds I just refused
　　Some gushing lady-almoner, –
Believe me, on these very grounds.
　　Good-bye, then. Ah, a rarity!
That cost me quite three hundred pounds, –
　　That Dürer figure, – 'Charity.'

[1873]

299

THOMAS HARDY
1840–1928

THOMAS HARDY was born in Dorset. He studied architecture, but intended to make his name as a writer. For thirty years he concentrated on his novels, only turning to poetry seriously in 1898 with the publication of *Wessex Poems*. Many of these had been written earlier and Hardy continued to mix old and new poems in each of his remaining seven books. His work is characterized by a curious home-expert quality, intricacy of metre vying with rugged oddity of diction. In this Hardy's nearest analogue is George Herbert, though Hardy is rougher in movement and crabs his adjectives rather than his verbs. Hardy's work too often suffers from a reading in bulk, and I have represented him sparingly. Despite this restriction, Hardy should be read as a minor major poet: in his limiting vice he is the exact opposite of Hopkins – with him it is too great a preoccupation with content, and too small a concern with form and arrangement, that finally blurs the outline of his achievement.

The Ruined Maid

'O 'Melia, my dear, this does everything crown!
Who could have supposed I should meet you in Town?
And whence such fair garments, such prosperi-ty?' –
'O didn't you know I'd been ruined?' said she.

– 'You left us in tatters, without shoes or socks,
Tired of digging potatoes, and spudding up docks;
And now you've gay bracelets and bright feathers three!' –
'Yes: that's how we dress when we're ruined,' said she.

– 'At home in the barton you said "thee" and "thou",
And "thik oon", and "theäs oon", and "t'other"; but now
Your talking quite fits 'ee for high compa-ny!' –
'Some polish is gained with one's ruin,' said she.

– 'Your hands were like paws then, your face blue and bleak
But now I'm bewitched by your delicate cheek,
And your little gloves fit as on any la-dy!'
'We never do work when we're ruined,' said she.

– 'You used to call home-life a hag-ridden dream,
And you'd sigh, and you'd sock; but at present you seem
To know not of megrims or melancho-ly!'
'True. One's pretty lively when ruined,' said she.

– 'I wish I had feathers, a fine sweeping gown,
And a delicate face, and could strut about Town!' –
'My dear – a raw country girl, such as you be,
Cannot quite expect that. You ain't ruined,' said she.

[1901]

The Convergence of the Twain

(Lines on the loss of the *Titanic*)

I

In a solitude of the sea
Deep from human vanity,
And the Pride of Life that planned her, stilly couches she.

II

Steel chambers, late the pyres
Of her salamandrine fires,
Cold currents thrid, and turn to rhythmic tidal lyres.

III

Over the mirrors meant
To glass the opulent
The sea-worm crawls – grotesque, slimed, dumb, indifferent.

IV

Jewels in joy designed
To ravish the sensuous mind
Lie lightless, all their sparkles bleared and black and blind.

V

Dim moon-eyed fishes near
Gaze at the gilded gear
And query: 'What does this vaingloriousness down here?'

VI

Well: while was fashioning
This creature of cleaving wing,
The Immanent Will that stirs and urges everything

VII

Prepared a sinister mate
For her – so gaily great –
A Shape of Ice, for the time far and dissociate.

VIII

And as the smart ship grew
In stature, grace, and hue,
In shadowy silent distance grew the Iceberg too.

IX

Alien they seemed to be:
No mortal eye could see
The intimate welding of their later history,

X

Or sign that they were bent
By paths coincident
On being anon twin halves of one august event.

XI

Till the Spinner of the Years
Said 'Now!' And each one hears,
And consummation comes, and jars two hemispheres.

[1914]

At Castle Boterel

As I drive to the junction of lane and highway,
  And the drizzle bedrenches the waggonette,
I look behind at the fading byway,
  And see on its slope, now glistening wet,
    Distinctly yet

Myself and a girlish form benighted
  In dry March weather. We climb the road
Beside a chaise. We had just alighted
  To ease the sturdy pony's load
    When he sighed and slowed.

What we did as we climbed, and what we talked of
  Matters not much, nor to what it led, –
Something that life will not be balked of
  Without rude reason till hope is dead,
    And feeling fled.

It filled but a minute. But was there ever
  A time of such quality, since or before,
In that hill's story? To one mind never,
  Though it has been climbed, foot-swift, foot-sore,
    By thousands more.

Primaeval rocks form the road's steep border,
  And much have they faced there, first and last,
Of the transitory in Earth's long order;
  But what they record in colour and cast
    Is – that we two passed.

And to me, though Time's unflinching rigour,
  In mindless rote, has ruled from sight
The substance now, one phantom figure
  Remains on the slope, as when that night
    Saw us alight.

I look and see it there, shrinking, shrinking,
  I look back at it amid the rain
For the very last time; for my sand is sinking,
  And I shall traverse old love's domain
     Never again.

               ⌈1914⌉

During Wind and Rain

    They sing their dearest songs –
    He, she, all of them – yea,
    Treble and tenor and bass,
      And one to play;
    With the candles mooning each face. . . .
      Ah, no; the years O!
How the sick leaves reel down in throngs!

    They clear the creeping moss –
    Elders and juniors – aye,
    Making the pathways neat
      And the garden gay;
    And they build a shady seat. . . .
      Ah, no; the years, the years;
See, the white storm-birds wing across!

    They are blithely breakfasting all –
    Men and maidens – yea,
    Under the summer tree,
      With a glimpse of the bay,
    While pet fowl come to the knee. .
      Ah, no; the years O!
And the rotten rose is ript from the wall.

They change to a high new house,
He, she, all of them – aye,
Clocks and carpets and chairs
    On the lawn all day,
And brightest things that are theirs. . . .
    Ah, no; the years, the years;
Down their carved names the rain-drop ploughs.

[1919]

GERARD MANLEY HOPKINS
1844–1889

GERARD MANLEY HOPKINS was born in Essex and died in Dublin. He was converted to Catholicism at Oxford, under the influence of Newman, and the remainder of his life was spent as a Jesuit. After his conversion, he gave up poetry for seven years, returning to it with his longest and most intricate poem *The Wreck of the Deutschland*. The richness of technique innovation embodied in this great ode and in all Hopkins's subsequent work is almost without precedent in English poetry. Nevertheless, as Hopkins himself saw, this does not all go to his credit. The invention of Sprung Rhythm – with its insight that a stressed syllable can carry up to three and not two unstressed syllables with it – is the chief contribution to metrics of the nineteenth century, ranking with Browning's discovery of the dramatic monologue as a tool for the enlargement of the stock of tones. However, in Hopkins's practice its combination with heavy alliteration of the kind used in Old English, and with the omission or inversion of parts of speech, sometimes leads to a grotesque over-carved effect which muddles or destroys not only the expected tone but any tone. Despite these qualifications, Hopkins remains a major Victorian poet, though more important for his form than his content. What finally places him a little lower than Tennyson or Arnold is his lack of any coherent original set of things to say. Paradoxically, this helped to make his work attractive at a time when recognizably 'Victorian' attitudes – domestic idealism, Imperialist fervour, decadence etc. – were suffering from a normal historical reaction of sympathy. Nevertheless, with the passage of time he may begin to seem less like the Donne of the nineteenth century than its Crashaw.

The Blessed Virgin compared to the Air we Breathe

Wild air, world-mothering air,
Nestling me everywhere,
That each eyelash or hair
Girdles; goes home betwixt

306

The fleeciest, frailest-flixed
Snowflake; that's fairly mixed
With, riddles, and is rife
In every least thing's life;
This needful, never spent,
And nursing element;
My more than meat and drink,
My meal at every wink;
This air, which, by life's law,
My lung must draw and draw
Now but to breathe its praise,
Minds me in many ways
Of her who not only
Gave God's infinity
Dwindled to infancy
Welcome in womb and breast,
Birth, milk, and all the rest
But mothers each new grace
That does now reach our race —
Mary Immaculate,
Merely a woman, yet
Whose presence, power is
Great as no goddess's
Was deemèd, dreamèd; who
This one work has to do —
Let all God's glory through,
God's glory which would go
Through her and from her flow
Off, and no way but so.

    I say that we are wound
With mercy round and round
As if with air: the same
Is Mary, more by name.
She, wild web, wondrous robe,
Mantles the guilty globe,
Since God has let dispense

Her prayers his providence:
Nay, more than almoner,
The sweet alms' self is her
And men are meant to share
Her life as life does air.
    If I have understood,
She holds high motherhood
Towards all our ghostly good
And plays in grace her part
About man's beating heart,
Laying, like air's fine flood,
The deathdance in his blood;
Yet no part but what will
Be Christ our Saviour still.
Of her flesh he took flesh:
He does take fresh and fresh,
Though much the mystery how,
Not flesh but spirit now
And makes, O marvellous!
New Nazareths in us,
Where she shall yet conceive
Him, morning, noon, and eve;
New Bethlems, and he born
There, evening, noon, and morn –
Bethlem or Nazareth,
Men here may draw like breath
More Christ and baffle death;
Who, born so, comes to be
New self and nobler me
In each one and each one
More makes, when all is done,
Both God's and Mary's Son.
    Again, look overhead
How air is azurèd;
O how! nay do but stand
Where you can lift your hand
Skywards: rich, rich it laps

Round the four fingergaps,
Yet such a sapphire-shot,
Charged, steepèd sky will not
Stain light. Yea, mark you this:
It does no prejudice.
The glass-blue days are those
When every colour glows,
Each shape and shadow shows.
Blue be it: this blue heaven
The seven or seven times seven
Hued sunbeam will transmit
Perfect, not alter it.
Or if there does some soft,
On things aloof, aloft,
Bloom breathe, that one breath more
Earth is the fairer for.
Whereas did air not make
This bath of blue and slake
His fire, the sun would shake,
A blear and blinding ball
With blackness bound, and all
The thick stars round him roll
Flashing like flecks of coal,
Quartz-fret, or sparks of salt,
In grimy vasty vault.
　　So God was god of old:
A mother came to mould
Those limbs like ours which are
What must make our daystar
Much dearer to mankind;
Whose glory bare would blind
Or less would win man's mind.
Through her we may see him
Made sweeter, not made dim,
And her hand leaves his light
Sifted to suit our sight.
　　Be thou then, O thou dear

Mother, my atmosphere;
My happier world, wherein
To wend and meet no sin;
Above me, round me lie
Fronting my froward eye
With sweet and scarless sky;
Stir in my ears, speak there
Of God's love, O live air,
Of patience, penance, prayer:
World-mothering air, air wild,
Wound with thee, in thee isled,
Fold home, fast fold thy child.

[1918]

God's Grandeur

The world is charged with the grandeur of God.
  It will flame out, like shining from shook foil;
  It gathers to a greatness, like the ooze of oil
Crushed. Why do men then now not reck his rod?
Generations have trod, have trod, have trod;
  And all is seared with trade; bleared, smeared with toil;
  And wears man's smudge and shares man's smell: the
    soil
Is bare now, nor can foot feel, being shod.

And for all this, nature is never spent;
  There lives the dearest freshness deep down things;
And though the last lights off the black West went
  Oh, morning, at the brown brink eastward, springs –
Because the Holy Ghost over the bent
  World broods with warm breast and with ah! bright
    wings.

[1918]

Spring and Fall:

to a young child

Margaret, are you gríeving
Over Goldengrove unleaving?
Leáves, líke the things of man, you
With your fresh thoughts care for, can you?
Áh! ás the heart grows older
It will come to such sights colder
By and by, nor spare a sigh
Though worlds of wanwood leafmeal lie;
And yet you wíll weep and know why.
Now no matter, child, the name:
Sórrow's spríngs áre the same.
Nor mouth had, no nor mind, expressed
What heart heard of, ghost guessed:
It ís the blight man was born for,
It is Margaret you mourn for.

[1918]

Inversnaid

This darksome burn, horseback brown,
His rollrock highroad roaring down,
In coop and in comb the fleece of his foam
Flutes and low to the lake falls home.

A windpuff-bonnet of fáwn-fróth
Turns and twindles over the broth
Of a pool so pitchblack, féll-frówning,
It rounds and rounds Despair to drowning.

Degged with dew, dappled with dew
Are the groins of the braes that the brook treads through,
Wiry heathpacks, flitches of fern,
And the beadbonny ash that sits over the burn.

What would the world be, once bereft
Of wet and of wildness? Let them be left,
O let them be left, wildness and wet;
Long live the weeds and the wilderness yet.

[1918]

'No worst, there is none. Pitched past pitch of grief'

No worst, there is none. Pitched past pitch of grief,
More pangs will, schooled at forepangs, wilder wring.
Comforter, where, where is your comforting?
Mary, mother of us, where is your relief?
My cries heave, herds-long; huddle in a main, a chief
Woe, world-sorrow; on an age-old anvil wince and sing –
Then lull, then leave off. Fury had shrieked 'No ling-
  ering! Let me be fell: force I must be brief'.

O the mind, mind has mountains; cliffs of fall
Frightful, sheer, no-man-fathomed. Hold them cheap
May who ne'er hung there. Nor does long our small
Durance deal with that steep or deep. Here! creep,
Wretch, under a comfort serves in a whirlwind: all
Life death does end and each day dies with sleep.

[1918]

'I wake and feel the fell of dark, not day'

I wake and feel the fell of dark, not day.
What hours. O what black hoürs we have spent
This night! what sights you, heart, saw; ways you went!
And more must, in yet longer light's delay.
    With witness I speak this. But where I say
Hours I mean years, mean life. And my lament
Is cries countless, cries like dead letters sent
To dearest him that lives alas! away.

I am gall, I am heartburn. God's most deep decree
Bitter would have me taste: my taste was me;
Bones built in me, flesh filled, blood brimmed the curse.
   Selfyeast of spirit a dull dough sours. I see
The lost are like this, and their scourge to be
As I am mine, their sweating selves; but worse.

                         [1918]

EUGENE LEE-HAMILTON
1845–1907

EUGENE LEE-HAMILTON was born in London and educated in France and Germany. He was in the Diplomatic Service until the age of twenty-eight, when he contracted a rare cerebro-spinal complaint (perhaps hysterical in origin) which compelled him to spend twenty years on a wheeled bed, suffering from paralysis, delusions and extreme pain. His poetry, first undertaken as a palliative for his sufferings, soon became the image of his disease in all its nightmare horror. The slow movement and Roman weight of his style (its chief merits) are partly the result of his method of composing in his head and dictating short phrases at a time. The sequence of *Imaginary Sonnets*, though marked by his usual preference for the macabre and the violent, is the most concrete and vivid series of its kind written in the nineteenth century. His lyrical monologues, of which *Ipsissimus* is one of the shortest, earn him the rank of Webster to Browning's Shakespeare.

Ipsissimus

Thou priest that art behind the screen
    Of this confessional, give ear:
I need God's help, for I have seen
    What turns my vitals limp with fear.
O Christ, O Christ, I must have done
More mortal sin than any one
    Who says his prayers in Venice here!

And yet by stealth I only tried
    To kill my enemy, God knows;
And who on earth has yet denied
    A man the right to kill his foes?
He won the race of the Gondoliers;
I hate him and the skin he wears;
    I hate him and the shade he throws.

I hate him through each day and hour;
   All ills that curse me seem his fault;
He makes my daily soup taste sour,
   He makes my daily bread taste salt.
And so I hung upon his track
At dusk, to stab him in the back
   In some lone street or archway vault.

But oh, give heed! – As I was stealing
   Upon his heels, with knife grasped tight,
There crept across my soul a feeling
   That I myself was kept in sight.
Each time I turned, dodge as I would,
A masked and unknown watcher stood,
   Who baffled all my plans that night.

What mask is this, I thought and thought,
   Who dogs me thus, when least I care?
His figure is nor tall nor short,
   And yet has a familiar air.
But oh, despite this watcher's eye,
I'll reach my man yet, by-and-by,
   And snuff his life out yet, elsewhere!

And though compelled to thus defer,
   I scheme another project soon;
I armed my boat with a hidden spur,
   To run him down in the lagoon.
At dusk I saw him row one day
Where low and wide the waters lay,
   Reflecting scarce the dim white moon.

No boat, as far as sight could strain,
   Loomed on the solitary sea;
I saw my oar each minute gain
   Upon my death-doomed enemy. . . .

315

When lo, a black-masked gondolier,
Silent and spectre-like, drew near,
   And stepped between my deed and me.

He seemed to rise from out the flood,
   And hovered near, to mar my game;
I knew him and his cursed hood,
   His cursed mask: he was the same.
So, balked once more, enraged and cowed,
Back through the still lagoon I rowed
   In mingled wonder, wrath, and shame.

Oh, were I not to come and pray
   Thee for thy absolution here
In the confessional to-day,
   My very ribs would burst with fear.
Leave not, good Father, in the lurch,
An honest son of Mother Church,
   Whose faith is firm and soul sincere.

Behind St Luke's, as the dead men know,
   A pale apothecary dwells,
Who deals in death both quick and slow,
   And baleful philtres, withering spells.
He sells alike to rich and poor
Who know what knocks to give his door,
   The yellow powder that rings the knells.

Well then, I went and knocked the knock
   With cautious hand, as I'd been taught;
The door revolved with silent lock,
   And I went in, suspecting naught.
But ho, the self-same form stood masked
Behind the counter, and unasked
   In silence proffered what I sought.

My knees and hands like aspens shook:
    I spilt the powder on the ground;
I dared not turn, I dared not look;
    My palsied tongue would make no sound.
Then through the door I fled at last,
With feet that seemed more slow than fast,
    And dared not even once turn round.

And yet I am an honest man,
    Who only sought to kill his foe:
Could I sit down and see each plan
    That I took up frustrated so?
God wot, as every scheme was balked,
And in the sun my man still walked,
    I felt my hatred grow and grow.

I thought, 'At dusk, with stealthy tread
    I'll seek his dwelling, and I'll creep
Upstairs, and hide beneath his bed,
    And in the night I'll strike him deep.'
And so I went; but at his door
The figure, masked just as before,
    Sat on the step, as if asleep.

Bent, spite all fear, upon my task,
    I tried to pass: there was no space.
Then rage prevailed; I snatched the mask
    From off the baffling figure's face. . . .
And (oh, unutterable dread!)
The face was mine, – mine white and dead, –
    Stiff with some frightful death's grimace.

What sins are mine, oh, luckless wight!
    That fate should play me such a trick,
And make me see a sudden sight
    That turns both soul and body sick?

Stretch out thy hands, thou Priest unseen
That sittest there behind the screen,
   And give me absolution quick!

O God, O God, his hands are dead!
   His hands are mine, oh, monstrous spell!
I feel them clammy on my head:
   Is he my own dead self as well?
Those hands are mine, – their scars, their shape:
O God, O God, there's no escape,
   And seeking Heaven, I fall on Hell!

[1884]

Henry I to the Sea

[A.D. 1120.]

O Sea, take all, since thou hast taken him
   Whose life to me was life. Let one wide wave
   Now sweep this land, and make a single grave
For king and people. Let the wild gull skim

Where now is England, and the sea-fish swim
   In every drowned cathedral's vaulted nave,
   As in a green and pillared ocean cave,
Submerged for ever and for ever dim.

And if the shuddering pilot ventures there
   And sees their pinnacles, like rocks to shun,
Above the waves, and green with tidal hair,

Then let him whisper that this thing was done
   By God, the Lord of Oceans, at the prayer
Of England's king, who mourned his only son.

[1888]

Luca Signorelli to his Son

[A.D. 1500.]

They brought thy body back to me quite dead,
  Just as thou hadst been stricken in the brawl.
  I let no tear, I let no curses fall,
But signed to them to lay thee on the bed.

Then, with clenched teeth, I stripped thy clothes soaked
    red;
  And taking up my pencil at God's call,
  All night I drew thy features, drew them all,
And every beauty of thy pale chill head.

For I required the glory of thy limbs,
  To lend it to archangel and to saint,
And of thy brow for brows with halo rims;

And thou shalt stand, in groups that I shall paint
  Upon God's walls; till, like procession hymns
Lost in the distance, ages make them faint.

[1888]

MICHAEL FIELD
1846–1914, 1862–1913

MICHAEL FIELD was the joint pen-name of an aunt-niece partnership, Miss Katherine Bradley and Miss Edith Cooper. Both died of cancer. Their reputation was founded as a closet-dramatist but their best work is in their expansions of Sappho and their lyrics on paintings.

Sweeter far than the harp,
more gold than gold

Πολὺ πακτίδος ἀδυμελεστέρα,
χρυσῶ χρυσοτέρα.

Thine elder that I am, thou must not cling
To me, nor mournful for my love entreat:
And yet, Alcæus, as the sudden spring
Is love, yea, and to veiled Demeter sweet.

Sweeter than tone of harp, more gold than gold
Is thy young voice to me; yet, ah, the pain
To learn I am beloved now I am old,
Who, in my youth, loved, as thou must, in vain.

[1889]

La Gioconda, by Leonardo Da Vinci,
in the Louvre

Historic, sidelong, implicating eyes;
A smile of velvet's lustre on the cheek;
Calm lips the smile leads upward: hand that lies
Glowing and soft, the patience in its rest
Of cruelty that waits and does not seek
For prey; a dusky forehead and a breast

320

Where twilight touches ripeness amorously:
Behind her, crystal rocks, a sea and skies
Of evanescent blue on cloud and creek;
Landscape that shines suppressive of its zest
For those vicissitudes by which men die.

[1892]

ALICE MEYNELL
1847–1922

ALICE MEYNELL was born in Barnes. She was converted to
Roman Catholicism as a girl. Throughout her career as a
poet she was able to maintain a thin flow of nearly perfect
lyrics. Her ear is as fine as Dowson's and she is able to
transmit intensity of religious feeling (for example, in *To The
Body*) by musical means. Her criticism of other nineteenth-
century and seventeenth-century poets is apt and strong.
Reading *The Wares of Autolycus*, in which many of her
reviews are collected, is an encouragement to treat the
content of her poetry with care: one's mind glides off the
smooth surface which sometimes masks a hard outline of
ideas.

Parted

Farewell to one now silenced quite,
Sent out of hearing, out of sight, –
　My friend of friends, whom I shall miss.
　He is not banished, though, for this, –
Nor he, nor sadness, nor delight.

Though I shall walk with him no more,
A low voice sounds upon the shore.
　He must not watch my resting-place
　But who shall drive a mournful face
From the sad winds about my door?

I shall not hear his voice complain
But who shall stop the patient rain?
　His tears must not disturb my heart,
　But who shall change the years, and part
The world from every thought of pain?

Although my life is left so dim,
The morning crowns the mountain-rim;
  Joy is not gone from summer skies,
  Nor innocence from children's eyes,
And all these things are part of him.

He is not banished, for the showers
Yet wake this green warm earth of ours.
  How can the summer but be sweet?
  I shall not have him at my feet,
And yet my feet are on the flowers.

[1875]

The Lady Poverty

The Lady Poverty was fair:
But she has lost her looks of late,
With change of times and change of air.
Ah slattern, she neglects her hair,
Her gown, her shoes. She keeps no state
As once when her pure feet were bare.

Or – almost worse, if worse can be –
She scolds in parlours; dusts and trims,
Watches and counts. Oh, is this she
Whom Francis met, whose step was free,
Who with Obedience carolled hymns,
In Umbria walked with Chastity?

Where is her ladyhood? Not here,
Not among modern kinds of men;
But in the stony fields, where clear
Through the thin trees the skies appear;
In delicate spare soil and fen,
And slender landscape and austere.

[1896]

Parentage

'When Augustus Cæsar legislated against the unmarried citizens of Rome, he declared them to be, in some sort, slayers of the people.'

Ah no, not these!
These, who were childless, are not they who gave
So many dead unto the journeying wave,
The helpless nurslings of the cradling seas;
Not they who doomed by infallible decrees
Unnumbered man to the innumerable grave.

But those who slay
Are fathers. Theirs are armies. Death is theirs,
The death of innocences and despairs;
The dying of the golden and the grey.
The sentence, when these speak it, has no Nay.
And she who slays is she who bears, who bears.

[1896]

To the Body

Thou inmost, ultimate
Council of judgement, palace of decrees,
Where the high senses hold their spiritual state,
Sued by earth's embassies,
And sign, approve, accept, conceive, create;

Create—thy senses close
With the world's pleas. The random odours reach
Their sweetness in the place of thy repose,
Upon thy tongue the peach,
And in thy nostrils breathes the breathing rose.

To thee, secluded one,
The dark vibrations of the sightless skies,
The lovely inexplicit colours, run;
The light gropes for those eyes.
O thou august! thou dost command the sun.

Music, all dumb, hath trod
Into thine ear her one effectual way;
And fire and cold approach to gain thy nod,
Where thou call'st up the day,
Where thou awaitest the appeal of God.

[1913]

The Launch

Forth, to the alien gravity,
Forth, to the laws of ocean, we,
Builders on earth by laws of land,
Entrust this creature of our hand
Upon the calculated sea.

Fast bound to shore we cling, we creep,
And make our ship ready to leap
Light to the flood, equipped to ride
The strange conditions of the tide—
New weight, new force, new world: the Deep.

Ah thus—not thus—the Dying, kissed,
Cherished, exhorted, shriven, dismissed;
By all the eager means we hold
We, warm, prepare him for the cold,
To keep the incalculable tryst.

[1913]

WILLIAM HENLEY
1849–1903

WILLIAM HENLEY was born in Gloucestershire. He suffered from tuberculosis but, after twenty months under the care of Lister at the Edinburgh Infirmary, he seems to have made a substantial recovery. Neither Henley's Imperialist verse nor his essays in French metres quite reach the top class: in the first field he is bettered by Newbolt, in the second by Dobson. The autobiographical sequence *In Hospital*, though 'modern' in the tone of W. D. Snodgrass or Elizabeth Jennings, is marred by weakness of construction and abstract phrasing. The Bill Sykes mood of *Madam Life's A Piece In Bloom* effectively combines Henley's cockney pose with his violence, but its concision and bite are unique in his work.

Madam Life's a Piece in Bloom

Madam Life's a piece in bloom
    Death goes dogging everywhere:
She's the tenant of the room,
    He's the ruffian on the stair.

You shall see her as a friend,
    You shall bilk him once or twice;
But he'll trap you in the end,
    And he'll stick you for her price.

With his kneebones at your chest,
    And his knuckles in your throat,
You would reason – plead – protest!
    Clutching at her petticoat;

But she's heard it all before,
    Well she knows you've had your fun,
Gingerly she gains the door,
    And your little job is done.

[*Collected Poems*, 1908]

ROBERT LOUIS STEVENSON
1850–1894

ROBERT LOUIS STEVENSON was born in Edinburgh and died in Samoa. He came of a family of Scottish engineers, and he clearly felt a mixture of pride in their achievement and guilt at not being able to add to it in a way they would understand. His touching poem beginning 'Say not of me' very gracefully conveys these mixed feelings. Stevenson had a fierce sense of commitment to the past and always wrote well about his father and his own lost childhood. His verse has tended to be overshadowed by the brilliance of his prose. In fact, it often strikes a deeper and more piercing note, running counter to the trend of the reign in working best when closest to his own life. Stevenson is a very central figure in the literature of Scotland: he embodies the love of clandestine violence which is exploited later by Buchan in Richard Hannay and by Fleming in James Bond. Most of Stevenson's adult life was spent as an invalid (he wrote much of *A Child's Garden of Verses* with his left hand after a haemorrhage while temporarily blind) and his driving interest in the life of power and action may have been accentuated by this.

My Bed is a Boat

My bed is like a little boat;
    Nurse helps me in when I embark;
She girds me in my sailor's coat
    And starts me in the dark.

At night, I go on board and say
    Good-night to all my friends on shore;
I shut my eyes and sail away
    And see and hear no more.

And sometimes things to bed I take,
    As prudent sailors have to do;
Perhaps a slice of wedding-cake,
    Perhaps a toy or two.

All night across the dark we steer:
But when the day returns at last,
Safe in my room, beside the pier,
I find my vessel fast.

[1885]

'Say not of me that
weakly I declined'

Say not of me that weakly I declined
The labours of my sires, and fled the sea,
The towers we founded and the lamps we lit,
To play at home with paper like a child.
But rather say: *In the afternoon of time*
A strenuous family dusted from its hands
The sand of granite, and beholding far
Along the sounding coast its pyramids
And tall memorials catch the dying sun,
Smiled well content, and to this childish task
Around the fire addressed its evening hours.

[1887]

'The tropics vanish, and
meseems that I'

The tropics vanish, and meseems that I,
From Halkerside, from topmost Allermuir,
Or steep Caerketton, dreaming gaze again.
Far set in fields and woods, the town I see
Spring gallant from the shallows of her smoke,
Cragged, spired, and turreted, her virgin fort
Beflagged. About, on seaward-drooping hills,
New folds of city glitter. Last, the Forth
Wheels ample waters set with sacred isles,
And populous Fife smokes with a score of towns.

There, on the sunny frontage of a hill,
Hard by the house of kings, repose the dead,
My dead, the ready and the strong of word.
Their works, the salt-encrusted, still survive;
The sea bombards their founded towers; the night
Thrills pierced with their strong lamps. The artificers,
One after one, here in this grated cell,
Where the rain erases and the rust consumes,
Fell upon lasting silence. Continents
And continental oceans intervene;
A sea uncharted, on a lampless isle,
Environs and confines their wandering child
In vain. The voice of generations dead
Summons me, sitting distant, to arise,
My numerous footsteps nimbly to retrace,
And, all mutation over, stretch me down
In that denoted city of the dead.
   APEMAMA.

[1887]

To S. C.*

I heard the pulse of the besieging sea
Throb far away all night. I heard the wind
Fly crying and convulse tumultuous palms.
I rose and strolled. The isle was all bright sand,
And flailing fans and shadows of the palm;
The heaven all moon and wind and the blind vault
The keenest planet slain, for Venus slept.
   The king, my neighbour, with his host of wives,
Slept in the precinct of the palisade;
Where single, in the wind, under the moon,
Among the slumbering cabins, blazed a fire,
Sole street-lamp and the only sentinel.
   To other lands and nights my fancy turned –

* Sidney Colvin.

329

To London first, and chiefly to your house,
The many-pillared and the well-beloved.
The yearning fancy lighted; there again
In the upper room I lay, and heard far off
The unsleeping city murmur like a shell;
The muffled tramp of the Museum guard
Once more went by me; I beheld again
Lamps vainly brighten the dispeopled street;
Again I longed for the returning morn,
The awaking traffic, the bestirring birds,
The consentaneous trill of tiny song
That weaves round monumental cornices
A passing charm of beauty. Most of all,
For your light foot I wearied, and your knock
That was the glad réveillé of my day.

Lo, now, when to your task in the great house
At morning through the portico you pass,
One moment glance, where by the pillared wall
Far-voyaging island gods, begrimed with smoke,
Sit now unworshipped, the rude monument
Of faiths forgot and races undivined:
Sit now disconsolate, remembering well
The priest, the victim, and the songful crowd,
The blaze of the blue noon, and that huge voice,
Incessant, of the breakers on the shore.
As far as these from their ancestral shrine,
So far, so foreign, your divided friends
Wander, estranged in body, not in mind.
    APEMAMA.

[1887]

Christmas at Sea

The sheets were frozen hard, and they cut the naked hand;
The decks were like a slide, where a seaman scarce could
   stand,
The wind was a nor'-wester, blowing squally off the sea;
And cliffs and spouting breakers were the only things a-lee.

They heard the surf a-roaring before the break of day;
But 'twas only with the peep of light we saw how ill we lay.
We tumbled every hand on deck instanter, with a shout,
And we gave her the maintops'l, and stood by to go about.

All day we tack'd and tack'd between the South Head and
   the North;
All day we haul'd the frozen sheets, and got no further
   forth;
All day as cold as charity, in bitter pain and dread,
For very life and nature we tack'd from head to head.

We gave the South a wider berth, for there the tide-race
   roar'd;
But every tack we made we brought the North Head close
   aboard;
So's we saw the cliffs and houses, and the breakers running
   high,
And the coastguard in his garden, with his glass against his
   eye.

The frost was on the village roofs as white as ocean foam;
The good red fires were burning bright in every 'longshore
   home;
The windows sparkled clear, and the chimneys volley'd out;
And I vow we sniff'd the victuals as the vessel went about.

The bells upon the church were rung with a mighty jovial
    cheer;
For it's just that I should tell you how (of all days in the
    year)
This day of our adversity was blessèd Christmas morn,
And the house above the coastguard's was the house where
    I was born.

O well I saw the pleasant room, the pleasant faces there,
My mother's silver spectacles, my father's silver hair;
And well I saw the firelight, like a flight of homely elves
Go dancing round the china-plates that stand upon the
    shelves!

And well I knew the talk they had, the talk that was of me,
Of the shadow on the household and the son that went to
    sea;
And O the wicked fool I seem'd, in every kind of way,
To be here and hauling frozen ropes on blessèd Christmas
    Day.

They lit the high sea-light, and the dark began to fall.
'All hands to loose topgallant sails!' I heard the captain call.
'By the Lord, she'll never stand it,' our first mate Jackson
    cried.
... 'It's the one way or the other, Mr Jackson,' he replied.

She stagger'd to her bearings, but the sails were new and
    good,
And the ship smelt up to windward just as though she
    understood.
As the winter's day was ending, in the entry of the night,
We clear'd the weary headland, and pass'd below the light.

And they heaved a mighty breath, every soul on board but
   me,
As they saw her nose again pointing handsome out to sea;
But all that I could think of, in the darkness and the cold,
Was just that I was leaving home and my folks were grow-
   ing old.

                                     [1896]

OSCAR WILDE

1856–1900

OSCAR FINGALL O'FLAHERTIE WILLS WILDE was born
in Dublin, the son of a well-known surgeon. He is perhaps
the most tragically brilliant figure in English literature after
Byron. His conviction and imprisonment for homosexuality
enrich with morbid glamour the spectacular gaiety of his
career as the Baudelairian dandy, author of the wittiest play
in English since Sheridan. *Requiescat* has the delicacy of a
cavalier lyric. *Ave Imperatrix* anticipates the rhetoric of the
Imperialist movement, but its tone is an odd mixture of
patriotism and compassion. The long poem *The Ballad of
Reading Gaol*, arising as it did out of Wilde's two years in
prison, has perhaps had more praise than it deserves: Wilde's
rhythm and antithesis can sometimes make sincerity sound
stagey.

Ave Imperatrix

Set in this stormy Northern sea,
　　Queen of these restless fields of tide,
England! what shall men say of thee,
　　Before whose feet the worlds divide?

The earth, a brittle globe of glass,
　　Lies in the hollow of thy hand,
And through its heart of crystal pass,
　　Like shadows through a twilight land,

The spears of crimson-suited war,
　　The long white-crested waves of fight,
And all the deadly fires which are
　　The torches of the lords of Night.

The yellow leopards, strained and lean,
　　The treacherous Russian knows so well,
With gaping blackened jaws are seen
　　Leap through the hail of screaming shell.

The strong sea-lion of England's wars
   Hath left his sapphire cave of sea,
To battle with the storm that mars
   The stars of England's chivalry.

The brazen-throated clarion blows
   Across the Pathan's reedy fen,
And the high steeps of Indian snows
   Shake to the tread of armèd men.

And many an Afghan chief, who lies
   Beneath his cool pomegranate-trees,
Clutches his sword in fierce surmise
   When on the mountain-side he sees

The fleet-foot Marri scout, who comes
   To tell how he hath heard afar
The measured roll of English drums
   Beat at the gates of Kandahar.

For southern wind and east wind meet
   Where, girt and crowned by sword and fire,
England with bare and bloody feet
   Climbs the steep road of wide empire.

O lonely Himalayan height,
   Grey pillar of the Indian sky,
Where saw'st thou last in clanging flight
   Our wingèd dogs of Victory?

The almond-groves of Samarcand,
   Bokhara, where red lilies blow,
And Oxus, by whose yellow sand
   The grave white-turbaned merchants go:

And on from thence to Ispahan,
  The gilded garden of the sun,
Whence the long dusty caravan
  Brings cedar wood and vermilion;

And that dread city of Cabool
  Set at the mountain's scarpèd feet,
Whose marble tanks are ever full
  With water for the noonday heat:

Where through the narrow straight Bazaar
  A little maid Circassian
Is led, a present from the Czar
  Unto some old and bearded khan, –

Here have our wild war-eagles flown,
  And flapped wide wings in fiery fight;
But the sad dove, that sits alone
  In England – she hath no delight.

In vain the laughing girl will lean
  To greet her love with love-lit eyes:
Down in some treacherous black ravine,
  Clutching his flag, the dead boy lies.

And many a moon and sun will see
  The lingering wistful children wait
To climb upon their father's knee;
  And in each house made desolate

Pale women who have lost their lord
  Will kiss the relics of the slain –
Some tarnished epaulette – some sword –
  Poor toys to soothe such anguished pain.

For not in quiet English fields
    Are these, our brothers, lain to rest,
Where we might deck their broken shields
    With all the flowers the dead love best.

For some are by the Delhi walls,
    And many in the Afghan land,
And many where the Ganges falls
    Through seven mouths of shifting sand.

And some in Russian waters lie,
    And others in the seas which are
The portals to the East, or by
    The wind-swept heights of Trafalgar.

O wandering graves! O restless sleep!
    O silence of the sunless day!
O still ravine! O stormy deep!
    Give up your prey! Give up your prey!

And thou whose wounds are never healed,
    Whose weary race is never won,
O Cromwell's England! must thou yield
    For every inch of ground a son?

Go! crown with thorns thy gold-crowned head,
    Change thy glad song to song of pain;
Wind and wild wave have got thy dead,
    And will not yield them back again.

Wave and wild wind and foreign shore
    Possess the flower of English land –
Lips that thy lips shall kiss no more,
    Hands that shall never clasp thy hand.

What profit now that we have bound
  The whole round world with nets of gold,
If hidden in our heart is found
  The care that groweth never old?

What profit that our galleys ride,
  Pine-forest-like, on every main?
Ruin and wreck are at our side,
  Grim warders of the House of Pain.

Where are the brave, the strong, the fleet?
  Where is our English chivalry?
Wild grasses are their burial-sheet,
  And sobbing waves their threnody.

O loved ones lying far away,
  What word of love can dead lips send!
O wasted dust! O senseless clay!
  Is this the end! is this the end!

Peace, peace! we wrong the noble dead
  To vex their solemn slumber so;
Though childless, and with thorn-crowned head,
  Up the steep road must England go,

Yet when this fiery web is spun,
  Her watchmen shall descry from far
The young Republic like a sun
  Rise from these crimson seas of war.

[1881]

Requiescat

Tread lightly, she is near
  Under the snow,
Speak gently, she can hear
  The daisies grow.

All her bright golden hair
　　Tarnished with rust,
She that was young and fair
　　Fallen to dust.

Lily-like, white as snow,
　　She hardly knew
She was a woman, so
　　Sweetly she grew.

Coffin board, heavy stone,
　　Lie on her breast,
I vex my heart alone,
　　She is at rest.

Peace, peace, she cannot hear
　　Lyre or sonnet,
All my life's buried here,
　　Heap earth upon it.

[1881]

AGNES MARY ROBINSON

1857–post 1922

AGNES MARY FRANCES ROBINSON was born at Leamington, and lived in London until her marriage with a French professor of Persian in 1888, when she moved to Paris. As Mrs Darmesteter, and later Mrs Duclaux, she continued to write poems. *Etruscan Tombs* is a good example of the Victorian short sonnet sequence, with a last line worthy of Hérédia.

Etruscan Tombs

I

To think the face we love shall ever die,
  And be the indifferent earth, and know us not!
To think that one of us shall live to cry
  On one long buried in a distant spot!

O wise Etruscans, faded in the night
  Yourselves, with scarce a rose-leaf on your trace,
You kept the ashes of the dead in sight,
  And shaped the vase to seem the vanished face.

But, O my Love, my life is such an urn
  That tender memories mould with constant touch,
Until the dust and earth of it they turn
  To your dear image that I love so much:

A sacred urn, filled with the sacred past,
That shall recall you while the clay shall last.

II

These cinerary urns with human head
  And human arms that dangle at their sides,
The earliest potters made them for their dead,
  To keep the mother's ashes or the bride's.

O rude attempt of some long-spent despair –
  With symbol and with emblem discontent –
To keep the dead alive and as they were,
  The actual features and the glance that went!

The anguish of your art was not in vain,
  For lo, upon these alien shelves removed
The sad immortal images remain,
  And show that once they lived and once you loved.

But oh, when I am dead may none for me
Invoke so drear an immortality!

III

Beneath the branches of the olive yard
  Are roots where cyclamen and violet grow;
Beneath the roots the earth is deep and hard,
  And there a king was buried long ago.

The peasants digging deeply in the mould
  Cast up the autumn soil about the place,
And saw a gleam of unexpected gold,
  And underneath the earth a living face.

With sleeping lids and rosy lips he lay
  Among the wreaths and gems that mark the king
One moment; then a little dust and clay
  Fell shrivelled over wreath and urn and ring.

A carven slab recalls his name and deeds,
Writ in a language no man living reads.

IV

Here lies the tablet graven in the past,
  Clear-charactered and firm and fresh of line.
See, not a word is gone; and yet how fast
  The secret no man living may divine!

What did he choose for witness in the grave?
    A record of his glory on the earth?
The wail of friends? The Pæans of the brave?
    The sacred promise of the second birth?

The tombs of ancient Greeks in Sicily
    Are sown with slender discs of graven gold
Filled with the praise of Death: 'Thrice happy he
    Wrapt in the milk-soft sleep of dreams untold!'

They sleep their patient sleep in altered lands,
The golden promise in their fleshless hands.

[1888]

JOHN DAVIDSON
1857–1909

JOHN DAVIDSON was born at Barrhead in Renfrewshire.
He left instructions in his will that no biography of him was
to be written. Davidson was a poet of extended talent never
fully realized. The Scottish quality of his verse is apparent
in its mixture of bitter flyting, surface erudition and coarse
humour. I rank his satire *The Crystal Palace* as the major
achievement of his ambitious last period, though there are
interesting, if inchoate, things in his series of long *Testaments*. Good shorter poems by Davidson (excluded to make
room for the less known *The Crystal Palace*) include the lyric
A Cinque Port, the social monologue *Thirty Bob A Week*
(rightly, and surprisingly, praised by Eliot) and the dream-
like ballad *A Runnable Stag*, with its curious foreboding of
his own suicide by drowning.

The Crystal Palace

Contraption, – that's the bizarre, proper slang,
Eclectic word, for this portentous toy,
The flying-machine, that gyrates stiffly, arms
A-kimbo, so to say, and baskets slung
From every elbow, skating in the air.
Irreverent, we; but Tartars from Thibet
May deem Sir Hiram the Grandest Lama, deem
His volatile machinery best, and most
Magnific, rotatory engine, meant
For penitence and prayer combined, whereby
Petitioner as well as orison
Are spun about in space: a solemn rite
Before the portal of that fane unique,
Victorian temple of commercialism,
Our very own eighth wonder of the world,
The Crystal Palace.

So sublime! Like some
Immense crustacean's gannoid skeleton,
Unearthed, and cleansed, and polished! Were it so
Our paleontological respect
Would shield it from derision; but when a shed,
Intended for a palace, looks as like
The fossil of a giant myriapod! . . .
'Twas Isabey – sarcastic wretch! – who told
A young aspirant, studying tandem art
And medicine, that he certainly was born
To be a surgeon: 'When you try,' he said,
'To paint a boat you paint a tumour.'

No
Idea of its purpose, and no word
Can make your glass and iron beautiful.
Colossal ugliness may fascinate
If something be expressed; and time adopts
Ungainliest stone and brick and ruins them
To beauty; but a building lacking life,
A house that must not mellow or decay? –
'Tis nature's outcast. Moss and lichens? Stains
Of weather? From the first Nature said 'No!
Shine there unblessed, a witness of my scorn!
I love the ashlar and the well-baked clay;
My seasons can adorn them sumptuously:
But you shall stand rebuked till men ashamed,
Abhor you, and destroy you and repent!'

But come: here's crowd; here's mod; a gala day!
The walks are black with people: no one hastes;
They all pursue their purpose business-like –
The polo-ground, the cycle-track; but most
Invade the palace glumly once again.
It is 'again'; you feel it in the air –
Resigned habitués on every hand:

And yet agog; abandoned, yet concerned!
They can't tell why they come; they only know
They must shove through the holiday somehow.

In the main floor the fretful multitude
Circulates from the north nave to the south
Across the central transept – swish and tread
And murmur, like a seaboard's mingled sound.
About the sideshows eddies swirl and swing:
Distorting mirrors; waltzing-tops – wherein
Couples are wildly spun contrariwise
To your revolving platforms; biographs,
Or rifle-ranges; panoramas: choose!
As stupid as it was last holiday?
They think so, – every whit! Outside, perhaps?
A spice of danger in the flying-machine?
A few who passed that whirligig, their hopes
On higher things, return disconsolate
To try the Tartar's volant oratory.
Others again, no more anticipant
Of any active business in their own
Diversion, joining stalwart folk who sought
At once the polo-ground, the cycle-track,
Accept the ineludible; while some
(Insidious anti-climax here) frequent
The water-entertainments – shallops, chutes
And rivers subterrene: – thus, passive, all,
Like savages bewitched, submit at last
To be the dupes of pleasure, sadly gay –
Victims, and not companions, of delight!

Not all! The garden-terrace: – hark, behold,
Music and dancing! People by themselves
Attempting happiness! A box of reeds –
Accordion, concertina, seraphine –
And practised fingers charm advertent feet!
The girls can dance, but, O their heavy-shod

345

Unwieldy swains! – No matter: – hatless heads,
With hair undone, eyes shut and cheeks aglow
On blissful shoulders lie; – such solemn youths
Sustaining ravished donahs! Round they swing,
In time or out, but unashamed and all
Enchanted with the glory of the world.
And look! Among the laurels on the lawns
Torn coats and ragged skirts, starved faces flushed
With passion and with wonder! – hid away
Avowedly; but seen – and yet not seen!
None laugh; none point; none notice: multitude
Remembers and forgives; unwisest love
Is sacrosanct upon a holiday.
Out of the slums, into the open air
Let loose for once, their scant economies
Already spent, what was there left to do?
O sweetly, tenderly, devoutly think,
Shepherd and Shepherdess in Arcady!

A heavy shower; the Palace fills; begins
The business and the office of the day,
The eating and the drinking – only real
Enjoyment to be had, they tell you straight
Now that the shifty weather fails them too.
But what's the pother here, the blank dismay?
Money has lost its value at the bars:
Like tavern-tokens when the Boar's Head rang
With laughter and the Mermaid swam in wine,
Tickets are now the only currency.
Before the buffets, metal tables packed
As closely as mosaic, with peopled chairs
Cementing them, where damsels in and out
Attend with food, like disembodied things
That traverse rock as easily as air –
These are the havens, these the happy isles!
A dozen people fight for every seat –
Without a quarrel, unturbulently: O,

A peaceable, a tame, a timorous crowd!
And yet relentless: this they know they need;
Here have they money's worth – some food, some drink;
And so alone, in couples, families, groups,
Consuming and consumed – for as they munch
Their victuals all their vitals ennui gnaws –
They sit and sit, and fain would sit it out
In tedious gormandize till firework-time.
But business beats them: those who sit must eat.
Tickets are purchased at besieged kiosks,
And when their value's spent – with such a grudge!–
They rise to buy again, and lose their seats;
For this is Mob, unhappy locust-swarm
Instinctive, apathetic, ravenous.

Beyond a doubt a most unhappy crowd!
Some scores of thousands searching up and down
The north nave and the south nave hungrily
For space to sit and rest to eat and drink:
Or captives in a labyrinth, or herds
Imprisoned in a vast arena; here
A moment clustered; there entangled; now
In reaches sped and now in whirlpools spun
With noises like the wind and like the sea,
But silent vocally: they hate to speak:
Crowd; Mob; a blur of faces featureless,
Of forms inane; a stranded shoal of folk.

Astounding in the midst of this to meet
Voltaire, the man who worshipped first, who made
Indeed, the only god men reverence now,
Public Opinion. There he sits alert –
A cast of Houdon's smiling philosophe.
Old lion-fox, old tiger-ape – what names
They gave him! – better charactered by one
Who was his heir: 'The amiable and gay'.

So said the pessimist who called life sour
And drank it to the dregs. Enough: Voltaire –
About to speak: hands of a mummy clutch
The fauteuil's arms; he listens to the last
Before reply; one foot advanced; a new
Idea radiant in his wrinkled face.

Lunch in the grill-room for the well-to-do,
The spendthrifts and the connoisseurs of food –
Gourmet, gourmand, bezonian, epicure.
Reserved seats at the window? – Surely; you
And I must have the best place everywhere.
A deluge smudges out the landscape. Watch
The waiters since the scenery's not on view.
A harvest-day with them, our Switzers – knights
Of the napkin! How they balance loaded trays
And though they push each other spill no drop!
And how they glare at lazy lunchers, snatch
Unfinished plates sans 'by your leave', and fling
The next dish down, before the dazzled lout
(The Switzer knows his man) has time to con
The menu, every tip precisely gaged,
Precisely earned, no service thrown away.
Sign of an extra douceur, reprimand
Is welcomed, and the valetudinous
Voluptuary served devoutly: he
With cauteries on his cranium; dyed moustache;
Teeth like a sea-wolf's, each a work of art
Numbered and valued singly; copper skin;
And neither eyelid's pouched: – why he alone
Is worth a half-day's wage! Waiters for him
Are pensioners of indigestion, paid
As secret criminals disburse blackmail,
As Attic gluttons sacrificed a cock
To Æsculapius to propitiate
Hygeia – if the classic flourish serves!

'Grilled soles?' – for us; – Kidneys to follow. – Now,
Your sole, sir; eat it with profound respect.
A little salt with one side; – scarce a pinch!
The other side with lemon; – tenderly!
Don't crush the starred bisection; – count the drops!
Those who begin with lemon miss the true
Aroma: quicken sense with salt, and then
The subtle, poignant, citric savour tunes
The delicate texture of the foam-white fish,
Evolving palatable harmony
That music might by happy chance express.
A crust of bread – (eat slowly: thirty chews,
Gladstonian rumination) – to change the key.
And now the wine – a well-decanted, choice
Château, *bon per*; a decade old; not more;
A velvet claret, piously unchilled.
A boiled potato with the kidney ... No!
Barbarian! Vandal! Sauce? 'Twould ruin all!
The kidney's the potato's sauce. Perpend:
You taste the esoteric attribute
In food; and know that all necessity
Is beauty's essence. Fill your glass: salute
The memory of the happy neolith
Who had the luck to hit on roast and boiled.
Finish the claret. – Now the rain has gone
The clouds are winnowed by the sighing south,
And hidden sunbeams through a silver woof
A warp of pallid bronze in secret ply.

Cigars and coffee in the billiard-room.
No soul here save the marker, eating chops;
The waiter and the damsel at the bar,
In listless talk. A most uncanny thing,
To enter suddenly a desolate cave
Upon the margent of the sounding Mob!
A hundred thousand people, class and mass,
In and about the palace, and not a pair

To play a hundred up! The billiard-room's
The smoking-room; and spacious too, like all
The apartments of the Palace: – why
Unused on holidays? The marker: aged;
Short, broad, but of a presence; reticent
And self-respecting; not at all the type: –
'O well,' says he; 'the business of the room
Fluctuates very little, year in, year out.
My customers are seasons mostly.' One
On the instant enters: a curate, very much
At ease in Zion – and in Sydenham.
He tells two funny stories – not of the room;
And talks about the stage. 'In London now,'
He thinks, 'the play's the thing.' He undertakes
To entertain and not to preach: you see,
It's with the theatre and the music-hall,
Actor and artiste, the parson must compete.
Every bank-holiday and special day
The Crystal Palace sees him. Yes; he feels
His hand's upon the public pulse on such
Occasions. O, a sanguine clergyman!

Heard in the billiard-room the sound of Mob,
Occult and ominous, besets the mind:
Something gigantic, something terrible
Passes without; repasses; lingers; goes;
Returns and on the threshold pants in doubt
Whether to knock and enter, or burst the door
In hope of treasure and a living prey.
The vainest fantasy! Rejoin the crowd:
At once the sound depreciates. Up and down
The north nave and the south nave hastily
Some tens of thousands walk, silent and sad,
A most unhappy people. – Hereabout
Cellini's Perseus ought to be. Not that;
That's stucco – and Canova's: a stupid thing;
The face and posture of a governess –

A nursery governess who's had the nerve
To pick a dead mouse up. It used to stand
Beside the billiard-room, against the wall,
A cast of Benvenuto's masterpiece –
That came out lame, as he foretold, despite
His dinner dishes in the foundry flung.
They shift their sculpture here haphazard. – That?
King Francis – by Clesinger – on a horse.
Absurd: most mounted statues are. – And this?
Verrochio's Coleone. Not absurd:
Grotesque and strong, the battle-harlot rides
A stallion; fore and aft, his saddle, peaked
Like a mitre, grips him as in a vice.
In heavy armour mailed; his lifted helm
Reveals his dreadful look; his brows are drawn;
Four wrinkles deeply trench his muscular face;
His left arm half-extended, and the reins
Held carelessly, although the gesture's tense;
His right hand wields a sword invisible;
Remorseless pressure of his lips protrudes
His mouth; he would decapitate the world.

The light is artificial now; the place
Phantasmal like a beach in hell where souls
Are ground together by an unseen sea.
A dense throng in the central transept, wedged
So tightly they can neither clap nor stamp,
Shouting applause at something, goad themselves
In sheer despair to think it rather fine:
'We came here to enjoy ourselves. Bravo,
Then! Are we not?' Courageous folk beneath
The brows of Michael Angelo's Moses dance
A cakewalk in the dim Renascence Court.
Three people in the silent Reading-room
Regard us darkly as we enter: three
Come in with us, stare vacantly about,
Look from the window and withdraw at once.

A drama; a balloon; a Beauty Show: –
People have seen them doubtless; but none of those
Deluded myriads walking up and down
The north nave and the south have anxiously –
And aimlessly, so silent and so sad.

The day wears; twilight ends; the night comes down.
A ruddy targelike moon in a purple sky,
And the crowd waiting on the fireworks. Come:
Enough of Mob for one while. This way out –
Past Linacre and Chatham, the second Charles,
Venus and Victory – and Sir William Jones
In placid contemplation of a State! –
Down the long corridor to the district train.

[1909]

FRANCIS THOMPSON
1859–1907

FRANCIS THOMPSON was born at Preston, the son of a
doctor. He was addicted to laudanum and, despite several
attempts to control and organize his addiction, died with his
full potentialities unrealized. His poetry enjoyed a fashionable
reputation, and was then brutally denigrated. *To The Dead
Cardinal* is free from his usual prolix verbiage and rich in
his grotesque metaphysical wit.

To The Dead Cardinal of Westminster

I will not perturbate
Thy Paradisal state
    With praise
    Of thy dead days;

To the new-heavened say, –
'Spirit, thou wert fine clay':
    This do,
    Thy praise who knew.

Therefore my spirit clings
Heaven's porter by the wings,
    And holds
    Its gated golds

Apart, with thee to press
A private business; –
    Whence,
    Deign me audience.

Anchorite, who didst dwell
With all the world for cell,
    My soul
    Round me doth roll

A sequestration bare.
Too far alike we were,
  Too far
  Dissimilar.

For its burning fruitage I
Do climb the tree o' the sky;
  Do prize
  Some human eyes.

You smelt the Heaven-blossoms,
And all the sweet embosoms
  The dear
  Uranian year.

Those Eyes my weak gaze shuns,
Which to the suns are Suns,
  Did
  Not affray your lid.

The carpet was let down
(With golden moultings strown)
  For you
  Of the angels' blue.

But I, ex-Paradised,
The shoulder of your Christ
  Find high
  To lean thereby.

So flaps my helpless sail,
Bellying with neither gale,
  Of Heaven
  Nor Orcus even.

Life is a coquetry
Of Death, which wearies me,
    Too sure
  Of the amour;

A tiring-room where I
Death's divers garments try,
    Till fit
  Some fashion sit.

It seemeth me too much
I do rehearse for such
    A mean
  And single scene.

The sandy glass hence bear —
Antique remembrancer;
    My veins
  Do spare its pains.

With secret sympathy
My thoughts repeat in me
    Infirm
  The turn o' the worm

Beneath my appointed sod;
The grave is in my blood;
    I shake
  To winds that take

Its grasses by the top;
The rains thereon that drop
    Perturb
  With drip acerb

My subtly answering soul;
The feet across its knoll
       Do jar
     Me from afar.

As sap foretastes the spring;
As Earth ere blossoming
       Thrills
     With far daffodils,

And feels her breast turn sweet
With the unconceivèd wheat;
       So doth
     My flesh foreloathe

The abhorrèd spring of Dis,
With seething presciences
       Affirm
     The preparate worm.

I have no thought that I,
When at the last I die,
       Shall reach
     To gain your speech.

But you, should that be so,
May very well, I know,
       May well
     To me in hell

With recognising eyes
Look from your Paradise —
     'God bless
     Thy hopelessness!'

Call, holy soul, O call
The hosts angelical,
      And say, –
   'See, far away

'Lies one I saw on earth;
One stricken from his birth
      With curse
   Of destinate verse.

'What place doth He ye serve
For such sad spirit reserve, –
      Given,
   In dark lieu of Heaven,

'The impitiable Dæmon,
Beauty, to adore and dream on,
      To be
   Perpetually

'Hers, but she never his?
He reapeth miseries;
      Foreknows
   His wages woes;

'He lives detachèd days;
He serveth not for praise;
      For gold
   He is not sold;

'Deaf is he to world's tongue;
He scorned for his song
      The loud
   Shouts of the crowd;

'He asketh not world's eyes;
Not to world's ears he cries;
    Saith, – "These
  Shut, if ye please";

'He measureth world's pleasure,
World's ease, as Saints might measure;
    For hire
  Just love entire

'He asks, not grudging pain;
And knows his asking vain,
    And cries –
  "Love! Love!" and dies,

'In guerdon of long duty,
Unowned by Love or Beauty;
    And goes –
  Tell, tell, who knows!

'Aliens from Heaven's worth,
Fine beasts who nose i' the earth,
    Do there
  Reward prepare.

'But are *his* great desires
Food but for nether fires?
    Ah me,
  A mystery!

'Can it be his alone,
To find, when all is known,
    That what
  He solely sought

'Is lost, and thereto lost
All that its seeking cost?
    That he
    Must finally,

'Through sacrificial tears,
And anchoretic years,
    Tryst
    With the sensualist?'

So ask; and if they tell
The secret terrible,
    Good friend,
    I pray thee send

Some high gold embassage
To teach my unripe age.
    Tell!
    Lest my feet walk hell.

[1893]

ALFRED EDWARD HOUSMAN
1859–1936

A. E. HOUSMAN was born in Worcestershire and educated at Oxford, where he failed Greats. He was an intellectual T. E. Lawrence, lacerating his mind and his emotions in the interests of objective standards, both in scholarship and in poetry. While preparing his great edition of Manilius, a Latin poet of smaller gifts than himself, he compiled an arsenal of prose invective to be deployed against potential enemies: the cold savagery of this prose reveals a rich energy he never fully released in his verse, which tends to monotony of tone, shallowness of ideas (compared, for example, with Hardy's) and mannerism of diction. Nevertheless, this verse tends to make an immediate impression and its clarity, rhythmical tightness and epigrammatic stoicism remain in a class by themselves.

'Her strong enchantments failing'

Her strong enchantments failing,
   Her towers of fear in wreck,
Her limbecks dried of poisons
   And the knife at her neck,

The Queen of air and darkness
   Begins to shrill and cry,
'O young man, O my slayer,
   To-morrow you shall die.'

O Queen of air and darkness,
   I think 'tis truth you say,
And I shall die to-morrow;
   But you will die to-day.

[1922]

'In Midnights of November'

In midnights of November,
    When Dead Man's Fair is nigh,
And danger in the valley,
    And anger in the sky,

Around the huddling homesteads
    The leafless timber roars,
And the dead call the dying
    And finger at the doors.

Oh, yonder faltering fingers
    Are hands I used to hold;
Their false companion drowses
    And leaves them in the cold.

Oh, to the bed of ocean,
    To Africk and to Ind,
I will arise and follow
    Along the rainy wind.

The night goes out and under
    With all its train forlorn;
Hues in the east assemble
    And cocks crow up the morn.

The living are the living
    And dead the dead will stay,
And I will sort with comrades
    That face the beam of day.

[1922]

'The fairies break their dances'

The fairies break their dances
    And leave the printed lawn,
And up from India glances
    The silver sail of dawn.

The candles burn their sockets,
    The blinds let through the day,
The young man feels his pockets
    And wonders what's to pay.

[1922]

Sinner's Rue

I walked alone and thinking,
    And faint the nightwind blew
And stirred on mounds at crossways
    The flower of sinner's rue.

Where the roads part they bury
    Him that his own hand slays,
And so the weed of sorrow
    Springs at the four cross ways.

By night I plucked it hueless,
    When morning broke 'twas blue:
Blue at my breast I fastened
    The flower of sinner's rue.

It seemed a herb of healing,
    A balsam and a sign,
Flower of a heart whose trouble
    Must have been worse than mine.

Dead clay that did me kindness,
 I can do none to you,
But only wear for breastknot
 The flower of sinner's rue.

[1922]

'The world goes none the lamer'

The world goes none the lamer,
 For ought that I can see,
Because this cursed trouble
 Has struck my days and me.

The stars of heaven are steady,
 The founded hills remain,
Though I to earth and darkness
 Return in blood and pain.

Farewell to all belongings
 I won or bought or stole;
Farewell, my lusty carcase,
 Farewell, my aery soul.

Oh worse remains for others,
 And worse to fear had I
Than here at four-and-twenty
 To lay me down and die.

[1936]

'Good creatures, do you love your lives'

Good creatures, do you love your lives
 And have you ears for sense?
Here is a knife like other knives,
 That cost me eighteen pence.

I need but stick it in my heart
  And down will come the sky,
And earth's foundations will depart
  And all you folk will die.

[1936]

'Because I liked you better'

Because I liked you better
  Than suits a man to say,
It irked you, and I promised
  To throw the thought away.

To put the world between us
  We parted, stiff and dry;
'Good-bye', said you, 'forget me.'
  'I will, no fear', said I.

If here, where clover whitens
  The dead man's knoll, you pass,
And no tall flower to meet you
  Starts in the trefoiled grass,

Halt by the headstone naming
  The heart no longer stirred,
And say the lad that loved you
  Was one that kept his word.

[1936]

'My dreams are of a field afar'

My dreams are of a field afar
  And blood and smoke and shot.
There in their graves my comrades are,
  In my grave I am not.

I too was taught the trade of man
    And spelt the lesson plain;
But they, when I forgot and ran,
    Remembered and remain.

[1936]

SIR HENRY NEWBOLT
1862–1938

HENRY JOHN NEWBOLT was born in Staffordshire and educated at Clifton. His poetry expresses the late nineteenth century public-school code with a special intensity. Metrical-skill combined with a subtle care for off-beat rhythm (as in *Messmates*, for example) sets his ballads above those by earlier militarist poets such as Aytoun and Doyle. He has one of the most vivid and resonant half-lines produced by the Imperialist tradition in the words 'the Gatling's jammed', with its hint of the kind of loyalty in the face of bungling which led to the charge of the Light Brigade.

Gillespie

Riding at dawn, riding alone,
   Gillespie left the town behind;
Before he turned by the westward road
   A horseman crossed him, staggering blind.

'The Devil's abroad in false Vellore,
   The Devil that stabs by night,' he said,
'Women and children, rank and file,
   Dying and dead, dying and dead.'

Without a word, without a groan,
   Sudden and swift Gillespie turned,
The blood roared in his ears like fire,
   Like fire the road beneath him burned.

He thundered back to Arcot gate,
   He thundered up through Arcot town,
Before he thought a second thought
   In the barrack yard he lighted down.

366

'Trumpeter, sound for the Light Dragoons,
　　Sound to saddle and spur,' he said;
'He that is ready may ride with me,
　　And he that can may ride ahead.'

Fierce and fain, fierce and fain,
　　Behind him went the troopers grim.
They rode as ride the Light Dragoons,
　　But never a man could ride with him.

Their rowels ripped their horses' sides,
　　Their hearts were red with a deeper goad;
But ever alone before them all
　　Gillespie rode, Gillespie rode.

Alone he came to false Vellore,
　　The walls were lined, the gates were barred;
Alone he walked where the bullets bit,
　　And called above to the Sergeant's guard.

'Sergeant, Sergeant, over the gate,
　　Where are your officers all?' he said;
Heavily came the Sergeant's voice,
　　'There are two living, and forty dead.'

'A rope, a rope,' Gillespie cried:
　　They bound their belts to serve his need;
There was not a rebel behind the wall
　　But laid his barrel and drew his bead.

There was not a rebel among them all
　　But pulled his trigger and cursed his aim,
For lightly swung and rightly swung
　　Over the gate Gillespie came.

He dressed the line, he led the charge,
    They swept the wall like a stream in spate,
And roaring over the roar they heard
    The galloper guns that burst the gate.

Fierce and fain, fierce and fain,
    The troopers rode the reeking flight:
The very stones remember still
    The end of them that stab by night.

They've kept the tale a hundred years,
    They'll keep the tale a hundred more:
Riding at dawn, riding alone,
    Gillespie came to false Vellore.

[1898]

Messmates

He gave us all a good-bye cheerily
    At the first dawn of day;
We dropped him down the side full drearily
    When the light died away.
It's a dead, dark watch that he's a-keeping there,
And a long, long night that lags a-creeping there,
Where the Trades and the tides roll over him
    And the great ships go by.

He's there alone with green seas rocking him
    For a thousand miles round;
He's there alone with dumb things mocking him,
    And we're homeward bound.
It's a long, lone watch that he's a-keeping there,
And a dead cold night that lags a-creeping there,
While the months and the years roll over him
    And the great ships go by.

I wonder if the tramps come near enough
  As they thrash to and fro,
And the battleships' bells ring clear enough
  To be heard down below;
If through all the lone watch that he's a-keeping there,
And the long, cold night that lags a-creeping there,
The voices of the sailor-men shall comfort him
  When the great ships go by.

[1898]

RUDYARD KIPLING
1865–1936

RUDYARD KIPLING was born in Bombay. His hard-hitting satires on life in the Indian Civil Service brought him precocious fame at the age of twenty-one. Only four years later he was publishing his best poems – including *Tommy* and *Danny Deever* – in London magazines. By the time of the Boer War he was the most widely read living English writer. If we are to believe Harold Macmillan, there were houses in Edwardian England where the only books known were Kipling and the Bible. Unfortunately, the award of the Nobel Prize in 1907, at the early age of forty-two, virtually marks the end of Kipling's career as a poet. Unlike his contemporary Yeats he had neither the inclination nor the flexibility of mind to respond easily to the fructifying influences of the younger generation. Fame isolated him into politics, and when he died in 1936 there was no literary figure to walk beside his coffin into the Abbey. The enduring merits of Kipling's early verse lie in its cunning synthesis of widely disparate influences: it merges the metrical speed and variety of Swinburne with the dialect humour of Barnes and the robust nationalist fervour of Macaulay. Its defects lie in its absence of scope for development, either by Kipling or others. The later poetry (with the exception of *Gertrude's Prayer*) recedes into the vernacular of nineteenth century metaphysics, shallow and unreal despite its obvious reflection of tragic physical and emotional stress.

The Story of Uriah

'Now there were two men in one city; the one rich and the other poor.'

> Jack Barrett went to Quetta
>   Because they told him to.
> He left his wife at Simla
>   On three-fourths his monthly screw
> Jack Barrett died at Quetta
>   Ere the next month's pay he drew.

Jack Barrett went to Quetta,
 He didn't understand
The reason of his transfer
 From the pleasant mountain-land:
The season was September,
 And it killed him out of hand.

Jack Barrett went to Quetta
 And there gave up the ghost:
Attempting two men's duty
 In that very healthy post;
And Mrs Barrett mourned for him
 Five lively months at most.

Jack Barrett's bones at Quetta
 Enjoy profound repose;
But I shouldn't be astonished
 If *now* his spirit knows
The reason of his transfer
 From the Himalayan snows.

And, when the Last Great Bugle Call
 Adown the Hurnai throbs,
When the last grim joke is entered
 In the big black Book of Jobs,
And Quetta graveyards give again
 Their victims to the air,
I shouldn't like to be the man
 Who sent Jack Barrett there.

         [1886]

The Galley-slave

Oh gallant was our galley from her carven steering-wheel
To her figurehead of silver and her beak of hammered steel;
The leg-bar chafed the ankle and we gasped for cooler air,
But no galley on the water with our galley could compare!

Our bulkheads bulged with cotton and our masts were
    stepped in gold –
We ran a mighty merchandise of niggers in the hold;
The white foam spun behind us, and the black shark swam
    below,
As we gripped the kicking sweep-head and we made that
    galley go.

It was merry in the galley, for we revelled now and then –
If they wore us down like cattle, faith, we fought and loved
    like men!
As we snatched her through the water, so we snatched a
    minute's bliss,
And the mutter of the dying never spoiled the lovers' kiss.

Our women and our children toiled beside us in the dark –
They died, we filed their fetters, and we heaved them to the
    shark –
We heaved them to the fishes, but so fast the galley sped
We had only time to envy, for we could not mourn our dead.

Bear witness, once my comrades, what a hard-bit gang
    were we –
The servants of the sweep-head but the masters of the sea!
By the hands that drove her forward as she plunged and
    yawed and sheered,
Woman, Man, or God or Devil, was there anything we
    feared?

Was it storm? Our fathers faced it and a wilder never blew;
Earth that waited for the wreckage watched the galley
    struggle through.
Burning noon or choking midnight, Sickness, Sorrow, Part-
    ing, Death?
Nay, our very babes would mock you had they time for idle
    breath.

But to-day I leave the galley and another takes my place;
There's my name upon the deck-beam – let it stand a little
  space.
I am free – to watch my messmates beating out to open
  main
Free of all that Life can offer – save to handle sweep again.

By the brand upon my shoulder, by the gall of clinging
  steel,
By the welt the whips have left me, by the scars that never
  heal;
By eyes grown old with staring through the sun-wash on
  the brine;
I am paid in full for service – would that service still were
  mine!

Yet they talk of times and seasons and of woe the years
  bring forth,
Of our galley swamped and shattered in the rollers of the
  North.
When the niggers break the hatches and the decks are gay
  with gore,
And a craven-hearted pilot crams her crashing on the shore.

She will need no half-mast signal, minute-gun, or rocket-
  flare,
When the cry for help goes seaward, she will find her
  servants there.
Battered chain-gangs of the orlop, grizzled drafts of years
  gone by,
To the bench that broke their manhood, they shall lash
  themselves and die.

Hale and crippled, young and aged, paid, deserted, shipped
  away –
Palace, cot, and lazaretto shall make up the tale that day,

When the skies are black above them, and the decks ablaze
    beneath,
And the top-men clear the raffle with their clasp-knives in
    their teeth.

It may be that Fate will give me life and leave to row once
    more –
Set some strong man free for fighting as I take awhile his
    oar.
But to-day I leave the galley. Shall I curse her service
    then?
God be thanked – whate'er comes after, I have lived and
    toiled with Men!

[1886]

Danny Deever

'What are the bugles blowin' for?' said Files-on-Parade.
'To turn you out, to turn you out,' the Colour Sergeant
    said.
'What makes you look so white, so white?' said Files-on-
    Parade.
'I'm dreadin' what I've got to watch,' the Colour-Sergeant
    said.
    For they're hangin' Danny Deever, you can hear the
        Dead March play,
    The regiment's in 'ollow square – they're hangin' him
        to-day;
    They've taken of his buttons off an' cut his stripes away,
    An' they're hangin' Danny Deever in the mornin'.

'What makes the rear-rank breathe so 'ard?' said Files-on-
    Parade.
'It's bitter cold, it's bitter cold,' the Colour-Sergeant said.
'What makes that front-rank man fall down?' says Files-
    on-Parade.

'A touch o' sun, a touch o' sun,' the Colour-Sergeant said.
  They are hangin' Danny Deever, they are marchin' of
    'im round,
  They 'ave 'alted Danny Deever by 'is coffin on the
    ground;
  An' 'e'll swing in 'arf a minute for a sneakin' shootin'
    hound –
  O they're hangin' Danny Deever in the mornin'!

''Is cot was right-'and cot to mine,' said Files-on-Parade.
''E's sleepin' out an' far to-night,' the Colour-Sergeant
  said.
'I've drunk 'is beer a score o' times,' said Files-on-Parade.
''E's drinkin' bitter beer alone,' the Colour Sergeant said.
  They are hangin' Danny Deever, you must mark 'im to
    'is place,
  For 'e shot a comrade sleepin' – you must look 'im in the
    face;
  Nine 'undred of 'is county an' the regiment's disgrace,
  While they're hangin' Danny Deever in the mornin'.

'What's that so black agin the sun?' said Files-on-Parade.
'It's Danny fightin' 'ard for life,' the Colour-Sergeant said.
'What's that that whimpers over'ead?' said Files-on-Parade.
'It's Danny's soul that's passin' now,' the Colour-Sergeant
  said.
  For they're done with Danny Deever, you can 'ear the
    quickstep play,
  The regiment's in column, an' they're marchin' us away;
  Ho! the young recruits are shakin', an' they'll want their
    beer to-day,
  After hangin' Danny Deever in the mornin'.

[1892]

375

Tommy

I went into a public-'ouse to get a pint o' beer,
The publican 'e up an' sez, 'We serve no red-coats here.'
The girls be'ind the bar they laughed an' giggled fit to die,
I outs into the street again, an' to myself sez I:
    O it's Tommy this, an' Tommy that, an' 'Tommy, go
      away';
    But it's 'Thank you, Mister Atkins,' when the band
      begins to play,
    The band begins to play, my boys, the band begins to
      play,
    O it's 'Thank you, Mister Atkins,' when the band begins
      to play.

I went into a theatre as sober as could be,
They gave a drunk civilian room, but 'adn't none for me;
They sent me to the gallery or round the music-'alls,
But when it comes to fightin', Lord! they'll shove me in the
    stalls!
    For it's Tommy this, an' Tommy that, an' 'Tommy,
      wait outside';
    But it's 'Special train for Atkins' when the trooper's on
      the tide,
    The troopship's on the tide, my boys, the troopship's on
      the tide,
    O it's 'Special train for Atkins' when the trooper's on the
      tide.

Yes, makin' mock o' uniforms that guard you while you
    sleep
Is cheaper than them uniforms, an' they're starvation
    cheap;
An' hustlin' drunken soldiers when they're goin' large a bit
Is five times better business than paradin' in full kit.

Then it's Tommy this, an' Tommy that, an' 'Tommy,
    'ow's yer soul?'
But it's 'Thin red line of 'eroes' when the drums begin
    to roll,
The drums begin to roll, my boys, the drums begin to
    roll,
O it's 'Thin red line of 'eroes' when the drums begin to
    roll.

We aren't no thin red 'eroes, nor we aren't no blackguards
    too,
But single men in barricks, most remarkable like you;
An' if sometimes our conduck isn't all your fancy paints,
Why, single men in barricks don't grow into plaster saints;
    While it's Tommy this, an' Tommy that, an' 'Tommy,
        fall be'ind,'
    But it's 'Please to walk in front, sir,' when there's
        trouble in the wind,
    There's trouble in the wind, my boys, there's trouble in
        the wind,
    O it's 'Please to walk in front, sir,' when there's trouble
        in the wind.

You talk o' better food for us, an' schools, an' fires, an' all:
We'll wait for extry rations if you treat us rational.
Don't mess about the cook-room slops, but prove it to our
    face
The Widow's Uniform is not the soldier-man's disgrace.
    For it's Tommy this, an' Tommy that, an' 'Chuck him
        out, the brute!'
    But it's 'Saviour of 'is country' when the guns begin to
        shoot;
    An' it's Tommy this, an' Tommy that, an' anything you
        please;
    An' Tommy ain't a bloomin' fool – you bet that Tommy
        sees!

                          [1892]

Ford o' Kabul river

Kabul town's by Kabul river —
  Blow the bugle, draw the sword —
There I lef my mate for ever,
    Wet an' drippin' by the ford.
      Ford, ford, ford o' Kabul river,
        Ford o' Kabul river in the dark!
      There's the river up and brimmin', an' there's 'arf a
        squadron swimmin'
        'Cross the ford o' Kabul river in the dark.

Kabul town 's a blasted place —
  Blow the bugle, draw the sword —
'Strewth I sha'n't forget 'is face
    Wet an' drippin' by the ford!
      Ford, ford, ford o' Kabul river,
        Ford o' Kabul river in the dark!
      Keep the crossing-stakes beside you, an' they will
        surely guide you
        'Cross the ford of Kabul river in the dark.

Kabul town is sun and dust —
  Blow the bugle, draw the sword —
I'd ha' sooner drownded fust
    'Stead of 'im beside the ford.
      Ford, ford, ford o' Kabul river,
        Ford o' Kabul river in the dark!
      You can 'ear the 'orses threshin', you can 'ear the men
        a-splashin',
        'Cross the ford o' Kabul river in the dark.

Kabul town was ours to take –
  Blow the bugle, draw the sword –
I'd ha' left it for 'is sake –
  'Im that left me by the ford.
    Ford, ford, ford o' Kabul river,
      Ford o' Kabul river in the dark!
    It's none so bloomin' dry there; ain't you never
      comin' nigh there,
      'Cross the ford o' Kabul river in the dark?

Kabul town'll go to hell –
  Blow the bugle, draw the sword –
'Fore I see him 'live an' well –
  'Im the best beside the ford.
    Ford, ford, ford, o' Kabul river,
      Ford 'o Kabul river in the dark!
    Gawd 'elp 'em if they blunder, for their boots 'll pull
      'em under,
      By the ford o' Kabul river in the dark.

Turn your 'orse from Kabul town –
  Blow the bugle, draw the sword –
'Im an' 'arf my troop is down,
  Down, an' drowned by the ford.
    Ford, ford, ford o' Kabul river,
      Ford o' Kabul river in the dark!
    There's the river low an' fallin', but it ain't no use o'
      callin'
      'Cross the ford o' Kabul river in the dark.

                  [1892]

The sacrifice of Er-Heb

Er-Heb beyond the Hills of Ao-Safai
Bears witness to the truth, and Ao-Safai
Hath told the men of Gorukh. Thence the tale
Comes westward o'er the peaks to India.

The story of Bisesa, Armod's child, –
A maiden plighted to the Chief in War,
The Man of Sixty Spears, who held the Pass
That leads to Thibet, but to-day is gone
To seek his comfort of the God called Budh
The Silent – showing how the Sickness ceased
Because of her who died to save the tribe.

Taman is One and greater than us all,
Taman is One and greater than all Gods:
Taman is Two in One and rides the sky,
Curved like a stallion's croup, from dusk to dawn,
And drums upon it with his heels, whereby
Is bred the neighing thunder in the hills.

This is Taman, the God of all Er-Heb,
Who was before all Gods, and made all Gods,
And presently will break the Gods he made,
And step upon the Earth to govern men
Who give him milk-dry ewes and cheat his Priests,
Or leave his shrine unlighted – as Er-Heb
Left it unlighted and forgot Taman,
When all the Valley followed after Kysh
And Yabosh, little Gods, but very wise,
And from the sky Taman beheld their sin.

He sent the Sickness out upon the hills
The Red Horse Sickness with the iron hooves.
To turn the Valley to Taman again.

And the Red Horse snuffed thrice into the wind,
The naked wind that had no fear of him;
And the Red Horse stamped thrice upon the snow,
The naked snow that had no fear of him;
And the Red Horse went out across the rocks
The ringing rocks that had no fear of him;
And downward, where the lean birch meets the snow,
And downward, where the grey pine meets the birch,
And downward, where the dwarf oak meets the pine,
Till at his feet our cup-like pastures lay.

That night, the slow mists of the evening dropped,
Dropped as a cloth upon a dead man's face,
And weltered in the valley, bluish-white
Like water very silent – spread abroad,
Like water very silent, from the Shrine
Unlighted of Taman to where the stream
Is dammed to fill our cattle-troughs – sent up
White waves that rocked and heaved and then were still,
Till all the Valley glittered like a marsh,
Beneath the moonlight, filled with sluggish mist
Knee-deep, so that men waded as they walked.

That night, the Red Horse grazed above the Dam,
Beyond the cattle-troughs. Men heard him feed,
And those that heard him sickened where they lay.

Thus came the sickness to Er-Heb, and slew
Ten men, strong men, and of the women four;
And the Red Horse went hillward with the dawn,
But near the cattle-troughs his hoof-prints lay.

That night, the slow mists of the evening dropped,
Dropped as a cloth upon the dead, but rose
A little higher, to a young girl's height;
Till all the valley glittered like a lake,
Beneath the moonlight, filled with sluggish mist.

That night, the Red Horse grazed beyond the Dam
A stone's-throw from the troughs. Men heard him feed,
And those that heard him sickened where they lay.
Thus came the sickness to Er-Heb, and slew
Of men a score, and of the women eight,
And of the children two.

                        Because the road
To Gorukh was a road of enemies,
And Ao-Safai was blocked with early snow,
We could not flee from out the Valley. Death
Smote at us in a slaughter-pen, and Kysh
Was mute as Yabosh, though the goats were slain;
And the Red Horse grazed nightly by the stream,
And later, outward, towards the Unlighted Shrine,
And those that heard him sickened where they lay.

Then said Bisesa to the Priests at dusk,
When the white mist rose up breast-high, and choked
The voices in the houses of the dead: –
'Yabosh and Kysh avail not. If the Horse
'Reach the Unlighted Shrine we surely die.
'Ye have forgotten of all Gods the Chief,
'Taman!' Here rolled the thunder through the Hill
And Yabosh shook upon his pedestal.
'Ye have forgotten of all Gods the chief
'Too long.' And all were dumb save one, who cried
On Yabosh with the Sapphire 'twixt His knees,
But found no answer in the smoky roof,
And, being smitten of the sickness, died
Before the altar of the Sapphire Shrine.

Then said Bisesa: – 'I am near to Death,
'And have the Wisdom of the Grave for gift
'To bear me on the path my feet must tread.
'If there be wealth on earth, then I am rich,
'For Armod is the first of all Er-Heb;
'If there be beauty on the earth,' – her eyes

Dropped for a moment to the temple floor, –
'Ye know that I am fair. If there be Love,
'Ye know that love is mine.' The Chief in War,
The Man of Sixty Spears, broke from the press,
And would have clasped her, but the Priests withstood,
Saying: – 'She has a message from Taman.'

Then said Bisesa: – 'By my wealth and love
'And beauty, I am chosen of the God
'Taman.' Here rolled the thunder through the Hills
And Kysh fell forward on the Mound of Skulls.

In darkness, and before our priests, the maid
Between the altars cast her bracelets down,
Therewith the heavy earrings Armod made,
When he was young, out of the water-gold
Of Gorukh – threw the breast-plate thick with jade
Upon the turquoise anklets – put aside
The bands of silver on her brow and neck;
And as the trinkets tinkled on the stones,
The thunder of Taman lowed like a bull.

Then said Bisesa, stretching out her hands,
As one in darkness fearing Devils: – 'Help!
'O Priests, I am a woman very weak.
'And who am I to know the will of Gods?
'Taman hath called me – whither shall I go?'
The Chief in War, the Man of Sixty Spears,
Howled in his torment, fettered by the Priests,
But dared not come to her to drag her forth,
And dared not lift his spear against the Priests.
Then all men wept.
              There was a Priest of Kysh
Bent with a hundred winters, hairless, blind,
And taloned as the great Snow-Eagle is.
His seat was nearest to the altar-fires,
And he was counted dumb among the Priests.
But, whether Kysh decreed, or from Taman

The impotent tongue found utterance we know
As little as the bats beneath the eaves.
He cried so that they heard who stood without: –
'To the Unlighted Shrine!' and crept aside
Into the shadow of his fallen God
And whimpered, and Bisesa went her way.

That night, the slow mists of the evening dropped,
Dropped as a cloth upon the dead, and rose
Above the roofs, and by the Unlighted Shrine
Lay as the slimy water of the troughs
When murrain thins the cattle of Er-Heb:
And through the mist men heard the Red Horse feed.

In Armod's house they burned Bisesa's dower,
And killed her black bull Tor, and broke her wheel,
And loosed her hair, as for the marriage-feast,
With cries more loud than mourning for the dead.

Across the fields, from Armod's dwelling-place,
We heard Bisesa weeping where she passed
To seek the Unlighted Shrine; the Red Horse neighed
And followed her, and on the river-mint
His hooves struck dead and heavy in our ears.

Out of the mists of evening, as the star
Of Ao-Safai climbs through the black snow-blur
To show the Pass is clear, Bisesa stepped
Upon the great grey slope of mortised stone,
The Causeway of Taman. The Red Horse neighed
Behind her to the Unlighted Shrine – then fled
North to the Mountain where his stable lies.
They know who dared the anger of Taman,
And watched that night above the clinging mists,
Far up the hill, Bisesa's passing in.

She set her hand upon the carven door,
Fouled by a myriad bats, and black with time,
Whereon is graved the Glory of Taman
In letters older than the Ao-Safai;
And twice she turned aside and twice she wept,
Cast down upon the threshold, clamouring
For him she loved – the Man of Sixty Spears,
And for her father, – and the black bull Tor,
Hers and her pride. Yea, twice she turned away
Before the awful darkness of the door,
And the great horror of the Wall of Man
Where Man is made the plaything of Taman,
An Eyeless Face that waits above and laughs.

But the third time she cried and put her palms
Against the hewn stone leaves, and prayed Taman
To spare Er-Heb and take her life for price.

They know who watched, the doors were rent apart
And closed upon Bisesa, and the rain
Broke like a flood across the Valley, washed
The mist away; but louder than the rain
The thunder of Taman filled men with fear.

Some say that from the Unlighted Shrine she cried
For succour, very pitifully, thrice,
And others that she sang and had no fear.
And some that there was neither song nor cry,
But only thunder and the lashing rain.

Howbeit, in the morning men rose up,
Perplexed with horror, crowding to the Shrine.
And when Er-Heb was gathered at the doors
The Priests made lamentation and passed in
To a strange Temple and a God they feared
But knew not.

From the crevices the grass
Had thrust the altar-slabs apart, the walls
Were grey with stains unclean, the roof-beams swelled
With many-coloured growth of rottenness,
And lichen veiled the Image of Taman
In leprosy. The Basin of the Blood
Above the altar held the morning sun:
A winking ruby on its heart: below,
Face hid in hands, the maid Bisesa lay.

Er-Heb beyond the Hills of Ao-Safai
Bears witness to the truth, and Ao-Safai
Hath told the men of Gorukh. Thence the tale
Comes westward o'er the peaks to India.

[1892]

White Horses

Where run your colts at pasture?
Where hide your mares to breed?
'Mid bergs about the Ice-cap
Or wove Sargasso weed;
By chartless reef and channel,
Or crafty coastwise bars,
But most the ocean-meadows
All purple to the stars!

Who holds the rein upon you?
The latest gale let free.
What meat is in your mangers?
The glut of all the sea.
'Twixt tide and tide's returning
Great store of newly dead, –
The bones of those that faced us,
And the hearts of those that fled.

Afar, off-shore and single,
   Some stallion, rearing swift,
Neighs hungry for new fodder,
   And calls us to the drift:
Then down the cloven ridges –
   A million hooves unshod –
Break forth the mad White Horses
   To seek their meat from God!

Girth-deep in hissing water
   Our furious vanguard strains –
Through mist of mighty tramplings
   Roll up the fore-blown manes –
A hundred leagues to leeward,
   Ere yet the deep is stirred,
The groaning rollers carry
   The coming of the herd!

Whose hand may grip your nostrils –
   Your forelock who may hold?
E'en they that use the broads with us –
   The riders bred and bold,
That spy upon our matings,
   That rope us where we run –
They know the strong White Horses
   From father unto son.

We breathe about their cradles,
   We race their babes ashore,
We snuff against their thresholds,
   We nuzzle at their door;
By day with stamping squadrons,
   By night in whinnying droves,
Creep up the wise White Horses,
   To call them from their loves.

And come they for your calling?
  No wit of man may save.
They hear the loosed White Horses
  Above their fathers' grave;
And, kin to those we crippled,
  And, sons of those we slew,
Spur down the wild white riders
  To school the herds anew.

What service have ye paid them,
  O jealous steeds and strong?
Save we that throw their weaklings,
  Is none dare work them wrong;
While thick around the homestead
  Our snow-backed leaders graze –
A guard behind their plunder,
  And a veil before their ways.

With march and countermarchings –
  With weight of wheeling hosts –
Stray mob or bands embattled –
  We ring the chosen coasts:
And, careless of our clamour
  That bids the stranger fly,
At peace within our pickets
  The wild white riders lie.

Trust ye the curdled hollows –
  Trust ye the neighing wind –
Trust ye the moaning groundswell –
  Our herds are close behind!

To bray your foeman's armies –
To chill and snap his sword –
Trust ye the wild White Horses,
The Horses of the Lord!

[1897]

WILLIAM BUTLER YEATS
1865–1939

WILLIAM BUTLER YEATS was born at Sandymount in
Dublin and died in the south of France. Although his
reputation as a minor poet was made in the 1890s, Yeats
only developed his full powers after 1908. In a sense the
grand rhetoric of his later verse can be seen as deriving from
a merger of elements in Synge and Symons but the seeds of
his later style are already present in poems of his own like
The Sorrow of Love. Yeats is represented here only by poems
written before 1900.

The Sorrow of Love

The brawling of a sparrow in the eaves,
The brilliant moon and all the milky sky,
And all that famous harmony of leaves,
Had blotted out man's image and his cry.

A girl arose that had red mournful lips
And seemed the greatness of the world in tears,
Doomed like Odysseus and the labouring ships
And proud as Priam murdered with his peers;

Arose, and on the instant clamorous eaves,
A climbing moon upon an empty sky,
And all that lamentation of the leaves,
Could but compose man's image and his cry.

[1893]

Who goes with Fergus?

Who will go drive with Fergus now,
And pierce the deep wood's woven shade,
And dance upon the level shore?

Young man, lift up your russet brow,
And lift your tender eyelids, maid,
And brood on hopes and fear no more.

And no more turn aside and brood
Upon love's bitter mystery;
For Fergus rules the brazen cars,
And rules the shadows of the wood,
And the white breast of the dim sea
And all dishevelled wandering stars.

[1893]

The Lamentation of the Old Pensioner

Although I shelter from the rain
Under a broken tree,
My chair was nearest to the fire
In every company
That talked of love or politics,
Ere Time transfigured me.

Though lads are making pikes again
For some conspiracy,
And crazy rascals rage their fill
At human tyranny,
My contemplations are of Time
That has transfigured me.

There's not a woman turns her face
Upon a broken tree,
And yet the beauties that I loved
Are in my memory;
I spit into the face of Time
That has transfigured me.

[1893]

ARTHUR SYMONS

1865–1945

ARTHUR WILLIAM SYMONS was born in Milford Haven. He suffered a nervous breakdown in 1908 which destroyed his already failing power to produce good verse. Nevertheless, his early work is more various than that of any other nineties poet, and at times piercingly morbid in a tone missed by Johnson and Dowson. Symons is a figure central to the understanding of the English decadence, which he worked hard to mould in his own image. His presentation of love as a disease gives his erotic verse a uniquely French note.

Scènes de la Vie de Bohème

EPISODE OF A NIGHT OF MAY

The coloured lanterns lit the trees, the grass,
The little tables underneath the trees,
And the rays dappled like a delicate breeze
    Each wine-illumined glass.

The pink light flickered, and a shadow ran
Along the ground as couples came and went;
The waltzing fiddles sounded from the tent,
    And *Giroflée* began.

They sauntered arm in arm, these two; the smiles
Grew chilly, as the best spring evenings do.
The words were warmer, but the words came few,
    And pauses fell at whiles.

But she yawned prettily. 'Come then,' said he.
He found a chair, Veuve Clicquot, some cigars.
They emptied glasses and admired the stars,
    The lanterns, night, the sea,

Nature, the newest opera, the dog
(So clever) who could shoulder arms and dance;
He mentioned Alphonse Daudet's last romance,
    Last Sunday's river-fog,

Love, Immortality; the talk ran down
To these mere lees: they wearied each of each,
And tortured ennui into hollow speech,
    And yawned, to hide a frown.

She jarred his nerves; he bored her – and so soon.
Both were polite, and neither cared to say
The word that mars a perfect night of May.
    They watched the waning moon.

                            [1889]

La Mélinite: Moulin-Rouge

Olivier Metra's Waltz of Roses
Sheds in rhythmic shower
The very petals of the flower;
And all is roses,
The rouge of petals in a shower.

Down the long hall the dance returning
Rounds the full circle, rounds
The perfect rose of lights and sounds,
The rose returning
Into the circle of its rounds.

Alone, apart, one dancer watches
Her mirrored, morbid grace;
Before the mirror, face to face,
Alone she watches
Her morbid, vague, ambiguous grace

393

Before the mirror's dance of shadows
She dances in a dream,
And she and they together seem
A dance of shadows,
Alike the shadows of a dream.

The orange-rosy lamps are trembling
Between the robes that turn;
In ruddy flowers of flame that burn
The lights are trembling:
The shadows and the dancers turn

And, enigmatically smiling,
In the mysterious night,
She dances for her own delight,
A shadow smiling
Back to a shadow in the night.

[1895]

At Dieppe: Grey and Green

TO WALTER SICKERT

The grey-green stretch of sandy grass,
Indefinitely desolate;
A sea of lead, a sky of slate;
Already autumn in the air, alas!

One stark monotony of stone,
The long hotel, acutely white,
Against the after-sunset light
Withers grey-green, and takes the grass's tone.

Listless and endless it outlies,
And means, to you and me, no more
Than any pebble on the shore,
Or this indifferent moment as it dies.

[1895]

White Heliotrope

The feverish room and that white bed,
The tumbled skirts upon a chair,
The novel flung half-open, where
Hat, hair-pins, puffs, and paints, are spread;

The mirror that has sucked your face
Into its secret deep of deeps,
And there mysteriously keeps
Forgotten memories of grace;

And you, half dressed and half awake,
Your slant eyes strangely watching me,
And I, who watch you drowsily,
With eyes that, having slept not, ache;

This (need one dread? nay, dare one hope?)
Will rise, a ghost of memory, if
Ever again my handkerchief
Is scented with White Heliotrope.

[1895]

Bianca

Her cheeks are hot, her cheeks are white;
The white girl hardly breathes to-night,
So faint the pulses come and go,
That waken to a smouldering glow
The morbid faintness of her white.

What drowsing heats of sense, desire
Longing and languorous, the fire
Of what white ashes, subtly mesh
The fascinations of her flesh
Into a breathing web of fire?

Only her eyes, only her mouth
Live, in the agony of drouth,
Athirst for that which may not be:
The desert of virginity
Aches in the hotness of her mouth.

I take her hands into my hands,
Silently, and she understands;
I set my lips upon her lips;
Shuddering to her finger-tips
She strains my hands within her hands.

I set my lips on hers; they close
Into a false and phantom rose;
Upon her thirsting lips I rain
A flood of kisses, and in vain;
Her lips inexorably close.

Through her closed lips that cling to mine,
Her hands that hold me and entwine,
Her body that abandoned lies,
Rigid with sterile ecstasies,
A shiver knits her flesh to mine.

Life sucks into a mist remote
Her fainting lips, her throbbing throat;
Her lips that open to my lips,
And, hot against my finger-tips,
The pulses leaping in her throat.

[1895]

Posthumous Coquetry

From *Théophile Gautier*

Let there be laid, when I am dead,
Ere 'neath the coffin-lid I lie,
Upon my cheek a little red
A little black about the eye.

For I in my close bier would fain,
As on the night his vows were made,
Rose-red eternally remain,
With khol beneath my blue eye laid.

Wind me no shroud of linen down
My body to my feet, but fold
The white folds of my muslin gown
With thirteen flounces, as of old.

This shall go with me where I go:
I wore it when I won his heart;
His first look hallowed it, and so,
For him, I laid the gown apart.

No immortelles, no broidered grace
Of tears upon my cushion be;
Lay me on my own pillow's lace,
My hair across it, like a sea.

That pillow, those mad nights of old,
Has seen our slumbering brows unite,
And 'neath the gondola's black fold
Has counted kisses infinite.

Between my hands of ivory,
Together set for prayer and rest,
Place then the opal rosary
The holy Pope at Rome has blest.

I will lie down then on that bed
And sleep the sleep that shall not cease;
His mouth upon my mouth has said
Pater and *Ave* for my peace.

[1895]

From *Amoris Victima*

And yet, there was a hunger in your eyes,
Once, when you turned upon me suddenly;
And suddenly you turned away from me,
Once, when, evoking other memories,
I said, 'You hate me: answer: do you not
Hate me?' and in your silence then I heard
The ruined echo of another word,
Love, Love, that wailed and would not be forgot.
And once you laughed, that laugh I understand,
Sadder than tears, a broken little laugh,
As if a sob had shivered it in half.
And once, when, pausing, I had laid my hand
Upon your hand my hand could always thrill,
The fingers stirred: ah! they remember still.

[1897]

Palm Sunday: Naples

Because it is the day of Palms,
Carry a palm for me,
Carry a palm in Santa Chiara,
And I will watch the sea;
There are no palms in Santa Chiara
To-day or any day for me.

I sit and watch the little sail
Lean side-ways on the sea,
The sea is blue from here to Sorrento
And the sea-wind comes to me,
And I see the white clouds lift from Sorrento
And the dark sail lean upon the sea.

I have grown tired of all these things,
And what is left for me?
I have no place in Santa Chiara,
There is no peace upon the sea;
But carry a palm in Santa Chiara,
Carry a palm for me.

[1899]

JOHN GRAY
1866–1934

JOHN GRAY was born at Woolwich and died in Edinburgh.
His Catholicism led him in time to take holy orders and
abandon the lush sensuousness of his nineties poetry for a
taut, more quirky style. Large claims for Gray's early verse
have been made – notably by Frank Kermode – but his
technique was slow to mature and the appeal of his book
Silverpoints (apart from its physical elegance) chiefly lies in
its anticipation of Eliot and Ransom.

Les Demoiselles De Sauve

Beautiful ladies through the orchard pass;
Bend under crutched-up branches, forked and low;
Trailing their samet palls o'er dew-drenched grass.

Pale blossoms, looking on proud Jacqueline,
Blush to the colour of her finger tips,
And rosy knuckles, laced with yellow lace.

High-crested Berthe discerns, with slant, clinched eyes,
Amid the leaves pink faces of the skies;
She locks her plaintive hands Sainte-Margot-wise.

Ysabeau follows last, with languorous pace;
Presses, voluptuous, to her bursting lips,
With backward stoop, a branch of eglantine.

Courtly ladies through the orchard pass;
Bow low, as in lords' halls; and springtime grass
Tangles a snare to catch the tapering toe.

[1893]

ERNEST DOWSON
1867–1900

ERNEST CHRISTOPHER DOWSON was born in Kent, the son of an East End dry-dock owner. Arthur Symons wrote a glamorizing account of his affair with the daughter of a Polish restaurant-owner in Soho, but the real blend of idealism and coarseness in his nature is hard to assess. He died worn out by excess. Dowson, through his care for metre, attains grace of sound and plangency of tone in his poetry. He is an artist in words, sometimes achieving a stern Horatian note (as in *You Would Have Understood Me*) but more often appealing for his lulling musical sweetness as a kind of *fin-de-siècle* Campion.

'They are not long, The weeping and the laughter'

Vitae summa brevis spem nos vetat incohare longam

They are not long, the weeping and the laughter,
 Love and desire and hate:
I think they have no portion in us after
  We pass the gate.

They are not long, the days of wine and roses:
 Out of a misty dream
Our path emerges for a while, then closes
  Within a dream.

         [1896]

Flos Lunae

I would not alter thy cold eyes,
Nor trouble the calm fount of speech
With aught of passion or surprise.
The heart of thee I cannot reach:
I would not alter thy cold eyes!

I would not alter thy cold eyes;
Nor have thee smile, nor make thee weep:
Though all my life droops down and dies,
Desiring thee, desiring sleep,
I would not alter thy cold eyes.

I would not alter thy cold eyes;
I would not change thee if I might,
To whom my prayers for incense rise,
Daughter of dreams! my moon of night!
I would not alter thy cold eyes.

I would not alter thy cold eyes,
With trouble of the human heart:
Within their glance my spirit lies,
A frozen thing, alone, apart;
I would not alter thy cold eyes.

[1896]

Non Sum Qualis Eram Bonae
Sub Regno Cynarae

Last night, ah, yesternight, betwixt her lips and mine
There fell thy shadow, Cynara! thy breath was shed
Upon my soul between the kisses and the wine;
And I was desolate and sick of an old passion,
    Yea, I was desolate and bowed my head:
I have been faithful to thee, Cynara! in my fashion.

All night upon mine heart I felt her warm heart beat,
Night-long within mine arms in love and sleep she lay;
Surely the kisses of her bought red mouth were sweet;
But I was desolate and sick of an old passion,
    When I awoke and found the dawn was gray:
I have been faithful to thee, Cynara! in my fashion.

I have forgot much, Cynara! gone with the wind,
Flung roses, roses riotously with the throng,
Dancing, to put thy pale, lost lilies out of mind;
But I was desolate and sick of an old passion,
   Yea, all the time, because the dance was long:
I have been faithful to thee, Cynara! in my fashion.

I cried for madder music and for stronger wine,
But when the feast is finished and the lamps expire,
Then falls thy shadow, Cynara! the night is thine;
And I am desolate and sick of an old passion,
   Yea, hungry for the lips of my desire:
I have been faithful to thee, Cynara! in my fashion.

[1896]

'You would have understood me,
had you waited'

Ah, dans ces mornes séjours
Les jamais sont les toujours
PAUL VERLAINE

You would have understood me, had you waited;
   I could have loved you, dear! as well as he:
Had we not been impatient, dear! and fated
    Always to disagree.

What is the use of speech? Silence were fitter:
   Lest we should still be wishing things unsaid.
Though all the words we ever spake were bitter,
    Shall I reproach you dead?

Nay, let this earth, your portion, likewise cover
   All the old anger, setting us apart:
Always, in all, in truth was I your lover;
    Always, I held your heart.

I have met other women who were tender,
    As you were cold, dear! with a grace as rare.
Think you, I turned to them, or made surrender,
    I who had found you fair?

Had we been patient, dear! ah, had you waited,
    I had fought death for you, better than he:
But from the very first, dear! we were fated
    Always to disagree.

Late, late, I come to you, now death discloses
    Love that in life was not to be our part:
On your low lying mound between the roses,
    Sadly I cast my heart.

I would not waken you: nay! this is fitter;
    Death and the darkness give you unto me;
Here we who loved so, were so cold and bitter,
    Hardly can disagree.

[1896]

Extreme Unction

Upon the eyes, the lips, the feet,
    On all the passages of sense,
The atoning oil is spread with sweet
    Renewal of lost innocence.

The feet, that lately ran so fast
    To meet desire, are soothly sealed;
The eyes, that were so often cast
    On vanity, are touched and healed.

From troublous sights and sounds set free;
    In such a twilight hour of breath,
Shall one retrace his life, or see,
    Through shadows, the true face of death?

Vials of mercy! Sacring oils!
　I know not where nor when I come,
Nor through what wanderings and toils,
　To crave of you Viaticum.

Yet, when the walls of flesh grow weak,
　In such an hour, it well may be,
Through mist and darkness, light will break,
　And each anointed sense will see.

[1896]

LIONEL JOHNSON

1867–1902

LIONEL PIGOT JOHNSON was born at Broadstairs. He died in London, ruined by excess of drink. The ivory coldness of his verse usually fails to achieve the sombre authority of Arnold, but in *By the Statue of King Charles at Charing Cross* he is able to convey Romantic hero-worship with a cool precision reminiscent of Marvell in the *Horatian Ode*.

By the Statue of King Charles at Charing Cross

Sombre and rich, the skies;
Great glooms, and starry plains.
Gently the night wind sighs;
Else a vast silence reigns.

The splendid silence clings
Around me: and around
The saddest of all kings
Crowned, and again discrowned.

Comely and calm, he rides
Hard by his own Whitehall:
Only the night wind glides:
No crowds, nor rebels, brawl.

Gone, too, his Court: and yet,
The stars his courtiers are:
Stars in their stations' set;
And every wandering star.

Alone he rides, alone,
The fair and fatal king:
Dark night is all his own,
That strange and solemn thing.

Which are more full of fate:
The stars; or those sad eyes?
Which are more still and great:
Those brows; or the dark skies?

Although his whole heart yearn
In passionate tragedy:
Never was face so stern
With sweet austerity.

Vanquished in life, his death
By beauty made amends:
The passing of his breath
Won his defeated ends.

Brief life, and hapless? Nay:
Through death, life grew sublime.
Speak after sentence? Yea:
And to the end of time.

Armoured he rides, his head
Bare to the stars of doom:
He triumphs now, the dead,
Beholding London's gloom.

Our wearier spirit faints,
Vexed in the world's employ:
His soul was of the saints;
And art to him was joy.

King, tried in fires of woe!
Men hunger for thy grace:
And through the night I go,
Loving thy mournful face.

Yet, when the city sleeps;
When all the cries are still:
The stars and heavenly deeps
Work out a perfect will.

[1895]

LORD ALFRED DOUGLAS
1870–1945

LORD ALFRED DOUGLAS was born at Ham Hill, near Worcester. His destructive homosexual tendencies (epitomized by his cruel affair with Wilde) and his later attempts to curb them after entering the Roman Catholic church, are interestingly objectified in his one good poem *Rejected*.

Rejected

Alas! I have lost my God,
   My beautiful God Apollo.
Wherever his footsteps trod
   My feet were wont to follow.

But oh! it fell out one day
   My soul was so heavy with weeping,
That I laid me down by the way;
   And he left me while I was sleeping.

And my soul awoke in the night,
   And I bowed my ear for his fluting,
And I heard but the breath of the flight
   Of wings and the night-birds hooting.

And night drank all her cup,
   And I went to the shrine in the hollow,
And the voice of my cry went up:
   'Apollo! Apollo! Apollo!'

But he never came to the gate,
   And the sun was hid in a mist,
And there came one walking late,
   And I knew it was Christ.

He took my soul and bound it
  With cords of iron wire,
Seven times round He wound it
  With the cords of my desire.

The cords of my desire,
  While my desire slept,
Were seven bands of wire
  To bind my soul that wept.

And He hid my soul at last
  In a place of stones and fears,
Where the hours like days went past
  And the days went by like years.

And after many days
  That which had slept awoke,
And desire burnt in a blaze,
  And my soul went up in the smoke.

And we crept away from the place
  And would not look behind,
And the angel that hides his face
  Was crouched on the neck of the wind.

And I went to the shrine in the hollow
  Where the lutes and the flutes were playing,
And I cried: 'I am come, Apollo,
  Back to thy shrine, from my straying.'

But he would have none of my soul
  That was stained with blood and with tears,
That had lain in the earth like a mole,
  In the place of great stones and fears.

And now I am lost in the mist
  Of the things that can never be,
For I will have none of Christ
  And Apollo will none of me.

[1899]

J. M. SYNGE

1871–1909

JAMES MILLINGTON SYNGE was born at Rathfarnham and died in Dublin. He anticipated his friend Yeats in the realistic – even brutal – presentation of Irish country life. His best work is in his plays, notably *The Playboy of The Western World*, but his handful of poems reveal a developing gift for the pithy combination of irony and violence.

Queens

Seven dog-days we let pass
Naming Queens in Glenmacnass
All the rare and royal names
Wormy sheepskin yet retains:
Etain, Helen, Maeve, and Fand,
Golden Deirdre's tender hand;
Bert, the big-foot, sung by Villon.
Cassandra, Ronsard found in Lyon.
Queens of Sheba, Meath, and Connaught.
Coifed with crown, or gaudy bonnet;
Queens whose finger once did stir men,
Queens were eaten of fleas and vermin,
Queens men drew like Monna Lisa,
Or slew with drugs in Rome and Pisa.
We named Lucrezia Crivelli,
And Titian's lady with amber belly,
Queens acquainted in learned sin,
Jane of Jewry's slender shin:
Queens who cut the boss of Glanna,
Judith of Scripture, and Gloriana,
Queens who wasted the East by proxy,
Or drove the ass-cart, a tinker's doxy.
Yet these are rotten – I ask their pardon –
And we've the sun on rock and garden;

These are rotten, so you're the Queen
Of all are living, or have been.

[1909]

Danny

One night a score of Erris men,
A score I'm told and nine,
Said, 'We'll get shut of Danny's noise
Of girls and widows dyin''.

'There's not his like from Binghamstown
To Boyle and Ballycroy,
At playing hell on decent girls,
At beating man and boy.

'He's left two pairs of female twins
Beyond in Killacreest,
And twice in Crossmolina fair
He's struck the parish priest.

'But we'll come round him in the night
A mile beyond the Mullet;
Ten will quench his bloody eyes,
And ten will choke his gullet.'

It wasn't long till Danny came,
From Bangor making way,
And he was damning moon and stars
And whistling grand and gay.

Till in a gap of hazel glen –
And not a hare in sight –
Out lepped the nine-and-twenty lads
Along his left and right.

413

Then Danny smashed the nose on Byrne,
He split the lips on three,
And bit across the right-hand thumb
On one Red Shawn Magee.

But seven tripped him up behind,
And seven kicked before,
And seven squeezed around his throat
Till Danny kicked no more.

Then some destroyed him with their heels,
Some tramped him in the mud,
Some stole his purse and timber pipe,
And some washed off his blood.

*   *   *

And when you're walking out the way
From Bangor to Belmullet,
You'll see a flat cross on a stone,
Where men choked Danny's gullet.

[1909]

On an Island

You've plucked a curlew, drawn a hen,
Washed the shirts of seven men,
You've stuffed my pillow, stretched the sheet,
And filled the pan to wash your feet,
You've cooped the pullets, wound the clock,
And rinsed the young men's drinking crock;
And now we'll dance to jigs and reels,
Nailed boots chasing girls' naked heels,
Until your father'll start to snore,
And Jude, now you're married, will stretch on the floor.

[1909]

AUBREY BEARDSLEY
1872–1898

AUBREY BEARDSLEY was born at Brighton and died in
Menton. He was the most brilliant satirical draughtsman of
his age and is perhaps the central figure in the history of *art
nouveau*. Surprisingly, the irony of his poetry, notably in
The Three Musicians, has been little contrasted with the
strenuously un-humorous note of the other decadents.

The Three Musicians

Along the path that skirts the wood,
  The three musicians wend their way,
Pleased with their thoughts, each other's mood,
  Franz Himmel's latest roundelay,
The morning's work, a new-found theme, their breakfast
    and the summer day.

One's a soprano, lightly frocked
  In cool, white muslin that just shows
Her brown silk stockings gaily clocked,
  Plump arms and elbows tipped with rose,
And frills of petticoats and things, and outlines as the warm
    wind blows.

Beside her a slim, gracious boy
  Hastens to mend her tresses' fall,.
And dies her favour to enjoy,
  And dies for *reclame* and recall
At Paris and St Petersburg, Vienna and St James's Hall.

The third's a Polish Pianist
  With big engagements everywhere,
A light heart and an iron wrist,
  And shocks and shoals of yellow hair,
And fingers that can trill on sixths and fill beginners with
    despair.

The three musicians stroll along
    And pluck the ears of ripened corn,
Break into odds and ends of song,
    And mock the woods with Siegfried's horn,
And fill the air with Gluck, and fill the tweeded tourist's
    soul with scorn.

The Polish genius lags behind,
    And, with some poppies in his hand,
Picks out the strings and wood and wind
    Of an imaginary band,
Enchanted that for once his men obey his beat and under-
    stand.

The charming cantatrice reclines
    And rests a moment where she sees
Her château's roof that hotly shines
    Amid the dusky summer trees,
And fans herself, half shuts her eyes, and smoothes the
    frock about her knees.

The gracious boy is at her feet,
    And weighs his courage with his chance;
His fears soon melt in noonday heat.
    The tourist gives a furious glance,
Red as his guide-book grows, moves on, and offers up a
    prayer for France.

            [1928]

Appendix

ANON

floreat semper

THIS fine poet – in his Victorian incarnation – was brought
to light by John Ashton in his *Modern Street Ballads*, pub-
lished in 1888. In 1861 there were claimed to be no less than
700 writers living solely by ballad singing and selling broad-
sheets. They were the heirs of the Scottish ballad-writers and
the ancestors of the modern folk-singer. *The Queen's Dream*
has a poised vulgarity that might have been the envy of Dob-
son or Hood. *The Three Butchers* is the mate of *King Harald's
Trance* in its blood-thick sexuality. *Van Dieman's Land*
compares interestingly with Kingsley's more sophisticated
treatment of a related theme in *The Last Buccanier*.

The Queen's Dream

Good people give attention, and listen for a while,
To an interesting ditty, which cannot fail to make you smile,
So all draw near, and lend an ear, while I relate a theme,
Concerning of Victoria, a strange and funny dream.

Chorus.
So these are dreams and visions
Of old England's blooming Queen.

At the Isle of Wight, the other night, as Vic lay in her bed,
Strange visions did to her appear, and dreams came in her
    head;
She drew Prince Albert by the nose, and gave a dreadful
    scream;
Oh, dear, she said, I'm filled with dread, I'd such a dread-
    ful dream.

Says Albert, Vic, what are you at? you've made my nose
    quite sore,
I'm in a mind, for half a pin, to kick you on the floor.

419

Such dreams for me will never do, you pepper'd me with
blows.
I never knew a wife to dream, and pull her husband's nose.

O, don't be vex'd, the Queen replied, you know I love you
well,
So listen awhile dear Albert, and my dreams to you I'll tell:
Last night, she said, I had a dream, as soon as I lay down,
I thought Napoleon had come o'er, to steal away my crown.

The vision of Napoleon appeared at my bed side,
He said that by my subjects he had been greatly belied,
But now, said he, I'll be revenged, I'll quickly make you
rue,
And I'll take away the laurels that were won at Waterloo.

When the vision of Napoleon, from my view did disappear,
To escape the French, I thought that we came to lodge
here,
I thought that we were so held down, by cursed poverty,
That I was forc'd to labour hard in a cotton factory.

Prince Albert, he stood quite amazed, and listened to the
Queen,
And said, dear Vic, I little thought that you had such a
dream,
Cheer up your heart, don't look so sad, you need not be
afraid,
For I'm sure the French will ne'er attempt, Old England
to invade.

The Queen to Albert then replied, I have not told you all,
For I dream't that Lord John Russell, altho' but very small,
Just like a Briton bold, then so nobly did advance,
And with his fist, knocked out the eye, of the Emperor of
France.

I dreamed that I was weaving on a pair of patent looms,
And I thought that you were going through the streets
a-selling brooms,
And I thought our blooming Prince of Wales was selling
milk and cream,
But, Albert dear, when I awoke, it was nothing but a dream.

Indeed, said Albert, dream no more, you fill my heart with
pain,
And I hope that you will never have such frightful dreams
again,
We've English and Irish soldiers, we can conquer all our
foes,
So, whenever you dream again Vic, pray don't you pull my
nose.

[1888]

Van Dieman's Land

Come all you gallant poachers, that ramble free from care,
That walk out on moonlight nights, with your dog, gun and
snare,
The jolly hares and pheasants, you have at your command,
Not thinking that your last career is to Van Dieman's Land.

Poor Tom Brown from Nottingham, Jack Williams and
poor Joe,
We are three daring poachers, the country does well know,
At night we are trepanned, by the keepers hid in sand,
Who for fourteen years transported us unto Van Dieman's
Land.

The first day that we landed upon this fatal shore,
The planters they came round us, full twenty score or more,
They rank'd us up like horses, and sold us out of hand,
And yok'd us up to ploughs, my boys, to plough Van
Dieman's Land.

Our cottages that we live in, are built of brick and clay,
And rotten straw for bedding, and we dare not say nay,
Our cots are fenc'd with fire, we slumber when we can,
To drive away wolves and tigers (?) upon Van Dieman's
    Land.

It's often when in slumber I have a pleasant dream,
With my sweet girl a-sitting down, all by a purling stream,
Through England I've been roaming, with her at command,
Now I awake broken hearted upon Van Dieman's Land.

God bless our wives and families, likewise that happy shore,
That isle of great contentment, which we shall see no more,
As for our wretched females, see them, we seldom can,
There's twenty, to one woman, upon Van Dieman's land.

There was a girl from Birmingham, Susan Summers was
    her name,
For fourteen years transported, we all well know the same,
Our planter bought her freedom, and married her out of
    hand,
She gave to us good usage upon Van Dieman's Land.

So all you gallant poachers, give ear unto my song,
It is a bit of good advice, although it is not long,
Throw by your dogs and snares, for to you I speak plain,
For if you knew our hardships, you would never poach
    again.

[1888]

The Three Butchers

It was Ips, Gips, and Johnson, as I've heard many say,
They had five hundred guineas, all on a market day:
As they rode over Northumberland, as hard as they could
    ride,
Oh, hark, Oh, hark, says Johnson, I hear a woman cry.

Then Johnson, being a valiant man, a man of courage bold,
He ranged the woods all over, till this woman he did be-
  hold,
How came you here? says Johnson, how came you here I
  pray,
I am come here to relieve you, if you will not me betray.

There have been ten swaggering blades, have hand and
  foot me bound,
And stripped me stark naked, with my hair pinn'd on the
  ground;
Then Johnson, being a valiant man, a man of courage bold,
He took his coat from off his back, to keep her from the
  cold.

As they rode over Northumberland, as hard as they could
  ride,
She put her fingers in her ears, and dismally she cried,
Then up start ten swaggering blades, with weapons in their
  hand,
And, riding up to Johnson, they bid him for to stand.

It's I'll not stand, said Ipson, then no indeed, not I,
Nor, I'll not stand, said Gipson, I'd sooner live than die.
Then I will stand, said Johnson, I'll stand the while I can,
I never yet was daunted, nor afraid of any man.

Then Johnson drew his glittering sword, with all his might
  and main,
So well he laid upon them, that eight of them were slain:
As he was fighting the other two, this woman he did not
  mind,
She took the knife all from his side, and ripped him up
  behind.

Now I must fall, says Johnson, I must fall unto the ground,
For relieving this wicked woman, she gave me my death
   wound;
Oh base woman, Oh base woman, whatever hast thou done,
Thou hast killed the finest butcher that ever the sun shone
   on.

This happened on a Market Day, as people were riding by,
To see this dreadful murder, they gave the hue and cry,
It's now this woman's taken, and bound in irons strong,
For killing the finest butcher that ever the sun shone on.

                                       [1888]

Tarpauling Jacket

I am a young jolly brisk sailor,
   Delights in all manner of sport,
When I'm in liquor I'm mellow,
   The girls I then merrily court.
But love is surrounded with trouble,
   And puts such strange thoughts in my head,
Is it not a terrible story,
   That love it should strike me stone dead?

      *   *   *

Here's a health to my friends and acquaintance,
   When death for me it doth come,
And let them behave in their station
   And send me a cask of good rum,
Let it be good royal stingo,
   With three barrels of beer,
To make my friends the more welcome
   When they meet me at derry down fair.

Let there be six sailors to carry me,
Let them be damnable drunk,
And as they are going to bury me,
Let them fall down with my trunk.
Let there be no sighing or sobbing,
But one single favour I crave,
Take me up in a tarpauling jacket,
And fiddle and dance to my grave.

[1937]

MARY C. GILLINGTON

floruit 1892–1917

MARY CLARISSA GILLINGTON published only one
collection of poems, jointly with her sister Alice, in 1892.
After her marriage she published a large number of books
on cookery and books for children under the name of May
Byron. *A Dead March* owes something to the revival of in-
terest in cavalier lyrics encouraged by Palgrave in *The
Golden Treasury*. In places it could almost be by Shirley.

A Dead March

Be hushed, all voices and untimely laughter;
 Let no least word be lightly said
 In the awful presence of the Dead,
  That slowly, slowly this way comes –
Arms piled on coffin, comrades marching after,
  Colours reversed, and muffled drums.

Be bared, all heads; feet, the procession follow
 Throughout the stilled and sorrowing town;
 Weep, woeful eyes, and be cast down;
  Tread softly, till the bearers stop
Under the cypress in the shadowy hollow,
  While last light fades o'er mountain top.

Lay down your burden here, whose life hath journeyed
 Afar, and where ye may not wot;
 Some little while around this spot
  Be dirges sung, and prayers low said,
Dead leaves disturbed, and clammy earth upturnëd;
  Then in his grave dead Love is laid.

Fling them upon him – withered aspirations,
 And battered hopes, and broken vows;
 He was the last of all his house,

Hath left behind no kith nor kin;
His blood-stained arms and faded decorations,
    His dinted helmet, – throw them in.

And all the time the twilight skies are turning
    To sullen ash and leaden grey;
    Cast the sods o'er him, come away;
        In vain upon his name you call, –
Though you all night should call with bitter yearning,
    He would not heed nor hear at all.

Pass homeward now, in musing melancholy,
    To find the house enfilled with gloom,
    And no lights lit in any room,
        And stinging herald drops of rain;
Choke up your empty heart with anguish wholly,
    For Love will never rise again.

                                            [1892]

WILLIAM McGONAGALL

1830–1902

WILLIAM McGONAGALL was born in Edinburgh. Some readers may suspect that the inclusion of his work is a joke, supposing his brand of doggerel to be fun but not poetry. By applying the simple test of whether his work is recognizable in small samples, it can easily be shown to be original. Like the Douanier Rousseau, McGonagall created a style out of a stupidity. He was the first – and perhaps so far the only widely known – naïve poet, and as such he deserves attention.

The famous Tay Whale

'Twas in the month of December, and in the year 1883,
That a monster whale came to Dundee,
Resolved for a few days to sport and play,
And devour the small fishes in the silvery Tay.

So the monster whale did sport and play
Among the innocent little fishes in the beautiful Tay,
Until he was seen by some men one day,
And they resolved to catch him without delay.

When it came to be known a whale was seen in the Tay,
Some men began to talk and to say,
We must try and catch this monster of a whale,
So come on, brave boys, and never say fail.

Then the people together in crowds did run,
Resolved to capture the whale and to have some fun!
So small boats were launched on the silvery Tay,
While the monster of the deep did sport and play.

Oh! it was a most fearful and beautiful sight,
To see it lashing the water with its tail all its might,
And making the water ascend like a shower of hail,
With one lash of its ugly and mighty tail.

Then the water did descend on the men in the boats,
Which wet their trousers and also their coats;
But it only made them the more determined to catch the
    whale,
But the whale shook at them his tail.

Then the whale began to puff and to blow,
While the men and the boats after him did go,
Armed well with harpoons for the fray,
Which they fired at him without dismay.

And they laughed and grinned just like wild baboons,
While they fired at him their sharp harpoons:
But when struck with the harpoons he dived below,
Which filled his pursuers' hearts with woe:

Because they guessed they had lost a prize,
Which caused the tears to well up in their eyes;
And in that their anticipations were only right,
Because he sped on to Stonehaven with all his might:

And was first seen by the crew of a Gourdon fishing boat.
Which they thought was a big coble upturned afloat;
But when they drew near they saw it was a whale,
So they resolved to tow it ashore without fail.

So they got a rope from each boat tied round his tail,
And landed their burden at Stonehaven without fail;
And when the people saw it their voices they did raise,
Declaring that the brave fishermen deserved great praise.

And my opinion is that God sent the whale in time of need,
No matter what other people may think or what is their
   creed;
I know fishermen in general are often very poor,
And God in His goodness sent it to drive poverty from their
   door.

So Mr John Wood has bought it for two hundred and
   twenty-six pound,
And has brought it to Dundee all safe and all sound;
Which measures forty feet in length from the snout to the
   tail,
So I advise the people far and near to see it without fail.

Then hurrah! for the mighty monster whale,
Which has got seventeen feet four inches from tip to tip of
   a tail!
Which can be seen for a sixpence or a shilling,
That is to say, if the people all are willing.

[1951]

1830 Poems Chiefly Lyrical: Alfred, Lord Tennyson
1837 Poems on Oriental Subjects: James Clarence Mangan
1842 Poems: Alfred, Lord Tennyson
     Dramatic Lyrics: Robert Browning
     (*Porphyria's Lover* first appeared in 1836)
     Lays of Ancient Rome: Thomas Babington Macaulay
1843 Studies of Sensation and Event: Ebenezer Jones
1844 Poems: Coventry Patmore
     Poems of Rural Life in the Dorset Dialect: William
          Barnes
1845 Dramatic Romances and Lyrics: Robert Browning
     Useful and Instructive Poetry: Lewis Carroll
1846 A Book of Nonsense: Edward Lear
1851 Legal Lyrics and Metrical Illustrations of the Scotch
          Forms of Process: George Outram
1853 Poems: Matthew Arnold
     Tamerton Church-Tower: Coventry Patmore
1854 The Angel in the House: Coventry Patmore
1855 Maud: Alfred, Lord Tennyson
     Men and Women: Robert Browning
     Poems, Second Series: Matthew Arnold
     Miscellanies: William Makepeace Thackeray
1856 England in Time of War: Sydney Dobell
1857 City Poems: Alexander Smith
     Aurora Leigh: Elizabeth Barrett Browning
     London Lyrics: Frederick Locker-Lampson
1858 The Defence of Guenevere: William Morris
     Andromeda: Charles Kingsley
1859 Poems of Rural Life in the Dorset Dialect, Second
          Series: William Barnes
     The Rubáiyát of Omar Khayyám: Edward Fitzgerald
1861 Christ's Company: Richard Watson Dixon
1862 Goblin Market: Christina Rossetti
     Poems: Arthur Hugh Clough
     (second edition with added poems, 1863)
1864 Dramatis Personae: Robert Browning
     Sonnets: Charles Tennyson-Turner

1865 Brother Fabian's Manuscript: Sebastian Evans
     Letters and Remains: Arthur Hugh Clough
1866 Poems and Ballads: Algernon Charles Swinburne
1867 New Poems: Matthew Arnold
1868 Small Tableaux: Charles Tennyson-Turner
     The Quest of the Sancgreall: Thomas Westwood
1869 The Holy Grail: Alfred, Lord Tennyson
1870 Portraits: Augusta Webster
     Bush Ballads and Galloping Rhymes: Adam Lindsay
        Gordon
1871 Nonsense Songs and Stories: Edward Lear
     Through the Looking-Glass: Lewis Carroll
1873 Vignettes in Rhyme: Austin Dobson
1875 Preludes: Alice Meynell
     Poems: William Bell Scott
     Legendary and Historic Ballads: Walter Thornbury
1878 Poems and Ballads, Second Series: Algernon Charles
        Swinburne
     The Unknown Eros: Coventry Patmore (enlarged
        edition)
1879 Poems of Rural Life in the Dorset Dialect (Collected):
        William Barnes
1880 Collected Sonnets: Charles Tennyson Turner
     Ballads: Alfred, Lord Tennyson
     The Heptalogia: Algernon Charles Swinburne
     The City of Dreadful Night: James Thomson
1881 Poems: Oscar Wilde
1883 Autumn Swallows: Ellice Hopkins
     Poems and Lyrics of the Joy of Earth: George
        Meredith
1884 Apollo and Marsyas: Eugene Lee-Hamilton
1885 At the Gate of the Convent: Alfred Austin
     A Child's Garden of Verses: Robert Louis Stevenson
1886 Collected Works: Dante Gabriel Rossetti
     (*A Trip to Paris and Belgium* was written in 1849)
     Departmental Ditties: Rudyard Kipling
1887 Ballads and Poems of Tragic Life: George Meredith
     Underwoods: Robert Louis Stevenson
1888 Imaginary Sonnets: Eugene Lee-Hamilton
     Songs, Ballads and a Garden Play: Agnes Mary
        Robinson

Modern Street Ballads: (edited by John Ashton: many date from before 1850)

1889 Days and Nights: Arthur Symons
Verses Written in India: Sir Alfred Lyall
Long Ago: Michael Field

1892 Poems: Mary C. Gillington (with Alice Gillington)
Sight and Song: Michael Field
Barrack-Room Ballads: Rudyard Kipling

1893 Silverpoints: John Gray
Poems: Francis Thompson
The Rose: William Butler Yeats
Poems Dramatic and Lyrical: Lord de Tabley
Old John: T. E. Brown

1895 Poems: Lionel Johnson
London Nights: Arthur Symons

1896 Verses: Ernest Dowson
Songs of Travel: Robert Louis Stevenson

1897 Amoris Victima: Arthur Symons

1898 The Island Race: Sir Henry Newbolt

1899 Images of Good and Evil: Arthur Symons
The City of the Soul: Lord Alfred Douglas

1901 Poems of the Past and the Present: Thomas Hardy

1902 Later Poems: Alice Meynell
(*The Lady Poverty* and *Parentage* were privately printed in 1896)

1903 The Five Nations: Rudyard Kipling

1904 Collected Poems: Christina Rossetti

1908 Collected Poems: William Henley

1909 Fleet Street: John Davidson
Poems and Translations: J. M. Synge

1912 The Oxford Book of Victorian Verse (edited by Sir Arthur Quiller-Couch: containing *Glenaradale* by Walter C. Smith, uncollected in his Collected Poems, 1904)

1913 Collected Poems: Alice Meynell

1914 Satires of Circumstance: Thomas Hardy

1918 Poems: Gerard Manley Hopkins
(*Spring and Fall* and *Inversnaid* appeared in The Poets and the Poetry of the Nineteenth Century: Bridges to Kipling, in 1893; most of Hopkins's poetry was written between 1875 and 1889)

1919 Moments of Vision: Thomas Hardy

1922   Last Poems: A. E. Housman
(many of these were written in the 1890s)

1928   An Anthology of Nineties Verse (edited by A. J. A. Symons: containing *The Three Musicians* by Aubrey Beardsley. This poem appeared in The Savoy in 1896)

1932   Collected Verse: Lewis Carroll

1936   More Poems: A. E. Housman
(many of these were written in the 1890s)

1937   Victorian Street Ballads: (edited by William Henderson: *Tarpauling Jacket* was current in the nineteenth century)

1951   Poetic Gems: William McGonagall

1957   The Silver Treasury of Light Verse (edited by Oscar Williams: *Oscar Wilde*, if correctly attributed to Swinburne, must have been written before 1909)

INDEX OF AUTHORS

INDEX OF FIRST LINES

Pedro de Alarcon	**The Three-Cornered Hat and Other Stories**
Leopoldo Alas	**La Regenta**
Ludovico Ariosto	**Orlando Furioso**
Giovanni Boccaccio	**The Decameron**
Baldassar Castiglione	**The Book of the Courtier**
Benvenuto Cellini	**Autobiography**
Miguel de Cervantes	**Don Quixote**
	Exemplary Stories
Dante	**The Divine Comedy** (in 3 volumes)
	La Vita Nuova
Bernal Diaz	**The Conquest of New Spain**
Carlo Goldoni	**Four Comedies (The Venetian Twins / The Artful Widow / Mirandolina / The Superior Residence)**
Niccolo Machiavelli	**The Discourses**
	The Prince
Alessandro Manzoni	**The Betrothed**
Giorgio Vasari	**Lives of the Artists** (in 2 volumes)

and

Five Italian Renaissance Comedies (Machiavelli / The Mandragola; Ariosto / Lena; Aretino / The Stablemaster; Gl'Intronatie / The Deceived; Guarini / The Faithful Shepherd)
The Jewish Poets of Spain
The Poem of the Cid
Two Spanish Picaresque Novels (Anon / Lazarille de Tormes; de Quevedo / The Swindler)

Honoré de Balzac	**Cousin Bette**
	Eugénie Grandet
	Lost Illusions
	Old Goriot
	Ursule Mirouet
Benjamin Constant	**Adolphe**
Corneille	**The Cid/Cinna/The Theatrical Illusion**
Alphonse Daudet	**Letters from My Windmill**
René Descartes	**Discourse on Method and Other Writings**
Denis Diderot	**Jacques the Fatalist**
Gustave Flaubert	**Madame Bovary**
	Sentimental Education
	Three Tales
Jean de la Fontaine	**Selected Fables**
Jean Froissart	**The Chronicles**
Théophile Gautier	**Mademoiselle de Maupin**
Edmond and Jules de	
Goncourt	**Germinie Lacerteux**
J.-K. Huysmans	**Against Nature**
Guy de Maupassant	**Selected Short Stories**
Molière	**The Misanthrope/The Sicilian/Tartuffe/A Doctor**
	in Spite of Himself/The Imaginary Invalid
Michel de Montaigne	**Essays**
Marguerite de Navarre	**The Heptameron**
Marie de France	**Lais**
Blaise Pascal	**Pensées**
Rabelais	**The Histories of Gargantua and Pantagruel**
Racine	**Iphigenia/Phaedra/Athaliah**
Arthur Rimbaud	**Collected Poems**
Jean-Jacques Rousseau	**The Confessions**
	Reveries of a Solitary Walker
Madame de Sevigné	**Selected Letters**
Voltaire	**Candide**
	Philosophical Dictionary
Émile Zola	**La Bête Humaine**
	Nana
	Thérèse Raquin